GREATEST AMERICAN HORROR STORIES

CLASSICS

Published 2025

FiNGERPRINT! CLASSICS

Prakash Books

Fingerprint Publishing
@FingerprintP
@fingerprintpublishingbooks
www.fingerprintpublishing.com

ISBN: 978 93 6214 748 6

of human morality. His works, such as "Young Goodman Brown" and "The Birth-Mark," delve into the psychological and moral implications of sin and guilt, earning him a place among the masters of American horror literature.

H.P. Lovecraft, born in 1890, is celebrated for his creation of cosmic horror—a subgenre that explores the insignificance of humanity in the face of vast, indifferent cosmic forces. Lovecraft's mythos, including the iconic entity Cthulhu, continues to inspire writers and artists across various media, solidifying his status as a visionary of the macabre.

O. Henry, born in 1862, is best known for his clever narratives with iconic endings. While not a traditional horror writer, his stories often contain elements of the uncanny and the macabre.

Lastly, Edith Wharton, born in 1862, is acclaimed for her incisive social commentary and psychological depth. Her forays into horror literature, such as "Afterward" and "The Eyes," explore the supernatural with subtlety and nuance, delving into themes of isolation, loss, and the uncanny.

Collectively, these authors have crafted a tapestry of terror that spans centuries, offering readers a glimpse into the darkest recesses of the human imagination.

American literature boasts narratives that have enthralled readers across generations—stories that plumb the depths of the human psyche, delving into realms of fear, dread, and the enigmatic. These stories have rightfully earned their place in the pantheon of horror fiction, crafted by illustrious storytellers such as Edgar Allan Poe, Ambrose Bierce, Washington Irving, Nathaniel Hawthorne, H.P. Lovecraft, O. Henry, and Edith Wharton. Their contributions have left an indelible mark on readers and writers alike. From haunted mansions to cosmic abysses, these narratives traverse diverse terrains, showcasing the breadth and depth of American horror literature.

Edgar Allan Poe, a master of the macabre, was born in Boston in 1809. His tumultuous life, marked by personal tragedies and literary innovations, laid the groundwork for much of modern horror literature. Poe's psychological insights and Gothic sensibilities continue to captivate readers, with classics like "The Tell-Tale Heart" and "The Fall of the House of Usher" enduring as staples of the genre.

Ambrose Bierce, a veteran of the Civil War, brought his experiences to bear on his writing, infusing his tales with a stark realism and biting satire. Born in 1842, Bierce's stories often explore the darker aspects of human nature, blending elements of horror and social commentary.

Washington Irving, one of America's first literary figures, was born in 1783. His contributions to horror literature include the iconic "The Legend of Sleepy Hollow," a tale steeped in the folklore of early America. Irving's ability to blend supernatural elements with vivid descriptions of colonial life established him as a pioneer of the genre.

Nathaniel Hawthorne, born in 1804, is renowned for his exploration of Puritanical themes and the complexities

"I have seen the dark universe yawning
Where the black planets roll without aim,
Where they roll in their horror unheeded,
Without knowledge, or lustre, or name."

— H. P. Lovecraft

About this Edition

This carefully curated collection showcases the timeless allure of American horror literature, spanning centuries and encompassing a diverse range of styles and themes. From Poe's macabre tales of madness and obsession to Lovecraft's horror and Wharton's eerie explorations of the supernatural, each story transports readers to the dark recesses of the human psyche. With haunting prose and unforgettable characters, this edition invites readers to experience the enduring legacy of American horror fiction.

Contents

Nathaniel Hawthrone

Edith Wharton

EDGAR ALLAN POE

1

The Tell-Tale Heart

True!—nervous—very, very dreadfully nervous I had been and am; but why *will* you say that I am mad? The disease had sharpened my senses—not destroyed—not dulled them. Above all was the sense of hearing acute. I heard all things in the heaven and in the earth. I heard many things in hell. How, then, am I mad? Hearken! and observe how healthily—how calmly I can tell you the whole story.

It is impossible to say how first the idea entered my brain; but once conceived, it haunted me day and night. Object there was none. Passion there was none. I loved the old man. He had never wronged me. He had never given me insult. For his gold I had no desire. I think it was his eye! yes, it was this! He had the eye of a vulture—a pale blue eye, with a film over it. Whenever it fell upon me, my blood ran cold; and so by degrees—very gradually—I made up my mind to take the life of the old man, and thus rid myself of the eye forever.

Now this is the point. You fancy me mad. Madmen know nothing. But you should have seen *me*. You should have seen how wisely I proceeded—with what caution—with what foresight—with what dissimulation I went to work! I was never kinder to the old man than during the whole week before I killed him. And every night, about midnight, I turned the latch of his door and opened it—oh so gently! And then, when I had made an opening sufficient for my head, I put in a dark lantern, all closed, closed, that no light shone out, and then I thrust in my head. Oh, you would have laughed to see how cunningly I thrust it in! I moved it slowly—very, very slowly, so that I might not disturb the old man's sleep. It took me an hour to place my whole head within the opening so far that I could see him as he lay upon his bed. Ha! would a madman have been so wise as this? And then, when my head was well in the room, I undid the lantern cautiously—oh, so cautiously—cautiously (for the hinges creaked)—I undid it just so much that a single thin ray fell upon the vulture eye. And this I did for seven long nights—every night just at midnight—but I found the eye always closed; and so it was impossible to do the work; for it was not the old man who vexed me, but his Evil Eye. And every morning, when the day broke, I went boldly into the chamber, and spoke courageously to him, calling him by name in a hearty tone, and inquiring how he has passed the night. So you see he would have been a very profound old man, indeed, to suspect that every night, just at twelve, I looked in upon him while he slept.

Upon the eighth night I was more than usually cautious in opening the door. A watch's minute hand moves more quickly than did mine. Never before that night had I *felt* the extent of my own powers—of my sagacity. I could scarcely contain my feelings of triumph. To think that there I was, opening the door, little by little, and he not even to dream of my secret deeds or thoughts. I fairly chuckled at the idea; and perhaps he heard me; for he moved on the bed suddenly, as if startled. Now you may think that I drew back—but no. His room was as black as pitch with the thick darkness (for the shutters were close fastened, through fear of robbers), and so I knew that he could not see the opening of the door, and I kept pushing it on steadily, steadily.

I had my head in, and was about to open the lantern, when my thumb slipped upon the tin fastening, and the old man sprang up in bed, crying out—"Who's there?"

I kept quite still and said nothing. For a whole hour I did not move a muscle, and in the meantime I did not hear him lie down. He was still sitting up in the bed listening;—just as I have done, night after night, hearkening to the death watches in the wall.

Presently I heard a slight groan, and I knew it was the groan of mortal terror. It was not a groan of pain or of grief—oh, no!—it was the low stifled sound that arises from the bottom of the soul when overcharged with awe. I knew the sound well. Many a night, just at midnight, when all the world slept, it has welled up from my own bosom, deepening, with its dreadful echo, the terrors that distracted me. I say I knew it well. I knew what the old man felt, and pitied him, although I chuckled at heart. I knew that he had been lying awake ever since the first slight noise, when he had turned in the bed. His fears had been ever since growing upon him. He had been trying to fancy them causeless, but could not. He had been saying to himself—"It is nothing but the wind in the chimney, it is only a mouse crossing the floor," or "It is merely a cricket which has made a single chirp." Yes, he had been trying to comfort himself with these suppositions: but he had found all in vain. *All in vain*; because Death, in approaching him had stalked with his black shadow before him, and enveloped the victim. And it was the mournful influence of the unperceived shadow that caused him to feel—although he neither saw nor heard—to *feel* the presence of my head within the room.

When I had waited a long time, very patiently, without hearing him lie down, I resolved to open a little—a very, very little crevice in the lantern. So I opened it—you cannot imagine how stealthily, stealthily—until, at length a simple dim ray, like the thread of the spider, shot from out the crevice and fell full upon the vulture eye.

It was open—wide, wide open—and I grew furious as I gazed upon it. I saw it with perfect distinctness—all a dull blue, with a hideous veil over it that chilled the very marrow in my bones; but I could see nothing else of the old man's face or person: for I had directed the ray as if by instinct, precisely upon the damned spot.

And have I not told you that what you mistake for madness is but over-acuteness of the sense?—now, I say, there came to my ears a low, dull, quick sound, such as a watch makes when enveloped in cotton. I knew that sound well, too. It was the beating of the old man's heart. It increased my fury, as the beating of a drum stimulates the soldier into courage.

But even yet I refrained and kept still. I scarcely breathed. I held the lantern motionless. I tried how steadily I could maintain the ray upon the eve. Meantime the hellish tattoo of the heart increased. It grew quicker and quicker, and louder and louder every instant. The old man's terror *must* have been extreme! It grew louder, I say, louder every moment!—do you mark me well I have told you that I am nervous: so I am. And now at the dead hour of the night, amid the dreadful silence of that old house, so strange a noise as this excited me to uncontrollable terror. Yet, for some minutes longer I refrained and stood still. But the beating grew louder, louder! I thought the heart must burst. And now a new anxiety seized me—the sound would be heard by a neighbor! The old man's hour had come! With a loud yell, I threw open the lantern and leaped into the room. He shrieked once—once only. In an instant I dragged him to the floor, and pulled the heavy bed over him. I then smiled gaily, to find the deed so far done. But, for many minutes, the heart beat on with a muffled sound. This, however, did not vex me; it would not be heard through the wall. At length it ceased. The old man was dead. I removed the bed and examined the corpse. Yes, he was stone, stone dead. I placed my hand upon the heart and held it there many minutes. There was no pulsation. He was stone dead. His eye would trouble me no more.

If still you think me mad, you will think so no longer when I describe the wise precautions I took for the concealment of the body. The night waned, and I worked hastily, but in silence. First of all I dismembered the corpse. I cut off the head and the arms and the legs.

I then took up three planks from the flooring of the chamber, and deposited all between the scantlings. I then replaced the boards so cleverly, so cunningly, that no human eye—not even *his*—could have detected anything wrong. There was nothing to wash out—no stain of any kind—no blood-spot whatever. I had been too wary for that. A tub had caught all—ha! ha!

When I had made an end of these labors, it was four o'clock—still dark as midnight. As the bell sounded the hour, there came a knocking at the street door. I went down to open it with a light heart—for what had I *now* to fear? There entered three men, who introduced themselves, with perfect suavity, as officers of the police. A shriek had been heard by a neighbor during the night; suspicion of foul play had been aroused; information had been lodged at the police office, and they (the officers) had been deputed to search the premises.

I smiled—for *what* had I to fear? I bade the gentlemen welcome. The shriek, I said, was my own in a dream. The old man, I mentioned, was absent in the country. I took my visiters all over the house. I bade them search—search *well*. I led them, at length, to *his* chamber. I showed them his treasures, secure, undisturbed. In the enthusiasm of my confidence, I brought chairs into the room, and desired them *here* to rest from their fatigues, while I myself, in the wild audacity of my perfect triumph, placed my own seat upon the very spot beneath which reposed the corpse of the victim.

The officers were satisfied. My *manner* had convinced them. I was singularly at ease. They sat, and while I answered cheerily, they chatted of familiar things. But, ere long, I felt myself getting pale and wished them gone. My head ached, and I fancied a ringing in my ears: but still they sat and still chatted. The ringing became more distinct:—It continued and became more distinct: I talked more freely to get rid of the feeling; but it continued and gained definiteness—until, at length, I found that the noise was *not* within my ears.

No doubt I now grew *very* pale; but I talked more fluently, and with a heightened voice. Yet the sound increased—and what could I do? It was *a low, dull, quick sound—much such a sound as a watch makes when enveloped in cotton.* I gasped for breath—and yet the officers heard it not. I talked more quickly, more vehemently; but the noise steadily increased. I arose and argued about trifles, in a high key and with violent gesticulations; but the noise steadily increased. Why *would* they not be gone? I paced the floor to and fro with heavy strides, as if excited to fury by the observations of the men—but the noise steadily increased. Oh God! what *could* I do? I foamed—I raved—I swore! I swung the chair upon which I had been sitting, and grated it upon the boards, but the noise arose over all and continually increased. It grew louder—louder—*louder*! And still the men chatted pleasantly, and smiled. Was it possible they heard not? Almighty God!—no, no! They heard!—they suspected!—they *knew*!—they were making a mockery of my horror!—this I thought, and this I think. But anything was better than this agony! Anything was more tolerable than this derision! I could bear those hypocritical smiles no longer! I felt that I must scream or die! and now—again!—hark! louder! louder! louder! *louder*!

"Villains!" I shrieked, "dissemble no more! I admit the deed! Tear up the planks! here, here!—It is the beating of his hideous heart!"

2

The Fall of the House of Usher

Son coeur est un luth suspendu;
Sitôt qu'on le touche il rèsonne.

—De Béranger

During the whole of a dull, dark, and soundless day in the autumn of the year, when the clouds hung oppressively low in the heavens, I had been passing alone, on horseback, through a singularly dreary tract of country; and at length found myself, as the shades of the evening drew on, within view of the melancholy House of Usher. I know not how it was—but, with the first glimpse of the building, a sense of insufferable gloom pervaded my spirit. I say insufferable; for the feeling was unrelieved by any of that half-pleasurable, because poetic, sentiment, with which the mind usually receives even the sternest natural images of the desolate or terrible. I looked upon the scene before me—upon the mere house, and the simple landscape features of the domain—upon the bleak walls—upon the vacant eye-like windows—upon a few rank sedges—and upon a few white trunks of decayed trees—with an utter depression of soul which I can compare to no earthly sensation more properly than to the after-dream of the reveler upon opium—the bitter lapse into everyday life—the hideous dropping off of the veil. There was an iciness, a sinking, a sickening of the heart—an unredeemed dreariness of thought which no goading of the imagination could torture into aught of the sublime. What was it—I paused to think—what was it that so unnerved me in the contemplation of the House of Usher? It was a mystery all insoluble; nor could I grapple with the shadowy fancies that crowded upon me as I pondered. I was forced to fall back upon the unsatisfactory conclusion, that while, beyond doubt, there *are* combinations of very simple natural objects which have the power of thus affecting us, still the analysis of this power lies among considerations beyond our depth. It was possible, I reflected, that a mere different arrangement of the particulars of the scene, of the details of the picture, would be sufficient to modify, or perhaps to annihilate its capacity for sorrowful impression; and, acting upon this idea, I reined my horse to the precipitous brink of a black and lurid tarn that lay in unruffled luster by the dwelling, and gazed down—but with a shudder even more thrilling than before—upon the remodeled and inverted images of the gray sedge, and the ghastly tree-stems, and the vacant and eye-like windows.

Nevertheless, in this mansion of gloom I now proposed to myself a sojourn of some weeks. Its proprietor, Roderick Usher, had been one of my boon companions in boyhood; but many years had elapsed since our last meeting. A letter, however, had lately reached me in a distant part of the country—a letter from him—which, in its wildly importunate nature, had admitted of no other than a personal reply. The MS. gave evidence of nervous agitation. The writer spoke of acute bodily illness—of a mental disorder which oppressed him—and of an earnest desire to see me, as his best, and indeed his only personal friend, with a view of attempting, by the cheerfulness of my society, some alleviation of his malady. It was the manner in which all this, and much more, was said—it was the apparent *heart* that went with his request—which allowed me no room for hesitation; and I accordingly obeyed forthwith what I still considered a very singular summons.

Although, as boys, we had been even intimate associates, yet I really knew little of my friend. His reserve had been always excessive and habitual. I was aware, however, that his very ancient family had been noted, time out of mind, for a peculiar sensibility of temperament, displaying itself, through long ages, in many works of exalted art, and manifested, of late, in repeated deeds of munificent yet unobtrusive charity, as well as in a passionate devotion to the intricacies, perhaps even more than to the orthodox and easily recognizable beauties, of musical science. I had learned, too, the very remarkable fact, that the stem of the Usher race, all time-honored as it was, had put forth, at no period, any enduring branch; in other words, that the entire family lay in the direct line of descent, and had always, with very trifling and very temporary variation, so lain. It was this deficiency, I considered, while running over in thought the perfect keeping of the character of the premises with the accredited character of the people, and while speculating upon the possible influence which the one, in the long lapse of centuries, might have exercised upon the other—it was this deficiency, perhaps, of collateral issue, and the consequent undeviating transmission, from sire to son, of the patrimony with the name, which had, at length, so identified the two as to merge the original title of the estate in the quaint and equivocal appellation of the "House of Usher"—an appellation which seemed to include, in the minds of the peasantry who used it, both the family and the family mansion.

I have said that the sole effect of my somewhat childish experiment—that of looking down within the tarn—had been to deepen the first singular impression. There can be no doubt that the consciousness of the rapid increase of my superstition—for why should I not so term it?—served mainly to accelerate the increase itself. Such, I have long known, is the paradoxical law of all sentiments having terror as a basis. And it might have been for this reason only, that, when I again uplifted my eyes to the house itself, from its image in the pool, there grew in my mind a strange fancy—a fancy so ridiculous, indeed, that I but mention it to show the vivid force of the sensations which oppressed me. I had so worked upon my imagination as really to believe that about the whole mansion and domain there hung an atmosphere peculiar to themselves and their immediate vicinity—an atmosphere which had no affinity with the air of heaven, but which had reeked up from the decayed trees, and the gray wall, and the silent tarn—a pestilent and mystic vapor, dull, sluggish, faintly discernible, and leaden-hued.

Shaking off from my spirit what *must* have been a dream, I scanned more narrowly the real aspect of the building. Its principal feature seemed to be that of an excessive antiquity. The discolouration of ages had been great. Minute fungi overspread the whole exterior, hanging in a fine tangled web-work from the eaves. Yet all this was apart from any extraordinary dilapidation.

No portion of the masonry had fallen; and there appeared to be a wild inconsistency between its still perfect adaptation of parts, and the crumbling condition of the individual stones. In this there was much that reminded me of the specious totality of old wood-work which has rotted for long years in some neglected vault, with no disturbance from the breath of the external air. Beyond this indication of extensive decay, however, the fabric gave little token of instability. Perhaps the eye of a scrutinizing observer might have discovered a barely perceptible fissure, which, extending from the roof of the building in front, made its way down the wall in a zigzag direction, until it became lost in the sullen waters of the tarn.

Noticing these things, I rode over a short causeway to the house. A servant in waiting took my horse, and I entered the Gothic archway of the hall. A valet, of stealthy step, thence conducted me, in silence, through many dark and intricate passages in my progress to the *studio* of his master. Much that I encountered on the way contributed, I know not how, to heighten the vague sentiments of which I have already spoken. While the objects around me—while the carvings of the ceilings, the somber tapestries of the walls, the ebon blackness of the floors, and the phantasmagoric armorial trophies which rattled as I strode, were but matters to which, or to such as which, I had been accustomed from my infancy—while I hesitated not to acknowledge how familiar was all this—I still wondered to find how unfamiliar were the fancies which ordinary images were stirring up. On one of the staircases, I met the physician of the family. His countenance, I thought, wore a mingled expression of low cunning and perplexity. He accosted me with trepidation and passed on. The valet now threw open a door and ushered me into the presence of his master.

The room in which I found myself was very large and lofty. The windows were long, narrow, and pointed, and at so vast a distance from the black oaken floor as to be altogether inaccessible from within. Feeble gleams of encrimsoned light made their way through the trellised panes, and served to render sufficiently distinct the more prominent objects around; the eye, however, struggled in vain to reach the remoter angles of the chamber, or the recesses of the vaulted and fretted ceiling. Dark draperies hung upon the walls. The general furniture was profuse, comfortless, antique, and tattered. Many books and musical instruments lay scattered about, but failed to give any vitality to the scene. I felt that I breathed an atmosphere of sorrow. An air of stern, deep, and irredeemable gloom hung over and pervaded all.

Upon my entrance, Usher arose from a sofa on which he had been lying at full length, and greeted me with a vivacious warmth which had much in it, I at first thought, of an overdone cordiality—of the constrained effort of the *ennuyé* man of the world. A glance, however, at his countenance, convinced me of his perfect sincerity. We sat down; and for some moments, while he spoke not, I gazed upon him with a feeling half of pity, half of awe. Surely, man had never before so terribly altered, in so brief a period, as had Roderick Usher! It was with difficulty that I could bring myself to admit the identity of the wan being before me with the companion of my early boyhood. Yet the character of his face had been at all times remarkable. A cadaverousness of complexion; an eye large, liquid, and luminous beyond comparison; lips somewhat thin and very pallid, but of a surpassingly beautiful curve; a nose of a delicate Hebrew model, but with a breadth of nostril unusual in similar formations; a finely molded chin, speaking, in its want of prominence, of a want of moral energy; hair of a more than web-like softness and tenuity; these features, with an inordinate expansion above the regions of the temple, made up altogether a countenance not easily to be forgotten. And now in the mere exaggeration of the prevailing character of these features, and of the expression they were wont to convey, lay so much of change that I doubted to whom I spoke. The now ghastly pallor of the skin, and the now miraculous luster of the eye, above all things startled and even awed me. The silken hair, too, had been suffered to grow all unheeded, and as, in its wild gossamer texture, it floated rather than fell about the face, I could not, even with effort, connect its arabesque expression with any idea of simple humanity.

In the manner of my friend I was at once struck with an incoherence—an inconsistency; and I soon found this to arise from a series of feeble and futile struggles to overcome an habitual trepidancy—an excessive nervous agitation. For something of this nature I had indeed been prepared, no less by his letter, than by reminiscences of certain boyish traits, and by conclusions deduced from his peculiar physical conformation and temperament. His action was alternately vivacious and sullen. His voice varied rapidly from a tremulous indecision (when the animal spirits seemed utterly in abeyance) to that species of energetic concision—that abrupt, weighty, unhurried, and hollow-sounding enunciation—that leaden, self-balanced and perfectly modulated guttural utterance, which may be observed in the lost drunkard, or the irreclaimable eater of opium, during the periods of his most intense excitement.

It was thus that he spoke of the object of my visit, of his earnest desire to see me, and of the solace he expected me to afford him. He entered, at some length, into what he conceived to be the nature of his malady. It was, he said, a constitutional and a family evil, and one for which he despaired to find a remedy—a mere nervous affection, he immediately added, which would undoubtedly soon pass off. It displayed itself in a host of unnatural sensations. Some of these, as he detailed them, interested and bewildered me; although, perhaps, the terms, and the general manner of the narration had their weight. He suffered much from a morbid acuteness of the senses; the most insipid food was alone endurable; he could wear only garments of certain texture; the odors of all flowers were oppressive; his eyes were tortured by even a faint light; and there were but peculiar sounds, and these from stringed instruments, which did not inspire him with horror.

To an anomalous species of terror I found him a bounden slave. "I shall perish," said he, "I *must* perish in this deplorable folly. Thus, thus, and not otherwise, shall I be lost. I dread the events of the future, not in themselves, but in their results. I shudder at the thought of any, even the most trivial, incident, which may operate upon this intolerable agitation of soul. I have, indeed, no abhorrence of danger, except in its absolute effect—in terror. In this unnerved—in this pitiable condition—I feel that the period will sooner or later arrive when I must abandon life and reason together, in some struggle with the grim phantasm, FEAR."

I learned, moreover, at intervals, and through broken and equivocal hints, another singular feature of his mental condition. He was enchained by certain superstitious impressions in regard to the dwelling which he tenanted, and whence, for many years, he had never ventured forth—in regard to an influence whose supposititious force was conveyed in terms too shadowy here to be re-stated—an influence which some peculiarities in the mere form and substance of his family mansion, had, by dint of long sufferance, he said, obtained over his spirit—an effect which the *physique* of the gray walls and turrets, and of the dim tarn into which they all looked down, had, at length, brought about upon the *morale* of his existence.

He admitted, however, although with hesitation, that much of the peculiar gloom which thus afflicted him could be traced to a more natural and far more palpable origin—to the severe and long-continued illness—indeed to the evidently approaching dissolution—of a tenderly beloved sister—his sole companion for long years—his last and only relative on earth. "Her decease," he said, with a bitterness which I can never forget, "would leave him (him the hopeless and the frail) the last of the ancient race of the Ushers." While he spoke, the Lady Madeline (for so was she called) passed slowly through a remote portion of the apartment, and, without having noticed my presence, disappeared. I regarded her with an utter astonishment not unmingled with dread—and yet I found it impossible to account for such feelings. A sensation of stupor oppressed me, as my eyes followed her retreating steps. When a door, at length, closed upon her, my glance sought instinctively and eagerly the countenance of the brother—but he had buried his face in his hands, and I could only perceive that a far more than ordinary wanness had overspread the emaciated fingers through which trickled many passionate tears.

The disease of the Lady Madeline had long baffled the skill of her physicians. A settled apathy, a gradual wasting away of the person, and frequent although transient affections of a partially cataleptical character, were the unusual diagnosis. Hitherto she had steadily borne up against the pressure of her malady, and had not betaken herself finally to bed; but, on the closing in of the evening of my arrival at the house, she succumbed (as her brother told me at night with inexpressible agitation) to the prostrating power of the destroyer; and I learned that the glimpse I had obtained of her person would thus probably be the last I should obtain—that the lady, at least while living, would be seen by me no more.

For several days ensuing, her name was unmentioned by either Usher or myself; and during this period I was busied in earnest endeavors to alleviate the melancholy of my friend. We painted and read together; or I listened, as if in a dream, to the wild improvisations of his speaking guitar. And thus, as a closer and still closer intimacy admitted me more unreservedly into the recesses of his spirit, the more bitterly did I perceive the futility of all attempt at cheering a mind from which darkness, as if an inherent positive quality, poured forth upon all objects of the moral and physical universe, in one unceasing radiation of gloom.

I shall ever bear about me a memory of the many solemn hours I thus spent alone with the master of the House of Usher. Yet I should fail in any attempt to convey an idea of the exact character of the studies, or of the occupations, in which he involved me, or led me the way. An excited and highly distempered ideality threw a sulphurous luster over all. His long improvised dirges will ring forever in my ears. Among other things,

I hold painfully in mind a certain singular perversion and amplification of the wild air of the last waltz of Von Weber. From the paintings over which his elaborate fancy brooded, and which grew, touch by touch, into vagueness at which I shuddered the more thrillingly, because I shuddered knowing not why;—from these paintings (vivid as their images now are before me) I would in vain endeavor to educe more than a small portion which should lie within the compass of merely written words. By the utter simplicity, by the nakedness of his designs, he arrested and overawed attention. If ever mortal painted an idea, that mortal was Roderick Usher. For me at least—in the circumstances then surrounding me—there arose out of the pure abstractions which the hypochondriac contrived to throw upon his canvass, an intensity of intolerable awe, no shadow of which felt I ever yet in the contemplation of the certainly glowing yet too concrete reveries of Fuseli.

One of the phantasmagoric conceptions of my friend, partaking not so rigidly of the spirit of abstraction, may be shadowed forth, although feebly, in words. A small picture presented the interior of an immensely long and rectangular vault or tunnel, with low walls, smooth, white, and without interruption or device. Certain accessory points of the design served well to convey the idea that this excavation lay at an exceeding depth below the surface of the earth. No outlet was observed in any portion of its vast extent, and no torch, or other artificial source of light was discernible; yet a flood of intense rays rolled throughout, and bathed the whole in a ghastly and inappropriate splendor.

I have just spoken of that morbid condition of the auditory nerve which rendered all music intolerable to the sufferer, with the exception of certain effects of stringed instruments. It was, perhaps, the narrow limits to which he thus confined himself upon the guitar, which gave birth, in great measure, to the fantastic character of his performances. But the fervid *facility* of his *impromptus* could not be so accounted for. They must have been, and were, in the notes, as well as in the words of his wild fantasias (for he not unfrequently accompanied himself with rhymed verbal improvisations), the result of that intense mental collectedness and concentration to which I have previously alluded as observable only in particular moments of the highest artificial excitement. The words of one of these rhapsodies I have easily remembered. I was, perhaps, the more forcibly impressed with it, as he gave it, because, in the under or mystic current of its meaning, I fancied that I perceived, and for the first time, a full consciousness on the part of Usher, of the tottering of his lofty reason upon her throne. The verses, which were entitled "The Haunted Palace,"* ran very nearly, if not accurately, thus:

I

In the greenest of our valleys,
    By good angels tenanted,
Once a fair and stately palace—
    Radiant palace—reared its head.
In the monarch Thought's dominion—
    It stood there!
Never seraph spread a pinion
    Over fabric half so fair.

II

Banners yellow, glorious, golden,
    On its roof did float and flow;
(This—all this—was in the olden
    Time long ago)
And every gentle air that dallied,
    In that sweet day,
Along the ramparts plumed and pallid,
    A winged odor went away.

III

Wanderers in that happy valley
    Through two luminous windows saw
Spirits moving musically
    To a lute's well-tunèd law,
Round about a throne, where sitting
    (Porphyrogene!)

---

* This poem was first published in the *American Museum* in April 1839.—Ed.

In state his glory well befitting,
The ruler of the realm was seen.

IV

And all with pearl and ruby glowing
Was the fair palace door,
Through which came flowing, flowing, flowing,
And sparkling evermore,
A troop of Echoes whose sweet duty
Was but to sing,
In voices of surpassing beauty,
The wit and wisdom of their king.

V

But evil things, in robes of sorrow,
Assailed the monarch's high estate;
(Ah, let us mourn, for never morrow
Shall dawn upon him, desolate!)
And, round about his home, the glory
That blushed and bloomed
Is but a dim-remembered story
Of the old time entombed.

VI

And travelers now within that valley,
Through the red-litten windows, see
Vast forms that move fantastically
To a discordant melody;
While, like a rapid ghastly river,
Through the pale door,
A hideous throng rush out forever,
And laugh—but smile no more.

I well remember that suggestions arising from this ballad, led us into a train of thought wherein there became manifest an opinion of Usher's which I mention not so much on account of its novelty (for other men* have thought thus), as on account of the pertinacity with which he maintained it. This opinion, in its general form, was that of the sentience of all vegetable things. But, in his disordered fancy, the idea had assumed a more daring character, and trespassed, under certain conditions, upon the kingdom of inorganization. I lack words to express the full extent, or the earnest *abandon* of his persuasion. The belief, however, was connected (as I have previously hinted) with the gray stones of the home of his forefathers. The conditions of the sentience had been here, he imagined, fulfilled in the method of collocation of these stones—in the order of their arrangement, as well as in that of the many *fungi* which overspread them, and of the decayed trees which stood around—above all, in the long undisturbed endurance of this arrangement, and in its reduplication in the still waters of the tarn. Its evidence—the evidence of the sentience—was to be seen, he said, (and I here started as he spoke) in the gradual yet certain condensation of an atmosphere of their own about the waters and the walls. The result was discoverable, he added, in that silent, yet importunate and terrible influence which for centuries had molded the destinies of his family, and which made *him* what I now saw him—what he was. Such opinions need no comment, and I will make none.

Our books—the books which, for years, had formed no small portion of the mental existence of the invalid—were, as might be supposed, in strict keeping with this character of phantasm. We pored together over such works as the *Ververt et Chartreuse* of Gresset; the *Belphegor* of Machiavelli; the *Heaven and Hell* of Swedenborg; the *Subterranean Voyage of Nicholas Klimm* by Holberg; the *Chiromancy* of Robert Flud, of Jean D'Indaginé, and of De la Chambre; the *Journey into the Blue Distance* of Tieck; and the *City of the Sun* of Campanella. One favorite volume was a small octavo edition of the *Directorium Inquisitorium*, by the Dominican Eymeric de Gironne; and there were passages in *Pomponius Mela*, about the old African Satyrs and Aegipans, over which Usher would sit dreaming for hours. His chief delight, however, was found in the perusal of an exceedingly rare and curious book in

* Watson, Dr. Percival, Spallanzani, and especially the Bishop of Landaff. See *Chemical Essays*, vol. v.

quarto Gothic—the manual of a forgotten church—the *Vigiliae Mortuorum secundum Chorum Ecclesiæ Maguntinae.*

I could not help thinking of the wild ritual of this work, and of its probable influence upon the hypochondriac, when, one evening, having informed me abruptly that the Lady Madeline was no more, he stated his intention of preserving her corpse for a fortnight, (previously to its final interment,) in one of the numerous vaults within the main walls of the building. The worldly reason, however, assigned for this singular proceeding, was one which I did not feel at liberty to dispute. The brother had been led to his resolution (so he told me) by consideration of the unusual character of the malady of the deceased, of certain obtrusive and eager inquiries on the part of her medical men, and of the remote and exposed situation of the burial-ground of the family. I will not deny that when I called to mind the sinister countenance of the person whom I met upon the staircase, on the day of my arrival at the house, I had no desire to oppose what I regarded as at best but a harmless, and by no means an unnatural, precaution.

At the request of Usher, I personally aided him in the arrangements for the temporary entombment. The body having been encoffined, we two alone bore it to its rest. The vault in which we placed it (and which had been so long unopened that our torches, half smothered in its oppressive atmosphere, gave us little opportunity for investigation) was small, damp, and entirely without means of admission for light; lying, at great depth, immediately beneath that portion of the building in which was my own sleeping apartment. It had been used, apparently, in remote feudal times, for the worst purposes of a donjon-keep, and, in later days, as a place of deposit for powder, or some other highly combustible substance, as a portion of its floor, and the whole interior of a long archway through which we reached it, were carefully sheathed with copper. The door, of massive iron, had been, also, similarly protected. Its immense weight caused an unusually sharp grating sound, as it moved upon its hinges.

Having deposited our mournful burden upon tressels within this region of horror, we partially turned aside the yet unscrewed lid of the coffin, and looked upon the face of the tenant. A striking similitude between the brother and sister now first arrested my attention; and Usher, divining, perhaps, my thoughts, murmured out some few words from which I learned that the deceased and himself had been twins, and that sympathies of a scarcely intelligible nature had always existed between them. Our glances, however, rested not long upon the dead—for we could not regard her unawed. The disease which had thus entombed the lady in the maturity of youth, had left, as usual in all maladies of a strictly cataleptical character, the mockery of a faint blush upon the bosom and the face, and that suspiciously lingering smile upon the lip which is so terrible in death. We replaced and screwed down the lid, and, having secured the door of iron, made our way, with toil, into the scarcely less gloomy apartments of the upper portion of the house.

And now, some days of bitter grief having elapsed, an observable change came over the features of the mental disorder of my friend. His ordinary manner had vanished. His ordinary occupations were neglected or forgotten. He roamed from chamber to chamber with hurried, unequal, and objectless step. The pallor of his countenance had assumed, if possible, a more ghastly hue—but the luminousness of his eye had utterly gone out. The once occasional huskiness of his tone was heard no more; and a tremulous quaver, as if of extreme terror, habitually characterized his utterance. There were times, indeed, when I thought his unceasingly agitated mind was laboring with some oppressive secret, to divulge which he struggled for the necessary courage. At times, again, I was obliged to resolve all into the mere inexplicable vagaries of madness, for I beheld him gazing upon vacancy for long hours, in an attitude of the profoundest attention, as if listening to some imaginary sound. It was no wonder that his condition terrified—that it infected me. I felt creeping upon me, by slow yet certain degrees, the wild influences of his own fantastic yet impressive superstitions.

It was, especially, upon retiring to bed late in the night of the seventh or eighth day after the placing of the lady Madeline within the donjon, that I experienced the full power of such feelings. Sleep came not near my couch—while the hours waned and waned away. I struggled to reason off the nervousness which had dominion over me. I endeavored to believe that much, if not all of what I felt, was due to the bewildering influence of the gloomy furniture of the room—of the dark and tattered draperies, which, tortured into motion by the breath of a rising tempest, swayed fitfully to and fro upon the walls, and rustled uneasily about the decorations of the bed. But my efforts were fruitless. An irrepressible tremor gradually pervaded my frame; and, at length, there sat upon my very heart an incubus of utterly causeless alarm. Shaking this off with a gasp and a struggle, I uplifted myself upon the pillows, and, peering earnestly within the intense darkness of the chamber, harkened—I know not why, except that an instinctive spirit prompted me—to certain low and indefinite sounds which came, through the pauses of the storm, at long intervals, I knew not whence. Overpowered by an intense sentiment of horror, unaccountable yet unendurable, I threw on my clothes with haste (for I felt that I should sleep no more during the night), and endeavored to arouse myself from the pitiable condition into which I had fallen, by pacing rapidly to and fro through the apartment.

I had taken but few turns in this manner, when a light step on an adjoining staircase arrested my attention. I presently recognized it as that of Usher. In an instant afterward he rapped, with a gentle touch, at my door, and entered, bearing a lamp. His countenance was, as usual, cadaverously wan—but, moreover, there was a species of mad hilarity in his eyes—an evidently restrained *hysteria* in his whole demeanor. His air appalled me—but anything was preferable to the solitude which I had so long endured, and I even welcomed his presence as a relief.

"And you have not seen it?" he said abruptly, after having stared about him for some moments in silence—"you have not then seen it?—but, stay! you shall." Thus speaking, and having carefully shaded his lamp, he hurried to one of the casements, and threw it freely open to the storm.

The impetuous fury of the entering gust nearly lifted us from our feet. It was, indeed, a tempestuous yet sternly beautiful night, and one wildly singular in its terror and its beauty. A whirlwind had apparently collected its force in our vicinity; for there were frequent and violent alterations in the direction of the wind; and the exceeding density of the clouds (which hung so low as to press upon the turrets of the house) did not prevent our perceiving the life-like velocity with which they flew careering from all points against each other, without passing away into the distance. I say that even their exceeding density did not prevent our perceiving this—yet we had no glimpse of the moon or stars—nor was there any flashing forth of the lightning. But the under surfaces of the huge masses of agitated vapor, as well as all terrestrial objects immediately around us, were glowing in the unnatural light of a faintly luminous and distinctly visible gaseous exhalation which hung about and enshrouded the mansion.

"You must not—you shall not behold this!" said I, shudderingly, to Usher, as I led him, with a gentle violence, from the window to a seat. "These appearances, which bewilder you, are merely electrical phenomena not uncommon—or it may be that they have their ghastly origin in the rank miasma of the tarn. Let us close this casement;—the air is chilling and dangerous to your frame. Here is one of your favorite romances. I will read, and you shall listen;—and so we will pass away this terrible night together."

The antique volume which I had taken up was the *Mad Trist* of Sir Launcelot Canning; but I had called it a favorite of Usher's more in sad jest than in earnest; for, in truth, there is little in its uncouth and unimaginative prolixity which could have had interest for the lofty and spiritual ideality of my friend. It was, however, the only book immediately at hand; and I indulged a vague hope that the excitement which now agitated the hypochondriac, might find relief (for the history of mental disorder is full of similar anomalies) even in the extremeness of the folly which I should read. Could I have judged, indeed, by the wild overstrained air of vivacity with which he harkened, or apparently harkened, to the words of the tale, I might well have congratulated myself upon the success of my design.

I had arrived at that well-known portion of the story where Ethelred, the hero of the Trist, having sought in vain for peaceable admission into the dwelling of the hermit, proceeds to make good an entrance by force. Here, it will be remembered, the words of the narrative run thus:

"And Ethelred, who was by nature of a doughty heart, and who was now mighty withal, on account of the powerfulness of the wine which he had drunken, waited no longer to hold parley with the hermit, who, in sooth, was of an obstinate and maliceful turn, but, feeling the rain upon his shoulders, and fearing the rising of the tempest, uplifted his mace outright, and, with blows, made quickly room in the plankings of the door for his gauntleted hand; and now pulling therewith sturdily, he so cracked, and ripped, and tore all asunder, that the noise of the dry and hollow-sounding wood alarumed and reverberated throughout the forest."

At the termination of this sentence I started, and for a moment, paused; for it appeared to me (although I at once concluded that my excited fancy had deceived me)—it appeared to me that, from some very remote portion of the mansion, there came, indistinctly, to my ears, what might have been, in its exact similarity of character, the echo (but a stifled and dull one certainly) of the very cracking and ripping sound which Sir Launcelot had so particularly described. It was, beyond doubt, the coincidence alone which had arrested my attention; for, amid the rattling of the sashes of the casements, and the ordinary commingled noises of the still increasing storm, the sound, in itself, had nothing, surely, which should have interested or disturbed me. I continued the story:

"But the good champion Ethelred, now entering within the door, was sore enraged and amazed to perceive no signal of the maliceful hermit; but, in the stead thereof, a dragon of a scaly and prodigious demeanor, and of a fiery tongue, which sate in guard before a palace of gold, with a floor of silver; and upon the wall there hung a shield of shining brass with this legend enwritten—

Who entereth herein, a conqueror hath bin;
Who slayeth the dragon, the shield he shall win.

And Ethelred uplifted his mace, and struck upon the head of the dragon, which fell before him, and gave up his pesty breath, with a shriek so horrid and harsh, and withal so piercing, that Ethelred had fain to close his ears with his hands against the dreadful noise of it, the like whereof was never before heard."

Here again I paused abruptly, and now with a feeling of wild amazement—for there could be no doubt whatever that, in this instance, I did actually hear (although from what direction it proceeded I found it impossible to say) a low and apparently distant, but harsh, protracted, and most unusual screaming or grating sound—the exact counterpart of what my fancy had already conjured up for the dragon's unnatural shriek as described by the romancer.

Oppressed, as I certainly was, upon the occurrence of this second and most extraordinary coincidence, by a thousand conflicting sensations, in which wonder and extreme terror were predominant, I still retained sufficient presence of mind to avoid exciting, by any observation, the sensitive nervousness of my companion. I was by no means certain that he had noticed the sounds in question; although, assuredly, a strange alteration had, during the last few minutes, taken place in his demeanor. From a position fronting my own, he had gradually brought round his chair, so as to sit with his face to the door of the chamber; and thus I could but partially perceive his features, although I saw that his lips trembled as if he were murmuring inaudibly. His head had dropped upon his breast—yet I knew that he was not asleep, from the wide and rigid opening of the eye as I caught a glance of it in profile. The motion of his body, too, was at variance with this idea—for he rocked from side to side with a gentle yet constant and uniform sway. Having rapidly taken notice of all this, I resumed the narrative of Sir Launcelot, which thus proceeded:

"And now, the champion, having escaped from the terrible fury of the dragon, bethinking himself of the brazen shield, and of the breaking up of the enchantment which was upon it, removed the carcass from out of the way before him, and approached valorously over the silver pavement of the castle to where the shield was upon the wall; which in sooth tarried not for his full coming, but feel down at his feet upon the silver floor, with a mighty great and terrible ringing sound."

No sooner had these syllables passed my lips, than—as if a shield of brass had indeed, at the moment, fallen heavily upon a floor of silver—I became aware of a distinct, hollow, metallic, and clangorous, yet apparently muffled reverberation. Completely unnerved, I leaped to my feet; but the measured rocking movement of Usher was undisturbed. I rushed to the chair in which he sat. His eyes were bent fixedly before him, and throughout his whole countenance there reigned a stony rigidity. But, as I placed my hand upon his shoulder, there came a strong shudder over his whole person; a sickly smile quivered about his lips; and I saw that he spoke in a low, hurried, and gibbering murmur, as if unconscious of my presence. Bending closely over him, I at length drank in the hideous import of his words.

"Not hear it?—yes, I hear it, and *have* heard it. Long—long—long—many minutes, many hours, many days, have I heard it—yet I dared not—oh, pity me, miserable wretch that I am!—I dared not—I *dared* not speak! *We have put her living in the tomb!* Said I not that my senses were acute? I *now* tell you that I heard her first feeble movements in the hollow coffin. I heard them—many, many days ago—yet I dared not—*I dared not speak!* And now—tonight—Ethelred—ha! ha!—the breaking of the hermit's door, and the death-cry of the dragon, and the clangor of the shield!—say, rather, the rending of her coffin, and the grating of the iron hinges of her prison, and her struggles within the coppered archway of the vault! Oh whither shall I fly? Will she not be here anon? Is she not hurrying to upbraid me for my haste? Have I not heard her footstep on the stair? Do I not distinguish that heavy and horrible beating of her heart? MADMAN!"—here he sprang furiously to his feet, and shrieked out his syllables, as if in the effort he were giving up his soul—"MADMAN! I TELL YOU THAT SHE NOW STANDS WITHOUT THE DOOR!"

As if in the superhuman energy of his utterance there had been found the potency of a spell—the huge antique panels to which the speaker pointed, threw slowly back, upon the instant, their ponderous and ebony jaws. It was the work of the rushing gust—but then without those doors there DID stand the lofty and enshrouded figure of the Lady Madeline of Usher. There was blood upon her white robes, and the evidence of some bitter struggle upon every portion of her emaciated frame. For a moment she remained trembling and reeling to and fro upon the threshold—then, with a low moaning cry, fell heavily inward upon the person of her brother, and in her violent and now final death-agonies, bore him to the floor a corpse, and a victim to the terrors he had anticipated.

From that chamber, and from that mansion, I fled aghast. The storm was still abroad in all its wrath as I found myself crossing the old causeway. Suddenly there shot along the path a wild light, and I turned to see whence a gleam so unusual could have issued; for the vast house and its shadows were alone behind me. The radiance was that of the full, setting, and blood-red moon, which now shone vividly through that once barely-discernible fissure, of which I have before spoken as extending from the roof of the building, in a zigzag direction, to the base. While I gazed, this fissure rapidly widened—there came a fierce breath of the whirlwind—the entire orb of the satellite burst at once upon my sight—my brain reeled as I saw the mighty walls rushing asunder—there was a long tumultuous shouting sound like the voice of a thousand waters—and the deep and dank tarn at my feet closed sullenly and silently over the fragments of the "HOUSE OF USHER."

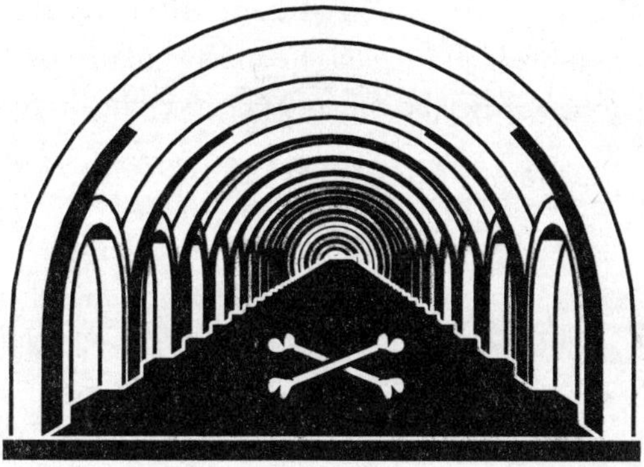

H.P.
LOVECRAFT

1

The Call of Cthulhu

"Of such great powers or beings there may be conceivably a survival . . . a survival of a hugely remote period when . . . consciousness was manifested, perhaps, in shapes and forms long since withdrawn before the tide of advancing humanity . . . forms of which poetry and legend alone have caught a flying memory and called them gods, monsters, mythical beings of all sorts and kinds . . . "

—Algernon Blackwood

I
The Horror in Clay

The most merciful thing in the world, I think, is the inability of the human mind to correlate all its contents. We live on a placid island of ignorance in the midst of black seas of infinity, and it was not meant that we should voyage far. The sciences, each straining in its own direction, have hitherto harmed us little; but some day the piecing together of dissociated knowledge will open up such terrifying vistas of reality, and of our frightful position therein, that we shall either go mad from the revelation or flee from the deadly light into the peace and safety of a new dark age.

Theosophists have guessed at the awesome grandeur of the cosmic cycle wherein our world and human race form transient incidents. They have hinted at strange survivals in terms which would freeze the blood if not masked by a bland optimism. But it is not from them that there came the single glimpse of forbidden eons which chills me when I think of it and maddens me when I dream of it. That glimpse, like all dread glimpses of truth, flashed out from an accidental piecing together of separated things—in this case an old newspaper item and the notes of a dead professor. I hope that no one else will accomplish this piecing out; certainly, if I live, I shall never knowingly supply a link in so hideous a chain. I think that the professor, too, intended to keep silent regarding the part he knew, and that he would have destroyed his notes had not sudden death seized him.

My knowledge of the thing began in the winter of 1926–27 with the death of my grand-uncle, George Gammell Angell, Professor Emeritus of Semitic languages in Brown University, Providence, Rhode Island. Professor Angell was widely known as an authority on ancient inscriptions, and had frequently been resorted to by the heads of prominent museums; so that his passing at the age of ninety-two may be recalled by many. Locally, interest was intensified by the obscurity of the cause of death. The professor had been stricken whilst returning from the Newport boat; falling suddenly, as witnesses said, after having been jostled by a nautical-looking negro who had come from one of the queer dark courts on the precipitous hillside which formed a short cut from the waterfront to the deceased's home in Williams Street. Physicians were unable to find any visible disorder, but concluded after perplexed debate that some obscure lesion of the heart, induced by the brisk ascent of so steep a hill by so elderly a man, was responsible for the end. At the time I saw no reason to dissent from this dictum, but latterly I am inclined to wonder—and more than wonder.

As my granduncle's heir and executor, for he died a childless widower, I was expected to go over his papers with some thoroughness; and for that purpose moved his entire set of files and boxes to my quarters in Boston. Much of the material which I correlated will be later published by the American Archeological Society, but there was one box which I found exceedingly puzzling, and which I felt much averse from showing to other eyes. It had been locked, and I did not find the key till it occurred to me to examine the personal ring which the professor carried always in his pocket. Then, indeed, I succeeded in opening it, but when I did so seemed only to be confronted by a greater and more closely locked barrier. For what could be the meaning of the queer clay bas-relief and the disjointed jottings, ramblings, and cuttings which I found? Had my uncle, in his latter years, become credulous of the most superficial impostures? I resolved to search out the eccentric sculptor responsible for this apparent disturbance of an old man's peace of mind.

The bas-relief was a rough rectangle less than an inch thick and about five by six inches in area; obviously of modern origin. Its designs, however, were far from modern in atmosphere and suggestion; for, although the vagaries of cubism and futurism are many and wild, they do not often reproduce that cryptic regularity which lurks in prehistoric writing. And writing of some kind the bulk of these designs seemed certainly to be; though my memory, despite much familiarity with the papers and collections of my uncle, failed in any way to identify this particular species, or even hint at its remotest affiliations.

Above these apparent hieroglyphics was a figure of evidently pictorial intent, though its impressionistic execution forbade a very clear idea of its nature. It seemed to be a sort of monster, or symbol representing a monster, of a form which only a diseased fancy could conceive. If I say that my somewhat extravagant imagination yielded simultaneous pictures of an octopus, a dragon, and a human caricature, I shall not be unfaithful to the spirit of the thing. A pulpy, tentacled head surmounted a grotesque and scaly body with rudimentary wings; but it was the *general outline* of the whole which made it most shockingly frightful. Behind the figure was a vague suggestion of a Cyclopean architectural background.

The writing accompanying this oddity was, aside from a stack of press cuttings, in Professor Angell's most recent hand; and made no pretense to literary style. What seemed to be the main document was headed "*CTHULHU CULT*" in characters painstakingly printed to avoid the erroneous reading of a word so unheard-of. This manuscript was divided into two sections, the first of which was headed "1925—Dream and Dream Work of H. A. Wilcox, 7 Thomas St., Providence, R. I.," and the second, "Narrative of Inspector John R. Legrasse, 121 Bienville St., New Orleans, La., at 1908 A. A. S. Mtg—Notes on Same, & Prof. Webb's Acct." The other manuscript papers were all brief notes, some of them accounts of the queer dreams of different persons, some of them citations from theosophical books and magazines (notably W. Scott-Eliott's *Atlantis and the Lost Lemuria*), and the rest comments on long-surviving secret societies and hidden cults, with references to passages in such mythological and anthropological source-books as Frazer's *Golden Bough* and Miss Murray's *Witch-Cult in Western Europe*. The cuttings largely alluded to outré mental illnesses and outbreaks of group folly or mania in the spring of 1925.

The first half of the principal manuscript told a very peculiar tale. It appears that on March 1st, 1925, a thin, dark young man of neurotic and excited aspect had called upon Professor Angell bearing the singular clay bas-relief, which was then exceedingly damp and fresh. His card bore the name of Henry Anthony Wilcox, and my uncle had recognized him as the youngest son of an excellent family slightly known to him, who had latterly been studying sculpture at the Rhode Island School of Design and living alone at the Fleur-de-Lys Building near that institution. Wilcox was a precocious youth of known genius but great eccentricity, and had from childhood excited attention through the strange stories and odd dreams he was in the habit of relating. He called himself "psychically hypersensitive", but the staid folk of the ancient commercial city dismissed him as merely "queer". Never mingling much with his kind, he had dropped gradually from social visibility, and was now known only to a small group of esthetes from other towns. Even the Providence Art Club, anxious to preserve its conservatism, had found him quite hopeless.

On the occasion of the visit, ran the professor's manuscript, the sculptor abruptly asked for the benefit of his host's archeological knowledge in identifying the hieroglyphics on the bas-relief. He spoke in a dreamy, stilted manner which suggested pose and alienated sympathy; and my uncle showed some sharpness in replying, for the conspicuous freshness of the tablet implied kinship with anything but archeology. Young Wilcox's rejoinder, which impressed my uncle enough to make him recall and record it verbatim, was of a fantastically poetic cast which must have typified his whole conversation, and which I have since found highly characteristic of him. He said, "It is new, indeed, for I made it last night in a dream of strange cities; and dreams are older than brooding Tyre, or the contemplative Sphinx, or garden-girdled Babylon."

It was then that he began that rambling tale which suddenly played upon a sleeping memory and won the fevered interest of my uncle. There had been a slight earthquake tremor the night before, the most considerable felt in New England for some years; and Wilcox's imagination had been keenly affected. Upon retiring, he had had an unprecedented dream of great Cyclopean cities of Titan blocks and sky-flung monoliths, all dripping with green ooze and sinister with latent horror. Hieroglyphics had covered the walls and pillars, and from some undetermined point below had come a voice that was not a voice; a chaotic sensation which only fancy could transmute into sound, but which he attempted to render by the almost unpronounceable jumble of letters, "*Cthulhu fhtagn*".

This verbal jumble was the key to the recollection which excited and disturbed Professor Angell. He questioned the sculptor with scientific minuteness; and studied with almost frantic intensity the bas-relief on which the youth had found himself working, chilled and clad only in his nightclothes, when waking had stolen bewilderingly over him. My uncle blamed his old age, Wilcox afterward said, for his slowness in recognizing both hieroglyphics and pictorial design. Many of his questions seemed highly out of place to his visitor, especially those which tried to connect the latter with strange cults or societies; and Wilcox could not understand the repeated promises of silence which he was offered in exchange for an admission of membership in some widespread mystical or paganly religious body. When Professor Angell became convinced that the sculptor was indeed ignorant of any cult or system of cryptic lore, he besieged his visitor with demands for future reports of dreams. This bore regular fruit, for after the first interview the manuscript records daily calls of the young man, during which he related startling fragments of nocturnal imagery whose burden was always some terrible Cyclopean vista of dark and dripping stone, with a subterrene voice or intelligence shouting monotonously in enigmatical sense-impacts uninscribable save as gibberish. The two sounds most frequently repeated are those rendered by the letters "*Cthulhu*" and "*R'lyeh*".

On March 23rd, the manuscript continued, Wilcox failed to appear; and inquiries at his quarters revealed that he had been stricken with an obscure sort of fever and taken to the home of his family in Waterman Street. He had cried out in the night, arousing several other artists in the building, and had manifested since then only alternations of unconsciousness and delirium. My uncle at once telephoned the family, and from that time forward kept close watch of the case; calling often at the Thayer Street office of Dr. Tobey, whom he learned to be in charge. The youth's febrile mind, apparently, was dwelling on strange things; and the doctor shuddered now and then as he spoke of them. They included not only a repetition of what he had formerly dreamed, but touched wildly on a gigantic thing "miles high" which walked or lumbered about. He at no time fully described this object, but occasional frantic words, as repeated by Dr. Tobey, convinced the professor that it must be identical with the nameless monstrosity he had sought to depict in his dream-sculpture. Reference to this object, the doctor added, was invariably a prelude to the young man's subsidence into lethargy. His temperature, oddly enough, was not greatly above normal; but the whole condition was otherwise such as to suggest true fever rather than mental disorder.

On April 2nd at about 3 p. m. every trace of Wilcox's malady suddenly ceased. He sat upright in bed, astonished to find himself at home and completely ignorant of what had happened in dream or reality since the night of March 22nd. Pronounced well by his physician, he returned to his quarters in three days; but to Professor Angell he was of no further assistance. All traces of strange dreaming had vanished with his recovery, and my uncle kept no record of his night-thoughts after a week of pointless and irrelevant accounts of thoroughly usual visions.

Here the first part of the manuscript ended, but references to certain of the scattered notes gave me much material for thought—so much, in fact, that only the ingrained skepticism then forming my philosophy can account for my continued distrust of the artist. The notes in question were those descriptive of the dreams of various persons covering the same period as that in which young Wilcox had had his strange visitations. My uncle, it seems, had quickly instituted a prodigiously far-flung body of inquiries amongst nearly all the friends whom he could question without impertinence, asking for nightly reports of their dreams, and the dates of any notable visions for some time past. The reception of his request seems to have been varied; but he must, at the very least, have received more responses than any ordinary man could have handled without a secretary. This original correspondence was not preserved, but his notes formed a thorough and really significant digest. Average people in society and business—New England's traditional "salt of the earth"—gave an almost completely negative result, though scattered cases of uneasy but formless nocturnal impressions appear here and there, always between March 23rd and April 2nd—the period of young Wilcox's delirium. Scientific men were little more affected, though four cases of vague description suggest fugitive glimpses of strange landscapes, and in one case there is mentioned a dread of something abnormal.

It was from the artists and poets that the pertinent answers came, and I know that panic would have broken loose had they been able to compare notes. As it was, lacking their original letters, I half suspected the compiler of having asked leading questions, or of having edited the correspondence in corroboration of what he had latently resolved to see. That is why I continued to feel that Wilcox, somehow cognizant of the old data which my uncle had possessed, had been imposing on the veteran scientist. These responses from esthetes told a disturbing tale. From February 28th to April 2nd a large proportion of them had dreamed very bizarre things, the intensity of the dreams being immeasurably the stronger during the period of the sculptor's delirium. Over a fourth of those who reported anything, reported scenes and half-sounds not unlike those which Wilcox had described; and some of the dreamers confessed acute fear of the gigantic nameless thing visible toward the last. One case, which the note describes with emphasis, was very sad. The subject, a widely known architect with leanings toward theosophy and occultism, went violently insane on the date of young Wilcox's seizure, and expired several months later after incessant screamings to be saved from some escaped denizen of hell. Had my uncle referred to these cases by name instead of merely by number, I should have attempted some corroboration and personal investigation; but as it was, I succeeded in tracing down only a few. All of these, however, bore out the notes in full. I have often wondered if all the objects of the professor's questioning felt as puzzled as did this fraction. It is well that no explanation shall ever reach them.

The press cuttings, as I have intimated, touched on cases of panic, mania, and eccentricity during the given period. Professor Angell must have employed a cutting bureau, for the number of extracts was tremendous, and the sources scattered throughout the globe. Here was a nocturnal suicide in London, where a lone sleeper had leaped from a window after a shocking cry. Here likewise a rambling letter to the editor of a paper in South America, where a fanatic deduces a dire future from visions he has seen. A dispatch from California describes a theosophist colony as donning white robes en masse for some "glorious fulfilment" which never arrives, whilst items from India speak guardedly of serious native unrest toward the end of March. Voodoo orgies multiply in Haiti, and African outposts report ominous mutterings. American officers in the Philippines find certain tribes bothersome about this time, and New York policemen are mobbed by hysterical Levantines on the night of March 22-23. The west of Ireland, too, is full of wild rumor and legendry, and a fantastic painter named Ardois-Bonnot hangs a blasphemous *Dream Landscape* in the Paris spring salon of 1926. And so numerous are the recorded troubles in insane asylums that only a miracle can have stopped the medical fraternity from noting strange parallelisms and drawing mystified conclusions. A weird bunch of cuttings, all told; and I can at this date scarcely envisage the callous rationalism with which I set them aside. But I was then convinced that young Wilcox had known of the older matters mentioned by the professor.

II
The Tale of Inspector Legrasse

The older matters which had made the sculptor's dream and bas-relief so significant to my uncle formed the subject of the second half of his long manuscript. Once before, it appears, Professor Angell had seen the hellish outlines of the nameless monstrosity, puzzled over the unknown hieroglyphics, and heard the ominous syllables which can be rendered only as "*Cthulhu*"; and all this in so stirring and horrible a connection that it is small wonder he pursued young Wilcox with queries and demands for data.

This earlier experience had come in 1908, seventeen years before, when the American Archeological Society held its annual meeting in St. Louis. Professor Angell, as befitted one of his authority and attainments, had had a prominent part in all the deliberations; and was one of the first to be approached by the several outsiders who took advantage of the convocation to offer questions for correct answering and problems for expert solution.

The chief of these outsiders, and in a short time the focus of interest for the entire meeting, was a commonplace-looking middle-aged man who had traveled all the way from New Orleans for certain special information unobtainable from any local source. His name was John Raymond Legrasse, and he was by profession an inspector of police. With him he bore the subject of his visit, a grotesque, repulsive, and apparently very ancient stone statuette whose origin he was at a loss to determine.

It must not be fancied that Inspector Legrasse had the least interest in archeology. On the contrary, his wish for enlightenment was prompted by purely professional considerations. The statuette, idol, fetish, or whatever it was, had been captured some months before in the wooded swamps south of New Orleans during a raid on a supposed voodoo meeting; and so singular and hideous were the rites connected with it, that the police could not but realize that they had stumbled on a dark cult totally unknown to them, and infinitely more diabolic than even the blackest of the African voodoo circles. Of its origin, apart from the erratic and unbelievable tales extorted from the captured members, absolutely nothing was to be discovered; hence the anxiety of the police for any antiquarian lore which might help them to place the frightful symbol, and through it track down the cult to its fountain-head.

Inspector Legrasse was scarcely prepared for the sensation which his offering created. One sight of the thing had been enough to throw the assembled men of science into a state of tense excitement, and they lost no time in crowding around him to gaze at the diminutive figure whose utter strangeness and air of genuinely abysmal antiquity hinted so potently at unopened and archaic vistas. No recognized school of sculpture had animated this terrible object, yet centuries and even thousands of years seemed recorded in its dim and greenish surface of unplaceable stone.

The figure, which was finally passed slowly from man to man for close and careful study, was between seven and eight inches in height, and of exquisitely artistic workmanship. It represented a monster of vaguely anthropoid outline, but with an octopuslike head whose face was a mass of feelers, a scaly, rubbery-looking body, prodigious claws on hind and fore feet, and long, narrow wings behind. This thing, which seemed instinct with a fearsome and unnatural malignancy, was of a somewhat bloated corpulence, and squatted evilly on a rectangular block or pedestal covered with undecipherable characters. The tips of the wings touched the back edge of the block, the seat occupied the center, whilst the long, curved claws of the doubled-up, crouching hind legs gripped the front edge and extended a quarter of the way down toward the bottom of the pedestal. The cephalopod head was bent forward, so that the ends of the facial feelers brushed the backs of huge forepaws which clasped the croucher's elevated knees. The aspect of the whole was abnormally lifelike, and the more subtly fearful because its source was so totally unknown. Its vast, awesome, and incalculable age was unmistakable; yet not one link did it show with any known type of art belonging to civilization's youth—or indeed to any other time.

Totally separate and apart, its very material was a mystery; for the soapy, greenish-black stone with its golden or iridescent flecks and striations resembled nothing familiar to geology or mineralogy. The characters along the base were equally baffling; and no member present, despite a representation of half the world's expert learning in this field, could form the least notion of even their remotest linguistic kinship. They, like the subject and material, belonged to something horribly remote and distinct from mankind as we know it; something frightfully suggestive of old and unhallowed cycles of life in which our world and our conceptions have no part.

And yet, as the members severally shook their heads and confessed defeat at the inspector's problem, there was one man in that gathering who suspected a touch of bizarre familiarity in the monstrous shape and writing, and who presently told with some diffidence of the odd trifle he knew. This person was the late William Channing Webb, professor of anthropology in Princeton University, and an explorer of no slight note.

Professor Webb had been engaged, forty-eight years before, in a tour of Greenland and Iceland in search of some Runic inscriptions which he failed to unearth; and whilst high up on the West Greenland coast had encountered a singular tribe or cult of degenerate Eskimos whose religion, a curious form of devil-worship, chilled him with its deliberate bloodthirstiness and repulsiveness. It was a faith of which other Eskimos knew little, and which they mentioned only with shudders, saying that it had come down from horribly ancient eons before ever the world was made. Besides nameless rites and human sacrifices there were certain queer hereditary rituals addressed to a supreme elder devil or *tornasuk*; and of this Professor Webb had taken a careful phonetic copy from an aged *angekok* or wizard-priest, expressing the sounds in Roman letters as best he knew how. But just now of prime significance was the fetish which this cult had cherished, and around which they danced when the aurora leaped high over the ice cliffs. It was, the professor stated, a very crude bas-relief of stone, comprising a hideous picture and some cryptic writing. And as far as he could tell, it was a rough parallel in all essential features of the bestial thing now lying before the meeting.

These data, received with suspense and astonishment by the assembled members, proved doubly exciting to Inspector Legrasse; and he began at once to ply his informant with questions. Having noted and copied an oral ritual among the swamp cult-worshipers his men had arrested, he besought the professor to remember as best he might the syllables taken down amongst the diabolist Eskimos. There then followed an exhaustive comparison of details, and a moment of really awed silence when both detective and scientist agreed on the virtual identity of the phrase common to two hellish rituals so many worlds of distance apart. What, in substance, both the Eskimo wizards and the Louisiana swamp-priests had chanted to their kindred idols was something very like this—the word-divisions being guessed at from traditional breaks in the phrase as chanted aloud:

"Ph'nglui mglw'nafh Cthulhu R'lyeh wgah'nagl fhtagn."

Legrasse had one point in advance of Professor Webb, for several among his mongrel prisoners had repeated to him what older celebrants had told them the words meant. This text, as given, ran something like this:

In his house at R'lyeh dead Cthulhu waits dreaming.

And now, in response to a general urgent demand, Inspector Legrasse related as fully as possible his experience with the swamp worshipers; telling a story to which I could see my uncle attached profound significance. It savored of the wildest dreams of myth-maker and theosophist, and disclosed an astonishing degree of cosmic imagination among such half-castes and pariahs as might be least expected to possess it.

On November 1st, 1907, there had come to New Orleans police a frantic summons from the swamp and lagoon country to the south. The squatters there, mostly primitive but good-natured descendants of Lafitte's men, were in the grip of stark terror from an unknown thing which had stolen upon them in the night. It was voodoo, apparently, but voodoo of a more terrible sort than they had ever known; and some of their women and children had disappeared since the malevolent tom-tom had begun its incessant beating far within the black haunted woods where no dweller ventured. There were insane shouts and harrowing screams, soul-chilling chants and dancing devil-flames; and, the frightened messenger added, the people could stand it no more.

So a body of twenty police, filling two carriages and an automobile, had set out in the late afternoon with the shivering squatter as a guide. At the end of the passable road they alighted, and for miles splashed on in silence through the terrible cypress woods where day never came. Ugly roots and malignant hanging nooses of Spanish moss beset them, and now and then a pile of dank stones or fragments of a rotting wall intensified by its hint of morbid habitation a depression which every malformed tree and every fungous islet combined to create. At length the squatter settlement, a miserable huddle of huts, hove in sight; and hysterical dwellers ran out to cluster around the group of bobbing lanterns. The muffled beat of tom-toms was now faintly audible far, far ahead; and a curdling shriek came at infrequent intervals when the wind shifted. A reddish glare, too, seemed to filter through the pale undergrowth beyond endless avenues of forest night. Reluctant even to be left alone again, each one of the cowed squatters refused point-blank to advance another inch toward the scene of unholy worship, so Inspector Legrasse and his nineteen colleagues plunged on unguided into black arcades of horror that none of them had ever trod before.

The region now entered by the police was one of traditionally evil repute, substantially unknown and untraversed by white men. There were legends of a hidden lake unglimpsed by mortal sight, in which dwelt a huge, formless white polypous thing with luminous eyes; and squatters whispered that bat-winged devils flew up out of caverns in inner earth to worship it at midnight. They said it had been there before D'Iberville, before La Salle, before the Indians, and before even the wholesome beasts and birds of the woods. It was nightmare itself, and to see it was to die. But it made men dream, and so they knew enough to keep away. The present voodoo orgy was, indeed, on the merest fringe of this abhorred area, but that location was bad enough; hence perhaps the very place of the worship had terrified the squatters more than the shocking sounds and incidents.

Only poetry or madness could do justice to the noises heard by Legrasse's men as they plowed on through the black morass toward the red glare and the muffled tom-toms. There are vocal qualities peculiar to men, and vocal qualities peculiar to beasts; and it is terrible to hear the one when the source should yield the other. Animal fury and orgiastic license here whipped themselves to demoniac heights by howls and squawking ecstasies that tore and reverberated through those nighted woods like pestilential tempests from the gulfs of hell. Now and then the less organized ululations would cease, and from what seemed a well-drilled chorus of hoarse voices would rise in singsong chant that hideous phrase or ritual:

Ph'nglui mglw'nafh Cthulhu R'lyeh wgah'nagl fhtagn.

Then the men, having reached a spot where the trees were thinner, came suddenly in sight of the spectacle itself. Four of them reeled, one fainted, and two were shaken into a frantic cry which the mad cacophony of the orgy fortunately deadened. Legrasse dashed swamp water on the face of the fainting man, and all stood trembling and nearly hypnotized with horror.

In a natural glade of the swamp stood a grassy island of perhaps an acre's extent, clear of trees and tolerably dry. On this now leaped and twisted a more indescribable horde of human abnormality than any but a Sime or an Angarola could paint. Void of clothing, this hybrid spawn were braying, bellowing and writhing about a monstrous ring-shaped bonfire; in the center of which, revealed by occasional rifts in the curtain of flame, stood a great granite monolith some eight feet in height; on top of which, incongruous in its diminutiveness, rested the noxious carven statuette. From a wide circle of ten scaffolds set up at regular intervals with the flame-girt monolith as a center hung, head downward, the oddly marred bodies of the helpless squatters who had disappeared. It was inside this circle that the ring of worshipers jumped and roared, the general direction of the mass motion being from left to right in endless bacchanale between the ring of bodies and the ring of fire.

It may have been only imagination and it may have been only echoes which induced one of the men, an excitable Spaniard, to fancy he heard antiphonal responses to the ritual from some far and unillumined spot deeper within the wood of ancient legendry and horror. This man, Joseph D. Galvez, I later met and questioned; and he proved distractingly imaginative. He indeed went so far as to hint of the faint beating of great wings, and of a glimpse of shining eyes and a mountainous white bulk beyond the remotest trees—but I suppose he had been hearing too much native superstition.

Actually, the horrified pause of the men was of comparatively brief duration. Duty came first; and although there must have been nearly a hundred mongrel celebrants in the throng, the police relied on their firearms and plunged determinedly into the nauseous rout. For five minutes the resultant din and chaos were beyond description. Wild blows were struck, shots were fired, and escapes were made; but in the end Legrasse was able to count some forty-seven sullen prisoners, whom he forced to dress in haste and fall into line between two rows of policemen. Five of the worshipers lay dead, and two severely wounded ones were carried away on improvised stretchers by their fellow-prisoners. The image on the monolith, of course, was carefully removed and carried back by Legrasse.

Examined at headquarters after a trip of intense strain and weariness, the prisoners all proved to be men of a very low, mixed-blooded, and mentally aberrant type. Most were seamen, and a sprinkling of negroes and mulattoes, largely West Indians or Brava Portuguese from the Cape Verde Islands, gave a coloring of voodooism to the heterogeneous cult. But before many questions were asked, it became manifest that something far deeper and older than negro fetishism was involved. Degraded and ignorant as they were, the creatures held with surprizing consistency to the central idea of their loathsome faith.

They worshiped, so they said, the Great Old Ones who lived ages before there were any men, and who came to the young world out of the sky. Those Old Ones were gone now, inside the earth and under the sea; but their dead bodies had told their secrets in dreams to the first man, who formed a cult which had never died. This was that cult, and the prisoners said it had always existed and always would exist, hidden in distant wastes and dark places all over the world until the time when the great priest Cthulhu, from his dark house in the mighty city of R'lyeh under the waters, should rise and bring the earth again beneath his sway. Some day he would call, when the stars were ready, and the secret cult would always be waiting to liberate him.

Meanwhile no more must be told. There was a secret which even torture could not extract. Mankind was not absolutely alone among the conscious things of earth, for shapes came out of the dark to visit the faithful few. But these were not the Great Old Ones. No man had ever seen the Old Ones. The carven idol was great Cthulhu, but none might say whether or not the others were precisely like him. No one could read the old writing now, but things were told by word of mouth. The chanted ritual was not the secret—that was never spoken aloud, only whispered. The chant meant only this: "In his house at R'lyeh dead Cthulhu waits dreaming."

Only two of the prisoners were found sane enough to be hanged, and the rest were committed to various institutions. All denied a part in the ritual murders, and averred that the killing had been done by Black-winged Ones which had come to them from their immemorial meeting-place in the haunted wood. But of those mysterious allies no coherent account could ever be gained. What the police did extract came mainly from an immensely aged mestizo named Castro, who claimed to have sailed to strange ports and talked with undying leaders of the cult in the mountains of China.

Old Castro remembered bits of hideous legend that paled the speculations of theosophists and made man and the world seem recent and transient indeed. There had been eons when other Things ruled on the earth, and They had had great cities. Remains of Them, he said the deathless Chinamen had told him, were still to be found as Cyclopean stones on islands in the Pacific. They all died vast epochs of time before man came, but there were arts which could revive Them when the stars had come round again to the right positions in the cycle of eternity. They had, indeed, come themselves from the stars, and brought Their images with Them.

These Great Old Ones, Castro continued, were not composed altogether of flesh and blood. They had shape—for did not this star-fashioned image prove it?—but that shape was not made of matter. When the stars were right, They could plunge from world to world through the sky; but when the stars were wrong, They could not live. But although They no longer lived, They would never really die. They all lay in stone houses in Their great city of R'lyeh, preserved by the spells of mighty Cthulhu for a glorious resurrection when the stars and the earth might once more be ready for Them. But at that time some force from outside must serve to liberate Their bodies. The spells that preserved Them intact likewise prevented Them from making an initial move, and They could only lie awake in the dark and think whilst uncounted millions of years rolled by. They knew all that was occurring in the universe, for Their mode of speech was transmitted thought. Even now They talked in Their tombs. When, after infinities of chaos, the first men came, the Great Old Ones spoke to the sensitive among them by molding their dreams; for only thus could Their language reach the fleshly minds of mammals.

Then, whispered Castro, those first men formed the cult around small idols which the Great Ones showed them; idols brought in dim eras from dark stars. That cult would never die till the stars came right again, and the secret priests would take great Cthulhu from His tomb to revive His subjects and resume His rule of earth. The time would be easy to know, for then mankind would have become as the Great Old Ones; free and wild and beyond good and evil, with laws and morals thrown aside and all men shouting and killing and reveling in joy. Then the liberated Old Ones would teach them new ways to shout and kill and revel and enjoy themselves, and all the earth would flame with a holocaust of ecstasy and freedom. Meanwhile the cult, by appropriate rites, must keep alive the memory of those ancient ways and shadow forth the prophecy of their return.

In the elder time chosen men had talked with the entombed Old Ones in dreams, but then something had happened. The great stone city R'lyeh, with its monoliths and sepulchers, had sunk beneath the waves; and the deep waters, full of the one primal mystery through which not even thought can pass, had cut off the spectral intercourse. But memory never died, and high priests said that the city would rise again when the stars were right. Then came out of the earth the black spirits of earth, moldy and shadowy, and full of dim rumors picked up in caverns beneath forgotten sea-bottoms. But of them old Castro dared not speak much. He cut himself off hurriedly, and no amount of persuasion or subtlety could elicit more in this direction. The *size* of the Old Ones, too, he curiously declined to mention. Of the cult, he said that he thought the center lay amid the pathless deserts of Arabia, where Irem, the City of Pillars, dreams hidden and untouched. It was not allied to the European witch-cult, and was virtually unknown beyond its members. No book had ever really hinted of it, though the deathless Chinamen said that there were double meanings in the *Necronomicon* of the mad Arab Abdul Alhazred which the initiated might read as they chose, especially the much-discussed couplet:

"That is not dead which can eternal lie,
And with strange eons even death may die."

Legrasse, deeply impressed and not a little bewildered, had inquired in vain concerning the historic affiliations of the cult. Castro, apparently, had told the truth when he said that it was wholly secret. The authorities at Tulane University could shed no light upon either cult or image, and now the detective had come to the highest authorities in the country and met with no more than the Greenland tale of Professor Webb.

The feverish interest aroused at the meeting by Legrasse's tale, corroborated as it was by the statuette, is echoed in the subsequent correspondence of those who attended, although scant mention occurs in the formal publication of the society. Caution is the first care of those accustomed to face occasional charlatanry and imposture. Legrasse for some time lent the image to Professor Webb, but at the latter's death it was returned to him and remains in his possession, where I viewed it not long ago. It is truly a terrible thing, and unmistakably akin to the dream-sculpture of young Wilcox.

That my uncle was excited by the tale of the sculptor I did not wonder, for what thoughts must arise upon hearing, after a knowledge of what Legrasse had learned of the cult, of a sensitive young man who had *dreamed* not only the figure and exact hieroglyphics of the swamp-found image and the Greenland devil tablet, but had come *in his dreams* upon at least three of the precise words of the formula uttered alike by Eskimo diabolists and mongrel Louisianans? Professor Angell's instant start on an investigation of the utmost thoroughness was eminently natural; though privately I suspected young Wilcox of having heard of the cult in some indirect way, and of having invented a series of dreams to heighten and continue the mystery at my uncle's expense. The dream-narratives and cuttings collected by the professor were, of course, strong corroboration; but the rationalism of my mind and the extravagance of the whole subject led me to adopt what I thought the most sensible conclusions. So, after thoroughly studying the manuscript again and correlating the theosophical and anthropological notes with the cult narrative of Legrasse, I made a trip to Providence to see the sculptor and give him the rebuke I thought proper for so boldly imposing upon a learned and aged man.

Wilcox still lived alone in the Fleur-de-Lys Building in Thomas Street, a hideous Victorian imitation of Seventeenth Century Breton architecture which flaunts its stuccoed front amidst the lovely Colonial houses on the ancient hill, and under the very shadow of the finest Georgian steeple in America. I found him at work in his rooms, and at once conceded from the specimens scattered about that his genius is indeed profound and authentic. He will, I believe, be heard from sometime as one of the great decadents; for he has crystallized in clay and will one day mirror in marble those nightmares and fantasies which Arthur Machen evokes in prose, and Clark Ashton Smith makes visible in verse and in painting.

Dark, frail, and somewhat unkempt in aspect, he turned languidly at my knock and asked me my business without rising. When I told him who I was, he displayed some interest; for my uncle had excited his curiosity in probing his strange dreams, yet had never explained the reason for the study. I did not enlarge his knowledge in this regard, but sought with some subtlety to draw him out.

In a short time I became convinced of his absolute sincerity, for he spoke of the dreams in a manner none could mistake. They and their subconscious residuum had influenced his art profoundly, and he showed me a morbid statue whose contours almost made me shake with the potency of its black suggestion. He could not recall having seen the original of this thing except in his own dream bas-relief, but the outlines had formed themselves insensibly under his hands. It was, no doubt, the giant shape he had raved of in delirium. That he really knew nothing of the hidden cult, save from what my uncle's relentless catechism had let fall, he soon made clear; and again I strove to think of some way in which he could possibly have received the weird impressions.

He talked of his dreams in a strangely poetic fashion; making me see with terrible vividness the damp Cyclopean city of slimy green stone—whose *geometry*, he oddly said, was *all wrong*—and hear with frightened expectancy the ceaseless, half-mental calling from underground: "*Cthulhu fhtagn*," "*Cthulhu fhtagn*."

These words had formed part of that dread ritual which told of dead Cthulhu's dream-vigil in his stone vault at R'lyeh, and I felt deeply moved despite my rational beliefs. Wilcox, I was sure, had heard of the cult in some casual way, and had soon forgotten it amidst the mass of his equally weird reading and imagining. Later, by virtue of its sheer impressiveness, it had found subconscious expression in dreams, in the bas-relief, and in the terrible statue I now beheld; so that his imposture upon my uncle had been a very innocent one. The youth was of a type, at once slightly affected and slightly ill-mannered, which I could never like; but I was willing enough now to admit both his genius and his honesty. I took leave of him amicably, and wish him all the success his talent promises.

The matter of the cult still remained to fascinate me, and at times I had visions of personal fame from researches into its origin and connections. I visited New Orleans, talked with Legrasse and others of that old-time raiding-party, saw the frightful image, and even questioned such of the mongrel prisoners as still survived. Old Castro, unfortunately, had been dead for some years. What I now heard so graphically at first hand, though it was really no more than a detailed confirmation of what my uncle had written, excited me afresh; for I felt sure that I was on the track of a very real, very secret, and very ancient religion whose discovery would make me an anthropologist of note. My attitude was still one of absolute materialism, *as I wish it still were*, and I discounted with almost inexplicable perversity the coincidence of the dream notes and odd cuttings collected by Professor Angell.

One thing which I began to suspect, and which I now fear I *know*, is that my uncle's death was far from natural. He fell on a narrow hill street leading up from an ancient waterfront swarming with foreign mongrels, after a careless push from a negro sailor. I did not forget the mixed blood and marine pursuits of the cult-members in Louisiana, and would not be surprized to learn of secret methods and poison needles as ruthless and as anciently known as the cryptic rites and beliefs. Legrasse and his men, it is true, have been let alone; but in Norway a certain seaman who saw things is dead. Might not the deeper inquiries of my uncle after encountering the sculptor's data have come to sinister ears? I thing Professor Angell died because he knew too much, or because he was likely to learn too much. Whether I shall go as he did remains to be seen, for I have learned much now.

III
The Madness from the Sea

If heaven ever wishes to grant me a boon, it will be a total effacing of the results of a mere chance which fixed my eye on a certain stray piece of shelf-paper. It was nothing on which I would naturally have stumbled in the course of my daily round, for it was an old number of an Australian journal, *Sydney Bulletin* for April 18, 1925. It had escaped even the cutting bureau which had at the time of its issuance been avidly collecting material for my uncle's research.

I had largely given over my inquiries into what Professor Angell called the "Cthulhu Cult," and was visiting a learned friend of Paterson, New Jersey, the curator of a local museum and a mineralogist of note. Examining one day the reserve specimens roughly set on the storage shelves in a rear room of the museum, my eye was caught by an odd picture in one of the old papers spread beneath the stones. It was the *Sydney Bulletin* I have mentioned, for my friend has wide affiliations in all conceivable foreign parts; and the picture was a half-tone cut of a hideous stone image almost identical with that which Legrasse had found in the swamp.

Eagerly clearing the sheet of its precious contents, I scanned the item in detail; and was disappointed to find it of only moderate length. What it suggested, however, was of portentous significance to my flagging quest; and I carefully tore it out for immediate action. It read as follows:

MYSTERY DERELICT FOUND AT SEA

Vigilant Arrives With Helpless Armed New Zealand Yacht in Tow. One Survivor and Dead Man Found Aboard. Tale of Desperate Battle and Deaths at Sea. Rescued Seaman Refuses Particulars of Strange Experience. Odd Idol Found in His Possession. Inquiry to Follow.

> The Morrison Co.'s freighter *Vigilant*, bound from Valparaiso, arrived this morning at its wharf in Darling Harbour, having in tow the battled and disabled but heavily armed steam yacht *Alert* of Dunedin, N. Z., which was sighted April 12th in S. Latitude 34° 21', W. Longitude 152° 17', with one living and one dead man aboard.
>
> The *Vigilant* left Valparaiso March 25th, and on April 2d was driven considerably south of her course by exceptionally heavy storms and monster waves. On April 12th the derelict was sighted; and though apparently deserted, was found upon boarding to contain one survivor in a half-delirious condition and one man who had evidently been dead for more than a week.
>
> The living man was clutching a horrible stone idol of unknown origin, about a foot in height, regarding whose nature authorities at Sydney University, the Royal Society, and the Museum in College Street all profess complete bafflement, and which the survivor says he found in the cabin of the yacht, in a small carved shrine of common pattern.
>
> This man, after recovering his senses, told an exceedingly strange story of piracy and slaughter. He is Gustaf Johansen, a Norwegian of some intelligence, and had been second mate of the two-masted schooner *Emma* of Auckland, which sailed for Callao February 20th, with a complement of eleven men.

The *Emma*, he says, was delayed and thrown widely south of her course by the great storm of March 1st, and on March 22d, in S. Latitude 49° 51', W. Longitude 128° 34', encountered the *Alert*, manned by a queer and evil-looking crew of Kanakas and half-castes. Being ordered peremptorily to turn back, Capt. Collins refused; whereupon the strange crew began to fire savagely and without warning upon the schooner with a peculiarly heavy battery of brass cannon forming part of the yacht's equipment.

The *Emma's* men showed fight, says the survivor, and though the schooner began to sink from shots beneath the waterline they managed to heave alongside their enemy and board her, grappling with the savage crew on the yacht's deck, and being forced to kill them all, the number being slightly superior, because of their particularly abhorrent and desperate though rather clumsy mode of fighting.

Three of the *Emma's* men, including Capt. Collins and First Mate Green, were killed; and the remaining eight under Second Mate Johansen proceeded to navigate the captured yacht, going ahead in their original direction to see if any reason for their ordering back had existed.

The next day, it appears, they raised and landed on a small island, although none is known to exist in that part of the ocean; and six of the men somehow died ashore, though Johansen is queerly reticent about this part of his story and speaks only of their falling into a rock chasm.

Later, it seems, he and one companion boarded the yacht and tried to manage her, but were beaten about by the storm of April 2nd.

From that time till his rescue on the 12th, the man remembers little, and he does not even recall when William Briden, his companion, died. Briden's death reveals no apparent cause, and was probably due to excitement or exposure.

Cable advices from Dunedin report that the *Alert* was well known there as an island trader, and bore an evil reputation along the waterfront. It was owned by a curious group of half-castes whose frequent meetings and night trips to the woods attracted no little curiosity; and it had set sail in great haste just after the storm and earth tremors of March 1st.

> Our Auckland correspondent gives the *Emma* and her crew an excellent reputation, and Johansen is described as a sober and worthy man.
>
> The admiralty will institute an inquiry on the whole matter beginning tomorrow, at which every effort will be made to induce Johansen to speak more freely than he has done hitherto.

This was all, together with the picture of the hellish image; but what a train of ideas it started in my mind! Here were new treasuries of data on the Cthulhu Cult, and evidence that it had strange interests at sea as well as on land. What motive prompted the hybrid crew to order back the *Emma* as they sailed about with their hideous idol? What was the unknown island on which six of the *Emma's* crew had died, and about which the mate Johansen was so secretive? What had the vice-admiralty's investigation brought out, and what was known of the noxious cult in Dunedin? And most marvelous of all, what deep and more than natural linkage of dates was this which gave a malign and now undeniable significance to the various turns of events so carefully noted by my uncle?

March 1st—our February 28th according to the International Date Line—the earthquake and storm had come. From Dunedin the *Alert* and her noisome crew had darted eagerly forth as if imperiously summoned, and on the other side of the earth poets and artists had begun to dream of a strange, dank Cyclopean city whilst a young sculptor had molded in his sleep the form of the dreaded Cthulhu. March 23rd the crew of the *Emma* landed on an unknown island and left six men dead; and on that date the dreams of sensitive men assumed a heightened vividness and darkened with dread of a giant monster's malign pursuit, whilst an architect had gone mad and a sculptor had lapsed suddenly into delirium! And what of this storm of April 2nd—the date on which all dreams of the dank city ceased, and Wilcox emerged unharmed from the bondage of strange fever? What of all this—and of those hints of old Castro about the sunken, star-born Old Ones and their coming reign; their faithful cult *and their mastery of dreams*? Was I tottering on the brink of cosmic horrors beyond man's power to bear? If so, they must be horrors of the mind alone, for in some way the second of April had put a stop to whatever monstrous menace had begun its siege of mankind's soul.

That evening, after a day of hurried cabling and arranging, I bade my host adieu and took a train for San Francisco. In less than a month I was in Dunedin; where, however, I found that little was known of the strange cult-members who had lingered in the old sea taverns. Waterfront scum was far too common for special mention; though there was vague talk about one inland trip these mongrels had made, during which faint drumming and red flame were noted on the distant hills.

In Auckland I learned that Johansen had returned *with yellow hair turned white* after a perfunctory and inconclusive questioning at Sydney, and had thereafter sold his cottage in West Street and sailed with his wife to his old home in Oslo. Of his stirring experience he would tell his friends no more than he had told the admiralty officials, and all they could do was to give me his Oslo address.

After that I went to Sydney and talked profitlessly with seamen and members of the vice-admiralty court. I saw the *Alert*, now sold and in commercial use, at Circular Quay in Sydney Cove, but gained nothing from its non-committal bulk. The crouching image with its cuttlefish head, dragon body, scaly wings, and hieroglyphed pedestal, was preserved in the Museum at Hyde Park; and I studied it long and well, finding it a thing of balefully exquisite workmanship, and with the same utter mystery, terrible antiquity, and unearthly strangeness of material which I had noted in Legrasse's smaller specimen. Geologists, the curator told me, had found it a monstrous puzzle; for they vowed that the world held no rock like it. Then I thought with a shudder of what old Castro had told Legrasse about the primal Great Ones: "They had come from the stars, and had brought Their images with Them."

Shaken with such a mental revolution as I had never before known, I now resolved to visit Mate Johansen in Oslo. Sailing for London, I re-embarked at once for the Norwegian capital; and one autumn day landed at the trim wharves in the shadow of the Egeberg.

Johansen's address, I discovered, lay in the Old Town of King Harold Haardrada, which kept alive the name of Oslo during all the centuries that the greater city masqueraded as "Christiania." I made the brief trip by taxicab, and knocked with palpitant heart at the door of a neat and ancient building with plastered front. A sad-faced woman in black answered my summons, and I was stung with disappointment when she told me in halting English that Gustaf Johansen was no more.

He had not long survived his return, said his wife, for the doings at sea in 1925 had broken him. He had told her no more than he had told the public, but had left a long manuscript—of "technical matters" as he said—written in English, evidently in order to safeguard her from the peril of casual perusal. During a walk through a narrow lane near the Gothenburg dock, a bundle of papers falling from an attic window had knocked him down. Two Lascar sailors at once helped him to his feet, but before the ambulance could reach him he was dead. Physicians found no adequate cause for the end, and laid it to heart trouble and a weakened constitution.

I now felt gnawing at my vitals that dark terror which will never leave me till I, too, am at rest; "accidentally" or otherwise. Persuading the widow that my connection with her husband's "technical matters" was sufficient to entitle me to his manuscript, I bore the document away and began to read it on the London boat.

It was a simple, rambling thing—a naive sailor's effort at a post-facto diary—and strove to recall day by day that last awful voyage. I can not attempt to transcribe it verbatim in all its cloudiness and redundance, but I will tell its gist enough to show why the sound of the water against the vessel's sides became so unendurable to me that I stopped my ears with cotton.

Johansen, thank God, did not know quite all, even though he saw the city and the Thing, but I shall never sleep calmly again when I think of the horrors that lurk ceaselessly behind life in time and in space, and of those unhallowed blasphemies from elder stars which dream beneath the sea, known and favored by a nightmare cult ready and eager to loose them on the world whenever another earthquake shall heave their monstrous stone city again to the sun and air.

Johansen's voyage had begun just as he told it to the vice-admiralty. The *Emma*, in ballast, had cleared Auckland on February 20th, and had felt the full force of that earthquake-born tempest which must have heaved up from the sea-bottom the horrors that filled men's dreams. Once more under control, the ship was making good progress when held up by the *Alert* on March 22nd, and I could feel the mate's regret as he wrote of her bombardment and sinking. Of the swarthy cult-fiends on the *Alert* he speaks with significant horror. There was some peculiarly abominable quality about them which made their destruction seem almost a duty, and

Johansen shows ingenuous wonder at the charge of ruthlessness brought against his party during the proceedings of the court of inquiry. Then, driven ahead by curiosity in their captured yacht under Johansen's command, the men sight a great stone pillar sticking out of the sea, and in S. Latitude 47° 9', W. Longitude 126° 43' come upon a coastline of mingled mud, ooze, and weedy Cyclopean masonry which can be nothing less than the tangible substance of earth's supreme terror—the nightmare corpse-city of R'lyeh, that was built in measureless eons behind history by the vast, loathsome shapes that seeped down from the dark stars. There lay great Cthulhu and his hordes, hidden in green slimy vaults and sending out at last, after cycles incalculable, the thoughts that spread fear to the dreams of the sensitive and called imperiously to the faithful to come on a pilgrimage of liberation and restoration. All this Johansen did not suspect, but God knows he soon saw enough!

I suppose that only a single mountain-top, the hideous monolith-crowned citadel whereon great Cthulhu was buried, actually emerged from the waters. When I think of the *extent* of all that may be brooding down there I almost wish to kill myself forthwith. Johansen and his men were awed by the cosmic majesty of this dripping Babylon of elder demons, and must have guessed without guidance that it was nothing of this or of any sane planet. Awe at the unbelievable size of the greenish stone blocks, at the dizzying height of the great carven monolith, and at the stupefying identity of the colossal statues and bas-reliefs with the queer image found in the shrine on the *Alert*, is poignantly visible in every line of the mate's frightened description.

Without knowing what futurism is like, Johansen achieved something very close to it when he spoke of the city; for instead of describing any definite structure or building, he dwells only on the broad impressions of vast angles and stone surfaces—surfaces too great to belong to anything right or proper for this earth, and impious with horrible images and hieroglyphs. I mention his talk about *angles* because it suggests something Wilcox had told me of his awful dreams. He had said that the *geometry* of the dream-place he saw was abnormal, non-Euclidean, and loathsomely redolent of spheres and dimensions apart from ours. Now an unlettered seaman felt the same thing whilst gazing at the terrible reality.

Johansen and his men landed at a sloping mud-bank on this monstrous Acropolis, and clambered slipperily up over titan oozy blocks which could have been no mortal staircase. The very sun of heaven seemed distorted when viewed through the polarizing miasma welling out from this sea-soaked perversion, and twisted menace and suspense lurked leeringly in those crazily elusive angles of carven rock where a second glance showed concavity after the first showed convexity.

Something very like fright had come over all the explorers before anything more definite than rock and ooze and weed was seen. Each would have fled had he not feared the scorn of the others, and it was only half-heartedly that they searched—vainly, as it proved—for some portable souvenir to bear away.

It was Rodriguez the Portuguese who climbed up the foot of the monolith and shouted of what he had found. The rest followed him, and looked curiously at the immense carved door with the now familiar squid-dragon bas-relief. It was, Johansen said, like a great barn-door; and they all felt that it was a door because of the ornate lintel, threshold, and jambs around it, though they could not decide whether it lay flat like a trap-door or slantwise like an outside cellar-door. As Wilcox would have said, the geometry of the place was all wrong. One could not be sure that the sea and the ground were horizontal, hence the relative position of everything else seemed fantasmally variable.

Briden pushed at the stone in several places without result. Then Donovan felt over it delicately around the edge, pressing each point separately as he went. He climbed interminably along the grotesque stone molding—that is, one would call it climbing if the thing was not after all horizontal—and the men wondered how any door in the universe could be so vast. Then, very softly and slowly, the acre-great panel began to give inward at the top; and they saw that it was balanced.

Donovan slid or somehow propelled himself down or along the jamb and rejoined his fellows, and everyone watched the queer recession of the monstrously carven portal. In this fantasy of prismatic distortion it moved anomalously in a diagonal way, so that all the rules of matter and perspective seemed upset.

The aperture was black with a darkness almost material. That tenebrousness was indeed a *positive quality*; for it obscured such parts of the inner walls as ought to have been revealed, and actually burst forth like smoke from its eon-long imprisonment, visibly darkening the sun as it slunk away into the shrunken and gibbous sky on flapping membranous wings. The odor arising from the newly opened depths was intolerable, and at length the quick-eared Hawkins thought he heard a nasty, slopping sound down there. Everyone listened, and everyone was listening still when It lumbered slobberingly into sight and gropingly squeezed Its gelatinous green immensity through the black doorway into the tainted outside air of that poison city of madness.

Poor Johansen's handwriting almost gave out when he wrote of this. Of the six men who never reached the ship, he thinks two perished of pure fright in that accursed instant. The Thing can not be described—there is no language for such abysms of shrieking and immemorial lunacy, such eldritch contradictions of all matter, force, and cosmic order. A mountain walked or stumbled. God! What wonder that across the earth a great architect went mad, and poor Wilcox raved with fever in that telepathic instant? The Thing of the idols, the green, sticky spawn of the stars, had awaked to claim his own. The stars were right again, and what an age-old cult had failed to do by design, a band of innocent sailors had done by accident. After vigintillions of years great Cthulhu was loose again, and ravening for delight.

Three men were swept up by the flabby claws before anybody turned. God rest them, if there be any rest in the universe. They were Donovan, Guerrera and Angstrom. Parker slipped as the other three were plunging frenziedly over endless vistas of green-crusted rock to the boat, and Johansen swears he was swallowed up by an angle of masonry which shouldn't have been there; an angle which was acute, but behaved as if it were obtuse. So only Briden and Johansen reached the boat, and pulled desperately for the *Alert* as the mountainous monstrosity flopped down the slimy stones and hesitated floundering at the edge of the water.

Steam had not been suffered to go down entirely, despite the departure of all hands for the shore; and it was the work of only a few moments of feverish rushing up and down between wheels and engines to get the *Alert* under way. Slowly, amidst the distorted horrors of that indescribable scene, she began to churn the lethal waters; whilst on the masonry of that charnel shore that was not of earth the titan Thing from the stars slavered and gibbered like Polypheme cursing the fleeing ship of Odysseus. Then, bolder than the storied Cyclops, great Cthulhu slid greasily into the water and began to pursue with vast wave-raising strokes of cosmic potency. Briden looked back and went mad, laughing shrilly as he kept on laughing at intervals till death found him one night in the cabin whilst Johansen was wandering deliriously.

But Johansen had not given out yet. Knowing that the Thing could surely overtake the *Alert* until steam was fully up, he resolved on a desperate chance; and, setting the engine for full speed, ran lightning-like on deck and reversed the wheel. There was a mighty eddying and foaming in the noisome brine, and as the steam mounted higher and higher the brave Norwegian drove his vessel head on against the pursuing jelly which rose above the unclean froth like the stern of a demon galleon. The awful squid-head with writhing feelers came nearly up to the bowsprit of the sturdy yacht, but Johansen drove on relentlessly.

There was a bursting as of an exploding bladder, a slushy nastiness as of a cloven sunfish, a stench as of a thousand opened graves, and a sound that the chronicler would not put on paper. For an instant the ship was befouled by an acrid and blinding green cloud, and then there was only a venomous seething astern; where—God in heaven!—the scattered plasticity of that nameless sky-spawn was nebulously *recombining* in its hateful original form, whilst its distance widened every second as the *Alert* gained impetus from its mounting steam.

That was all. After that Johansen only brooded over the idol in the cabin and attended to a few matters of food for himself and the laughing maniac by his side. He did not try to navigate after the first bold flight, for the reaction had taken something out of his soul. Then came the storm of April 2nd, and a gathering of the clouds about his consciousness. There is a sense of spectral whirling through liquid gulfs of infinity, of dizzying rides through reeling universes on a comet's tail, and of hysterical plunges from the pit to the moon and from the moon back again to the pit, all livened by a cachinnating chorus of the distorted, hilarious elder gods and the green, bat-winged mocking imps of Tartarus.

Out of that dream came rescue—the *Vigilant*, the vice-admiralty court, the streets of Dunedin, and the long voyage back home to the old house by the Egeberg. He could not tell—they would think him mad. He would write of what he knew before death came, but his wife must not guess. Death would be a boon if only it could blot out the memories.

That was the document I read, and now I have placed it in the tin box beside the bas-relief and the papers of Professor Angell. With it shall go this record of mine—this test of my own sanity, wherein is pieced together that which I hope may never be pieced together again. I have looked upon all that the universe has to hold of horror, and even the skies of spring and the flowers of summer must ever afterward be poison to me. But I do not think my life will be long. As my uncle went, as poor Johansen went, so I shall go. I know too much, and the cult still lives.

Cthulhu still lives, too, I suppose, again in that chasm of stone which has shielded him since the sun was young. His accursed city is sunken once more, for the *Vigilant* sailed over the spot after the April storm; but his ministers on earth still bellow and prance and slay around idol-capped monoliths in lonely places. He must have been trapped by the sinking whilst within his black abyss, or else the world would by now be screaming with fright and frenzy. Who knows the end? What has risen may sink, and what has sunk may rise. Loathsomeness waits and dreams in the deep, and decay spreads over the tottering cities of men. A time will come—but I must not and can not think! Let me pray that, if I do not survive this manuscript, my executors may put caution before audacity and see that it meets no other eye.

NOTE

Found among the papers of the late
Francis Wayland Thurston, of Boston.

2

At the Mountains of Madness

I am forced into speech because men of science have refused to follow my advice without knowing why. It is altogether against my will that I tell my reasons for opposing this contemplated invasion of the antarctic—with its vast fossil hunt and its wholesale boring and melting of the ancient ice caps. And I am the more reluctant because my warning may be in vain.

Doubt of the real facts, as I must reveal them, is inevitable; yet, if I suppressed what will seem extravagant and incredible there would be nothing left. The hitherto withheld photographs, both ordinary and aërial, will count in my favor, for they are damnably vivid and graphic. Still, they will be doubted because of the great lengths to which clever fakery can be carried. The ink drawings, of course, will be jeered at as obvious impostures; notwithstanding a strangeness and technique which art experts ought to remark and puzzle over.

In the end I must rely on the judgment and standing of the few scientific leaders who have, on the one hand, sufficient independence of thought to weigh my data on its own hideously convincing merits or in the light of certain primordial and highly baffling myth cycles; and on the other hand, sufficient influence to deter the exploring world in general from any rash and over-ambitious program in the region of those mountains of madness.

It is an unfortunate fact that relatively obscure men like myself and my associates, connected only with a small university, have little chance of making an impression where matters of a wildly bizarre or highly controversial natures are concerned.

It is further against us that we are not, in the strictest sense, specialists in the fields which came primarily to be concerned. As a geologist, my object in leading the Miskatonic University Expedition was wholly that of securing deep-level specimens of rock and soil from various parts of the antarctic continent, aided by the remarkable drill devised by Professor Frank H. Pabodie of our engineering department.

I had no wish to be a pioneer in any other field than this, but I did hope that the use of this new mechanical appliance at different points along previously explored paths would bring to light materials of a sort hitherto unreached by the ordinary methods of collection.

Pabodie's drilling apparatus, as the public already knows from our reports, was unique and radical in its lightness, portability, and capacity to combine the ordinary Artesian drill principle with the principle of the small circular rock drill in such a way as to cope quickly with strata of varying hardness.

Steel head, jointed rods, gasoline motor, collapsible wooden derrick, dynamiting paraphernalia, cording, rubbish-removal auger, and sectional piping for bores five inches wide and up to one thousand feet deep all formed, with needed accessories, no greater load than three seven-dog sledges could carry. This was made possible by the clever aluminum alloy of which most of the metal objects were fashioned.

Four large Dornier aëroplanes, designed especially for the tremendous altitude flying necessary on the antarctic plateau and with added fuel-warming and quick-starting devices worked out by Pabodie, could transport our entire expedition from a base at the edge of the great ice barrier to various suitable inland points, and from these points a sufficient quota of dogs would serve us.

We planned to cover as great an area as one antarctic season—or longer, if absolutely necessary—would permit, operating mostly in the mountain ranges and on the plateau south of Ross Sea; regions explored in varying degree by Shackleton, Amundsen, Scott, and Byrd. With frequent changes of camp, made by aëroplane and involving distances great enough to be of geological significance, we expected to unearth a quite unprecedented amount of material—especially in the pre-Cambrian strata of which so narrow a range of antarctic specimens had previously been secured.

We wished also to obtain as great as possible a variety of the upper fossiliferous rocks, since the primal life history of this bleak realm of ice and death is of the highest importance to our knowledge of the earth's past. That the antarctic continent was once temperate and even tropical, with a teeming vegetable and animal life of which the lichens, marine fauna, arachnida, and penguins of the northern edge are the only survivors, is a matter of common information; and we hoped to expand that information in variety, accuracy, and detail. When a simple boring revealed fossiliferous signs, we would enlarge the aperture by blasting, in order to get specimens of suitable size and condition.

Our borings, of varying depth according to the promise held out by the upper soil or rock, were to be confined to exposed, or nearly exposed, land surfaces—these inevitably being slopes and ridges because of the mile or two-mile thickness of solid ice overlying the lower levels.

We could not afford to waste drilling depth on any considerable amount of more glaciation, though Pabodie had worked out a plan for sinking copper electrodes in thick clusters of borings and melting off limited areas of ice with current from a gasoline-driven dynamo.

It is this plan—which we could not put into effect except experimentally on an expedition such as ours—that the coming Starkweather-Moore Expedition proposes to follow, despite the warnings I have issued since our return from the antarctic.

The public knows of the Miskatonic Expedition through our frequent wireless reports to the *Arkham Advertiser* and Associated Press, and through the later articles by Pabodie and myself. We consisted of four men from the University—Pabodie, Lake of the biology department, Atwood of the physics department—also a meteorologist—and myself, representing geology and having nominal command, also sixteen assistants: seven graduate students from Miskatonic and nine skilled mechanics.

Of these sixteen, twelve were qualified aëroplane pilots, all but two of whom were competent wireless operators. Eight of them understood navigation with compass and sextant, as did Pabodie, Atwood and I. In addition, of course, our two ships—wooden exwhalers, reinforced for ice conditions and having auxiliary steam—were fully manned.

The Nathaniel Derby Pickman Foundation, aided by a few special contributions, financed the expedition; hence our preparations were extremely thorough, despite the absence of great publicity.

The dogs, sledges, machines, camp materials, and unassembled parts of our five planes were delivered in Boston, and there our ships were loaded.

We were marvelously well-equipped for our specific purposes, and in all matters pertaining to supplies, regimen, transportation, and camp construction we profited by the excellent example of our many recent and exceptionally brilliant predecessors. It was the unusual number and fame of these predecessors which made our own expedition—ample though it was—so little noticed by the world at large.

As the newspapers told, we sailed from Boston Harbor on September 2nd, 1930, taking a leisurely course down the coast and through the Panama Canal, and stopping at Samoa and Hobart, Tasmania, at which latter place we took on final supplies.

None of our exploring party had ever been in the polar regions before, hence we all relied greatly on our ship captains—J. B. Douglas, commanding the brig *Arkham*, and serving as commander of the sea party, and Georg Thorfinnssen, commanding the barque *Miskatonic*—both veteran whalers in antarctic waters.

As we left the inhabited world behind the sun sank lower and lower in the north, and stayed longer and longer above the horizon each day. At about 62° South Latitude we sighted our first icebergs—tablelike objects with vertical sides—and just before reaching the antarctic circle, which we crossed on October 20th with appropriately quaint ceremonies, we were considerably troubled with field ice.

The falling temperature bothered me considerably after our long voyage through the tropics, but I tried to brace up for the worse rigors to come. On many occasions the curious atmospheric effects enchanted me vastly; these included a strikingly vivid mirage—the first I had ever seen—in which distant bergs became the battlements of unimaginable cosmic castles.

Pushing through the ice, which was fortunately neither extensive nor thickly packed, we regained open water at South Latitude 67°, East Longitude 175°. On the morning of October 26th a strong land blink appeared on the south, and before noon we all felt a thrill of excitement at beholding a vast, lofty, and snow-clad mountain chain which opened out and covered the whole vista ahead. At last we had encountered an outpost of the great unknown continent and its cryptic world of frozen death.

These peaks were obviously the Admiralty Range discovered by Ross, and it would now be our task to round Cape Adare and sail down the east coast of Victoria Land to our contemplated base on the shore of McMurdo Sound, at the foot of the volcano Erebus in South Latitude 77° 9'.

The last lap of the voyage was vivid and fancy-stirring. Great barren peaks of mystery loomed up constantly against the west as the low northern sun of noon or the still lower horizon-grazing southern sun of midnight poured its hazy reddish rays over the white snow, bluish ice and water lanes, and black bits of exposed granite slope.

Through the desolate summits swept raging, intermittent gusts of the terrible antarctic wind, whose cadences sometimes held vague suggestions of a wild and half-sentient musical piping, with notes extending over a wide range, and which for some subconscious mnemonic reason seemed to me disquieting and even dimly terrible.

Something about the scene reminded me of the strange and disturbing Asian paintings of Nicholas Roerich, and of the still stranger and more disturbing descriptions of the evilly fabled plateau of Leng which occur in the dreaded *Necronomicon* of the mad Arab Abdul Alhazred. I was rather sorry, later on, that I had ever looked into that monstrous book at the college library.

On the 7th of November, sight of the westward range having been temporarily lost, we passed Franklin Island; and the next day descried the cones of Mts. Erebus and Terror on Ross Island ahead, with the long line of the Parry Mountains beyond. There now stretched off to the east the low, white line of the great ice barrier, rising perpendicularly to a height of two hundred feet like the rocky cliffs of Quebec, and marking the end of southward navigation.

In the afternoon we entered McMurdo Sound and stood off the coast in the lee of smoking Mt. Erebus. The scoriaceous peak towered up some twelve thousand seven hundred feet against the eastern sky, like a Japanese print of the sacred Fujiyama, while beyond it rose the white, ghostlike height of Mt. Terror, ten thousand nine hundred feet in altitude, and now extinct as a volcano.

Puffs of smoke from Erebus came intermittently, and one of the graduate assistants—a brilliant young fellow named Danforth—pointed out what looked like lava on the snowy slope, remarking that this mountain, discovered in 1840, had undoubtedly been the source of Poe's image when he wrote seven years later:

"—the lavas that restlessly roll
Their sulphurous currents down Yaanek
In the ultimate climes of the pole—
That groan as they roll down Mount Yaanek
In the realms of the boreal pole."

Danforth was a great reader of bizarre material, and had talked a good deal of Poe. I was interested myself because of the antarctic scene of Poe's only long story—the disturbing and enigmatical *Arthur Gordon Pym*. On the barren shore, and on the lofty ice barrier in the background, myriad of grotesque penguins squawked and flapped their fins, while many fat seals were visible on the water, swimming or sprawling across large cakes of slowly drifting ice.

Using small boats, we effected a difficult landing on Ross Island shortly after midnight, on the morning of the 9th, carrying a line of cable from each of the ships and preparing to unload supplies by means of a breeches-buoy arrangement.

Our sensations on first treading antarctic soil were poignant and complex, even though at this particular point the Scott and Shackleton expeditions had preceded us.

Our camp on the frozen shore below the volcano's slope was only a provisional one, headquarters being kept aboard the *Arkham*. We landed all our drilling apparatus, dogs, sledges, tents, provisions, gasoline tanks, experimental ice-melting outfit, cameras, both ordinary and aërial, aëroplane parts, and other accessories, including three small portable wireless outfits—besides those in the planes—capable of communicating with the *Arkham's* large outfit from any part of the antarctic continent that we would be likely to visit.

The ship's outfit, communicating with the outside world, was to convey press reports to the *Arkham Advertiser's* powerful wireless station on Kingsport Head, Mass. We hoped to complete our work during a single antarctic summer; but if this proved impossible we would winter on the

Arkham, sending the *Miskatonic* north before the freezing of the ice for another summer's supplies.

I need not repeat what the newspapers have already published about our early work: of our ascent of Mt. Erebus; our successful mineral borings at several points on Ross Island and the singular speed with which Pabodie's apparatus accomplished them, even through solid rock layers; our provisional test of the small ice-melting equipment; our perilous ascent of the great barrier with sledges and supplies; and our final assembling of five huge aëroplanes at the camp atop the barrier.

The health of our land party—twenty men and fifty-five Alaskan sledge dogs—was remarkable, though of course we had so far encountered no really destructive temperatures or windstorms.

For the most part, the thermometer varied between zero and 20° or 25° above, and our experience with New England winters had accustomed us to rigors of this sort. The barrier camp was semipermanent, and destined to be a storage cache for gasoline, provisions, dynamite, and other supplies.

Only four of our planes were needed to carry the actual exploring material, the fifth being left with a pilot and two men, from the ships, at the storage cache to form a means of reaching us from the *Arkham* in case all our exploring planes were lost.

Later, when not using all the other planes for moving apparatus, we would employ one or two in a shuttle transportation service between this cache and another permanent base on the great plateau from six hundred to seven hundred miles southward, beyond Beardmore Glacier.

Despite the almost unanimous accounts of appalling winds and tempests that pour down from the plateau, we determined to dispense with intermediate bases, taking our chances in the interest of economy and probable efficiency.

Wireless reports have spoken of the breathtaking, four-hour, nonstop flight of our squadron on November 21st over the lofty shelf ice, with vast peaks rising on the west, and the unfathomed silences echoing to the sound of our engines.

Wind troubled us only moderately, and our radio compasses helped us through the one opaque fog we encountered. When the vast rise loomed ahead, between Latitudes 83° and 84°, we knew we had reached Beardmore Glacier, the largest valley glacier in the world, and that the frozen sea was now giving place to a frowning and mountainous coast line.

At last we were truly entering the white, æon-dead world of the ultimate south. Even as we realized it we saw the peak of Mt. Nansen in the eastern distance, towering up to its height of almost fifteen thousand feet.

The successful establishment of the southern base above the glacier in Latitude 86° 7', East Longitude 174° 23', and the phenomenally rapid and effective borings and blastings made at various points reached by our sledge trips and short aëroplane flights, are matters of history; as is the arduous and triumphant ascent of Mt. Nansen by Pabodie and two of the graduate students—Gedney and Carroll—on December 13th to 15th.

We were some eight thousand five hundred feet above sea-level. When experimental drillings revealed solid ground only twelve feet down through the snow and ice at certain points, we made considerable use of the small melting apparatus and sunk bores and performed dynamiting at many places, where no previous explorer had ever thought of securing mineral specimens.

The pre-Cambrian granites and beacon sandstones thus obtained confirmed our belief that this plateau was homogeneous, with the great bulk of the continent to the west, but somewhat different from the parts lying eastward below South America—which we then thought to form a separate and smaller continent divided from the larger one by a frozen junction of Ross and Weddell Seas, though Byrd has since disproved the report.

In certain of the sandstones, dynamited and chiseled after boring revealed their nature, we found some highly interesting fossil markings and fragments; notably ferns, seaweeds, trilobites, crinoids, and such mollusks as linguellæ and gastropods—all of which seemed of real significance in connection with the region's primordial history. There was also a queer triangular, striated marking, about a foot in greatest diameter, which Lake pieced together from three fragments of slate brought up from a deep-blasted aperture.

These fragments came from a point to the westward, near the Queen Alexandra Range; and Lake, as a biologist, seemed to find their curious marking unusually puzzling and provocative, though to my geological eye it looked not unlike some of the ripple effects reasonably common in the sedimentary rocks.

Since slate is no more than a metamorphic formation into which a sedimentary stratum is pressed, and since the pressure itself produces odd distorting effects on any markings which may exist, I saw no reason for extreme wonder over the striated depression.

On January 6, 1931, Lake, Pabodie, Daniels, all six of the students, four mechanics, and myself flew directly over the south pole in two of the great planes, being forced down once by a sudden high wind, which, fortunately, did not develop into a typical storm. This was, as the papers have stated, one of several observation flights, during others of which we tried to discern new topographical features in areas unreached by previous explorers.

Our early flights were disappointing in this latter respect, though they afforded us some magnificent examples of the richly fantastic and deceptive mirages of the polar regions, of which our sea voyage had given us some brief foretastes.

Distant mountains floated in the sky as enchanted cities, and often the whole white world would dissolve into a gold, silver, and scarlet land of Dunsanian dreams and adventurous expectancy under the magic of the low midnight sun.

On cloudy days we had considerable trouble in flying, owing to the tendency of snowy earth and sky to merge into one mystical opalescent void with no visible horizon to mark the junction of the two.

At length we resolved to carry out our original plan of flying five hundred miles eastward with all four exploring planes and establishing a fresh sub-base at a point which would probably be on the smaller continental division, as we mistakenly conceived it. Geological specimens obtained there would be desirable for purposes of comparison.

Our health so far had remained excellent—lime juice well offsetting the steady diet of tinned and salted food, and temperatures generally above zero enabling us to do without our thickest furs.

It was now midsummer, and with haste and care we might be able to conclude work by March and avoid a tedious wintering through the long antarctic night. Several savage windstorms had burst upon us from the west, but we had escaped damage through the skill of Atwood in devising rudimentary aëroplane shelters and windbreaks of heavy snow blocks, and in reinforcing the principal camp buildings with snow. Our good luck and efficiency had indeed been almost uncanny.

The outside world knew, of course, of our program, and was told also of Lake's strange and dogged insistence on a westward—or rather, northwestward—prospecting trip before our radical shift to the new base.

It seems that he had pondered a great deal and with alarmingly radical daring over that triangular striated marking in the slate; reading into it certain contradictions in nature and geological period which whetted his curiosity to the utmost, and made him avid to sink more borings and blastings in the west-stretching formation to which the exhumed fragments evidently belonged.

He was strangely convinced that the marking was the print of some bulky, unknown, and radically unclassifiable organism of considerably advanced evolution, notwithstanding that the rock which bore it was of so vastly ancient a date—Cambrian if not actually pre-Cambrian—as to preclude the probable existence not only of all highly evolved life, but of any life at all above the unicellular or at most the trilobite stage. These fragments, with their odd marking, must have been five hundred million to a thousand million years old.

II

Popular imagination, I judge, responded actively to our wireless bulletins of Lake's start northwestward into regions never trodden by human foot or penetrated by human imagination, though we did not mention his wild hopes of revolutionizing the entire sciences of biology and geology.

His preliminary sledging and boring journey of January 11th to 18th with Pabodie and five others—marred by the loss of two dogs in an upset when crossing one of the great pressure ridges in the ice—had brought up more and more of the Archæan slate; and even I was interested by the singular profusion of evident fossil markings in that unbelievably ancient stratum.

These markings, however, were of very primitive life forms involving no great paradox except that any life forms should occur in rock as definitely pre-Cambrian as this seemed to be; hence I still failed to see the good sense of Lake's demand for an interlude in our time-saving program—an interlude requiring the use of all four planes, many men, and the whole of the expedition's mechanical apparatus.

I did not, in the end, veto the plan, though I decided not to accompany the northwestward party despite Lake's plea for my geological advice. While they were gone, I would remain at the base with Pabodie and five men and work out final plans for the eastward shift. In preparation for this transfer, one of the planes had begun to move up a good gasoline supply from McMurdo Sound; but this could wait temporarily. I kept with me one sledge and nine dogs, since it is unwise to be at any time without possible transportation in an utterly tenantless world of æon-long death.

Lake's subexpedition into the unknown, as every one will recall, sent out its own reports from the short-wave transmitters on the planes; these being simultaneously picked up by our apparatus at the southern base and by the *Arkham* at McMurdo Sound, whence they were relayed to the outside world on wave lengths up to fifty meters.

The start was made January 22nd at 4 a.m.; and the first wireless message we received came only two hours later, when Lake spoke of descending and starting a small-scale ice-melting and bore at a point some three hundred miles away from us. Six hours after that a second and very excited message told of the frantic, beaverlike work whereby a shallow shaft had been sunk and blasted, culminating in the discovery of slate fragments with several markings approximately like the one which had caused the original puzzlement.

Three hours later a brief bulletin announced the resumption of the flight in the teeth of a raw and piercing gale; and when I dispatched a message of protest against further hazards, Lake replied curtly that his new specimens made any hazard worth taking.

I saw that his excitement had reached the point of mutiny, and that I could do nothing to check this headlong risk of the whole expedition's success; but it was appalling to think of his plunging deeper and deeper into that treacherous and sinister white immensity of tempests and unfathomed mysteries which stretched off for some fifteen hundred miles to the half-known, half-suspected coast line of Queen Mary and Knox Lands.

Then, in about an hour and a half more, came that doubly excited message from Lake's moving plane, which almost reversed my sentiments and made me wish I had accompanied the party:

> 10:05 p.m. On the wing. After snowstorm, have spied mountain range ahead higher than any hitherto seen. May equal Himalayas, allowing for height of plateau. Probable Latitude 76° 15', Longitude

> 113° 10' E. Reaches far as can see to right and left. Suspicion of two smoking cones. All peaks black and bare of snow. Gale blowing off them impedes navigation.

After that Pabodie, the men, and I hung breathlessly over the receiver. Thought of this titanic mountain rampart seven hundred miles away inflamed our deepest sense of adventure; and we rejoiced that our expedition, if not ourselves personally, had been its discoverers. In half an hour Lake called us again:

> Moulton's plane forced down on plateau in foothills, but nobody hurt and perhaps can repair. Shall transfer essentials to other three for return or further moves if necessary, but no more heavy plane travel needed just now. Mountains surpass anything in imagination. Am going up scouting in Carroll's plane, with all weight out.
>
> You can't imagine anything like this. Highest peaks must go over thirty-five thousand feet. Everest out of the running, Atwood to work out height with theodolite while Carroll and I go up. Probably wrong about cones, for formations look stratified. Possibly pre-Cambrian slate with other strata mixed in. Queer sky line effects—regular sections of cubes clinging to highest peaks. Whole thing marvelous in red-gold light of low sun. Like land of mystery in a dream or gateway to forbidden world of untrodden wonder. Wish you were here to study.

Though it was technically sleeping time, not one of us listeners thought for a moment of retiring. It must have been a good deal the same at McMurdo Sound, where the supply cache and the *Arkham* were also getting the messages; for Captain Douglas gave out a call congratulating everybody on the important find, and Sherman, the cache operator, seconded his sentiments. We were sorry, of course, about the damaged aëroplane, but hoped it could be easily mended. Then, at eleven p.m., came another call from Lake:

> Up with Carroll over highest foothills. Don't dare try really tall peaks in present weather, but shall later. Frightful work climbing, and hard going at this altitude, but worth it. Great range fairly solid, hence can't get any glimpses beyond. Main summits exceed

> Himalayas, and very queer. Range looks like pre-Cambrian slate, with plain signs of many other upheaved strata. Was wrong about volcanism. Goes farther in either direction than we can see. Swept clear of snow above about twenty-one thousand feet.
>
> Odd formations on slopes of highest mountains. Great low square blocks with exactly vertical sides, and rectangular lines of low, vertical ramparts, like the old Asian castles clinging to steep mountains in Roerich's paintings. Impressive from distance. Flew close to some, and Carroll thought they were formed of smaller separate pieces, but that is probably weathering. Most edges crumbled and rounded off as if exposed to storms and climate changes for millions of years.
>
> Parts, especially upper parts, seem to be of lighter-colored rock than any visible strata on slopes proper, hence an evidently crystalline origin. Close flying shows many cave mouths, some unusually regular in outline, square or semicircular. You must come and investigate. Think I saw rampart squarely on top of one peak. Height seems about thirty thousand to thirty-five thousand feet. Am up twenty-one thousand five hundred myself, in devilish, gnawing cold. Wind whistles and pipes through passes and in and out of caves, but no flying danger so far.

From then on for another half hour Lake kept up a running fire of comment, and expressed his intention of climbing some of the peaks on foot. I replied that I would join him as soon as he could send a plane, and that Pabodie and I would work out the best gasoline plan—just where and how to concentrate our supply in view of the expedition's altered character.

Obviously, Lake's boring operations, as well as his aëroplane activities, would need a great deal delivered at the new base which he was to establish at the foot of the mountains; and it was possible that the eastward flight might not be made, after all, this season. In connection with this business I called Captain Douglas and asked him to get as much as possible out of the ships and up the barrier with the single dog team we had left there. A direct route across the unknown region between Lake and McMurdo Sound was what we really ought to establish.

Lake called me later to say that he had decided to let the camp stay where Moulton's plane had been forced down, and where repairs had already progressed somewhat. The ice sheet was very thin, with dark ground here and there visible, and he would sink some borings and blasts at that very point before making any sledge trips or climbing expeditions.

He spoke of the ineffable majesty of the whole scene, and the queer state of his sensations at being in the lee of vast, silent pinnacles, whose ranks shot up like a wall reaching the sky at the world's rim.

Atwood's theodolite observations had placed the height of the five tallest peaks at from thirty thousand to thirty-four thousand feet.

The windswept nature of the terrain clearly disturbed Lake, for it argued the occasional existence of prodigious gales, violent beyond anything we had so far encountered. His camp lay a little more than five miles from where the higher foothills rose abruptly.

I could almost trace a note of subconscious alarm in his words—flashed across a glacial void of seven hundred miles—as he urged that we all hasten with the matter and get the strange, new region disposed of as soon as possible. He was about to rest now, after a continuous day's work of almost unparalleled speed, strenuousness, and results.

In the morning I had a three-cornered wireless talk with Lake and Captain Douglas at their widely separated bases. It was agreed that one of Lake's planes would come to my base for Pabodie, the five men, and myself, as well as for all the fuel it could carry. The rest of the fuel question, depending on our decision about an easterly trip, could wait for a few days, since Lake had enough for immediate camp heat and borings.

Eventually the old southern base ought to be restocked, but if we postponed the easterly trip we would not use it till the next summer, and, meanwhile, Lake must send a plane to explore a direct route between his new mountains and McMurdo Sound.

Pabodie and I prepared to close our base for a short or long period, as the case might be. If we wintered in the antarctic we would probably fly straight from Lake's base to the *Arkham* without returning to this spot. Some of our conical tents had already been reinforced by blocks of hard snow, and now we decided to complete the job of making a permanent village. Owing to a very liberal tent supply, Lake had with him all that his base would need, even after our arrival. I wirelessed that Pabodie and I would be ready for the northwestward move after one day's work and one night's rest.

Our labors, however, were not very steady after four p.m., for about that time Lake began sending in the most extraordinary and excited messages. His working day had started unpropitiously, since an aëroplane survey of the nearly exposed rock surfaces showed an entire absence of those Archæan and primordial strata for which he was looking, and which formed so great a part of the colossal peaks that loomed up at a tantalizing distance from the camp.

Most of the rocks glimpsed were apparently Jurassic and Comanchean sandstones and Permian and Triassic schists, with now and then a glossy black outcropping suggesting a hard and slaty coal.

This rather discouraged Lake, whose plans all hinged on unearthing specimens more than five hundred million years older. It was clear to him that in order to recover the Archæan slate vein in which he had found the odd markings, he would have to make a long sledge trip from these foothills to the steep slopes of the gigantic mountains themselves.

He had resolved, nevertheless, to do some local boring as part of the expedition's general program; hence, he set up the drill and put five men to work with it while the rest finished settling the camp and repairing the damaged aëroplane. The softest visible rock—a sandstone about a quarter of a mile from the camp—had been chosen for the first sampling; and the drill made excellent progress without much supplementary blasting.

It was about three hours afterward, following the first really heavy blast of the operation, that the shouting of the drill crew was heard; and that young Gedney—the acting foreman—rushed into the camp with the startling news.

They had struck a cave. Early in the boring the sandstone had given place to a vein of Comanchean limestone, full of minute fossil cephalopods, corals, echini, and spirifera, and with occasional suggestions of siliceous sponges and marine vertebrate bones—the latter probably of teliosts, sharks, and ganoids.

This, in itself, was important enough, as affording the first vertebrate fossils the expedition had yet secured; but when shortly afterward the drill head dropped through the stratum into apparent vacancy, a wholly new and doubly intense wave of excitement spread among the excavators.

A good-sized blast had laid open the subterrane secret; and now, through a jagged aperture perhaps five feet across and three feet thick, there yawned before the avid searchers a section of shallow limestone hollowing worn more than fifty million years ago by the trickling ground waters of a bygone tropic world.

The hollowed layer was not more than seven or eight feet deep, but extended off indefinitely in all directions and had a fresh, slightly moving air which suggested its membership in an extensive subterranean system. Its roof and floor were abundantly equipped with large stalactites and stalagmites, some of which met in columnar form.

But important above all else was the vast deposit of shells and bones, which in places nearly choked the passage. Washed down from unknown jungles of Mesozoic tree ferns and fungi, and forests of Tertiary cycads, fan palms, and primitive angiosperms, this osseous medley contained representatives of more Cretaceous, Eocene, and other animal species than the greatest palæontologist could have counted or classified in a year. Mollusks, crustacean armor, fishes, amphibians, reptiles, birds, and early mammals—great and small, known and unknown.

No wonder Gedney ran back to the camp shouting, and no wonder every one else dropped work and rushed headlong through the biting cold to where the tall derrick marked a new-found gateway to secrets of inner earth and vanished æons.

When Lake had satisfied the first keen edge of his curiosity he scribbled a message in his notebook and had young Moulton run back to the camp to dispatch it by wireless.

This was my first word of the discovery, and it told of the identification of early shells, bones of ganoids and placoderms, remnants of labyrinthodonta and thecoiidea, great mosasaur skull fragments, dinosaur vertebræ and armor plates, pterodactyl teeth and wing bones, Archaeopteryx débris, Miocene sharks' teeth, primitive bird skulls, and other bones of archaic mammals such as Palæotheres, Xiphodons, Eohippi, Oreodons, and Titanotheriidæ.

There was nothing as recent as a mastodon, elephant, true camel, deer, or bovine animal; hence Lake concluded that the last deposits had occurred during the Oligocene Age, and that the hollowed stratum had lain in its present dried, dead, and inaccessible state for at least thirty million years.

On the other hand, the prevalence of very early life forms was singular in the highest degree. Though the limestone formation was, on the evidence of such typical imbedded fossils as ventriculites, positively and unmistakably Comanchean and not a particle earlier; the free fragments in the hollow space included a surprising proportion from organisms hitherto considered as peculiar to far older periods—even rudimentary fishes, mollusks, and corals as remote as the Silurian or Ordovician.

The inevitable inference was that in this part of the world there had been a remarkable and unique degree of continuity between the life of over three hundred million years ago and that of only thirty million years ago. How far this continuity had extended beyond the Oligocene Age when the cavern was closed was of course past all speculation.

In any event, the coming of the frightful ice in the Pleistocene some five hundred thousand years ago—a mere yesterday as compared with the age of this cavity—must have put an end to any of the primal forms which had locally managed to outlive their common terms.

Lake was not content to let his first message stand, but had another bulletin written and dispatched across the snow to the camp before Moulton could get back. After that Moulton stayed at the wireless in one of the planes, transmitting to me—and to the *Arkham* for relaying to the outside world—the frequent postscripts which Lake sent him by a succession of messengers.

Those who followed the newspapers will remember the excitement created among men of science by that afternoon's reports—reports which have finally led, after all these years, to the organization of that very Starkweather-Moore Expedition which I am so anxious to dissuade from its purposes. I had better give the messages literally as Lake sent them, and as our base operator McTighe translated them from his pencil shorthand:

> Fowler makes discovery of highest importance in sandstone and limestone fragments from blasts. Several distinct triangular striated prints like those in archæan slate, proving that source survived from over six hundred million years ago to Comanchean times without more than moderate morphological changes and decrease in average size. Comanchean prints apparently more primitive or decadent, if anything, than older ones. Emphasize importance of discovery in press. Will mean to biology what Einstein has meant to mathematics and physics. Joins up with my previous work and amplifies conclusions.

Appears to indicate, as I suspected, that earth has seen whole cycle or cycles of organic life before known one that begins with Archæozoic cells. Was evolved and specialized not later than a thousand million years ago, when planet was young and recently uninhabitable for any life forms of normal protoplasmic structure. Question arises when, where, and how development took place.

Later. Examining certain skeletal fragments of large land and marine saurians and primitive mammals, find singular local wounds or injuries to bony structure not attributable to any known predatory or carnivorous animal of any period. Of two sorts—straight, penetrant bores, and apparently hacking incisions. One or two cases of cleanly severed bones. Not many specimens affected. Am sending to camp for electric torches. Will extend search area underground by hacking away stalactites.

Still later. Have found peculiar soapstone fragment about six inches across and an inch and a half thick, wholly unlike any visible local formation—greenish, but no evidences to place its period. Has curious smoothness and regularity. Shaped like five-pointed star with tips broken off, and signs of other cleavage at inward angles and in center of surface. Small, smooth depression in center of unbroken surface. Arouses much curiosity as to source and weathering. Probably some freak of water action. Carroll, with magnifier, thinks he can make out additional markings of geologic significance. Groups of tiny dots in regular patterns. Dogs growing uneasy as we work, and seem to hate this soapstone. Must see if it has any peculiar odor. Will report again when Mills gets back with light and we start on underground area.

10:15 p.m. Important discovery. Orrendorf and Watkins, working underground at 9:45 with light, found monstrous barrel-shaped fossil of wholly unknown nature; probably vegetable unless overgrown specimen of unknown marine radiata. Tissue evidently preserved by mineral salts. Tough as leather, but astonishing flexibility retained in places. Marks of broken-off parts at ends and around sides. Six feet end to end, three and five tenths feet central diameter, tapering to one foot at each end. Like a barrel with five bulging ridges in place of staves. Lateral breakages, as of thinnish stalks, are at equator in middle of these ridges. In furrows between ridges are curious growths—combs or wings that fold up and spread out like fans. All greatly damaged but one, which gives almost seven-foot wing spread. Arrangement reminds one of certain monsters of primal myth, especially fabled Elder Things in *Necronomicon.*

These wings seem to be membranous, stretched on framework of glandular tubing. Apparent minute orifices in frame tubing at wing tips. Ends of body shriveled, giving no clue to interior or to what has been broken off there. Must dissect when we get back to camp. Can't decide whether vegetable or animal. Many features obviously of almost incredible primitiveness. Have set all hands cutting stalactites and looking for further specimens. Additional scarred bones found, but these must wait. Having trouble with dogs. They can't endure the new specimen, and would probably tear it to pieces if we didn't keep it at a distance from them.

11:30 p.m. Attention, Dyer, Pabodie, Douglas. Matter of highest—I might say transcendent—importance. *Arkham* must relay to Kingsport Head Station at once. Strange barrel growth is the archæan thing that left prints in rocks. Mills, Boudreau, and Fowler discover cluster of thirteen more at underground point forty feet from aperture. Mixed with curiously rounded and configured soapstone fragments smaller than one previously found—star-shaped, but no marks of breakage except at some of the points.

Of organic specimens, eight apparently perfect, with all appendages. Have brought all to surface, leading off dogs to distance. They cannot stand the things. Give close attention to description and repeat back for accuracy. Papers must get this right.

Objects are eight feet long all over. Six-foot, five-ridged barrel torso three and five tenths feet central diameter, one foot end diameters. Dark gray, flexible, and infinitely tough. Seven-foot membranous wings of same color, found folded, spread out of furrows between ridges. Wing framework tubular or glandular, or lighter gray, with orifices at wing tips. Spread wings have serrated edge. Around equator, one at central apex of each of the five vertical, stavelike ridges, are five systems of light-gray flexible arms or tentacles found tightly folded to torso but expansible to maximum length of over three feet. Like arms of primitive crinoid. Single stalks three inches diameter branch after six inches into five substalks, each of which branches after eight inches into five small, tapering tentacles or tendrils, giving each stalk a total of twenty-five tentacles.

At top of torso blunt, bulbous neck of lighter gray, with gill-like suggestions, holds yellowish five-pointed starfish-shaped apparent head covered with three-inch wiry cilia of various prismatic colors.

Head thick and puffy, about two feet point to point, with three-inch flexible yellowish tubes projecting from each point. Slit in exact center of top probably breathing aperture. At end of each tube is spherical expansion where yellowish membrane rolls back on handling to reveal glassy, red-irised globe, evidently an eye.

Five slightly longer reddish tubes start from inner angles of starfish-shaped head and end in saclike swellings of same color which, upon pressure, open to bell-shaped orifices two inches maximum diameter and lined with sharp, white tooth-like projections—probable mouths. All these tubes, cilia, and points of starfish head, found folded tightly down; tubes and points clinging to bulbous neck and torso. Flexibility surprising despite vast toughness.

At bottom of torso, rough but dissimilarly functioning counterparts of head arrangements exist. Bulbous light-gray pseudoneck, without gill suggestions, holds greenish five-pointed starfish arrangement.

Tough, muscular arms four feet long and tapering from seven inches diameter at base to about two and five tenths at point. To each point is attached small end of a greenish five-veined membranous triangle eight inches long and six wide at farther end. This is the paddle, fin, or pseudofoot which had made prints in rocks from a thousand million to fifty or sixty million years old.

From inner angles of starfish arrangement project two-foot reddish tubes tapering from three inches diameter at base to one at tip. Orifices at tips. All these parts infinitely tough and leathery, but extremely flexible. Four-foot arms with paddles undoubtedly used for locomotion of some sort, marine or otherwise. When moved, display suggestions of exaggerated muscularity. As found, all these projections tightly folded over pseudoneck and end of torso, corresponding to projections at other end.

Cannot yet assign positively to animal or vegetable kingdom, but odds now favor animal. Probably represents incredibly advanced evolution of radiata without loss of certain primitive features. Echinoderm resemblances unmistakable despite local contradictory evidences.

Wing structure puzzles in view of probable marine habitat, but may have use in water navigation. Symmetry is curiously vegetablelike, suggesting vegetable's essential up-and-down structure rather than animal's fore-and-aft structure. Fabulously early date of evolution, preceding even simplest archæan Protozoa hitherto known, baffles all conjecture as to origin.

Complete specimens have such uncanny resemblance to certain creatures of primal myth that suggestion of ancient existence outside antarctic becomes inevitable. Dyer and Pabodie have read *Necronomicon* and seen Clark Ashton Smith's nightmare paintings based on text, and will understand when I speak of Elder Things supposed to have created all earth life as jest or mistake. Students have always thought conception formed from morbid imaginative treatment of very ancient tropical radiata. Also like prehistoric folklore things Wilmarth has spoken of—Cthulhu cult appendages, etc.

Vast field of study opened. Deposits probably of late Cretaceous or early Eocene period, judging from associated specimens. Massive stalagmites deposited above them. Hard work hewing out, but toughness prevented damage. State of preservation miraculous, evidently owing to limestone action. No more found so far, but will resume search later. Job now to get fourteen huge specimens to camp without dogs, which bark furiously and can't be trusted near them.

With nine men—three left to guard the dogs—we ought to manage the three sledges fairly well, though wind is bad. Must establish plane communication with McMurdo Sound and begin shipping material. But I've got to dissect one of these things before we take any rest. Wish I had a real laboratory here. Dyer better kick himself for having tried to stop my westward trip. First the world's greatest mountains, and then this. If this last isn't the high spot of the expedition, I don't know what is. We're made scientifically. Congrats, Pabodie, on the drill that opened up the cave. Now will *Arkham* please repeat description?

The sensations of Pabodie and myself at receipt of this report were almost beyond description, nor were our companions much behind us in enthusiasm. McTighe, who had hastily translated a few high spots as they came from the droning receiving set, wrote out the entire message from his shorthand version, as soon as Lake's operator signed off.

All appreciated the epoch-making significance of the discovery, and I sent Lake congratulations as soon as the *Arkham's* operator had repeated back the descriptive parts as requested; and my example was followed by Sherman from his station at the McMurdo Sound supply cache, as well as by Captain Douglas of the *Arkham.*

Later, as head of the expedition, I added some remarks to be relayed through the *Arkham* to the outside world. Of course, rest was an absurd thought amidst this excitement; and my only wish was to get to Lake's camp as quickly as I could. It disappointed me when he sent word that a rising mountain gale made early aërial travel impossible.

But within an hour and a half interest again rose to banish disappointment. Lake, sending more messages, told of the completely successful transportation of the fourteen great specimens to the camp. It had been a hard pull, for the things were surprisingly heavy; but nine men had accomplished it very neatly. Now some of the party were hurriedly building a snow corral at a safe distance from the camp, to which the dogs could be brought for greater convenience in feeding. The specimens were laid out on the hard snow near the camp, save for one on which Lake was making crude attempts at dissection.

This dissection seemed to be a greater task than had been expected, for, despite the heat of a gasoline stove in the newly raised laboratory tent, the deceptively flexible tissues of the chosen specimen—a powerful and intact one—lost nothing of their more than leathery toughness. Lake was puzzled as to how he might make the requisite incisions without violence destructive enough to upset all the structural niceties he was looking for.

He had, it is true, seven more perfect specimens; but these were too few to use up recklessly unless the cave might later yield an unlimited supply. Accordingly, he removed the specimen and dragged in one which, though having remnants of the starfish arrangements at both ends, was badly crushed and partly disrupted along one of the great torso furrows.

Results, quickly reported over the wireless, were baffling and provocative indeed. Nothing like delicacy or accuracy was possible with instruments hardly able to cut the anomalous tissue, but the little that was achieved left us all awed and bewildered.

Existing biology would have to be wholly revised, for this thing was no product of any cell growth science knows about. There had been scarcely any mineral replacement, and despite an age of perhaps forty million years the internal organs were wholly intact.

The leathery, undeteriorative, and almost indestructible quality was an inherent attribute of the thing's form of organization, and pertained to some paleocene cycle of invertebrate evolution utterly beyond our powers of speculation.

At first all that Lake found was dry, but as the heated tent produced its thawing effect, organic moisture of pungent and offensive odor was encountered toward the thing's uninjured side. It was not blood, but a thick, dark-green fluid apparently answering the same purpose. By the time Lake reached this stage all thirty-seven dogs had been brought to the still uncompleted corral near the camp, and even at that distance set up a savage barking and show of restlessness at the acrid, diffusive smell.

Far from helping to place the strange entity, this provisional dissection merely deepened its mystery. All guesses about its external members had been correct, and on the evidence of these one could hardly hesitate to call the thing animal, but internal inspection brought up so many vegetable evidences that Lake was left hopelessly at sea. It had digestion and circulation, and eliminated waste matter through the reddish tubes of its starfish-shaped base.

Cursorily, one would say that its respiratory apparatus handled oxygen rather than carbon dioxide; and there were odd evidences of air-storage chambers and methods of shifting respiration from the external orifice to at least two other fully developed breathing systems—gills and pores.

Clearly, it was amphibian and probably adapted to long airless hibernation periods as well. Vocal organs seemed present in connection with the main respiratory system, but they presented anomalies beyond immediate solution. Articulate speech, in the sense of syllable utterance, seemed barely conceivable, but musical piping notes covering a wide range were highly probable. The muscular system was almost pre-naturally developed.

The nervous system was so complex and highly developed as to leave Lake aghast. Though excessively primitive and archaic in some respects, the thing had a set of gangliar centers and connectives arguing the very extremes of specialized development.

Its five-lobed brain was surprisingly advanced, and there were signs of a sensory equipment, served in part through the wiry cilia of the head, involving factors alien to any other terrestrial organism. Probably it had more than five senses, so that its habits could not be predicted from any existing analogy.

It must, Lake thought, have been a creature of keen sensitiveness and delicately differentiated functions in its primal world—much like the ants and bees of to-day. It reproduced like the vegetable cryptogams, especially the pteridophyta; having spore cases at the tips of the wings and evidently developing from a thallus or prothallus.

But to give it a name at this stage was mere folly. It looked like a radiate, but was clearly something more. It was partly vegetable, but had three fourths of the essentials of animal structure. That it was marine in origin, its symmetrical contour and certain other attributes clearly indicated; yet one could not be exact as to the limit of its later adaptations.

The wings, after all, held a persistent suggestion of the aërial. How it could have undergone its tremendously complex evolution on a new-born earth in time to leave prints in archæan rocks was so far beyond conception as to make Lake whimsically recall the primal myths about Great Old Ones who filtered down from the stars and concocted earth life as a joke or mistake; and the wild tales of cosmic hill things from outside told by a folklorist colleague in Miskatonic's English department.

Naturally, he considered the possibility of the pre-Cambrian prints having been made by a less evolved ancestor of the present specimens, but quickly rejected this too-facile theory upon considering the advanced structural qualities of the older fossils. If anything, the later contours showed decadence rather than higher evolution.

The size of the pseudofeet had decreased, and the whole morphology seemed coarsened and simplified. Moreover, the nerves and organs, just examined, held singular suggestions of retrogression from forms still more complex. Atrophied and vestigial parts were surprisingly prevalent. Altogether, little could be said to have been solved; and Lake fell back on mythology for a provisional name—jocosely dubbing his finds "The Elder Ones."

At about two-thirty a.m., having decided to postpone further work and get a little rest, he covered the dissected organism with a tarpaulin, emerged from the laboratory tent, and studied the intact specimens with renewed interest.

The ceaseless antarctic sun had begun to limber up their tissues a trifle, so that the head points and tubes of two or three showed signs of unfolding; but Lake did not believe there was any danger of immediate decomposition in the almost subzero air. He did, however, move all the undissected specimens closer together and throw a spare tent over them in order to keep off the direct solar rays. That would also help to keep their possible scent away from the dogs, whose hostile unrest was really becoming a problem, even at their substantial distance and behind the higher and higher snow walls, which an increased quota of the men were hastening to raise around their quarters.

He had to weight down the corners of the tent cloth with heavy blocks of snow to hold it in place amidst the rising gale, for the titan mountains seemed about to deliver some gravely severe blasts. Early apprehensions about sudden antarctic winds were revived, and under Atwood's supervision precautions were taken to bank the tents, new dog corral, and crude aëroplane shelters with snow, on the mountainward side. These latter shelters, begun with hard snow blocks during odd moments, were by no means as high as they should have been; and Lake finally detached all hands from other tasks to work on them.

It was after four when Lake at last prepared to sign off and advised us all to share the rest period his outfit would take when the shelter walls were a little higher. He held some friendly chat with Pabodie over the ether, and repeated his praise of the really marvelous drills that had helped him make his discovery. Atwood also sent greetings and praises.

I gave Lake a warm word of congratulation, owning up that he was right about the western trip, and we all agreed to get in touch by wireless at ten in the morning. If the gale was then over, Lake would send a plane for the party at my base. Just before retiring I dispatched a final message to the *Arkham*, with instructions about toning down the day's news for the outside world, since the full details seemed radical enough to rouse a wave of incredulity until further substantiated.

III

None of us, I imagine, slept very heavily or continuously that morning. Both the excitement of Lake's discovery and the mounting fury of the wind were against such a thing. So savage was the blast even where we were, that we could not help wondering how much worse it was at Lake's camp, directly under the vast unknown peaks that bred and delivered it.

McTighe was awake at ten o'clock and tried to get Lake on the wireless, as agreed, but some electrical condition in the disturbed air to the westward seemed to prevent communication. We did, however, get the *Arkham*, and Douglas told me that he had likewise been vainly trying to reach Lake. He had not known about the wind, for very little was blowing at McMurdo Sound, despite its persistent rage where we were.

Throughout the day we all listened anxiously and tried to get Lake at intervals, but invariably without results. About noon a positive frenzy of wind stampeded out of the west, causing us to fear for the safety of our camp; but it eventually died down, with only a moderate relapse at two p.m.

After three o'clock it was very quiet, and we redoubled our efforts to get Lake. Reflecting that he had four planes, each provided with an excellent short-wave outfit, we could not imagine any ordinary accident capable of crippling all his wireless equipment at once. Nevertheless, the stony silence continued, and when we thought of the delirious force the wind must have had in his locality we could not help making the most direful conjectures.

By six o'clock our fears had become intense and definite, and after a wireless consultation with Douglas and Thorfinnssen I resolved to take steps toward investigation. The fifth aëroplane, which we had left at the McMurdo Sound supply cache with Sherman and two sailors, was in good shape and ready for instant use, and it seemed that the very emergency for which it had been saved was now upon us.

I got Sherman by wireless and ordered him to join me with the plane and the two sailors at the southern base as quickly as possible, the air conditions being apparently highly favorable. We then talked over the personnel of the coming investigation party, and decided that we would include all hands, together with the sledge and dogs which I had kept with me. Even so great a load would not be too much for one of the huge planes built to our special orders for heavy machinery transportation. At intervals I still tried to reach Lake with the wireless, but all to no purpose.

Sherman, with the sailors Gunnarsson and Larsen, took off at seven thirty; and reported a quiet flight from several points on the wing. They arrived at our base at midnight, and all hands at once discussed the next move. It was risky business sailing over the antarctic in a single aëroplane without any line of bases, but no one drew back from what seemed like the plainest necessity. We turned in at two o'clock for a brief rest after some preliminary loading of the plane, but were up again in four hours to finish the loading and packing.

At seven fifteen a.m., January 25th, we started northwestward under McTighe's pilotage with ten men, seven dogs, a sledge, a fuel and food supply, and other items including the plane's wireless outfit. The atmosphere was clear, fairly quiet, and relatively mild in temperature, and we anticipated very little trouble in reaching the latitude and longitude designated by Lake as the site of his camp. Our apprehensions were over what we might find, or fail to find, at the end of our journey, for silence continued to answer all calls dispatched to the camp.

Every incident of that four-and-a-half-hour flight is burned into my recollection because of its crucial position in my life. It marked my loss, at the age of fifty-four, of all that peace and balance which the normal mind possesses through its accustomed conception of external nature and nature's laws.

Thenceforward the ten of us—but the student Danforth and myself above all others—were to face a hideously amplified world of lurking horrors which nothing can erase from our emotions, and which we would refrain from sharing with mankind in general if we could. The newspapers have printed the bulletins we sent from the moving plane, telling of our nonstop course, our two battles with treacherous upper-air gales, our glimpse of the broken surface where Lake had sunk his mid-journey shaft three days before, and our sight of a group of those strange fluffy snow cylinders noted by Amundsen and Byrd as rolling in the wind across the endless leagues of frozen plateau.

There came a point, though, when our sensations could not be conveyed in any words the press would understand, and a later point when we had to adopt an actual rule of strict censorship.

The sailor Larsen was first to spy the jagged line of witchlike cones and pinnacles ahead, and his shouts sent every one to the windows of the great cabined plane. Despite our speed, they were very slow in gaining prominence; hence we knew that they must be infinitely far off, and visible only because of their abnormal height.

Little by little, however, they rose grimly into the western sky, allowing us to distinguish various bare, bleak, blackish summits, and to catch the curious sense of phantasy which they inspired as seen in the reddish antarctic light against the provocative background of iridescent ice-dust clouds.

In the whole spectacle there was a persistent, pervasive hint of stupendous secrecy and potential revelation. It was as if these stark, nightmare spires marked the pylons of a frightful gateway into forbidden spheres of dream, and complex gulfs of remote time, space, and ultradimensionality. I could not help feeling that they were evil things—mountains of madness whose farther slopes looked out over some accursed ultimate abyss.

That seething, half-luminous cloud background held ineffable suggestions of a vague, ethereal beyondness far more than terrestrially spatial, and gave appalling reminders of the utter remoteness, separateness, desolation, and æon-long death of this untrodden and unfathomed austral world.

It was young Danforth who drew our notice to the curious regularities of the higher mountain sky line—regularities like clinging fragments of perfect cubes, which Lake had mentioned in his messages, and which indeed justified his comparison with the dreamlike suggestions of primordial temple ruins, on cloudy Asian mountaintops so subtly and strangely painted by Roerich.

There was indeed something hauntingly Roerichlike about this whole unearthly continent of mountainous mystery. I had felt it in October when we first caught sight of Victoria Land, and I felt it afresh now. I felt, too, another wave of uneasy consciousness of archæan mythical resemblances, of how disturbingly this lethal realm corresponded to the evilly famed plateau of Leng in the primal writings.

Mythologists have placed Leng in Central Asia, but the racial memory of man—or of his predecessors—is long, and it may well be that certain tales have come down from lands and mountains and temples of horror earlier than Asia and earlier than any human world we know.

A few daring mystics have hinted at a pre-Pleistocene origin for the fragmentary Pnakotic Manuscripts, and have suggested that the devotees of Tsathoggua were as alien to mankind as Tsathoggua itself.

Leng, wherever in space or time it might brood, was not a region I would care to be in or near, nor did I relish the proximity of a world that had ever bred such ambiguous and archæan monstrosities as those Lake had just mentioned. At the moment I felt sorry that I had ever read the abhorred *Necronomicon*, or talked so much with that unpleasantly erudite folklorist Wilmarth at the university.

This mood undoubtedly served to aggravate my reaction to the bizarre mirage which burst upon us from the increasingly opalescent zenith as we drew near the mountains and began to make out the cumulative undulations of the foothills. I had seen dozens of polar mirages during the preceding weeks, some of them quite as uncanny and fantastically vivid as the present sample, but this one had a wholly novel and obscure quality of menacing symbolism, and I shuddered as the seething labyrinth of fabulous walls and towers and minarets loomed out of the troubled ice vapors above our heads.

The effect was that of a Cyclopean city of no architecture known to man or to human imagination, with vast aggregations of night-black masonry embodying monstrous perversions of geometrical laws. There were truncated cones, sometimes terraced or fluted, surmounted by tall cylindrical shafts here and there bulbously enlarged and often capped with tiers of thinnish scalloped disks, and strange, beetling, tablelike constructions suggesting piles of multitudinous rectangular slabs or circular plates or five-pointed stars with each one overlapping the one beneath.

There were composite cones and pyramids either alone or surmounting cylinders or cubes or flatter truncated cones and pyramids, and occasional needlelike spires in curious clusters of five.

All of these febrile structures seemed knit together by tubular bridges crossing from one to the other at various dizzy heights, and the implied scale of the whole was terrifying and oppressive in its sheer giganticism.

The general type of mirage was not unlike some of the wilder forms observed and drawn by the arctic whaler Scoresby in 1820, but at this time and place, with those dark, unknown mountain peaks soaring stupendously ahead, that anomalous elder-world discovery in our minds, and the pall of probable disaster enveloping the greater part of our expedition, we all seemed to find in it a taint of latent malignity and infinitely evil portent.

I was glad when the mirage began to break up, though in the process the various nightmare turrets and cones assumed distorted, temporary forms of even vaster hideousness. As the whole illusion dissolved to churning opalescence, we began to look earthward again, and saw that our journey's end was not far off.

The unknown mountains ahead rose dizzily up like a fearsome rampart of giants, their curious regularities showing with startling clearness even without a field glass. We were over the lowest foothills now, and could see amidst the snow, ice, and bare patches of their main plateau a couple of darkish spots which we took to be Lake's camp and boring.

The higher foothills shot up between five and six miles away, forming a range almost distinct from the terrifying line of more than Himalayan peaks beyond them. At length Ropes—the student who had relieved McTighe at the controls—began to head downward toward the left-hand dark spot whose size marked it as the camp. As he did so, McTighe sent out the last uncensored wireless message the world was to receive from our expedition.

Every one, of course, has read the brief and unsatisfying bulletins of the rest of our antarctic sojourn.

Some hours after our landing we sent a guarded report of the tragedy we found, and reluctantly announced the wiping out of the whole Lake party by the frightful wind of the preceding day, or of the night before that. There were eleven known dead, young Gedney was missing.

People pardoned our hazy lack of details through realization of the shock the sad event must have caused us, and believed us when we explained that the mangling action of the wind had rendered all eleven bodies unsuitable for transportation outside.

Indeed, I flatter myself that even in the midst of our distress, utter bewilderment, and soul-clutching horror, we scarcely went beyond the truth in any specific instance. The tremendous significance lies in what we dared not tell; what I would not tell now but for the need of warning others off from nameless terrors.

It is a fact that the wind had wrought dreadful havoc. Whether all could have lived through it, even without the other thing, is gravely open to doubt. The storm, with its fury of madly driven ice particles, must have been beyond anything our expedition had encountered before.

One aëroplane shelter—all, it seems, had been left in a far too flimsy and inadequate state—was nearly pulverized; and the derrick at the distant boring was entirely shaken to pieces.

The exposed metal of the grounded planes and drilling machinery was bruised into a high polish, and two of the small tents were flattened despite their snow banking. Wooden surfaces left out in the blast were pitted and denuded of paint, and all signs of tracks in the snow were completely obliterated.

It is also true that we found none of the archæan biological objects in a condition to take outside as a whole. We did gather some minerals from a vast, tumbled pile, including several of the greenish soapstone fragments whose odd five-pointed rounding and faint patterns of grouped dots caused so many doubtful comparisons, and some fossil bones, among which were the most typical of the curiously injured specimens.

None of the dogs survived, their hurriedly built snow inclosure near the camp being almost wholly destroyed. The wind may have done that, though the greater breakage, on the side next to the camp, which was not the windward one, suggests an outward leap or break of the frantic beasts themselves.

All three sledges were gone, and we have tried to explain that the wind may have blown them off into the unknown. The drill and ice-melting machinery at the boring were too badly damaged to warrant salvage, so we used them to choke up that subtly disturbing gateway to the past which Lake had blasted.

We likewise left at the camp the two most shaken up of the planes; since our surviving party had only four real pilots—Sherman, Danforth, McTighe, and Ropes—in all, with Danforth in a poor nervous shape to navigate. We brought back all the books, scientific equipment, and other incidentals we could find, though much was rather unaccountably blown away. Spare tents and furs were either missing or badly out of condition.

It was approximately four p.m., after wide plane cruising had forced us to give Gedney up for lost, that we sent our guarded message to the *Arkham* for relaying; and I think we did well to keep it as calm and noncommittal as we succeeded in doing.

The most we said about agitation concerned our dogs, whose frantic uneasiness near the biological specimens was to be expected from poor Lake's accounts. We did not mention, I think, their display of the same uneasiness when sniffing around the queer greenish soapstones and certain other objects in the disordered region—objects including scientific instruments, aëroplanes, and machinery, both at the camp and at the boring, whose parts had been loosened, moved, or otherwise tampered with by winds that must have harbored singular curiosity and investigativeness.

About the fourteen biological specimens we were pardonably indefinite. We said that the only ones we discovered were damaged, but that enough was left of them to prove Lake's description wholly and impressively accurate. It was hard work keeping our personal emotions out of this matter—and we did not mention numbers or say exactly how we had found those which we did find. We had by that time agreed not to transmit anything suggesting madness on the part of Lake's men, and it surely looked like madness to find six imperfect monstrosities carefully buried upright in nine-foot snow graves under five-pointed mounds punched over with groups of dots in patterns exactly like those on the queer greenish soapstones dug up from Mesozoic or Tertiary times. The eight perfect specimens mentioned by Lake seemed to have been completely blown away.

We were careful, too, about the public's general peace of mind; hence Danforth and I said little about that frightful trip over the mountains the next day. It was the fact that only a radically lightened plane could possibly cross a range of such height which mercifully limited that scouting tour to the two of us.

On our return at one a.m., Danforth was close to hysterics, but kept an admirably stiff upper lip. It took no persuasion to make him promise not to show our sketches and the other things we brought away in our pockets, not to say anything more to the others than what we had agreed to relay outside, and to hide our camera films for private development later on; so that part of my present story will be as new to Pabodie, McTighe, Ropes, Sherman, and the rest as it will be to that world in general. Indeed—Danforth is closer mouthed than I: for he saw, or thinks he saw, one thing he will not tell even me.

As all know, our report included a tale of a hard ascent—a confirmation of Lake's opinion that the great peaks are of archæan slate and other very primal crumpled strata unchanged since at least middle Comanchean time, a conventional comment on the regularity of the clinging cube and rampart formations, a decision that the cave mouths indicate dissolved calcareous veins, a conjecture that certain slopes and passes would permit of the scaling and crossing of the entire range by seasoned mountaineers, and a remark that the mysterious other side holds a lofty and immense superplateau as ancient and unchanging as the mountains themselves—twenty thousand feet in elevation, with grotesque rock formations protruding through a thin glacial layer and with low gradual foothills between the general plateau surface and the sheer precipices of the highest peaks.

This body of data is in every respect true so far as it goes, and it completely satisfied the men at the camp. We laid our absence of sixteen hours—a longer time than our announced flying, landing, reconnoitering, and rock-collecting program called for—to a long mythical spell of adverse wind conditions, and told truly of our landing on the farther foothills.

Fortunately our tale sounded realistic and prosaic enough not to tempt any of the others into emulating our flight. Had any tried to do that, I would have used every ounce of my persuasion to stop them—and I do not know what Danforth would have done.

While we were gone, Pabodie, Sherman, Ropes, McTighe, and Williamson had worked like beavers over Lake's two best planes, fitting them again for use, despite the altogether unaccountable juggling of their operative mechanism.

We decided to load all the planes the next morning and start back for our old base as soon as possible. Even though indirect, that was the safest way to work toward McMurdo Sound; for a straight-line flight across the most utterly unknown stretches of the æon-dead continent would involve many additional hazards.

Further exploration was hardly feasible in view of our tragic decimation and the ruin of our drilling machinery. The doubts and horrors around us—which we did not reveal—made us wish only to escape from this austral world of desolation and brooding madness as swiftly as we could.

As the public knows, our return to the world was accomplished without further disasters. All planes reached the old base on the evening of the next day—January 27th—after a swift nonstop flight; and on the 28th we made McMurdo Sound in two laps, the one pause being very brief, and occasioned by a faulty rudder, in the furious wind over the ice shelf after we had cleared the great plateau.

In five days more, the *Arkham* and *Miskatonic*, with all hands and equipment on board, were shaking clear of the thickening field ice and working up Ross Sea, with the mocking mountains of Victoria Land looming westward against a troubled antarctic sky and twisting the wind's wails into a wide-ranged musical piping which chilled my soul to the quick.

Less than a fortnight later we left the last hint of polar land behind us and thanked heaven that we were clear of a haunted, accursed realm where life and death, space and time, have made black and blasphemous alliances in the unknown epochs since matter first writhed and swam on the planet's scarce-cooled crust.

Since our return we have all constantly worked to discourage antarctic exploration, and have kept certain doubts and guesses to ourselves with splendid unity and faithfulness. Even young Danforth, with his nervous breakdown, has not flinched or babbled to his doctors.

Indeed, as I have said, there is one thing he thinks he alone saw which he will not tell even me, though I think it would help his psychological state if he would consent to do so. It might explain and relieve much, though perhaps the thing was no more than the delusive aftermath of an earlier shock. That is the impression I gather after those rare, irresponsible moments when he whispers disjointed things to me—things which he repudiates vehemently as soon as he gets a grip on himself again.

It will be hard work deterring others from the great white south, and some of our efforts may directly harm our cause by drawing inquiring notice. We might have known from the first that human curiosity is undying, and that the results we announced would be enough to spur others ahead on the same age-long pursuit of the unknown.

Lake's reports of those biological monstrosities had aroused naturalists and palæontologists to the highest pitch, though we were sensible enough not to show the detached parts we had taken from the actual buried specimens, or our photographs of those specimens as they were found. We also refrained from showing the more puzzling of the scarred bones and greenish soapstones; while Danforth and I have closely guarded the pictures we took or drew on the superplateau across the range, and the crumpled things we smoothed, studied in terror, and brought away in our pockets.

But now that Starkweather-Moore party is organizing, and with a thoroughness far beyond anything our outfit attempted—if not dissuaded, they will get to the innermost nucleus of the antarctic and melt and bore till they bring up that which we know may end the world. So I must break through all reticences at last—even about that ultimate, nameless thing beyond the mountains of madness.

IV

It is only with vast hesitancy and repugnance that I let my mind go back to Lake's camp and what we really found there—and to that other thing beyond the awful mountain wall.

I have told of the wind-ravaged terrain, the damaged shelters, the disarranged machinery, the varied uneasiness of our dogs, the missing sledges and other items, the deaths of men and dogs, the absence of Gedney, and the six insanely buried biological specimens, strangely sound in texture for all their structural injuries, from a world forty million years dead. I do not recall whether I mentioned that upon checking up the canine bodies we found one dog missing. We did not think much about that till later—indeed, only Danforth and I have thought of it at all.

The principal things I have been keeping back relate to the bodies, and to certain subtle points which may or may not lend a hideous and incredible kind of rationale to the apparent chaos.

At the time, I tried to keep the men's minds off those points; for it was so much simpler—so much more normal—to lay everything to an outbreak of madness on the part of some of Lake's party. From the look of things, that demon mountain wind must have been enough to drive any man mad in the midst of this center of all earthly mystery and desolation.

The crowning abnormality, of course, was the condition of the bodies—men and dogs alike. They had all been in some terrible kind of conflict, and were torn and mangled in fiendish and altogether inexplicable ways. Death, so far as we could judge, had in each case come from strangulation or laceration.

The dogs had evidently started the trouble, for the state of their ill-built corral bore witness to its forcible breakage from within. It had been set some distance from the camp because of the hatred of the animals for those hellish archæan organisms, but the precaution seemed to have been taken in vain. When left alone in that monstrous wind, behind flimsy walls of insufficient height, they must have stampeded—whether from the wind itself, or from some subtle, increasing odor emitted by the nightmare specimens, one could not say.

But whatever had happened, it was hideous and revolting enough. Perhaps I had better put squeamishness aside and tell the worst at last—though with a categorical statement of opinion, based on the first-hand observations and most rigid deductions of both Danforth and myself, that the then missing Gedney was in no way responsible for the loathsome horrors we found.

I have said that the bodies were frightfully mangled. Now I must add that some were incised and subtracted from in the most curious, cold-blooded, and inhuman fashion. It was the same with dogs and men. All the healthier, fatter bodies, quadrupedal or bipedal, had had their most solid masses of tissue cut out and removed, as by a careful butcher; and around them was a strange sprinkling of salt—taken from the ravaged provision chests on the planes—which conjured up the most horrible associations.

The thing had occurred in one of the crude aëroplane shelters from which the plane had been dragged out, and subsequent winds had effaced all tracks which could have supplied any plausible theory. Scattered bits of clothing, roughly slashed from the human incision subjects, hinted no clues.

It is useless to bring up the half impression of certain faint snow prints in one shielded corner of the ruined inclosure—because that impression did not concern human prints at all, but was clearly mixed up with all the talk of fossil prints which poor Lake had been giving throughout the preceding weeks. One had to be careful of one's imagination in the lee of those overshadowing mountains of madness.

As I have indicated, Gedney and one dog turned out to be missing in the end. When we came on that terrible shelter we had missed two dogs and two men; but the fairly unharmed dissecting tent, which we entered after investigating the monstrous graves, had something to reveal.

It was not as Lake had left it, for the covered parts of the primal monstrosity had been removed from the improvised table. Indeed, we had already realized that one of the six imperfect and insanely buried things we had found—the one with the trace of a peculiarly hateful odor—must represent the collected sections of the entity which Lake had tried to analyze.

On and around that laboratory table were strewn other things, and it did not take long for us to guess that those things were the carefully, though oddly and inexpertly dissected parts of one man and one dog. I shall spare the feelings of survivors by omitting mention of the man's identity.

Lake's anatomical instruments were missing, but there were evidences of their careful cleansing. The gasoline stove was also gone, though around it we found a curious litter of matches. We buried the human parts beside the other ten men, and the canine parts with the other thirty-five dogs. Concerning the bizarre smudges on the laboratory table, and on the jumble of roughly handled illustrated books scattered near it, we were much too bewildered to speculate.

This formed the worst of the camp horror, but other things were equally perplexing. The disappearance of Gedney, the one dog, the eight uninjured biological specimens, the three sledges, and certain instruments, illustrated technical and scientific books, writing materials, electric torches and batteries, food and fuel, heating apparatus, spare tents, fur suits, and the like, was utterly beyond sane conjecture; as were likewise the spatter-fringed ink blots on certain pieces of paper, and the evidences of curious alien fumbling and experimentation around the planes and all other mechanical devices both at the camp and at the boring. The dogs seemed to abhor this oddly disordered machinery.

Then, too, there was the upsetting of the larder, the disappearance of certain staples, and the jarringly comical heap of tin cans pried open in the most unlikely ways and at the most unlikely places. The profusion of scattered matches, intact, broken, or spent, formed another minor enigma—as did the two or three tent cloths and fur suits which we found lying about with peculiar and unorthodox slashings conceivably due to clumsy efforts at unimaginable adaptations.

The maltreatment of the human and canine bodies, and the crazy burial of the damaged archæan specimens, were all of a piece with this apparent disintegrative madness. In view of just such an eventuality as the present one, we carefully photographed all the main evidences of insane disorder at the camp; and shall use the prints to buttress our pleas against the departure of the proposed Starkweather-Moore Expedition.

Our first act after finding the bodies in the shelter was to photograph and open the row of insane graves with the five-pointed snow mounds. We could not help noticing the resemblance of these monstrous mounds, with their clusters of grouped dots, to poor Lake's descriptions of the strange greenish soapstones; and when we came on some of the soapstones themselves in the great mineral pile we found the likeness very close indeed.

The whole general formation, it must be made clear, seemed abominably suggestive of the starfish head of the archæan entities; and we agreed that the suggestion must have worked potently upon the sensitized minds of Lake's overwrought party.

For madness—centering in Gedney as the only possible surviving agent—was the explanation spontaneously adopted by everybody so far as spoken utterance was concerned; though I will not be so naïve as to deny that each of us may have harbored wild guesses which sanity forbade him to formulate completely.

Sherman, Pabodie, and McTighe made an exhaustive aëroplane cruise over all the surrounding territory in the afternoon, sweeping the horizon with field glasses in quest of Gedney and of the various missing things; but nothing came to light.

The party reported that the titan-barrier range extended endlessly to right and left alike, without any diminution in height or essential structure. On some of the peaks, though, the regular cube and rampart formations were bolder and plainer, having doubly fantastic similitudes to Roerich-painted Asian hill ruins. The distribution of cryptical cave mouths on the black snow-denuded summits seemed roughly even as far as the range could be traced.

In spite of all the prevailing horrors we were left with enough sheer scientific zeal and adventurousness to wonder about the unknown realm beyond those mysterious mountains.

As our guarded messages stated, we rested at midnight after our day of terror and bafflement—but not without a tentative plan for one or more range-crossing altitude flights in a lightened plane with aërial camera and geologist's outfit, beginning the following morning.

It was decided that Danforth and I try it first, and we awaked at seven a.m. intending an early trip; though heavy winds—mentioned in our brief bulletin to the outside world—delayed our start till nearly nine o'clock.

I have already repeated the noncommittal story we told the men at camp—and relayed outside—after our return sixteen hours later. It is now my terrible duty to amplify this account by filling in the merciful blanks with hints of what we really saw in that hidden transmontane world—hints of the revelations which have finally driven Danforth to a nervous collapse.

I wish he would add a really frank word about the thing which he thinks he alone saw—even though it was probably a nervous delusion—and which was perhaps the last straw that put him where he is; but he is firm against that. All I can do is to repeat his later disjointed whispers about what set him shrieking as the plane soared back through the wind-tortured mountain pass after that real and tangible shock which I shared.

This will form my last word. If the plain signs of surviving elder horrors in what I disclose be not enough to keep others from meddling with the inner antarctic—or at least from prying too deeply beneath the surface of that ultimate waste of forbidden secrets and unhuman, æon-cursed desolation—the responsibility for unnamable and perhaps immeasurable evils will not be mine.

Danforth and I, studying the notes made by Pabodie in his afternoon flight and checking up with a sextant, had calculated that the lowest available pass in the range lay somewhat to the right of us, within sight of camp, and about twenty-three thousand or twenty-four thousand feet above sea-level. For this point, then, we first headed in the lightened plane as we embarked on our flight of discovery.

The camp itself, on foothills which sprang from a high continental plateau, was some twelve thousand feet in altitude; hence the actual height increase necessary was not so vast as it might seem. Nevertheless we were acutely conscious of the rarefied air and intense cold as we rose; for, on account of visibility conditions, we had to leave the cabin windows open. We were dressed, of course, in our heaviest furs.

As we drew near the forbidding peaks, dark and sinister above the line of crevasse-riven snow and interstitial glaciers, we noticed more and more the curiously regular formations clinging to the slopes; and thought again of the strange Asian paintings of Nicholas Roerich.

The ancient and wind-weathered rock strata fully verified all of Lake's bulletins, and proved that these pinnacles had been towering up in exactly the same way since a surprisingly early time in earth's history—perhaps over fifty million years. How much higher they had once been, it was futile to guess; but everything about this strange region pointed to obscure atmospheric influences unfavorable to change, and calculated to retard the usual climatic processes of rock disintegration.

But it was the mountainside tangle of regular cubes, ramparts, and cave mouths which fascinated and disturbed us most. I studied them with a field glass and took aërial photographs while Danforth drove; and at times I relieved him at the controls—though my aviation knowledge was purely an amateur's—in order to let him use the binoculars.

We could easily see that much of the material of the things was a lightish archæan quartzite, unlike any formation visible over broad areas of the general surface; and that their regularity was extreme and uncanny to an extent which poor Lake had scarcely hinted.

As he had said, their edges were crumbled and rounded from untold æons of savage weathering; but their preternatural solidity and tough material had saved them from obliteration. Many parts, especially those closest to the slopes, seemed identical in substance with the surrounding rock surface.

The whole arrangement looked like the ruins of Macchu Picchu in the Andes, or the primal foundation walls of Kish as dug up by the Oxford-Field Museum Expedition in 1929; and both Danforth and I obtained that occasional impression of separate Cyclopean blocks which Lake had attributed to his flight-companion Carroll.

How to account for such things in this place was frankly beyond me, and I felt queerly humbled as a geologist. Igneous formations often have strange regularities—like the famous Giants' Causeway in Ireland—but this stupendous range, despite Lake's original suspicion of smoking cones, was above all else nonvolcanic in evident structure.

The curious cave mouths, near which the odd formation seemed most abundant, presented another, albeit a lesser puzzle because of their regularity of outline. They were, as Lake's bulletin had said, often approximately square or semicircular; as if the natural orifices had been shaped to greater symmetry by some magic hand. Their numerousness and wide distribution were remarkable, and suggested that the whole region was honeycombed with tunnels dissolved out of limestone strata.

Such glimpses as we secured did not extend far within the caverns, but we saw that they were apparently clear of stalactites and stalagmites. Outside, those parts of the mountain slopes adjoining the apertures seemed invariably smooth and regular; and Danforth thought that the slight cracks and pittings of the weathering tended toward unusual patterns.

Filled as he was with the horrors and strangenesses discovered at the camp, he hinted that the pittings vaguely resembled those baffling groups of dots sprinkled over the primeval greenish soapstones, so hideously duplicated on the madly conceived snow mounds above those six buried monstrosities.

We had risen gradually in flying over the higher foothills and along toward the relatively low pass we had selected. As we advanced we occasionally looked down at the snow and ice of the land route, wondering whether we could have attempted the trip with the simpler equipment of earlier days.

Somewhat to our surprise we saw that the terrain was far from difficult as such things go; and that despite the crevasses and other bad spots it would not have been likely to deter the sledges of a Scott, a Shackleton, or an Amundsen. Some of the glaciers appeared to lead up to wind-bared passes with unusual continuity, and upon reaching our chosen pass we found that its case formed no exception.

Our sensations of tense expectancy as we prepared to round the crest and peer out over an untrodden world can hardly be described on paper; even though we had no cause to think the regions beyond the range essentially different from those already seen and traversed. The touch of evil mystery in these barrier mountains, and in the beckoning sea of opalescent sky glimpsed betwixt their summits, was a highly subtle and attenuated matter not to be explained in literal words. Rather was it an affair of vague psychological symbolism and æsthetic association—a thing mixed up with exotic poetry and paintings, and with archaic myths lurking in shunned and forbidden volumes.

Even the wind's burden held a peculiar strain of conscious malignity; and for a second it seemed that the composite sound included a bizarre musical whistling, or piping over a wide range as the blast swept in and out of the omnipresent and resonant cave mouths. There was a cloudy note of reminiscent repulsion in this sound, as complex and unplaceable as any of the other dark impressions.

We were now, after a slow ascent, at a height of twenty-three thousand five hundred and seventy feet according to the aneroid; and had left the region of clinging snow definitely below us. Up here were only dark, bare rock slopes and the start of rough-ribbed glaciers—but with those provocative cubes, ramparts, and echoing cave mouths to add a portent of the unnatural, the fantastic, and the dreamlike.

Looking along the line of high peaks, I thought I could see the one mentioned by poor Lake, with a rampart exactly on top. It seemed to be half lost in a queer antarctic haze—such a haze, perhaps, as had been responsible for Lake's early notion of volcanism.

The pass loomed directly before us, smooth and windswept between its jagged and malignly frowning pylons. Beyond it was a sky fretted with swirling vapors and lighted by the low polar sun—the sky of that mysterious farther realm upon which we felt no human eye had ever gazed.

A few more feet of altitude and we would behold that realm. Danforth and I, unable to speak except in shouts amidst the howling, piping wind that raced through the pass and added to the noise of the unmuffled engines, exchanged eloquent glances. And then, having gained those last few feet, we did indeed stare across the momentous divide and over the unsampled secrets of an elder and utterly alien earth.

V

I think that both of us simultaneously cried out in mixed awe, wonder, terror, and disbelief in our own senses as we finally cleared the pass and saw what lay beyond. Of course, we must have had some natural theory in the back of our heads to steady our faculties for the moment. Probably we thought of such things as the grotesquely weathered stones of the Garden of the Gods in Colorado, or the fantastically symmetrical wind-carved rocks of the Arizona desert. Perhaps we even half thought the sight a mirage like that we had seen the morning before on first approaching those mountains of madness.

We must have had some such normal notions to fall back upon as our eyes swept that limitless, tempest-scarred plateau and grasped the almost endless labyrinth of colossal, regular, and geometrically eurythmic stone masses which reared their crumbled and pitted crests above a glacial sheet not more than forty or fifty feet deep at its thickest, and in places obviously thinner.

The effect of the monstrous sight was indescribable, for some fiendish violation of known natural law seemed certain at the outset. Here, on a hellishly ancient table-land fully twenty thousand feet high, and in a climate deadly to habitation since a prehuman age not less than five hundred thousand years ago, there stretched nearly to the vision's limit a tangle of orderly stone which only the desperation of mental self-defense could possibly attribute to any but a conscious and artificial cause.

We had previously dismissed, so far as serious thought was concerned, any theory that the cubes and ramparts of the mountainsides were other than natural in origin. How could they be otherwise, when man himself could scarcely have been differentiated from the great apes at the time when this region succumbed to the present unbroken reign of glacial death?

Yet now the sway of reason seemed irrefutably shaken, for this Cyclopean maze of squared, curved, and angled blocks had features which cut off all comfortable refuge. It was, very clearly, the blasphemous city of the mirage in stark, objective, and ineluctable reality. That damnable portent had had a material basis after all—there had been some horizontal stratum of ice dust in the upper air, and this shocking stone survival had projected its image across the mountains according to the simple laws of reflection. Of course, the phantom had been twisted and exaggerated, and had contained things which the real source did not contain; yet now, as we saw that real source, we thought it even more hideous and menacing than its distant image.

Only the incredible, unhuman massiveness of these vast stone towers and ramparts had saved the frightful thing from utter annihilation in the hundreds of thousands—perhaps millions—of years it had brooded there amidst the blasts of a bleak upland. "Corona Mundi—Roof of the World——" All sorts of fantastic phrases sprang to our lips as we looked dizzily down at the unbelievable spectacle.

I thought again of the eldritch primal myths that had so persistently haunted me since my first sight of this dead antarctic world—of the demonic plateau of Leng, of the Mi-Go, or Abominable Snow Men of the Himalayas, of the Pnakotic Manuscripts with their prehuman implications, of the Cthulhu cult, of the *Necronomicon*, and of the Hyperborean legends of formless Tsathoggua and the worse than formless star spawn associated with that semientity.

For boundless miles in every direction the thing stretched off with very little thinning; indeed, as our eyes followed it to the right and left along the base of the low, gradual foothills which separated it from the actual mountain rim, we decided that we could see no thinning at all except for an interruption at the left of the pass through which we had come. We had merely struck, at random, a limited part of something of incalculable extent.

The foothills were more sparsely sprinkled with grotesque stone structures, linking the terrible city to the already familiar cubes and ramparts which evidently formed its mountain outposts. These latter, as well as the queer cave mouths, were as thick on the inner as on the outer sides of the mountains.

The nameless stone labyrinth consisted, for the most part, of walls from ten to one hundred and fifty feet in ice-clear height, and of a thickness varying from five to ten feet. It was composed mostly of prodigious blocks of dark primordial slate, schist, and sandstone—blocks in many cases as large as 4 × 6 × 8 feet—though in several places it seemed to be carved out of a solid, uneven bed rock of pre-Cambrian slate.

The buildings were far from equal in size, there being innumerable honeycomb arrangements of enormous extent as well as smaller separate structures.

The general shape of these things tended to be conical, pyramidal, or terraced; though there were many perfect cylinders, perfect cubes, clusters of cubes, and other rectangular forms, and a peculiar sprinkling of angled edifices whose five-pointed ground plan roughly suggested modern fortifications. The builders had made constant and expert use of the principle of the arch, and domes had probably existed in the city's heyday.

The whole tangle was monstrously weathered, and the glacial surface from where the towers projected was strewn with fallen blocks and immemorial débris. Where the glaciation was transparent we could see the lower parts of the gigantic piles, and we noticed the ice-preserved stone bridges which connected the different towers at varying distances above the ground. On the exposed walls we could detect the scarred places where other and higher bridges of the same sort had existed.

Closer inspection revealed countless largish windows; some of which were closed with shutters of a petrified material originally wood, though most gaped open in a sinister and menacing fashion.

Many of the ruins, of course, were roofless, and with uneven though wind-rounded upper edges; whilst others, of a more sharply conical or pyramidal model or else protected by higher surrounding structures, preserved intact outlines despite the omnipresent crumbling and pitting. With the field glass we could barely make out what seemed to be sculptural decorations in horizontal bands—decorations including those curious groups of dots whose presence on the ancient soapstones now assumed a vastly larger significance.

In many places the buildings were totally ruined and the ice sheet deeply riven from various geologic causes. In other places the stonework was worn down to the very level of the glaciation. One broad swath, extending from the plateau's interior to a cleft in the foothills about a mile to the left of the pass we had traversed, was wholly free from buildings. It probably represented, we concluded, the course of some great river which in Tertiary times—millions of years ago—had poured through the city and into some prodigious subterranean abyss of the great barrier range. Certainly, this was above all a region of caves, gulfs, and underground secrets beyond human penetration.

Looking back to our sensations, and recalling our dazedness at viewing this monstrous survival from æons we had thought prehuman, I can only wonder that we preserved the semblance of equilibrium which we did. Of course, we knew that something—chronology, scientific theory, or our own consciousness—was woefully awry; yet we kept enough poise to guide the plane, observe many things quite minutely, and take a careful series of photographs which may yet serve both us and the world in good stead.

In my case, ingrained scientific habit may have helped; for above all my bewilderment and sense of menace there burned a dominant curiosity to fathom more of this age-old secret—to know what sort of beings had built and lived in this incalculably gigantic place, and what relation to the general world of its time or of other times so unique a concentration of life could have had.

For this place could be no ordinary city. It must have formed the primary nucleus and center of some archaic and unbelievable chapter of earth's history whose outward ramifications, recalled only dimly in the most obscure and distorted myths, had vanished utterly amidst the chaos of terrene convulsions long before any human race we know had shambled out of apedom.

Here sprawled a Palæogæan megalopolis compared with which the fabled Atlantis and Lemuria, Commoriom and Uzuldaroum, and Olathoë in the land of Lomar are recent things of to-day—not even of yesterday; a megalopolis ranking with such whispered prehuman blasphemies as Valusia, R'lyeh, Ib in the land of Mnar, and the Nameless City of Arabia Deserta.

As we flew above that tangle of stark Titan towers my imagination sometimes escaped all bounds and roved aimlessly in realms of fantastic associations—even weaving links betwixt this lost world and some of my own wildest dreams concerning the mad horror at the camp.

The plane's fuel tank, in the interest of greater lightness, had been only partly filled; hence we now had to exert caution in our explorations. Even so, however, we covered an enormous extent of ground—or rather, air—after swooping down to a level where the wind became virtually negligible.

There seemed to be no limit to the mountain range, or to the length of the frightful stone city which bordered its inner foothills. Fifty miles of flight in each direction showed no major change in the labyrinth of rock and masonry that clawed up corpselike through the eternal ice.

There were, though, some highly absorbing diversifications; such as the carvings on the canyon where that broad river had once pierced the foothills and approached its sinking place in the great range.

The headlands at the stream's entrance had been boldly carved into Cyclopean pylons; and something about the ridgy, barrel-shaped designs stirred up oddly vague, hateful, and confusing semiremembrances in both Danforth and me.

We also came upon several star-shaped open spaces, evidently public squares, and noted various undulations in the terrain. Where a sharp hill rose, it was generally hollowed out into some sort of rambling stone edifice; but there were at least two exceptions. Of these latter, one was too badly weathered to disclose what had been on the jutting eminence, while the other still bore a fantastic conical monument carved out of the solid rock and roughly resembling such things as the well-known Snake Tomb in the ancient valley of Petra.

Flying inland from the mountains, we discovered that the city was not of infinite width, even though its length along the foothills seemed endless. After about thirty miles the grotesque stone buildings began to thin out, and in ten more miles we came to an unbroken waste virtually without signs of sentient artifice. The course of the river beyond the city seemed marked by a broad, depressed line, while the land assumed a somewhat greater ruggedness, seeming to slope slightly upward as it receded in the mist-hazed west.

So far we had made no landing, yet to leave the plateau without an attempt at entering some of the monstrous structures would have been inconceivable. Accordingly, we decided to find a smooth place on the foothills near our navigable pass, there grounding the plane and preparing to do some exploration on foot.

Though these gradual slopes were partly covered with a scattering of ruins, low flying soon disclosed an ample number of possible landing places. Selecting that nearest to the pass, since our next flight would be across the great range and back to camp, we succeeded about twelve thirty p.m. in coming down on a smooth, hard snow field wholly devoid of obstacles and well adapted to a swift and favorable take-off later on.

It did not seem necessary to protect the plane with a snow banking for so brief a time and in so comfortable an absence of high winds at this level; hence we merely saw that the landing skis were safely lodged, and that the vital parts of the mechanism were guarded against the cold.

For our foot journey we discarded the heaviest of our flying furs, and took with us a small outfit consisting of pocket compass, hand camera, light provisions, voluminous notebooks and paper, geologist's hammer and chisel, specimen bags, coil of climbing rope, and powerful electric torches with extra batteries; this equipment having been carried in the plane on the chance that we might be able to effect a landing, take ground pictures, make drawings and topographical sketches, and obtain rock specimens from some bare slope, outcropping, or mountain cave.

Fortunately, we had a supply of extra paper to tear up, place in a spare specimen bag, and use on the ancient principle of hare and hounds for marking our course in any interior mazes we might be able to penetrate. This had been brought in case we found some cave system with air quiet enough to allow such a rapid and easy method in place of the usual rock-chipping method of trail blazing.

Walking cautiously downhill over the crusted snow, toward the stupendous stone labyrinth that loomed against the opalescent west, we felt almost as keen a sense of imminent marvels as we had felt on approaching the unfathomed mountain pass four hours previously.

True, we had become visually familiar with the incredible secret concealed by the barrier peaks; yet the prospect of actually entering primordial walls reared by conscious beings perhaps millions of years ago—before any known race of men could have existed—was none the less awesome and potentially terrible in its implications of cosmic abnormality.

Though the thinness of the air at this prodigious altitude made exertion somewhat more difficult than usual, both Danforth and I found ourselves bearing up very well, and felt equal to almost any task which might fall to our lot.

It took only a few steps to bring us to a shapeless ruin worn level with the snow, while ten or fifteen rods farther on there was a huge, roofless rampart still complete in its gigantic five-pointed outline, and rising to an irregular height of ten or eleven feet. For this latter we headed; and when at last we were actually able to touch its weathered Cyclopean blocks, we felt that we had established an unprecedented and almost blasphemous link with forgotten æons normally closed to our species.

This rampart, shaped like a star and perhaps three hundred feet from point to point, was built of Jurassic sandstone blocks of irregular size, averaging 6 x 8 feet in surface. There was a row of arched loopholes or windows about four feet wide and five feet high, spaced quite symmetrically along the points of the star and at its inner angles, and with the bottoms about four feet from the glaciated surface.

Looking through these, we could see that the masonry was fully five feet thick, that there were no partitions remaining within, and that there were traces of banded carvings or bas-reliefs on the interior walls—facts we had indeed guessed before, when flying low over this rampart and others like it. Though lower parts must have originally existed, all traces of such things were now wholly obscured by the deep layer of ice and snow at this point.

We crawled through one of the windows and vainly tried to decipher the nearly effaced mural designs, but did not attempt to disturb the glaciated floor. Our orientation flights had indicated that many buildings in the city proper were less ice-choked, and that we might perhaps find wholly clear interiors leading down to the true ground level if we entered those structures still roofed at the top.

Before we left the rampart we photographed it carefully, and studied its mortarless Cyclopean masonry with complete bewilderment. We wished that Pabodie were present, for his engineering knowledge might have helped us guess how such titanic blocks could have been handled in that unbelievably remote age when the city and its outskirts were built up.

The half-mile walk downhill to the actual city, with the upper wind shrieking vainly and savagely through the skyward peaks in the background, was something of which the smallest details will always remain engraved on my mind. Only in fantastic nightmares could any human beings but Danforth and me conceive such optical effects.

Between us and the churning vapors of the west lay that monstrous tangle of dark stone towers, its outré and incredible forms impressing us afresh at every new angle of vision. It was a mirage in solid stone, and were it not for the photographs I would still doubt that such a thing could be. The general type of masonry was identical with that of the rampart we had examined; but the extravagant shapes which this masonry took in its urban manifestations were past all description.

Even the pictures illustrate only one or two phases of its endless variety, preternatural massiveness, and utterly alien exoticism. There were geometrical forms for which an Euclid could scarcely find a name—cones of all degrees of irregularity and truncation, terraces of every sort of provocative disproportion, shafts with odd bulbous enlargements, broken columns in curious groups, and five-pointed or five-ridged arrangements of mad grotesqueness.

As we drew nearer we could see beneath certain transparent parts of the ice sheet, and detect some of the tubular stone bridges that connected the crazily sprinkled structures at various heights. Of orderly streets there seemed to be none, the only broad open swath being a mile to the left, where the ancient river had doubtless flowed through the town into the mountains.

Our field glasses showed the external, horizontal bands of nearly effaced sculptures and dot groups to be very prevalent, and we could half imagine what the city must once have looked like—even though most of the roofs and tower tops had necessarily perished.

As a whole, it had been a complex tangle of twisted lanes and alleys, all of them deep canyons, and some little better than tunnels because of the overhanging masonry or overarching bridges.

Now, outspread below us, it loomed like a dream phantasy against a westward mist through whose northern end the low, reddish antarctic sun of early afternoon was struggling to shine; and when, for a moment, that sun encountered a denser obstruction and plunged the scene into temporary shadow, the effect was subtly menacing in a way I can never hope to depict. Even the faint howling and piping of the unfelt wind in the great mountain passes behind us took on a wilder note of purposeful malignity.

The last stage of our descent to the town was unusually steep and abrupt, and a rock outcropping at the edge where the grade changed led us to think that an artificial terrace had once existed there. Under the glaciation, we believed, there must be a flight of steps or its equivalent.

When at last we plunged into the town itself, clambering over fallen masonry and shrinking from the oppressive nearness and dwarfing height of omnipresent crumbling and pitted walls, our sensations again became such that I marvel at the amount of self-control we retained.

Danforth was frankly jumpy, and began making some offensively irrelevant speculations about the horror at the camp—which I resented all the more because I could not help sharing certain conclusions forced upon us by many features of this morbid survival from nightmare antiquity.

The speculations worked on his imagination, too; for in one place—where a débris-littered alley turned a sharp corner—he insisted that he saw faint traces of ground markings which he did not like; whilst elsewhere he stopped to listen to a subtle, imaginary sound from some undefined point—a muffled musical piping, he said, not unlike that of the wind in the mountain caves, yet somehow disturbingly different.

The ceaseless five-pointedness of the surrounding architecture and of the few distinguishable mural arabesques had a dimly sinister suggestiveness we could not escape, and gave us a touch of terrible subconscious certainty concerning the primal entities which had reared and dwelt in this unhallowed place.

Nevertheless, our scientific and adventurous souls were not wholly dead, and we mechanically carried out our program of chipping specimens from all the different rock types represented in the masonry. We wished a rather full set in order to draw better conclusions regarding the age of the place.

Nothing in the great outer walls seemed to date from later than the Jurassic and Comanchean periods, nor was any piece of stone in the entire place of a greater recency than the Pliocene age. In stark certainty, we were wandering amidst a death which had reigned at least five hundred thousand years, and in all probability even longer.

As we proceeded through this maze of stone-shadowed twilight we stopped at all available apertures to study interiors and investigate entrance possibilities. Some were above our reach, whilst others led only into ice-choked ruins as unroofed and barren as the rampart on the hill.

One, though spacious and inviting, opened on a seemingly bottomless abyss without visible means of descent. Now and then we had a chance to study the petrified wood of a surviving shutter, and were impressed by the fabulous antiquity implied in the still discernible grain. These things had come from Mesozoic gymnosperms and conifers—especially Cretaceous cycads—and from fan palms and early angiosperms of plainly Tertiary date. Nothing definitely later than the Pliocene could be discovered.

In the placing of these shutters—whose edges showed the former presence of queer and long-vanished hinges—usage seemed to be varied—some being on the outer and some on the inner side of the deep embrasures. They seemed to have become wedged in place, thus surviving the rusting of their former and probably metallic fixtures and fastenings.

After a time we came across a row of windows—in the bulges of a colossal five-edged cone of undamaged apex—which led into a vast, well-preserved room with stone flooring; but these were too high in the room to permit descent without a rope. We had a rope with us, but did not wish to bother with this twenty-foot drop unless obliged to—especially in this thin plateau air where great demands were made upon the heart action.

This enormous room was probably a hall or concourse of some sort, and our electric torches showed bold, distinct, and potentially startling sculptures arranged round the walls in broad, horizontal bands separated by equally broad strips of conventional arabesques. We took careful note of this spot, planning to enter here unless a more easily gained interior was encountered.

Finally, though, we did encounter exactly the opening we wished; an archway about six feet wide and ten feet high, marking the former end of an aërial bridge which had spanned an alley about five feet above the present level of glaciation. These archways, of course, were flush with upper-story floors, and in this case one of the floors still existed.

The building thus accessible was a series of rectangular terraces on our left facing westward. That across the alley, where the other archway yawned, was a decrepit cylinder with no windows and with a curious bulge about ten feet above the aperture. It was totally dark inside, and the archway seemed to open on a well of illimitable emptiness.

Heaped débris made the entrance to the vast left-hand building doubly easy, yet for a moment we hesitated before taking advantage of the long-wished chance. For though we had penetrated into this tangle of archaic mystery, it required fresh resolution to carry us actually inside a complete and surviving building of a fabulous elder world whose nature was becoming more and more hideously plain to us.

In the end, however, we made the plunge, and scrambled up over the rubble into the gaping embrasure. The floor beyond was of great slate slabs, and seemed to form the outlet of a long, high corridor with sculptured walls.

Observing the many inner archways which led off from it, and realizing the probable complexity of the nest of apartments within, we decided that we must begin our system of hare-and-hound trail blazing. Hitherto our compasses, together with frequent glimpses of the vast mountain range between the towers in our rear, had been enough to prevent our losing our way; but from now on, the artificial substitute would be necessary.

Accordingly we reduced our extra paper to shreds of suitable size, placed these in a bag to be carried by Danforth, and prepared to use them as economically as safety would allow. This method would probably gain us immunity from straying, since there did not appear to be any strong air currents inside the primordial masonry. If such should develop, or if our paper supply should give out, we could of course fall back on the more secure though more tedious and retarding method of rock chipping.

Just how extensive a territory we had opened up, it was impossible to guess without a trial. The close and frequent connection of the different buildings made it likely that we might cross from one to another on bridges underneath the ice, except where impeded by local collapses and geologic rifts, for very little glaciation seemed to have entered the massive constructions.

Almost all the areas of transparent ice had revealed the submerged windows as tightly shuttered, as if the town had been left in that uniform state until the glacial sheet came to crystallize the lower part for all succeeding time. Indeed, one gained a curious impression that this place had been deliberately closed and deserted in some dim, bygone æon, rather than overwhelmed by any sudden calamity or even gradual decay. Had the coming of the ice been foreseen, and had a nameless population left *en masse* to seek a less doomed abode?

The precise physiographic conditions attending the formation of the ice sheet at this point would have to wait for later solution. It had not, very plainly, been a grinding drive. Perhaps the pressure of accumulated snows had been responsible, and perhaps some flood from the river, or from the bursting of some ancient glacial dam in the great range, had helped to create the special state now observable. Imagination could conceive almost anything in connection with this place.

VI

It would be cumbrous to give a detailed, consecutive account of our wanderings inside that cavernous, æon-dead honeycomb of primal masonry—that monstrous lair of elder secrets which now echoed for the first time, after uncounted epochs, to the tread of human feet.

This is especially true because so much of the horrible drama and revelation came from a mere study of the omnipresent mural carvings. Our flash-light photographs of those carvings will do much toward proving the truth of what we are now disclosing, and it is lamentable that we had not a larger film supply with us. As it was, we made crude notebook sketches of certain salient features after all our films were used up.

The building which we had entered was one of great size and elaborateness, and gave us an impressive notion of the architecture of that nameless geologic past. The inner partitions were less massive than the outer walls, but on the lower levels were excellently preserved. Labyrinthine complexity, involving curiously irregular differences in floor levels, characterized the entire arrangement; and we should certainly have been lost at the very outset but for the trail of torn paper left behind us.

We decided to explore the more decrepit upper parts first of all, hence climbed aloft in the maze for a distance of some one hundred feet, to where the topmost tier of chambers yawned snowily and ruinously open to the polar sky. Ascent was effected over the steep, transversely ribbed stone ramps or inclined planes which everywhere served in lieu of stairs.

The rooms we encountered were of all imaginable shapes and proportions, ranging from five-pointed stars to triangles and perfect cubes. It might be safe to say that their general average was about 30 × 30 feet in floor area, and twenty feet in height, though many larger apartments existed.

After thoroughly examining the upper regions and the glacial level we descended, story by story, into the submerged part, where indeed we soon saw we were in a continuous maze of connected chambers and passages probably leading over unlimited areas outside this particular building.

The Cyclopean massiveness and giganticism of everything about us became curiously oppressive; and there was something vaguely but deeply unhuman in all the contours, dimensions, proportions, decorations, and constructional nuances of the blasphemously archaic stonework. We soon realized, from what the carvings revealed, that this monstrous city was many million years old.

We cannot yet explain the engineering principles used in the anomalous balancing and adjustment of the vast rock masses, though the function of the arch was clearly much relied on. The rooms we visited were wholly bare of all portable contents, a circumstance which sustained our belief in the city's deliberate desertion. The prime decorative feature was the almost universal system of mural sculpture, which tended to run in continuous horizontal bands three feet wide and arranged from floor to ceiling in alternation with bands of equal width given over to geometrical arabesques.

There were exceptions to this rule of arrangement, but its preponderance was overwhelming. Often, however, a series of smooth cartouches containing oddly patterned groups of dots would be sunk along one of the arabesque bands.

The technique, we soon saw, was mature, accomplished, and æsthetically evolved to the highest degree of civilized mastery, though utterly alien in every detail to any known art tradition of the human race. In delicacy of execution no sculpture I have ever seen could approach it. The minutest details of elaborate vegetation, or of animal life, were rendered with astonishing vividness despite the bold scale of the carvings; whilst the conventional designs were marvels of skillful intricacy.

The arabesques displayed a profound use of mathematical principles, and were made up of obscurely symmetrical curves and angles based on the quantity of five.

The pictorial bands followed a highly formalized tradition, and involved a peculiar treatment of perspective, but had an artistic force that moved us profoundly notwithstanding the intervening gulf of vast geologic periods.

Their method of design hinged on a singular juxtaposition of the cross section with the two-dimensional silhouette, and embodied an analytical psychology beyond that of any known race of antiquity. It is useless to try to compare this art with any represented in our museums. Those who see our photographs will probably find its closest analogue in certain grotesque conceptions of the most daring futurists.

The arabesque tracery consisted altogether of depressed lines, whose depth on unweathered walls varied from one to two inches. When cartouches with dot groups appeared—evidently as inscriptions in some unknown and primordial language and alphabet—the depression of the smooth surface was perhaps an inch and a half, and of the dots perhaps a half inch more. The pictorial bands were in countersunk low relief, their background being depressed about two inches from the original wall surface.

In some specimens marks of a former coloration could be detected, though for the most part the untold æons had disintegrated and banished any pigments which may have been applied. The more one studied the marvelous technique the more one admired the things. Beneath their strict conventionalization one could grasp the minute and accurate observation and graphic skill of the artists; and indeed, the very conventions themselves served to symbolize and accentuate the real essence or vital differentiation of every object delineated.

We felt, too, that besides these recognizable excellences there were others lurking beyond the reach of our perceptions. Certain touches here and there gave vague hints of latent symbols and stimuli which another mental and emotional background, and a fuller or different sensory equipment, might have made of profound and poignant significance to us.

The subject matter of the sculptures obviously came from the life of the vanished epoch of their creation, and contained a large proportion of evident history. It is this abnormal historic-mindedness of the primal race—a chance circumstance operating, through coincidence, miraculously in our favor—which made the carvings so awesomely informative to us, and which caused us to place their photography and transcription above all other considerations.

In certain rooms the dominant arrangement was varied by the presence of maps, astronomical charts, and other scientific designs on an enlarged scale—these things giving a naïve and terrible corroboration to what we gathered from the pictorial friezes and dados.

In hinting at what the whole revealed, I can only hope that my account will not arouse a curiosity greater than sane caution on the part of those who believe me at all. It would be tragic if any were to be allured to that realm of death and horror by the very warning meant to discourage them.

Interrupting these sculptured walls were high windows and massive twelve-foot doorways; both now and then retaining the petrified wooden planks—elaborately carved and polished—of the actual shutters and doors. All metal fixtures had long ago vanished, but some of the doors remained in place and had to be forced aside as we progressed from room to room.

Window frames with odd transparent panes—mostly elliptical—survived here and there, though in no considerable quantity. There were also frequent niches of great magnitude, generally empty, but once in a while containing some bizarre object carved from green soapstone which was either broken or perhaps held too inferior to warrant removal.

Other apertures were undoubtedly connected with bygone mechanical facilities—heating, lighting, and the like—of a sort suggested in many of the carvings. Ceilings tended to be plain, but had sometimes been inlaid with green soapstone or other tiles, mostly fallen now. Floors were also paved with such tiles, though plain stonework predominated.

As I have said, all furniture and other movables were absent; but the sculptures gave a clear idea of the strange devices which had once filled these tomblike, echoing rooms. Above the glacial sheet the floors were generally thick with detritus, litter, and débris, but farther down this condition decreased.

In some of the lower chambers and corridors there was little more than gritty dust or ancient incrustations, while occasional areas had an uncanny air of newly swept immaculateness. Of course, where rifts or collapses had occurred, the lower levels were as littered as the upper ones.

A central court—as we had seen in other structures, from the air—saved the inner regions from total darkness; so that we seldom had to use our electric torches in the upper rooms except when studying sculptured details. Below the ice cap, however, the twilight deepened; and in many parts of the tangled ground level there was an approach to absolute blackness.

To form even a rudimentary idea of our thoughts and feelings as we penetrated this æon-silent maze of unhuman masonry one must correlate a hopelessly bewildering chaos of fugitive moods, memories, and impressions. The sheer appalling antiquity and lethal desolation of the place were enough to overwhelm almost any sensitive person, but added to these elements were the recent unexplained horror at the camp, and the revelations all too soon effected by the terrible mural sculptures around us.

The moment we came upon a perfect section of carving, where no ambiguity of interpretation could exist, it took only a brief study to give us the hideous truth—a truth which it would be naïve to claim Danforth and I had not independently suspected before, though we had carefully refrained from even hinting it to each other. There could now be no further merciful doubt about the nature of the beings which had built and inhabited this monstrous dead city millions of years ago, when man's ancestors were primitive archaic mammals, and vast Dinosauria roamed the tropical steppes of Europe and Asia.

We had previously clung to a desperate alternative and insisted—each to himself—that the omnipresence of the five-pointed motif meant only some cultural or religious exaltation of the archæan natural object which had so patently embodied the quality of five-pointedness; as the decorative motifs of Minoan Crete exalted the sacred bull, those of Egypt the scarabæus, those of Rome the wolf and the eagle, and those of various savage tribes some chosen totem animal.

But this lone refuge was now stripped from us, and we were forced to face definitely the reason-shaking realization which the reader of these pages has doubtless long ago anticipated. I can scarcely bear to write it down in black and white even now, but perhaps that will not be necessary.

The things once rearing and dwelling in this frightful masonry in the age of Dinosauria were not indeed Dinosauria, but far worse. Mere Dinosauria were new and almost brainless objects—but the builders of the city were wise and old, and had left certain traces in rocks even then laid down well nigh a thousand million years—rocks laid down before the true life of earth had advanced beyond plastic groups of cells—rocks laid down before the true life of earth had existed at all.

They were the makers and enslavers of that life, and above all doubt the originals of the fiendish elder myths which things like the Pnakotic Manuscripts and the *Necronomicon* affrightedly hint about. They were the great "Old Ones" that had filtered down from the stars when earth was young—the beings whose substance an alien evolution had shaped, and whose powers were such as this planet had never bred. And to think that only the day before Danforth and I had actually looked upon fragments of their millennially fossilized substance—and that poor Lake and his party had seen their complete outlines——

It is, of course, impossible for me to relate in proper order the stages by which we picked up what we know of that monstrous chapter of prehuman life. After the first shock of the certain revelation, we had to pause a while to recuperate, and it was fully three o'clock before we got started on our actual tour of systematic research.

The sculptures in the building we entered were of relatively late date—perhaps two million years ago—as checked up by geological, biological, and astronomical features—and embodied an art which would be called decadent in comparison with that of specimens we found in older buildings, after crossing bridges under the glacial sheet.

One edifice hewn from the solid rock seemed to go back forty or possibly even fifty million years—to the lower Eocene or upper Cretaceous—and contained bas-reliefs of an artistry surpassing anything else, with one tremendous exception, that we encountered. That was, we have since agreed, the oldest domestic structure we traversed.

Were it not for the support of those flashlights soon to be made public, I would refrain from telling what I found and inferred, lest I be confined as a madman. Of course, the infinitely early parts of the patchwork tale—representing the preterrestrial life of the star-headed beings on other planets, in other galaxies, and in other universes—can readily be interpreted as the fantastic mythology of those beings themselves; yet such parts sometimes involved designs and diagrams so uncannily close to the latest findings of mathematics and astrophysics that I scarcely know what to think. Let others judge when they see the photographs I shall publish.

Naturally, no one set of carvings which we encountered told more than a fraction of any connected story, nor did we even begin to come upon the various stages of that story in their proper order. Some of the vast rooms were independent units so far as their designs were concerned, whilst in other cases a continuous chronicle would be carried through a series of rooms and corridors.

The best of the maps and diagrams were on the walls of a frightful abyss below even the ancient ground level—a cavern perhaps two hundred feet square and sixty feet high, which had almost undoubtedly been an educational center of some sort.

There were many provoking repetitions of the same material in different rooms and buildings, since certain chapters of experience, and certain summaries or phases of racial history, had evidently been favorites with different decorators or dwellers. Sometimes, though, variant versions of the same theme proved useful in settling debatable points and filling up gaps.

I still wonder that we deduced so much in the short time at our disposal. Of course, we even now have only the barest outline—and much of that was obtained later on from a study of the photographs and sketches we made.

It may be the effect of this later study—the revived memories and vague impressions acting in conjunction with his general sensitiveness and with that final supposed horror-glimpse whose essence he will not reveal even to me—which has been the immediate source of Danforth's present breakdown.

But it had to be; for we could not issue our warning intelligently without the fullest possible information, and the issuance of that warning is a prime necessity. Certain lingering influences in that unknown antarctic world of disordered time and alien natural law make it imperative that further exploration be discouraged.

VII

The full story, so far as deciphered, will eventually appear in an official bulletin of Miskatonic University. Here I shall sketch only the salient highlights in a formless, rambling way. Myth or otherwise, the sculptures told of the coming of those star-headed things to the nascent, lifeless earth out of cosmic space—their coming, and the coming of many other alien entities such as at certain times embark upon spatial pioneering.

They seemed able to traverse the interstellar ether on their vast membranous wings—thus oddly confirming some curious hill folklore long ago told me by an antiquarian colleague. They had lived under the sea a good deal, building fantastic cities and fighting terrific battles with nameless adversaries by means of intricate devices employing unknown principles of energy.

Evidently their scientific and mechanical knowledge far surpassed man's to-day, though they made use of its more widespread and elaborate forms only when obliged to.

Some of the sculptures suggested that they had passed through a stage of mechanized life on other planets, but had receded upon finding its effects emotionally unsatisfying. Their preternatural toughness of organization and simplicity of natural wants made them peculiarly able to live on a high plane without the more specialized fruits of artificial manufacture, and even without garments, except for occasional protection against the elements.

It was under the sea, at first for food and later for other purposes, that they first created earth life—using available substances according to long-known methods.

The more elaborate experiments came after the annihilation of various cosmic enemies. They had done the same thing on other planets, having manufactured not only necessary foods, but certain multicellular protoplasmic masses capable of molding their tissues into all sorts of temporary organs under hypnotic influence and thereby forming ideal slaves to perform the heavy work of the community.

These viscous masses were without doubt what Abdul Alhazred whispered about as the "Shoggoths" in his frightful *Necronomicon*, though even that mad Arab had not hinted that any existed on earth except in the dreams of those who had chewed a certain alkaloidal herb.

When the star-headed Old Ones on this planet had synthesized their simple food forms and bred a good supply of Shoggoths, they allowed other cell groups to develop into other forms of animal and vegetable life for sundry purposes, extirpating any whose presence became troublesome.

With the aid of the Shoggoths, whose expansions could be made to lift prodigious weights, the small, low cities under the sea grew to vast and imposing labyrinths of stone not unlike those which later rose on land. Indeed, the highly adaptable Old Ones had lived much on land in other parts of the universe, and probably retained many traditions of land construction.

As we studied the architecture of all these sculptured Palæogæan cities, including that whose æon-dead corridors we were even then traversing, we were impressed by a curious coincidence which we have not yet tried to explain, even to ourselves. The tops of the buildings, which in the actual city around us had, of course, been weathered into shapeless ruins ages ago, were clearly displayed in the bas-reliefs, and showed vast clusters of needlelike spires, delicate finials on certain cone and pyramid apexes, and tiers of thin, horizontal scalloped disks capping cylindrical shafts.

This was exactly what we had seen in that monstrous and portentous mirage, cast by a dead city whence such sky-line features had been absent for thousands and ten of thousands of years, which loomed on our ignorant eyes across the unfathomed mountains of madness as we first approached poor Lake's ill-fated camp.

Of the life of the Old Ones, both under the sea and after part of them migrated to land, volumes could be written. Those in shallow water had continued the fullest use of the eyes at the ends of their five main head tentacles, and had practiced the arts of sculpture and of writing in quite the usual way—the writing accomplished with a stylus on waterproof waxen surfaces.

Those lower down in the ocean depths, though they used a curious phosphorescent organism to furnish light, pieced out their vision with obscure special senses operating through the prismatic cilia on their heads—senses which rendered all the Old Ones partly independent of light in emergencies. Their forms of sculpture and writing had changed curiously during the descent, embodying certain apparently chemical coating processes—probably to secure phosphorescence—which the bas-reliefs could not make clear to us.

The beings moved in the sea partly by swimming—using the lateral crinoid arms—and partly by wriggling with the lower tier of tentacles containing the pseudofeet. Occasionally they accomplished long swoops with the auxiliary use of two or more sets of their fan-like folding wings.

On land they locally used the pseudofeet, but now and then flew to great heights or over long distances with their wings. The many slender tentacles into which the crinoid arms branched were infinitely delicate, flexible, strong, and accurate in muscular-nervous coördination—ensuring the utmost skill and dexterity in all artistic and other manual operations.

The toughness of the things was almost incredible. Even the terrific pressure of the deepest sea bottoms appeared powerless to harm them. Very few seemed to die at all except by violence, and their burial places were very limited. The facts that they covered their vertically inhumed dead with five-pointed inscribed mounds set up thoughts in Danforth and me which made a fresh pause and recuperation necessary after the sculptures revealed it.

The beings multiplied by means of spores—like vegetable pteridophyta, as Lake had suspected—but, owing to their prodigious toughness and longevity, and consequent lack of replacement needs, they did not encourage the large-scale development of new prothallia except when they had new regions to colonize.

The young matured swiftly, and received an education evidently beyond any standard we can imagine. The prevailing intellectual and æsthetic life was highly evolved, and produced a tenaciously enduring set of customs and institutions which I shall describe more fully in my coming monograph. These varied slightly according to sea or land residence, but had the same foundations and essentials.

Though able, like vegetables, to derive nourishment from inorganic substances; they vastly preferred organic and especially animal food. They ate uncooked marine life under the sea, but cooked their viands on land. They hunted game and raised meat herds—slaughtering with sharp weapons whose odd marks on certain fossil bones our expedition had noted.

They resisted all ordinary temperatures marvelously, and in their natural state could live in water down to freezing. When the great chill of the Pleistocene drew on, however—nearly a million years ago—the land dwellers had to resort to special measures, including artificial heating—until, at last, the deadly cold appears to have driven them back into the sea.

For their prehistoric flights through cosmic space, legend said, they had absorbed certain chemicals and become almost independent of eating, breathing, or heat conditions—but by the time of the great cold they had lost track of the method. In any case, they could not have prolonged the artificial state indefinitely without harm.

Being nonpairing and semivegetable in structure, the Old Ones had no biological basis for the family phase of mammal life, but seemed to organize large households on the principles of comfortable space-utility and—as we deduced from the pictured occupations and diversions of codwellers—congenial mental association.

In furnishing their homes they kept everything in the center of the huge rooms, leaving all wall spaces free for decorative treatment. Lighting, in the case of the land inhabitants, was accomplished by a device probably electro-chemical in nature.

Both on land and under water they used curious tables, chairs and couches like cylindrical frames—for they rested and slept upright with folded-down tentacles—and racks for the hinged sets of dotted surfaces forming their books.

Government was evidently complex and probably socialistic, though no certainties in this regard could be deduced from the sculptures we saw. There was extensive commerce, both local and between different cities—certain small, flat counters, five-pointed and inscribed, serving as money. Probably the smaller of the various greenish soapstones found by our expedition were pieces of such currency.

Though the culture was mainly urban, some agriculture and much stock raising existed. Mining and a limited amount of manufacturing were also practiced. Travel was very frequent, but permanent migration seemed relatively rare except for the vast colonizing movements by which the race expanded.

For personal locomotion no external aid was used, since in land, air, and water movement alike the Old Ones seemed to possess excessively vast capacities for speed. Loads, however, were drawn by beasts of burden—Shoggoths under the sea, and a curious variety of primitive vertebrates in the later years of land existence.

These vertebrates, as well as an infinity of other life forms—animal and vegetable, marine, terrestrial, and aërial—were the products of unguided evolution acting on life cells made by the Old Ones, but escaping beyond their radius of attention. They had been suffered to develop unchecked because they had not come in conflict with the dominant beings. Bothersome forms, of course, were mechanically exterminated.

It interested us to see in some of the very last and most decadent sculptures a shambling, primitive mammal, used sometimes for food and sometimes as an amusing buffoon by the land dwellers, whose vaguely simian and human foreshadowings were unmistakable. In the building of land cities the huge stone blocks of the high towers were generally lifted by vast-winged pterodactyls of a species heretofore unknown to palæontology.

The persistence with which the Old Ones survived various geologic changes and convulsions of the earth's crust was little short of miraculous.

Though few or none of their first cities seem to have remained beyond the Archæan Age, there was no interruption in their civilization or in the transmission of their records.

Their original place of advent to the planet was the Antarctic Ocean, and it is likely that they came not long after the matter forming the moon was wrenched from the neighboring South Pacific. According to one of the sculptured maps, the whole globe was then under water, with stone cities scattered farther and farther from the antarctic as æons passed.

Another map shows a vast bulk of dry land around the south pole, where it is evident that some of the beings made experimental settlements, though their main centers were transferred to the nearest sea bottom.

Later maps, which display this land mass as cracking and drifting, and sending certain detached parts northward, uphold in a striking way the theories of continental drift lately advanced by Taylor, Wegener, and Joly.

With the upheaval of new land in the South Pacific, tremendous events began. Some of the marine cities were hopelessly shattered, yet that was not the worst misfortune. Another race—a land race of beings shaped like octopi and probably corresponding to the fabulous prehuman spawn of Cthulhu—soon began filtering down from cosmic infinity and precipitated a monstrous war which for a time drove the Old Ones wholly back to the sea—a colossal blow in view of the increasing land settlements.

Later, peace was made, and the new lands were given to the Cthulhu spawn whilst the Old Ones held the sea and the older lands. New land cities were founded—the greatest of them in the antarctic, for this region of first arrival was sacred.

From then on, as before, the antarctic remained the center of the Old Ones' civilization, and all the cities built there by the Cthulhu spawn were blotted out.

Then, suddenly, the lands of the Pacific sank again, taking with them the frightful stone city of R'lyeh and all the cosmic octopi, so that the Old Ones were again supreme on the planet, except for one shadowy fear about which they did not like to speak.

At a rather later age their cities dotted all the land and water areas of the globe—hence the recommendation in my coming monograph that some archæologist make systematic borings with Pabodie's type of apparatus in certain widely separated regions.

The steady trend down the ages was from water to land—a movement encouraged by the rise of new land masses, though the ocean was never wholly deserted. Another cause of the landward movement was the new difficulty in breeding and managing the Shoggoths upon which successful sea life depended.

With the march of time, as the sculptures sadly confessed, the art of creating new life from inorganic matter had been lost, so that the Old Ones had to depend on the molding of forms already in existence. On land the great reptiles proved highly tractable; but the Shoggoths of the sea, reproducing by fission and acquiring a dangerous degree of accidental intelligence, presented for a time a formidable problem.

They had always been controlled through the hypnotic suggestion of the Old Ones, and had modeled their tough plasticity into various useful temporary limbs and organs; but now their self-modeling powers were sometimes exercised independently, and in various imitative forms implanted by past suggestion. They had, it seems, developed a semistable brain whose separate and occasionally stubborn volition echoed the will of the Old Ones without always obeying it.

Sculptured images of these Shoggoths filled Danforth and me with horror and loathing. They were normally shapeless entities composed of a viscous jelly which looked like an agglutination of bubbles, and each averaged about fifteen feet in diameter when a sphere. They had, however, a constantly shifting shape and volume—throwing out temporary developments or forming apparent organs of sight, hearing, and speech in imitation of their masters, either spontaneously or according to suggestion.

They seem to have become peculiarly intractable toward the middle of the Permian Age, perhaps one hundred and fifty million years ago, when a veritable war of resubjugation was waged upon them by the marine Old Ones. Pictures of this war, and of the headless, slime-coated fashion in which the Shoggoths typically left their slain victims, held a marvelously fearsome quality despite the intervening abyss of untold ages.

The Old Ones had used curious weapons of molecular disturbance against the rebel entities, and in the end had achieved a complete victory. Thereafter the sculptures showed a period in which Shoggoths were tamed and broken by armed Old Ones as the wild horses of the American west were tamed by cowboys.

Though during the rebellion the Shoggoths had shown an ability to live out of water, this transition was not encouraged—since their usefulness on land would hardly have been commensurate with the trouble of their management.

During the Jurassic Age the Old Ones met fresh adversity in the form of a new invasion from outer space—this time by half-fungous, half-crustacean creatures—creatures undoubtedly the same as those figuring in certain whispered hill legends of the north, and remembered in the Himalayas as the Mi-Go, or Abominable Snow Men.

To fight these beings the Old Ones attempted, for the first time since their terrene advent, to sally forth again into the planetary ether; but, despite all traditional preparations, found it no longer possible to leave the earth's atmosphere. Whatever the old secret of interstellar travel had been, it was now definitely lost to the race.

In the end the Mi-Go drove the Old Ones out of all the northern lands, though they were powerless to disturb those in the sea. Little by little the slow retreat of the elder race to their original antarctic habitat was beginning.

It was curious to note from the pictured battles that both the Cthulhu spawn and the Mi-Go seem to have been composed of matter more widely different from that which we know than was the substance of the Old Ones. They were able to undergo transformations and reintegrations impossible for their adversaries, and seem therefore to have originally come from even remoter gulfs of cosmic space.

The Old Ones, but for their abnormal toughness and peculiar vital properties, were strictly material, and must have had their absolute origin within the known space-time continuum—whereas the first sources of the other beings can only be guessed at with bated breath. All this, of course, assuming that the nonterrestrial linkages and the anomalies ascribed to the invading foes are not pure mythology. Conceivably, the Old Ones might have invented a cosmic framework to account for their occasional defeats, since historical interest and pride obviously formed their chief psychological element. It is significant that their annals failed to mention many advanced and potent races of beings whose mighty cultures and towering ethics figure persistently in certain obscure legends.

The changing state of the world through long geologic ages appeared with startling vividness in many of the sculptured maps and scenes. In certain cases existing science will require revision, while in other cases its bold deductions are magnificently confirmed.

As I have said, the hypothesis of Taylor, Wegener, and Joly that all the continents are fragments of an original antarctic land mass which cracked from centrifugal force and drifted apart over a technically viscous lower surface—an hypothesis suggested by such things as the complimentary outlines of Africa and South America, and the way the great mountain chains are rolled and shoved up—receives striking support from this uncanny source.

Maps evidently showing the Carboniferous of a hundred million or more years ago displayed significant rifts and chasms destined later to separate Africa from the once continuous realms of Europe (then the Valusia of primal legend), Asia, the Americas, and the antarctic continent.

Other charts—and most significantly one in connection with the founding fifty million years ago of the vast dead city around us—showed all the present continents well differentiated. And in the latest discoverable specimen—dating perhaps from the Pliocene Age—the approximate world of to-day appeared quite clearly despite the linkage of Alaska with Siberia, of North America with Europe through Greenland, and of South America with the antarctic continent through Graham Land.

In the Carboniferous map the whole globe—ocean floor and rifted land mass alike—bore symbols of the Old Ones' vast stone cities, but in the later charts the gradual recession toward the antarctic became very plain.

The final Pliocene specimen showed no land cities except on the antarctic continent and the tip of South America, nor any ocean cities north of the fiftieth parallel of South Latitude. Knowledge and interest in the northern world, save for a study of coast lines probably made during long exploration flights on those fan-like membranous wings, had evidently declined to zero among the Old Ones.

Destruction of cities through the up-thrust of mountains, the centrifugal rending of continents, the seismic convulsions of land or sea bottom, and other natural causes was a matter of common record; and it was curious to observe how fewer and fewer replacements were made as the ages wore on.

The vast dead megalopolis that yawned around us seemed to be the last general center of the race—built early in the Cretaceous Age after a titanic earth buckling had obliterated a still vaster predecessor not far distant.

It appeared that this general region was the most sacred spot of all, where reputedly the first Old Ones had settled on a primal sea bottom. In the new city—many of whose features we could recognize in the sculptures, but which stretched fully a hundred miles along the mountain range in each direction beyond the farthest limits of our aërial survey—there were reputed to be preserved certain sacred stones forming part of the first sea-bottom city, which were thrust up to light after long epochs in the course of the general crumpling of strata.

VIII

Naturally, Danforth and I studied with special interest and a peculiarly personal sense of awe everything pertaining to the immediate district in which we were. Of this local material there was naturally a vast abundance.

On the tangled ground level of the city we were lucky enough to find a house of very late date whose walls, though somewhat damaged by a neighboring rift, contained sculptures of decadent workmanship carrying the story of the region, much beyond the Pliocene map, whence we derived our last general glimpse of the prehuman world. This was the last place we examined in detail, since what we found there set upon us a fresh, immediate objective.

Certainly, we were in one of the strangest, weirdest, and most terrible of all the corners of earth's globe. Of all existing lands it was infinitely the most ancient. The conviction grew upon us that this hideous upland must indeed be the fabled nightmare plateau of Leng which even the mad author of the *Necronomicon* was reluctant to discuss.

The great mountain chain was tremendously long—starting as a low range at Luitpold Land on the coast of Weddell Sea and virtually crossing the entire continent. The really high part stretched in a mighty arc from about Latitude 82°, E. Longitude 60° to Latitude 70°, East Longitude 115°, with its concave side toward our camp and its seaward end in the region of that long, ice-locked coast whose hills were glimpsed by Wilkes and Mawson at the antarctic circle.

Yet even more monstrous exaggerations of nature seemed disturbingly close at hand. I have said that these peaks are higher than the Himalayas, but the sculptures forbid me to say that they are earth's highest. That grim honor is beyond doubt reserved for something which half the sculptures hesitated to record at all, whilst others approached it with obvious repugnance and trepidation.

It seems that there was one part of the ancient land—the first part that ever rose from the waters after the earth had flung off the moon and the Old Ones had seeped down from the stars—which had come to be shunned as vaguely and namelessly evil. Cities built there had crumbled before their time, and had been found suddenly deserted.

Then when the first great earth buckling had convulsed the region in the Comanchean Age, a frightful line of peaks had shot suddenly up amidst the most appalling din and chaos—and earth had received her loftiest and most terrible mountains.

If the scale of the carvings was correct, these abhorred things must have been much over forty thousand feet high—radically vaster than even the shocking mountains of madness we had crossed. They extended, it appeared, from about Latitude 77°, E. Longitude 70° to Latitude 70°, E. Longitude 100°—less than three hundred miles away from the dead city, so that we would have spied their dreaded summits in the dim western distance had it not been for that vague, opalescent haze. Their northern end must likewise be visible from the long antarctic circle coast line at Queen Mary Land.

Some of the Old Ones, in the decadent days, had made strange prayers to those mountains—but none ever went near them or dared to guess what lay beyond. No human eye had ever seen them, and as I studied the emotions conveyed in the carvings I prayed that none ever might.

There are protecting hills along the coast beyond them—Queen Mary and Kaiser Wilhelm Lands—and I thank Heaven no one has been able to land and climb those hills. I am not as sceptical about old tales and fears as I used to be, and I do not laugh now at the prehuman sculptor's notion that lightning paused meaningfully now and then at each of the brooding crests, and that an unexplained glow shone from one of those terrible pinnacles all through the long polar night. There may be a very real and very monstrous meaning in the old Pnakotic whispers about Kadath in the Cold Waste.

But the terrain close at hand was hardly less strange, even if less namelessly accursed. Soon after the founding of the city the great mountain range became the seat of the principal temples, and many carvings showed what grotesque and fantastic towers had pierced the sky where now we saw only the curiously clinging cubes and ramparts.

In the course of ages the caves had appeared, and had been shaped into adjuncts of the temples. With the advance of still later epochs all the limestone veins of the region were hollowed out by ground waters, so that the mountains, the foothills, and the plains below them were a veritable network of connected caverns and galleries. Many graphic sculptures told of explorations deep underground, and of the final discovery of the Stygian sunless sea that lurked at earth's bowels.

This vast nighted gulf had undoubtedly been worn by the great river which flowed down from the nameless and horrible westward mountains, and which had formerly turned at the base of the Old Ones' range and flowed beside that chain into the Indian Ocean between Budd and Totten Lands on Wilkes's coast line. Little by little it had eaten away the limestone hill base at its turning, till at last its sapping currents reached the caverns of the ground waters and joined with them in digging a deeper abyss.

Finally its whole bulk emptied into the hollow hills and left the old bed toward the ocean dry. Much of the later city as we now found it had been built over that former bed. The Old Ones, understanding what had happened, and exercising their always keen artistic sense, had carved into ornate pylons those headlands of the foothills where the great stream began its descent into eternal darkness.

This river, once crossed by scores of noble stone bridges, was plainly the one whose extinct course we had seen in our aëroplane survey. Its position in different carvings of the city helped us to orient ourselves to the scene as it had been at various stages of the region's age-long, æon-dead history, so that we were able to sketch a hasty but careful map of the salient features—squares, important buildings, and the like—for guidance in further explorations.

We could soon reconstruct in fancy the whole stupendous thing as it was a million or ten million or fifty million years ago, for the sculptures told us exactly what the buildings and mountains and squares and suburbs and landscape setting and luxuriant Tertiary vegetation had looked like.

It must have had a marvelous and mystic beauty, and as I thought of it I almost forgot the clammy sense of sinister oppression with which the city's inhuman age and massiveness and deadness and remoteness and glacial twilight had choked and weighed on my spirit.

Yet, according to certain carvings the denizens of that city had themselves known the clutch of oppressive terror; for there was a somber and recurrent type of scene in which the Old Ones were shown in the act of recoiling affrightedly from some object—never allowed to appear in the design—found in the great river and indicated as having been washed down through waving, vine-draped cycad forests from those horrible westward mountains.

It was only in the one late-built house with the decadent carvings that we obtained any foreshadowing of the final calamity leading to the city's desertion. Undoubtedly there must have been many sculptures of the same age elsewhere, even allowing for the slackened energies and aspirations of a stressful and uncertain period; indeed, very certain evidence of the existence of others came to us shortly afterward. But this was the first and only set we directly encountered.

We meant to look farther later on; but as I have said, immediate conditions dictated another present objective. There would, though, have been a limit—for after all hope of a long future occupancy of the place had perished among the Old Ones, there could not but have been a complete cessation of mural decoration. The ultimate blow, of course, was the coming of the great cold which once held most of the earth in thrall, and which has never departed from the ill-fated poles—the great cold that, at the world's other extremity, put an end to the fabled lands of Lomar and Hyperborea.

Just when this tendency began in the antarctic it would be hard to say in terms of exact years. Nowadays we set the beginning of the general glacial periods at a distance of about five hundred thousand years from the present, but at the poles the terrible scourge must have commenced much earlier. All quantitative estimates are partly guesswork, but it is quite likely that the decadent sculptures were made considerably less than a million years ago, and that the actual desertion of the city was complete long before the conventional opening of the Pleistocene—five hundred thousand years ago—as reckoned in terms of the earth's whole surface.

In the decadent sculptures there were signs of thinner vegetation everywhere, and of a decreased country life on the part of the Old Ones. Heating devices were shown in the houses, and winter travelers were represented as muffled in protective fabrics. Then we saw a series of cartouches—the continuous band arrangement being frequently interrupted in these late carvings—depicting a constantly growing migration to the nearest refuges of greater warmth—some fleeing to cities under the sea off the far-away coast, and some clambering down through networks of limestone caverns in the hollow hills to the neighboring black abyss of subterrane waters.

In the end, it seems to have been the neighboring abyss which received the greatest colonization. This was partly due, no doubt, to the traditional sacredness of this special region, but may have been more conclusively determined by the opportunities it gave for continuing the use of the great temples on the honeycombed mountains, and for retaining the vast land city as a place of summer residence and base of communication with various mines.

The linkage of old and new abodes was made more effective by means of several gradings and improvements along the connecting routes, including the chiseling of numerous direct tunnels from the ancient metropolis to the black abyss—sharply down-pointing tunnels whose mouths we carefully drew, according to our most thoughtful estimates, on the guide map we were compiling.

It was obvious that at least two of these tunnels lay within a reasonable exploring distance of where we were—both being on the mountainward edge of the city, one less than a quarter of a mile toward the ancient rivercourse, and the other perhaps twice that distance in the opposite direction.

The abyss, it seems, had shelving shores of dry land at certain places, but the Old Ones built their new city under water—no doubt because of its greater certainty of uniform warmth. The depth of the hidden sea appears to have been very great, so that the earth's internal heat could insure its habitability for an indefinite period.

The beings seem to have had no trouble in adapting themselves to part-time—and eventually, of course, whole-time—residence under water, since they had never allowed their gill systems to atrophy.

There were many sculptures which showed how they had always frequently visited their submarine kinsfolk elsewhere, and how they had habitually bathed on the deep bottom of their great river. The darkness of inner earth could likewise have been no deterrent to a race accustomed to long antarctic nights.

Decadent though their style undoubtedly was, these latest carvings had a truly epic quality where they told of the building of the new city in the cavern sea. The Old Ones had gone about it scientifically—quarrying insoluble rocks from the heart of the honeycombed mountains, and employing expert workers from the nearest submarine city to perform the construction according to the best methods.

These workers brought with them all that was necessary to establish the new venture—Shoggoth tissue from which to breed stone lifters and subsequent beasts of burden for the cavern city, and other protoplasmic matter to mold into phosphorescent organisms for lighting purposes.

At last a mighty metropolis rose on the bottom of that Stygian sea, its architecture much like that of the city above, and its workmanship displaying relatively little decadence because of the precise mathematical element inherent in building operations.

The newly bred Shoggoths grew to enormous size and singular intelligence, and were represented as taking and executing orders with marvelous quickness. They seemed to converse with the Old Ones by mimicking their voices—a sort of musical piping over a wide range, if poor Lake's dissection had indicated aright—and to work more from spoken commands than from hypnotic suggestions as in earlier times.

They were, however, kept in admirable control. The phosphorescent organisms supplied light with vast effectiveness, and doubtless atoned for the loss of the familiar polar auroras of the outer-world night.

Art and decoration were pursued, though, of course, with a certain decadence. The Old Ones seemed to realize this falling off themselves, and in many cases anticipated the policy of Constantine the Great by transplanting especially fine blocks of ancient carving from their land city, just as the emperor, in a similar age of decline, stripped Greece and Asia of their finest art to give his new Byzantine capital greater splendors than its own people could create. That the transfer of sculptured blocks had not been more extensive, was doubtless owing to the fact that the land city was not at first wholly abandoned.

By the time total abandonment did occur—and it surely must have occurred before the polar Pleistocene was far advanced—the Old Ones had perhaps become satisfied with their decadent art—or had ceased to recognize the superior merit of the older carvings. At any rate, the æon-silent ruins around us had certainly undergone no wholesale sculptural denudation, though all the best separate statues, like other movables, had been taken away.

The decadent cartouches and dados telling this story were, as I have said, the latest we could find in our limited search. They left us with a picture of the Old Ones shuttling back and forth betwixt the land city in summer and the sea-cavern city in winter, and sometimes trading with the sea-bottom cities off the antarctic coast.

By this time the ultimate doom of the land city must have been recognized, for the sculptures showed many signs of the cold's malign encroachments. Vegetation was declining, and the terrible snows of the winter no longer melted completely even in midsummer.

The saurian live stock were nearly all dead, and the mammals were standing it none too well. To keep on with the work of the upper world it had become necessary to adapt some of the amorphous and curiously cold-resistant Shoggoths to land life—a thing the Old Ones had formerly been reluctant to do. The great river was now lifeless, and the upper sea had lost most of its denizens except the seals and whales. All the birds had flown away, save only the great, grotesque penguins.

What had happened afterward we could only guess. How long had the new sea-cavern city survived? Was it still down there, a stony corpse in eternal blackness? Had the subterranean waters frozen at last? To what fate had the ocean-bottom cities of the outer world been delivered? Had any of the Old Ones shifted north ahead of the creeping ice cap? Existing geology shows no trace of their presence. Had the frightful Mi-Go been still a menace in the outer land world of the north? Could one be sure of what might or might not linger, even to this day, in the lightless and unplumbed abysses of earth's deepest water?

Those things had seemingly been able to withstand any amount of pressure—and men of the sea have fished up curious objects at times. And has the killer-whale theory really explained the savage and mysterious scars on antarctic seals noticed a generation ago by Borchgrevingk?

The specimens found by poor Lake did not enter into these guesses, for their geologic setting proved them to have lived at what must have been a very early date in the land city's history. They were, according to their location, certainly not less than thirty million years old, and we reflected that in their day the sea-cavern city, and indeed the cavern itself, had had no existence.

They would have remembered an older scene, with lush Tertiary vegetation everywhere, a younger land city of flourishing arts around them, and a great river sweeping northward along the base of the mighty mountains toward a far-away tropic ocean.

And yet we could not help thinking about these specimens—especially about the eight perfect ones that were missing from Lake's hideously ravaged camp. There was something abnormal about that whole business—the strange things we had tried so hard to lay to somebody's madness—those frightful graves—the amount *and nature* of the missing material—Gedney—the unearthly toughness of those archaic monstrosities, and the queer vital freaks the sculptures now showed the race to have——Danforth and I had seen a good deal in the last few hours, and were prepared to believe and keep silent about many appalling and incredible secrets of primal nature.

IX

I have said that our study of the decadent sculptures brought about a change in our immediate objective. This, of course, had to do with the chiseled avenues to the black inner world, of whose existence we had not known before, but which we were now eager to find and traverse.

From the evident scale of the carvings we deduced that a steeply descending walk of about a mile through either of the neighboring tunnels would bring us to the brink of the dizzy, sunless cliffs about the great abyss, down whose side paths, improved by the Old Ones, led to the rocky shore of the hidden and nighted ocean. To behold this fabulous gulf in stark reality was a lure which seemed impossible of resistance once we knew of the thing—yet we realized we must begin the quest at once if we expected to include it in our present trip.

In was now eight p.m., and we had not enough battery replacements to let our torches burn on forever. We had done so much of our studying and copying below the glacial level that our battery supply had had at least five hours of nearly continuous use, and despite the special dry cell formula would obviously be good for only about four more—though by keeping one torch unused, except for especially interesting or difficult places, we might manage to eke out a safe margin beyond that.

It would not do to be without a light in these Cyclopean catacombs, hence in order to make the abyss trip we must give up all further mural deciphering. Of course, we intended to revisit the place for days and perhaps weeks of intensive study and photography—curiosity having long ago gotten the better of horror—but just now we must hasten.

Our supply of trail-blazing paper was far from unlimited, and we were reluctant to sacrifice spare notebooks or sketching paper to augment it, but we did let one large notebook go. If worst came to worst, we could resort to rock chipping—and, of course, it would be possible, even in case of really lost direction, to work up to full daylight by one channel or another if granted sufficient time for plentiful trial and error. So, at last, we set off eagerly in the indicated direction of the nearest tunnel.

According to the carvings from which we had made our map, the desired tunnel mouth could not be much more than a quarter of a mile from where we stood; the intervening space showing solid-looking buildings quite likely to be penetrable still at a subglacial level. The opening itself would be in the basement—on the angle nearest the foothills—of a vast five-pointed structure of evidently public and perhaps ceremonial nature, which we tried to identify from our aërial survey of the ruins.

No such structure came to our minds as we recalled our flight, hence we concluded that its upper parts had been greatly damaged, or that it had been totally shattered in an ice rift we had noticed. In the latter case the tunnel would probably turn out to be choked, so that we would have to try the next nearest one—the one less than a mile to the north.

The intervening river course prevented our trying any of the more southern tunnels on this trip; and indeed, if both of the neighboring ones were choked it was doubtful whether our batteries would warrant an attempt on the next northerly one—about a mile beyond our second choice.

As we threaded our dim way through the labyrinth with the aid of map and compass—traversing rooms and corridors in every stage of ruin or preservation, clambering up ramps, crossing upper floors and bridges and clambering down again, encountering choked doorways and piles of débris, hastening now and then along finely preserved and uncannily immaculate stretches, taking false leads and retracing our way (in such cases removing the blind paper trail we had left), and once in a while striking the bottom of an open shaft through which daylight poured or trickled down—we were repeatedly tantalized by the sculptured walls along our route.

We had wormed our way very close to the computed site of the tunnel's mouth—having crossed a second-story bridge to what seemed plainly the tip of a pointed wall, and descended to a ruinous corridor especially rich in decadently elaborate and apparently ritualistic sculptures of late workmanship—when, about eight thirty p.m., Danforth's keen young nostrils gave us the first hint of something unusual.

If we had had a dog with us, I suppost we would have been warned before. At first we could not precisely say what was wrong with the formerly crystal-pure air, but after a few seconds our memories reached only too definitely. Let me try to state the thing without flinching. There was an odor—and that odor was vaguely, subtly, and unmistakably akin to what had nauseated us upon opening the insane grave of the horror poor Lake had dissected.

Of course, the revelation was not as clearly cut at the time as it sounds now. There were several conceivable explanations, and we did a good deal of indecisive whispering. Most important of all, we did not retreat without further investigation; for having come this far, we were loath to be balked by anything short of certain disaster.

Anyway, what we must have suspected was altogether too wild to believe. Such things did not happen in any normal world. It was probably sheer irrational instinct which made us dim our single torch—tempted no longer by the decadent and sinister sculptures that leered menacingly from the oppressive walls—and which softened our progress to a cautious tiptoeing and crawling over the increasingly littered floor and heaps of débris.

Danforth's eyes as well as nose proved better than mine, for it was likewise he who first noticed the queer aspect of the débris after we had passed many half-choked arches leading to chambers and corridors on the ground level. It did not look quite as it ought after countless thousands of years of desertion, and when we cautiously turned on more light we saw that a kind of swath seemed to have been lately tracked through it. The irregular nature of the latter precluded any definite marks, but in the smoother places there were suggestions of the dragging of heavy objects. Once we thought there was a hint of parallel tracks, as if of runners. This was what made us pause again.

It was during that pause that we caught—simultaneously this time—the other odor ahead. Paradoxically, it was both a less frightful and a more frightful odor—less frightful intrinsically, but infinitely appalling in this place under the known circumstances—unless, of course, Gedney——

For the odor was the plain and familiar one of common petrol—everyday gasoline.

Our motivation after that is something I will leave to psychologists. We knew now that some terrible extension of the camp horrors must have crawled into this nighted burial place of the æons, hence could not doubt any longer the existence of nameless conditions—present or at least recent—just ahead. Yet in the end we did let sheer burning curiosity—or anxiety—or autohypnotism—or vague thoughts of responsibility toward Gedney—of what not—drive us on.

Danforth whispered again of the print he thought he had seen at the alley turning in the ruins above; and of the faint musical piping—potentially of tremendous significance in the light of Lake's dissection report, despite its close resemblance to the cave-mouth echoes of the windy peaks—which he thought he had shortly afterward half heard from unknown depths below.

I, in my turn, whispered of how the camp was left—of what had disappeared, and of how the madness of a lone survivor might have conceived the inconceivable—a wild trip across the monstrous mountains and a descent into the unknown, primal masonry——

But we could not convince each other, or even ourselves, of anything definite. We had turned off all light as we stood still, and vaguely noticed that a trace of deeply filtered upper daylight kept the blackness from being absolute.

Having automatically begun to move ahead, we guided ourselves by occasional flashes from our torch. The disturbed débris formed an impression we could not shake off, and the smell of gasoline grew stronger. More and more ruin met our eyes and hampered our feet, until very soon we saw that the forward way was about to cease. We had been all too correct in our pessimistic guess about that rift glimpsed from the air. Our tunnel quest was a blind one, and we were not even going to be able to reach the basement out of which the abyssward aperture opened.

The torch, flashing over the grotesquely carved walls of the blocked corridor in which we stood, showed several doorways in various states of obstruction; and from one of them the gasoline odor—quite submerging that other hint of odor—came with especial distinctness. As we looked more steadily, we saw that beyond a doubt there had been a slight and recent clearing away of débris from that particular opening. Whatever the lurking horror might be, we believed the direct avenue toward it was now plainly manifest. I do not think any one will wonder that we waited an appreciable time before making any further motion.

And yet, when we did venture inside that black arch, our first impression was one of anticlimax. For amidst the littered expanse of that sculptured crypt—a perfect cube with sides of about twenty feet—there remained no recent object of instantly discernible size; so that we looked instinctively, though in vain, for a farther doorway.

In another moment, however, Danforth's sharp vision had discovered a place where the floor débris had been disturbed. We turned on both torches full strength. Though what we saw in that light was actually simple and trifling, I am none the less reluctant to tell of it because of what it implied.

It was a rough leveling of the débris, upon which several small objects lay carelessly scattered, and at one corner of which a considerable amount of gasoline must have been spilled lately enough to leave a strong odor even at this extreme superplateau altitude. In other words, it could not be other than a sort of camp—a camp made by questing beings who, like us, had been turned back by the unexpectedly choked way to the abyss.

Let me be plain. The scattered objects were, so far as substance was concerned, all from Lake's camp, and consisted of: tin cans as queerly opened as those we had seen at that ravaged place, many spent matches, three illustrated books more or less curiously smudged, an empty ink bottle with its pictorial and instructional carton, a broken fountain pen, some oddly snipped fragments of fur and tent cloth, a used electric battery with circular of directions, a folder that came with our type of tent heater, and a sprinkling of crumpled papers.

It was all bad enough, but when we smoothed out the papers and looked at what was on them we felt we had come to the worst. We had found certain inexplicably blotted papers at the camp which might have prepared us, yet the effect of the sight, down there in the prehuman vaults of a nightmare city, was almost too much to bear.

A mad Gedney might have made the groups of dots in imitation of those found on the greenish soapstones, just as the dots on those insane five-pointed grave mounds might have been made; and he might conceivably have prepared rough, hasty sketches—varying in their accuracy—or lack of it—which outlined the neighboring parts of the city and traced the way from a circularly represented place outside our previous route—a place we identified as a great cylindrical tower in the carvings and as a vast circular gulf glimpsed in our aërial survey—to the present five-pointed structure and the tunnel mouth therein.

He might, I repeat, have prepared such sketches; for those before us were quite obviously compiled, as our own had been, from late sculptures somewhere in the glacial labyrinth, though not from the ones which we had seen and used. But what this art-blind bungler could never have done was to execute those sketches in a strange and assured technique perhaps superior, despite haste and carelessness, to any of the decadent carvings from which they were taken—the characteristic and unmistakable technique of the Old Ones themselves in the dead city's heyday.

There are those who will say Danforth and I were utterly mad not to flee for our lives after that; since our conclusions were now—notwithstanding their wildness—completely fixed, and of a nature I need not even mention to those who have read my account as far as this. Perhaps we were mad—for have I not said those horrible peaks were mountains of madness? But I think I can detect something of the same spirit—albeit in a less extreme form—in the men who stalk deadly beasts through African jungles to photograph them or study their habits. Half paralyzed with terror though we were, there was nevertheless fanned within us a blazing flame of awe and curiosity which triumphed in the end.

Of course, we did not mean to face that—or those—which we knew had been there, but we felt that they must be gone by now. They would by this time have found the other neighboring entrance to the abyss, and have passed within, to whatever night-black fragments of the past might await them in the ultimate gulf—the ultimate gulf they had never seen. Or if that entrance, too, was blocked, they would have gone on to the north seeking another. They were, we remembered, partly independent of light.

Looking back to that moment, I can scarcely recall just what precise form our new emotions took—just what change of immediate objective it was that so sharpened our sense of expectancy. We certainly did not mean to face what we feared—yet I will not deny that we may have had a lurking, unconscious wish to spy certain things from some hidden vantage point.

Probably we had not given up our zeal to glimpse the abyss itself, though there was interposed a new goal in the form of that great circular place shown on the crumpled sketches we had found. We had at once recognized it as a monstrous cylindrical tower in the carvings, but appearing only as a prodigious, round aperture from above.

Something about the impressiveness of its rendering, even in these hasty diagrams, made us think that its subglacial levels must still form a feature of peculiar importance. Perhaps it embodied architectural marvels as yet unencountered by us. It was certainly of incredible age, according to the sculptures in which it figured—being indeed among the first things built in the city. Its carvings, if preserved, could not but be highly significant. Moreover, it might form a good present link with the upper world—a shorter route than the one we were so carefully blazing and probably that by which those others had descended.

At any rate, the thing we did was to study the terrible sketches—which quite perfectly confirmed our own—and start back over the indicated course to the circular place; the course which our nameless predecessors must have traversed twice before us. The other neighboring gate to the abyss would lie beyond that. I need not speak of our journey—during which we continued to leave an economical trail of paper—for it was precisely the same in kind as that by which we had reached the cul-de-sac, except that it tended to adhere more closely to the ground level and even descend to basement corridors.

Every now and then we could trace certain disturbing marks in the débris or litter underfoot; and, after we had passed outside the radius of the gasoline scent, we were again faintly conscious—spasmodically—of that more hideous and more persistent scent. After the way had branched from our former course, we sometimes gave the rays of our single torch a furtive sweep along the walls; noting in almost every case the well-nigh omnipresent sculptures, which indeed seem to have formed a main æsthetic outlet for the Old Ones.

About nine-thirty p.m., while traversing a vaulted corridor whose increasingly glaciated floor seemed somewhat below the ground level and whose roof grew lower as we advanced, we began to see strong daylight ahead and were able to turn off our torch. It appeared that we were coming to the vast, circular place, and that our distance from the upper air could not be very great.

The corridor ended in an arch, surprisingly low for these megalithic ruins, but we could see much through it even before we emerged. Beyond, there stretched a prodigious round space—fully two hundred feet in diameter—strewn with débris and containing many choked archways corresponding to the one we were about to cross. The walls were—in available spaces—boldly sculptured into a spiral band of heroic proportions; and displayed, despite the destructive weathering caused by the openness of the spot, an artistic splendor far beyond anything we had encountered before. The littered floor was quite heavily glaciated, and we fancied that the true bottom lay at a considerably lower depth.

But the salient object of the place was the titanic stone ramp which, eluding the archways by a sharp turn outward into the open floor, wound spirally up the stupendous cylindrical wall like an inside counterpart of those once climbing outside the monstrous towers or zikkurats of antique Babylon. Only the rapidity of our flight, and the perspective which confounded the descent with the tower's inner wall, had prevented our noticing this feature from the air, and thus caused us to seek another avenue to the subglacial level.

Pabodie might have been able to tell what sort of engineering held it in place, but Danforth and I could merely admire and marvel. We could see mighty stone corbels and pillars here and there, but what we saw seemed inadequate to the function performed. The thing was excellently preserved up to the present top of the tower—a highly remarkable circumstance in view of its exposure—and its shelter had done much to protect the bizarre and disturbing cosmic sculptures on the walls.

As we stepped out into the awesome half daylight of this monstrous cylinder bottom—fifty million years old, and without doubt the most primally ancient structure ever to meet our eyes—we saw that the ramp-traversed sides stretched dizzily up to a height of fully sixty feet.

This, we recalled from our aërial survey, meant an outside glaciation of some forty feet; since the yawning gulf we had seen from the plane had been at the top of an approximately twenty-foot mound of crumbled masonry, somewhat sheltered for three fourths of its circumference by the massive curving walls of a line of higher ruins. According to the sculptures the original tower had stood in the center of an immense circular plaza, and had been perhaps five hundred or six hundred feet high, with tiers of horizontal disks near the top, and a row of needlelike spires along the upper rim.

Most of the masonry had obviously toppled outward rather than inward—a fortunate happening, since otherwise the ramp might have been shattered and the whole interior choked. As it was, the ramp showed sad battering; whilst the choking was such that all the archways seemed to have been half cleared.

It took us only a moment to conclude that this was indeed the route by which those others had descended, and that this would be the logical route for our own ascent, despite the long trail of paper we had left elsewhere. The tower's mouth was no farther from the foothills and our waiting plane than was the great terraced building we had entered, and any further subglacial exploration we might make on this trip would lie in this general region.

Oddly, we were still thinking about possible later trips—even after all we had seen and guessed. Then, as we picked our way cautiously over the débris of the great floor, there came a sight which for the time excluded all other matters.

It was the neatly huddled array of three sledges in that farther angle of the ramp's lower and outward-projecting course which had hitherto been screened from our view. There they were—the three sledges missing from Lake's camp—shaken by a hard usage which must have included forcible dragging along great reaches of snowless masonry and débris, as well as much hand portage over utterly unnavigable places.

They were carefully and intelligently packed and strapped, and contained things memorably familiar enough: the gasoline stove, fuel cans, instrument cases, provision tins, tarpaulins obviously bulging with books, and some bulging with less obvious contents—everything derived from Lake's equipment.

After what we had found in that other room, we were in a measure prepared for this encounter. The really great shock came when we stepped over and undid one tarpaulin, whose outlines had peculiarly disquieted us. It seems that others as well as Lake had been interested in collecting typical specimens; for there were two here, both stiffly frozen, perfectly preserved, patched with adhesive plaster where some wounds around the neck had occurred, and wrapped with care to prevent further damage. They were the bodies of young Gedney and the missing dog.

X

Many people will probably judge us callous as well as mad for thinking about the northward tunnel and the abyss so soon after our somber discovery, and I am not prepared to say that we would have immediately revived such thoughts but for a specific circumstance which broke in upon us and set up a whole new train of speculations.

We had replaced the tarpaulin over poor Gedney and were standing in a kind of mute bewilderment when the sounds finally reached our consciousness—the first sounds we had heard since descending out of the open where the mountain wind whined faintly from its unearthly heights. Well-known and mundane though they were, their presence in this remote world of death was more unexpected and unnerving than any grotesque or fabulous tones could possibly have been—since they gave a fresh upsetting to all our notions of cosmic harmony.

Had it been some trace of that bizarre musical piping over a wide range, which Lake's dissection report had led us to expect in those others—and which, indeed, our overwrought fancies had been reading into every wind howl we had heard since coming on the camp horror—it would have had a kind of hellish congruity with the æon-dead region around us. A voice from other epochs belongs in a graveyard of other epochs.

As it was, however, the noise shattered all our profoundly seated adjustments—all out tacit acceptance of the inner antarctic as a waste utterly and irrevocably void of every vestige of normal life.

What we heard was not the fabulous note of any buried blasphemy of elder earth from whose supernal toughness an age-denied polar sun had evoked a monstrous response. Instead, it was a thing so mockingly normal and so unerringly familiarized by our sea days off Victoria Land and our camp days at McMurdo Sound that we shuddered to think of it here, where such things ought not to be. To be brief—it was simply the raucous squawking of a penguin.

The muffled sound floated from subglacial recesses nearly opposite to the corridor whence we had come—regions manifestly in the direction of that other tunnel to the vast abyss. The presence of a living water bird in such a direction—in a world whose surface was one of age-long and uniform lifelessness—could lead to only one conclusion; hence our first thought was to verify the objective reality of the sound. It was, indeed, repeated, and seemed at times to come from more than one throat.

Seeking its source, we entered an archway from which much débris had been cleared; resuming our trail blazing—with an added paper supply taken with curious repugnance from one of the tarpaulin bundles on the sledges—when we left daylight behind.

As the glaciated floor gave place to a litter of detritus, we plainly discerned some curious, dragging tracks; and once Danforth found a distinct print of a sort whose description would be only too superfluous. The course indicated by the penguin cries was precisely what our map and compass prescribed as an approach to the more northerly tunnel mouth, and we were glad to find that a bridgeless thoroughfare on the ground and basement levels seemed open.

The tunnel, according to the chart, ought to start from the basement of a large pyramidal structure which we seemed vaguely to recall from our aërial survey as remarkably well-preserved. Along our path the single torch showed a customary profusion of carvings, but we did not pause to examine any of these.

Suddenly a bulky white shape loomed up ahead of us, and we flashed on the second torch. It is odd how wholly this new quest had turned our minds from earlier fears of what might lurk near. Those other ones, having left their supplies in the great circular place, must have planned to return after their scouting trip toward or into the abyss; yet we had now discarded all caution concerning them as completely as if they had never existed.

This white, waddling thing was fully six feet high, yet we seemed to realize at once that it was not one of those others. They were larger and dark, and, according to the sculptures, their motion over land surfaces was a swift, assured matter despite the queerness of their sea-born tentacle equipment. But to say that the white thing did not profoundly frighten us would be vain. We were indeed clutched for an instant by a primitive dread almost sharper than the worst of our reasoned fears regarding those others.

Then came a flash of anticlimax as the white shape sidled into a lateral archway to our left, to join two others of its kind which had summoned it in raucous tones. For it was only a penguin—albeit of a huge, unknown species larger than the greatest of the known king penguins, and monstrous in its combined albinism and virtual eyelessness.

When we had followed the thing into the archway and turned both our torches on the indifferent and unheeding group of three, we saw that they were all eyeless albinos of the same unknown and gigantic species.

Their size reminded us of some of the archaic penguins depicted in the Old Ones' sculptures, and it did not take us long to conclude that they were descended from the same stock—undoubtedly surviving through a retreat to some warmer inner region whose perpetual blackness had destroyed their pigmentation and atrophied their eyes to mere useless slits.

That their present habitat was the vast abyss we sought, was not for a moment to be doubted; and this evidence of the gulf's continued warmth and habitability filled us with the most curious and subtly perturbing fancies.

We wondered, too, what had caused these three birds to venture out of their usual domain. The state and silence of the great dead city made it clear that it had at no time been a habitual seasonal rookery, whilst the manifest indifference of the trio to our presence made it seem odd that any passing party of those others should have startled them.

Was it possible that those others had taken some aggressive notion or tried to increase their meat supply? We doubted whether that pungent odor which the dogs had hated could cause an equal antipathy in these penguins; since their ancestors had obviously lived on excellent terms with the Old Ones—an amicable relationship which must have survived in the abyss below as long as any of the Old Ones remained.

Regretting—in a flare-up of the old spirit of pure science—that we could not photograph these anomalous creatures, we shortly left them to their squawking and pushed on toward the abyss whose openness was now so positively proved to us, and whose exact direction occasional penguin tracks made clear.

Not long afterward a steep descent in a long, low, doorless, and peculiarly sculptureless corridor led us to believe that we were approaching the tunnel mouth at last. We had passed two more penguins.

Then the corridor ended in a prodigious open space which made us gasp involuntarily—a perfect inverted hemisphere, obviously deep underground, fully a hundred feet in diameter and fifty feet high, with low archways opening around all parts of the circumference but one, and that one yawning cavernously with a black, arched aperture which broke the symmetry of the vault to a height of nearly fifteen feet. It was the entrance to the great abyss.

In this vast hemisphere, whose concave roof was impressively though decadently carved to a likeness of the primordial celestial dome, a few albino penguins waddled—aliens there, but indifferent and unseeing. The black tunnel yawned indefinitely off at a steep, descending grade, its aperture adorned with grotesquely chiseled jambs and lintel.

From that cryptical mouth we fancied a current of slightly warmer air and perhaps even a suspicion of vapor proceeded; and we wondered what living entities other than penguins the limitless void below, and the contiguous honeycombings of the land and the titan mountains, might conceal.

We wondered, too, whether the trace of mountaintop smoke at first suspected by poor Lake, as well as the odd haze we had ourselves perceived around the rampart-crowned peak, might not be caused by the tortuous-channeled rising of some such vapor from the unfathomed regions of earth's core.

Entering the tunnel, we saw that its outline was—at least at the start—about fifteen feet each way—sides, floor, and arched roof composed of the usual megalithic masonry. The sides were sparsely decorated with cartouches of conventional designs in a later, decadent style; and all the construction and carving were marvellously well-preserved.

The floor was quite clear, except for a slight detritus bearing outgoing penguin tracks and the inward tracks of those others. The farther one advanced, the warmer it became; so that we were soon unbuttoning our heavy garments. We wondered whether there were any actually igneous manifestations below, and whether the waters of that sunless sea were hot.

After a short distance the masonry gave place to solid rock, though the tunnel kept the same proportions and presented the same aspect of carved regularity. Occasionally its varying grade became so steep that grooves were cut in the floor.

Several times we noted the mouths of small lateral galleries not recorded in our diagrams; none of them such as to complicate the problem of our return, and all of them welcome as possible refuges in case we met unwelcome entities on their way back from the abyss.

The nameless scent of such things was very distinct. Doubtless it was suicidally foolish to venture into that tunnel under the known conditions, but the lure of the unplumbed is stronger in certain persons than most suspect—indeed, it was just such a lure which had brought us to this unearthly polar waste in the first place.

We saw several penguins as we passed along, and speculated on the distance we would have to traverse. The carvings had led us to expect a steep downhill walk of about a mile to the abyss, but our previous wanderings had shown us that matters of scale were not wholly to be depended on.

After about a quarter of a mile that nameless scent became greatly accentuated, and we kept very careful track of the various lateral openings we passed. There was no visible vapor as at the mouth, but this was doubtless due to the lack of contrasting cooler air. The temperature was rapidly ascending, and we were not surprised to come upon a careless heap of material shudderingly familiar to us. It was composed of furs and tent cloths taken from Lake's camp, and we did not pause to study the bizarre forms into which the fabrics had been slashed.

Slightly beyond this point we noticed a decided increase in the size and number of the side galleries, and concluded that the densely honeycombed region beneath the higher foothills must now have been reached.

The nameless scent was now curiously mixed with another and scarcely less offensive odor—of what nature we could not guess, though we thought of decaying organisms and perhaps unknown subterrane fungi.

Then came a startling expansion of the tunnel for which the carvings had not prepared us—a broadening and rising into a lofty, natural-looking elliptical cavern with a level floor, some seventy-five feet long and fifty broad, and with many immense side passages leading away into cryptical darkness.

Though this cavern was natural in appearance, an inspection with both torches suggested that it had been formed by the artificial destruction of several walls between adjacent honeycombings. The walls were rough, and the high, vaulted roof was thick with stalactites; but the solid rock floor had been smoothed off, and was free from all débris, detritus, or even dust to a positively abnormal extent.

Except for the avenue through which we had come, this was true of the floors of all the great galleries opening off from it; and the singularity of the condition was such as to set us vainly puzzling.

The curious new fetor which had supplemented the nameless scent was excessively pungent here; so much so that it destroyed all trace of the other. Something about this whole place, with its polished and almost glistening floor, struck us as more vaguely baffling and horrible than any of the monstrous things we have previously encountered.

The regularity of the passage immediately ahead, prevented all confusion as to the right course amidst this plethora of equally great cave mouths. Nevertheless we resolved to resume our paper trail blazing if any further complexity should develop; for dust tracks, of course, could no longer be expected.

Upon resuming our direct progress we cast a beam of torchlight over the tunnel walls—and stopped short in amazement at the supremely radical change which had come over the carvings in this part of the passage. We realized, of course, the great decadence of the Old Ones' sculpture at the time of the tunneling, and had indeed noticed the inferior workmanship of the arabesques in the stretches behind us.

But now, in this deeper section beyond the cavern, there was a sudden difference wholly transcending explanation—a difference in basic nature as well as in mere quality, and involving so profound and calamitous a degradation of skill that nothing in the hitherto observed rate of decline could have led one to expect it.

This new and degenerate work was coarse, bold, and wholly lacking in delicacy of detail. It was countersunk with exaggerated depth in bands following the same general line as the sparse cartouches of the earlier sections, but the height of the reliefs did not reach the level of the general surface.

Danforth had the idea that it was a second carving—a sort of palimpsest formed after the obliteration of a previous design. In nature it was wholly decorative and conventional, and consisted of crude spirals and angles roughly following the quintile mathematical tradition of the Old Ones, yet seeming more like a parody than a perpetuation of that tradition.

Since we could not afford to spend any considerable time in study, we resumed our advance after a cursory look.

We saw and heard fewer penguins, but thought we caught a vague suspicion of an infinitely distant chorus of them somewhere deep within the earth. The new and inexplicable odor was abominably strong, and we could detect scarcely a sign of that other nameless scent.

Puffs of visible vapor ahead bespoke increasing contrasts in temperature, and the relative nearness of the sunless sea cliffs of the great abyss. Then, quite unexpectedly, we saw certain obstructions on the polished floor ahead—obstructions which were quite definitely not penguins—and turned on our second torch after making sure that the objects were quite stationary.

XI

Still another time have I come to a place where it is very difficult to proceed. I ought to be hardened by this stage; but there are some experiences and intimations which scar too deeply to permit of healing, and leave only such added sensitiveness that memory re-inspired all the original horror.

We saw, as I have said, certain obstructions on the polished floor ahead; and I may add that our nostrils were assailed almost simultaneously by a very curious intensification of the strange, prevailing fetor, now quite plainly mixed with the nameless stench of those others which had gone before us.

The light of the second torch left no doubt of what the obstructions were, and we dared approach them only because we could see, even from a distance, that they were quite as past all harming power as had been the six similar specimens unearthed from the monstrous star-mounded graves at poor Lake's camp.

They were, indeed, as lacking in completeness as most of those we had unearthed—though it grew plain from the thick, dark-green pool gathering around them that their incompleteness was of infinitely greater recency. There seemed to be only four of them, whereas Lake's bulletins would have suggested no less than eight as forming the group which had preceded us. To find them in this state was wholly unexpected, and we wondered what sort of monstrous struggle had occurred down here in the dark.

Penguins, attacked in a body, retaliate savagely with their beaks; and our ears now made certain the existence of a rookery far beyond. Had those others disturbed such a place and aroused murderous pursuit? The obstructions did not suggest it, for penguin beaks against the tough tissues Lake had dissected could hardly account for the terrible damage our approaching glance was beginning to make out. Besides, the huge blind birds we had seen appeared to be singularly peaceful.

Had there, then, been a struggle among those others, and were the absent four responsible? If so, where were they? Were they close at hand and likely to form an immediate menace to us? We glanced anxiously at some of the smooth-floored lateral passages as we continued our slow and frankly reluctant approach.

Whatever the conflict was, it had clearly been that which had frightened the penguins into their unaccustomed wandering. It must, then, have arisen near that faintly heard rookery in the incalculable gulf beyond, since there were no signs that any birds had normally dwelt here.

Perhaps, we reflected, there had been a hideous running fight, with the weaker party seeking to get back to the cached sledges when their pursuers finished them. One could picture the demonic fray between namelessly monstrous entities as it surged out of the black abyss with great clouds of frantic penguins squawking and scurrying ahead.

I say that we approached those sprawling and incomplete obstructions slowly and reluctantly. Would to Heaven we had never approached them at all, but had run back at top speed out of that blasphemous tunnel with the greasily smooth floors and the degenerate murals aping and mocking the things they had superseded—run back, before we had seen what we did see, and before our minds were burned with something which will never let us breathe easily again!

Both of our torches were turned on the prostrate objects, so that we soon realized the dominant factor in their incompleteness. Mauled, compressed, twisted, and ruptured as they were, their chief common injury was total decapitation.

From each one the tentacled starfish head had been removed; and as we drew near we saw that the manner of removal looked more like some hellish tearing or suction than like any ordinary form of cleavage.

Their noisome dark-green ichor formed a large, spreading pool; but its stench was half overshadowed by that newer and stranger stench, here more pungent than at any other point along our route.

Only when we had come very close to the sprawling obstructions could we trace that second, unexplainable fetor to any immediate source—and the instant we did so Danforth, remembering certain very vivid sculptures of the Old Ones' history in the Permian Age one hundred and fifty million years ago, gave vent to a nerve-tortured cry which echoed hysterically through that vaulted and archaic passage with the evil, palimpsest carvings.

I came only just short of echoing his cry myself; for I had seen those primal sculptures, too, and had shudderingly admired the way the nameless artist had suggested that hideous slime coating found on certain incomplete and prostrate Old Ones—those whom the frightful Shoggoths had characteristically slain and sucked to a ghastly headlessness in the great war of resubjugation.

They were infamous, nightmare sculptures even when telling of age-old, bygone things; for Shoggoths and their work ought not to be seen by human beings or portrayed by any beings.

The mad author of the *Necronomicon* had nervously tried to swear that none had been bred on this planet, and that only drugged dreamers had ever conceived them. Formless protoplasm able to mock and reflect all forms and organs and processes—viscous agglutinations of bubbling cells—rubbery fifteen-foot spheroids infinitely plastic and ductile—slaves of suggestion, builders of cities—more and more sullen, more and more intelligent, more and more amphibious, more and more imitative! Great Heaven! What madness made even those blasphemous Old Ones willing to use and to carve such things?

And now, when Danforth and I saw the freshly glistening and reflectively iridescent black slime which clung thickly to those headless bodies and stank obscenely with that new, unknown odor whose cause only a diseased fancy could envisage—clung to those bodies and sparkled less voluminously on a smooth part of the accursedly resculptured wall in a series of grouped dots—we understood the quality of cosmic fear to its uttermost depths.

It was not fear of those four missing others—for all too well did we suspect they would do no harm again. Poor devils! After all, they were not evil things of their kind. They were the men of another age and another order of being. Nature had played a hellish jest on them—as it will on any others that human madness, callousness, or cruelty may hereafter drag up in that hideously dead or sleeping polar waste—and this was their tragic homecoming.

They had not been even savages—for what indeed had they done? That awful awakening in the cold of an unknown epoch—perhaps an attack by the furry, frantically barking quadrupeds, and a dazed defense against them and the equally frantic white simians with the queer wrappings and paraphernalia! Poor Lake. Poor Gedney. And poor Old Ones! Scientists to the last—what had they done that we would not have done in their place? Lord, what intelligence and persistence! What a facing of the incredible, just as those carven kinsmen and forbears had faced things only a little less incredible! Radiates, vegetables, monstrosities, star spawn—whatever they had been, they were men!

They had crossed the icy peaks on whose templed slopes they had once worshiped and roamed among the tree ferns. They had found their dead city brooding under its curse, and had read its carven latter days as we had done. They had tried to reach their living fellows in fabled depths of blackness they had never seen—and what had they found?

All this flashed in unison through the thoughts of Danforth and me as we looked from those headless, slime-coated shapes to the loathsome palimpsest sculptures and the diabolical dot groups of fresh slime on the wall beside them—looked and understood what must have triumphed and survived down there in the Cyclopean water city of that nighted, penguin-fringed abyss, whence even now a sinister curling mist had begun to belch pallidly as if in answer to Danforth's hysterical scream.

The shock of recognizing that monstrous slime and headlessness had frozen us into mute, motionless statues, and it is only through later conversations that we have learned of the complete identity of our thoughts at that moment.

It seemed æons that we stood there, but actually it could not have been more than ten or fifteen seconds. That hateful, pallid mist curled forward as if veritably driven by some remoter advancing bulk—and then came a sound which upset much of what we had just decided, and in so doing broke the spell and enabled us to run like mad past squawking, confused penguins over our former trail back to the city, along ice-sunken megalithic corridors to the great open circle, and up that archaic spiral ramp in a frenzied, automatic plunge for the sane outer air and light of day.

The new sound, as I have intimated, upset much that we had decided; because it was what poor Lake's dissection had led us to attribute to those we had just judged dead. It was, Danforth later told me, precisely what he had caught in infinitely muffled form when at that spot beyond the alley corner above the glacial level; and it certainly had a shocking resemblance to the wind pipings we had both heard around the lofty mountain caves.

At the risk of seeming puerile I will add another thing, too, if only because of the surprising way Danforth's impression chimed with mine. Of course, common reading is what prepared us both to make the interpretation, though Danforth has hinted at queer notions about unsuspected and forbidden sources to which Poe may have had access when writing his "Arthur Gordon Pym" a century ago.

It will be remembered that in that fantastic tale there is a word of unknown but terrible and prodigious significance connected with the antarctic and screamed eternally by the gigantic, spectrally snowy birds of that malign region's core. "*Tekeli-li! Tekeli-li!*" That, I may admit, is exactly what we thought we heard conveyed by that sudden sound behind the advancing white mist—that insidious, musical piping over a singularly wide range.

We were in full flight before three notes or syllables had been uttered, though we knew that the swiftness of the Old Ones would enable any scream-roused and pursuing survivor of the slaughter to overtake us in a moment if it really wished to do so.

We had a vague hope, however, that nonaggressive conduct and a display of kindred reason might cause such a being to spare us in case of capture, if only from scientific curiosity.

After all, if such a one had nothing to fear for itself it would have no motive in harming us. Concealment being futile at this juncture, we used our torch for a running glance behind, and perceived that the mist was thinning. Would we see at last, a complete and living specimen of those others? Again came that insidious musical piping—"*Tekeli-li! Tekeli-li!*"

Then, noting that we were actually gaining on our pursuer, it occurred to us that the entity might be wounded. We could take no chances, however, since it was very obviously approaching in answer to Danforth's scream, rather than in flight from any other entity. The timing was too close to admit of doubt.

Of the whereabouts of that less conceivable and less mentionable nightmare—that fetid, unglimpsed mountain of slime-spewing protoplasm whose race had conquered the abyss and sent land pioneers to recarve and squirm through the burrows of the hills—we could form no guess; and it cost us a genuine pang to leave this probably crippled Old One—perhaps a lone survivor—to the peril of recapture and a nameless fate.

Thank Heaven we did not slacken our run. The curling mist had thickened again, and was driving ahead with increased speed; whilst the straying penguins in our rear were squawking and screaming and displaying signs of a panic really surprising in view of their relatively minor confusion when we had passed them.

Once more came that sinister, wide-ranged piping—"*Tekeli-li! Tekeli-li!*" We had been wrong. The thing was not wounded, but had merely paused on encountering the bodies of its fallen kindred and the hellish slime inscription above them. We could never know what that demon message was—but those burials at Lake's camp had shown how much importance the beings attached to their dead.

Our recklessly used torch now revealed ahead of us the large open cavern where various ways converged, and we were glad to be leaving those morbid palimpsest sculptures—almost felt even when scarcely seen—behind.

Another thought which the advent of the cave inspired was the possibility of losing our pursuer at this bewildering focus of large galleries. There were several of the blind albino penguins in the open space, and it seemed clear that their fear of the oncoming entity was extreme to the point of unaccountability.

If at that point we dimmed our torch to the very lowest limit of traveling need, keeping it strictly in front of us, the frightened squawking motions of the huge birds in the mist might muffle our footfalls, screen our true course, and somehow set up a false lead.

Amidst the churning, spiraling fog, the littered and unglistening floor of the main tunnel beyond this point, as differing from the other morbidly polished burrows, could hardly form a highly distinguishing feature; even, so far as we could conjecture, for those indicated special senses which made the Old Ones partly, though imperfectly, independent of light in emergencies.

In fact, we were somewhat apprehensive lest we go astray ourselves in our haste. For we had, of course, decided to keep straight on toward the dead city; since the consequences of loss in those unknown foothill honeycombings would be unthinkable.

The fact that we survived and emerged is sufficient proof that the thing did take a wrong gallery whilst we providentially hit on the right one. The penguins alone could not have saved us, but in conjunction with the mist they seem to have done so. Only a benign fate kept the curling vapors thick enough at the right moment, for they were constantly shifting and threatening to vanish.

Indeed, they did lift for a second just before we emerged from the nauseously resculptured tunnel into the cave; so that we actually caught one first and only half glimpse of the oncoming entity as we cast a final, desperately fearful glance backward before dimming the torch and mixing with the penguins in the hope of dodging pursuit. If the fate which screened us was benign, that which gave us the half glimpse was infinitely the opposite; for to that flash of semivision can be traced a full half of the horror which has ever since haunted us.

Our exact motive in looking back again was perhaps no more than the immemorial instinct of the pursued to gauge the nature and course of its pursuer; or perhaps it was an automatic attempt to answer a subconscious question raised by one of our senses.

In the midst of our flight, with all our faculties centered on the problem of escape, we were in no condition to observe and analyze details; yet even so our latent brain cells must have wondered at the message brought them by our nostrils. Afterward, we realized what it was—that our retreat from the fetid slime coating on those headless obstructions, and the coincident approach of the pursuing entity, had not brought us the exchange of stenches which logic called for.

In the neighborhood of the prostrate things that new and lately unexplainable fetor had been wholly dominant; but by this time it ought to have largely given place to the nameless stench associated with those others. This it had not done—for instead, the newer and less bearable smell was now virtually undiluted, and growing more and more poisonously insistent each second.

So we glanced back—simultaneously, it would appear; though no doubt the incipient motion of one prompted the imitation of the other. As we did so we flashed both torches full strength at the momentarily thinned mist; either from sheer primitive anxiety to see all we could, or in a less primitive but equally unconscious effort to dazzle the entity before we dimmed our light and dodged among the penguins of the labyrinth center ahead.

Unhappy act! Not Orpheus himself, or Lot's wife, paid much more dearly for a backward glance. And again came that shocking, wide-ranged piping—"*Tekeli-li! Tekeli-li!*"

Danforth was totally unstrung, and the first thing I remember of the rest of the journey was hearing him light-headedly chant a hysterical formula in which I alone of mankind could have found anything but insane irrelevance. It reverberated in falsetto echoes among the squawks of the penguins; reverberated through the vaulting ahead, and—thank Heaven—through the now empty vaultings behind. He could not have begun it at once—else we would not have been alive and blindly racing. I shudder to think of what a shade of difference in his nervous reactions might have brought.

"South Station Under—Washington Under—Park Street Under—Kendall—Central—Harvard——" The poor fellow was chanting the familiar stations of the Boston-Cambridge tunnel that burrowed through our peaceful native soil thousands of miles away in New England, yet to me the ritual had neither irrelevance nor home feeling. It had only horror, because I knew unerringly the monstrous, nefandous analogy that had suggested it.

We had expected, upon looking back, to see a terrible and incredible moving entity if the mists were thin enough; but of that entity we had formed a clear idea. What we did see—for the mists were indeed all too malignly thinned—was something altogether different, and immeasurably more hideous and detestable. It was the utter, objective embodiment of the fantastic novelist's 'thing that should not be'; and its nearest comprehensible analogue is a vast, onrushing subway train as one sees it from a station platform—the great black front looming colossally out of infinite subterraneous distance, constellated with strangely colored lights and filling the prodigious burrow.

But we were not on a station platform. We were on the track ahead as the nightmare, plastic column of fetid black iridescence oozed tightly onward through its fifteen-foot sinus, gathering unholy speed and driving before it a spiral, rethickening cloud of the pallid abyss vapor.

It was a terrible, indescribable thing, vaster than any subway train—a shapeless congeries of protoplasmic bubbles, faintly self-luminous, and with myriads of temporary eyes forming and unforming as pustules of greenish light all over the tunnel-filling front that bore down upon us, crushing the frantic penguins and slithering over the glistening floor that it and its kind had swept so evilly free of all litter.

Still came that eldritch, mocking cry—"*Tekeli-li! Tekeli-li!*" And at last we remembered that the demonic Shoggoths—given life, though, and plastic organ patterns solely by the Old Ones, and having no language save that which the dot groups expressed—had likewise no voice save the imitated accents of their bygone masters.

XII

Danforth and I have recollections of emerging into the great sculptured hemisphere and of threading our back trail through the Cyclopean rooms and corridors of the dead city; yet these are purely dream fragments involving no memory of volition, details, or physical exertion.

There was something vaguely appropriate about our departure from those buried epochs; for as we wound our panting way up the sixty-foot cylinder of primal masonry we glimpsed beside us a continuous procession of heroic sculptures in the dead race's early and undecayed technique—a farewell from the Old Ones, written fifty million years ago.

Finally, scrambling out at the top, we found ourselves on a great mound of tumbled blocks, with the curved walls of higher stonework rising westward, and the brooding peaks of the great mountains showing beyond the more crumbled structures toward the east.

The sky above was a churning and opalescent mass of tenuous ice vapors, and the cold clutched at our vitals.

In less than a quarter of an hour we had found the steep grade to the foothills—the probable ancient terrace—by which we had descended, and could see the dark bulk of our great plane amidst the sparse ruins on the rising slope ahead.

Halfway uphill toward our goal we paused for a momentary breathing spell, and turned to look again at the fantastic tangle of incredible stone shapes below us—once more outlined mystically against an unknown west. As we did so we saw that the sky beyond had lost its morning haziness; the restless ice vapors having moved up to the zenith, where their mocking outlines seemed on the point of settling into some bizarre pattern which they feared to make quite definite or conclusive.

There now lay revealed on the ultimate white horizon behind the grotesque city a dim, elfin line of pinnacled violet whose needle-pointed heights loomed dreamlike against the beckoning rose color of the western sky. Up toward this shimmering rim sloped the ancient table-land, the depressed course of the bygone river traversing it as an irregular ribbon of shadow.

For a second we gasped in admiration of the scene's unearthly cosmic beauty, and then vague horror began to creep into our souls. For this far violet line could be nothing else than the terrible mountains of the forbidden land—highest of earth's peaks and focus of earth's evil; harborers of nameless horrors and Archæan secrets; shunned and prayed to by those who feared to carve their meaning; untrodden by any living thing of earth, but visited by the sinister lightnings and sending strange beams across the plains in the polar night.

If the sculptured maps and pictures in that prehuman city had told truly, these cryptic violet mountains could not be much less than three hundred miles away; yet none the less sharply did their dim elfin essence jut above that remote and snowy rim, like the serrated edge of a monstrous alien planet about to rise into unaccustomed heavens.

Looking at them, I thought nervously of certain sculptured hints of what the great bygone river had washed down into the city from their accursed sloping—and wondered how much sense and how much folly had lain in the fears of those Old Ones who carved them so reticently.

I recalled how their northerly end must come near the coast at Queen Mary Land, where even at that moment Sir Douglas Mawson's expedition was doubtless working less than a thousand miles away; and hoped that no evil fate would give Sir Douglas and his men a glimpse of what might lie beyond the protecting coastal range. Such thoughts formed a measure of my overwrought condition at the time—and Danforth seemed to be even worse.

Yet before we had passed the great star-shaped ruin and reached our plane our fears had become transferred to the lesser, but vast enough, range whose re-crossing lay ahead of us.

From these foothills the black, ruin-crusted slopes reared up starkly and hideously against the east, again reminding us of those strange Asian paintings of Nicholas Roerich; and when we thought of the damnable honeycombings inside them, and of the frightful amorphous entities that might have pushed their fetidly squirming sway even to the topmost hollow pinnacles, we could not face without panic the prospect of again sailing by those suggestive skyward cave mouths where the wind made sounds like an evil musical piping over a wide range.

To make matters worse, we saw distinct traces of local mist around several of the summits—as poor Lake must have done when he made that early mistake about volcanism—and thought shiveringly of that kindred mist from which we had just escaped—of that, and of the blasphemous, horror-fostering abyss whence all such vapors came.

All was well with the plane, and we clumsily hauled on our heavy flying furs. Danforth got the engine started without trouble, and we made a very smooth take-off over the nightmare city.

At a very high level there must have been great disturbance, since the ice-dust clouds of the zenith were doing all sorts of fantastic things; but at twenty-four thousand feet, the height we needed for the pass, we found navigation quite practicable.

As we drew close to the jutting peaks the wind's strange piping again became manifest, and I could see Danforth's hands trembling at the controls. Rank amateur though I was, I thought at that moment that I might be a better navigator than he in effecting the dangerous crossing between pinnacles; and when I made motions to change seats and take over his duties he did not protest.

I tried to keep all my skill and self-possession about me, and stared at the sector of reddish farther sky betwixt the walls of the pass.

But Danforth, released from his piloting and keyed up to a dangerous nervous pitch, could not keep quiet. I felt him turning and wriggling about as he looked back at the terrible receding city, ahead at the cave-riddled, cube-barnacled peaks, sidewise at the bleak sea of snowy, rampart-strown foothills, and upward at the seething, grotesquely clouded sky.

It was then, just as I was trying to steer safely through the pass, that his mad shrieking brought us so close to disaster, by shattering my tight hold on myself and causing me to fumble helplessly with the controls for a moment. A second afterward my resolution triumphed and we made the crossing safely——Yet I am afraid that Danforth will never be the same again.

I have said that Danforth refused to tell me what final horror made him scream out so insanely—a horror which, I feel sadly sure, is mainly responsible for his present breakdown. We had snatches of shouted conversation above the wind's piping and the engine's buzzing as we reached the safe side of the range and swooped slowly down toward the camp, but that had mostly to do with the pledges of secrecy we had made as we prepared to leave the nightmare city.

All that Danforth has ever hinted is that the final horror was a mirage. It was not, he declares, anything connected with the cubes and caves of those echoing, vaporous, wormily honeycombed mountains of madness which we crossed; but a single fantastic, demonic glimpse, among the churning westward zenith clouds, of what lay back of those other violet westward mountains which the Old Ones had shunned and feared.

He has on rare occasions whispered disjointed and irresponsible things about "the black pit," "the carven rim," "the proto-Shoggoths," "the windowless solids with five dimensions," "the nameless cylinders," "the elder pharos," "Yog-Sothoth," "the primal white jelly," "the color out of space," "the wings," "the eyes in darkness," "the moon-ladder," "the original, the eternal, the undying," and other bizarre conceptions; but when he is fully himself he repudiates all this and attributes it to his curious and macabre reading of earlier years. Danforth, indeed, is known to be among the few who have ever dared go completely through that worm-riddled copy of the *Necronomicon* kept under lock and key in the college library.

The higher sky, as we crossed the range, was surely vaporous and disturbed enough; and although I did not see the zenith I can well imagine that its swirls of ice dust may have taken strange forms. Imagination, knowing how vividly distant scenes can sometimes be reflected, refracted, and magnified by such layers of restless cloud, might easily have supplied the rest—and, of course, Danforth did not hint any of these specific horrors till after his memory had had a chance to draw on his bygone reading. He could never have seen so much in one instantaneous glance.

At the time, his shrieks were confined to the repetition of a single, mad word of all too obvious source: "*Tekeli-li! Tekeli-li!*"

O. HENRY

1

The Furnished Room

Restless, shifting, fugacious as time itself is a certain vast bulk of the population of the red brick district of the lower West Side. Homeless, they have a hundred homes. They flit from furnished room to furnished room, transients forever—transients in abode, transients in heart and mind. They sing 'Home, Sweet Home' in ragtime; they carry their *lares et penates* in a bandbox; their vine is entwined about a picture hat; a rubber plant is their fig tree.

Hence the houses of this district, having had a thousand dwellers, should have a thousand tales to tell, mostly dull ones, no doubt; but it would be strange if there could not be found a ghost or two in the wake of all these vagrant guests.

One evening after dark a young man prowled among these crumbling red mansions, ringing their bells. At the twelfth he rested his lean hand-baggage upon the step and wiped the dust from his hatband and forehead. The bell sounded faint and far away in some remote, hollow depths.

To the door of this, the twelfth house whose bell he had rung, came a housekeeper who made him think of an unwholesome, surfeited worm that had eaten its nut to a hollow shell and now sought to fill the vacancy with edible lodgers.

He asked if there was a room to let.

"Come in," said the housekeeper. Her voice came from her

throat; hert hroat seemed lined with fur. "I have the third-floor back, vacant since a week back. Should you wish to look at it?"

The young man followed her up the stairs. A faint light from no particular source mitigated the shadows of the halls. They trod noiselessly upon a stair carpet that its own loom would have forsworn. It seemed to have become vegetable; to have degenerated in that rank, sunless air to lush lichen or spreading moss that grew in patches to the staircase and was viscid under the foot like organic matter. At each turn of the stairs were vacant niches in the wall. Perhaps plants had once been set within them. If so they had died in that foul and tainted air. It may be that statues of the saints had stood there, but it was not difficult to conceive that imps and devils had dragged them forth in the darkness and down to the unholy depths of some furnished pit below.

"This is the room," said the housekeeper, from her furry throat. "It's a nice room. It ain't often vacant. I had some most elegant people in it last summer—no trouble at all, and paid in advance to the minute. The water's at the end of the hall. Sprowls and Mooney kept it three months. They done a vaudeville sketch. Miss B'retta Sprowls—you may have heard of her—Oh, that was just the stage names—right there over the dresser is where the marriage certificate hung, framed. The gas is here, and you see there is plenty of closet room. It's a room everybody likes. It never stays idle long."

"Do you have many theatrical people rooming here?" asked the young man.

"They comes and goes. A good proportion of my lodgers is connected with the theatres. Yes, sir, this is the theatrical district. Actor people never stays long anywhere. I get my share. Yes, they comes and goes."

He engaged the room, paying for a week in advance. He was tired, he said, and would take possession at once. He counted out the money. The room had been made ready, she said, even to towels and water. As the housekeeper moved away he put, for the thousandth time, the question that he carried at the end of his tongue.

"A young girl—Miss Vashner—Miss Eloise Vashner—do you remember such a one among your lodgers? She would be singing on the stage, most likely. A fair girl, of medium height and slender, with reddish, gold hair and a dark mole near her left eyebrow."

"No, I don't remember the name. Them stage people has names they change as often as their rooms. They comes and they goes. No, I don't call that one to mind."

No. Always no. Five months of ceaseless interrogation and the inevitable negative. So much time spent by day in questioning managers, agents, schools and choruses; by night among the audiences of theatres from all-star casts down to music halls so low that he dreaded to find what he most hoped for. He who had loved her best had tried to find her. He was sure that since her disappearance from home this great, water-girt city held her somewhere, but it was like a monstrous quicksand, shifting its particles constantly, with no foundation, its upper granules of today buried tomorrow in ooze and slime.

The furnished room received its latest guest with a first glow of pseudo-hospitality, a hectic, haggard, perfunctory welcome like the specious smile of a demirep. The sophistical comfort came in reflected gleams from the decayed furniture, the ragged brocade upholstery of a couch and two chairs, a foot-wide cheap pier-glass between the two windows, from one or two gilt picture frames and a brass bedstead in a corner.

The guest reclined, inert, upon a chair, while the room, confused in speech as though it were an apartment in Babel, tried to discourse to him of its divers tenantry.

A polychromatic rug like some brilliant-flowered rectangular, tropical islet lay surrounded by a billowy sea of soiled matting. Upon the gay-papered wall were those pictures that pursue the homeless one from house to house—The Huguenot Lovers, The First Quarrel, The Wedding Breakfast, Psyche at the Fountain. The mantel's chastely severe outline was ingloriously veiled behind some pert drapery drawn rakishly askew like the sashes of the Amazonian ballet. Upon it was some desolate flotsam cast aside by the room's marooned when a lucky sail had borne them to a fresh port—a trifling vase or two, pictures of actresses, a medicine bottle, some stray cards out of a deck.

One by one, as the characters of a cryptograph become explicit, the little signs left by the furnished room's procession of guests developed a significance. The threadbare space in the rug in front of the dresser told that lovely women had marched in the throng. Tiny fingerprints on the wall spoke of little prisoners trying to feel their way to sun and air. A splattered stain, raying like the shadow of a bursting bomb, witnessed where a hurled glass or bottle had splintered with its contents against the wall. Across the pier glass had been scrawled with a diamond in staggering letters the name 'Marie.' It seemed that the succession of dwellers in the furnished room had turned in fury—perhaps tempted beyond forbearance by its garish coldness—and wreaked upon it their passions. The furniture was chipped and bruised; the couch, distorted by bursting springs, seemed a horrible monster that had been slain during the stress of some grotesque convulsion. Some more potent upheaval had cloven a great slice from the marble mantel. Each plank in the floor owned its particular cant and shriek as from a separate and individual agony. It seemed incredible that all this malice and injury had been wrought upon the room by those who had called it for a time their home; and yet it may have been the cheated home instinct surviving blindly, the resentful rage at false household gods that had kindled their wrath. A hut that is our own we can sweep and adorn and cherish.

The young tenant in the chair allowed these thoughts to file, soft-shod, through his mind, while there drifted into the room furnished sounds and furnished scents. He heard in one room a tittering and incontinent, slack laughter; in others the monologue of a scold, the rattling of dice, a lullaby, and one crying dully; above him a banjo tinkled with spirit. Doors banged somewhere; the elevated trains roared intermittently; a cat yowled miserably upon a back fence. And he breathed the breath of the house—a dank savour rather than a smell—a cold, musty effluvium as from underground vaults mingled with the reeking exhalations of linoleum and mildewed and rotten woodwork.

Then, suddenly, as he rested there, the room was filled with the strong, sweet odour of mignonette. It came as upon a single buffet of wind with such sureness and fragrance and emphasis that it almost seemed a living visitant. And the man cried aloud: "What, dear?" as if he had been called, and sprang up and faced about. The rich odour clung to him and wrapped him around. He reached out his arms for it, all his senses for the time confused and commingled. How could one be peremptorily called by an odour? Surely it must have been a sound. But, was it not the sound that had touched, that had caressed him?

"She has been in this room," he cried, and he sprang to wrest from it a token, for he knew he would recognize the smallest thing that had belonged to her or that she had touched. This enveloping scent of mignonette, the odour that she had loved and made her own—whence came it?

The room had been but carelessly set in order. Scattered upon the flimsy dresser scarf were half a dozen hairpins—those discreet, indistinguishable friends of womankind, feminine of gender, infinite of mood and uncommunicative of tense. These he ignored, conscious of their triumphant lack of identity. Ransacking the drawers of the dresser he came upon a discarded, tiny, ragged handkerchief. He pressed it to his face. It was racy and insolent with heliotrope; he hurled it to the floor. In another drawer he found odd buttons, a theatre programme, a pawnbroker's card, two lost marshmallows, a book on the divination of dreams. In the last was a woman's black satin hair bow, which halted him, poised between ice and fire. But the black satin hair bow also is femininity's demure, impersonal, common ornament, and tells no tales.

And then he traversed the room like a hound on the scent, skimming the walls, considering the corners of the bulging matting on his hands and knees, rummaging mantel and tables, the curtains and hangings, the drunken cabinet in the corner, for a visible sign, unable to perceive that she was there beside, around, against, within, above him, clinging to him, wooing him, calling him so poignantly through the finer senses that even his grosser ones became cognizant of the call. Once again he answered loudly: "Yes, dear!" and turned, wild-eyed, to gaze on vacancy, for he could not yet discern form and colour and love and outstretched arms in the odour of mignonette. Oh, God! Whence that odour, and since when have odours had a voice to call? Thus he groped.

He burrowed in crevices and corners, and found corks and cigarettes. These he passed in passive contempt. But once he found in a fold of the matting a half-smoked cigar, and this he ground beneath his heel with a green and trenchant oath. He sifted the room from end to end. He found dreary and ignoble small records of many a peripatetic tenant; but of her whom he sought, and who may have lodged there, and whose spirit seemed to hover there, he found no trace.

And then he thought of the housekeeper.

He ran from the haunted room downstairs and to a door that showed a crack of light. She came out to his knock. He smothered his excitement as best he could.

"Will you tell me, madam," he besought her, "who occupied the room I have before I came?"

"Yes, sir. I can tell you again. 'Twas Sprowls and Mooney, as I said. Miss B'retta Sprowls it was in the theatres, but Missis Mooney she was. My house is well known for respectability. The marriage certificate hung, framed, on a nail over—"

"What kind of a lady was Miss Sprowls—in looks, I mean?"

"Why, black-haired, sir, short, and stout, with a comical face. They left a week ago Tuesday."

"And before they occupied it?"

"Why, there was a single gentleman connected with the draying business. He left owing me a week. Before him was Missis Crowder and her two children, that stayed four months; and back of them was old Mr. Doyle, whose sons paid for him. He kept the room six months. That goes back a year, sir, and further I do not remember."

He thanked her and crept back to his room. The room was dead. The essence that had vivified it was gone. The perfume of mignonette had departed. In its place was the old, stale odour of moldy house furniture, of atmosphere in storage.

The ebbing of his hope drained his faith. He sat staring at the yellow, singing gaslight. Soon he walked to the bed and began to tear the sheets into strips. With the blade of his knife he drove them tightly into every crevice around windows and door. When all was snug and taut he turned out the light, turned the gas full on again and laid himself gratefully upon the bed.

It was Mrs. McCool's night to go with the can for beer. So she fetched it and sat with Mrs. Purdy in one of those subterranean retreats where housekeepers foregather and the worm dieth seldom.

"I rented out my third-floor-back this evening," said Mrs. Purdy, across a fine circle of foam. "A young man took it. He went up to bed two hours ago."

"Now, did ye, Mrs. Purdy, ma'am?" said Mrs. McCool, with intense admiration. "You do be a wonder for rentin' rooms of that kind. And did ye tell him, then?" she concluded in a husky whisper, laden with mystery.

"Rooms," said Mrs. Purdy, in her furriest tones, "are furnished for to rent. I did not tell him, Mrs. McCool."

"'Tis right ye are, ma'am; 'tis by renting rooms we kape alive. Ye have the rale sense for business, ma'am. There be many people will rayjict the rentin' of a room if they be tould a suicide has been after dyin' in the bed of it."

"As you say, we has our living to be making," remarked Mrs. Purdy.

"Yis, ma'am; 'tis true. 'Tis just one wake ago this day I helped ye lay out the third-floor-back. A pretty slip of a colleen she was to be killin' herself wid the gas—a swate little face she had, Mrs. Purdy, ma'am."

"She'd a-been called handsome, as you say," said Mrs. Purdy, assenting but critical, "but for that mole she had a-growin' by her left eyebrow. Do fill up your glass again, Mrs. McCool."

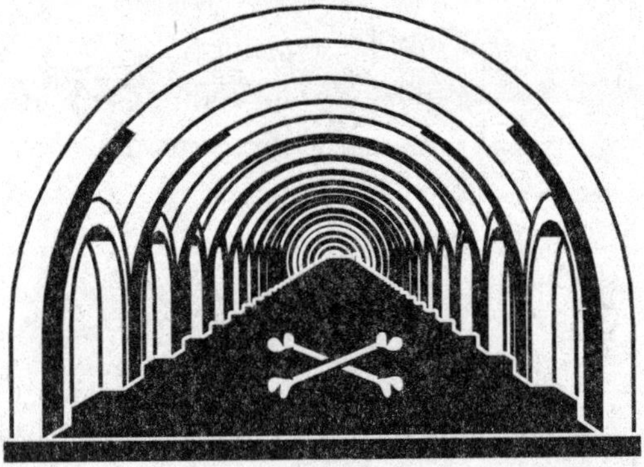

WASHINGTON IRVING

1

The Legend of Sleepy Hollow

Found Among the Papers of the
Late Diedrich Knickerbocker.

A pleasing land of drowsy head it was,
Of dreams that wave before the half-shut eye;
And of gay castles in the clouds that pass,
Forever flushing round a summer sky.

Castle of Indolence.

In the bosom of one of those spacious coves which indent the eastern shore of the Hudson, at that broad expansion of the river denominated by the ancient Dutch navigators the Tappan Zee, and where they always prudently shortened sail and implored the protection of St. Nicholas when they crossed, there lies a small market town or rural port, which by some is called Greensburgh, but which is more generally and properly known by the name of Tarry Town. This name was given, we are told, in former days, by the good housewives of the adjacent country, from the inveterate propensity of their husbands to linger about the village tavern on market days. Be that as it may, I do not vouch for the fact, but merely advert to it, for the sake of being precise and authentic. Not far from this village, perhaps about two miles, there is a little valley or rather lap of land among high hills, which is one of the quietest places in the whole world. A small brook glides through it, with just murmur enough to lull one to repose; and the occasional whistle of a quail or tapping of a woodpecker is almost the only sound that ever breaks in upon the uniform tranquillity.

I recollect that, when a stripling, my first exploit in squirrel-shooting was in a grove of tall walnut-trees that shades one side of the valley. I had wandered into it at noontime, when all nature is peculiarly quiet, and was startled by the roar of my own gun, as it broke the Sabbath stillness around and was prolonged and reverberated by the angry echoes. If ever I should wish for a retreat whither I might steal from the world and its distractions, and dream quietly away the remnant of a troubled life, I know of none more promising than this little valley.

From the listless repose of the place, and the peculiar character of its inhabitants, who are descendants from the original Dutch settlers, this sequestered glen has long been known by the name of SLEEPY HOLLOW, and its rustic lads are called the Sleepy Hollow Boys throughout all the neighboring country. A drowsy, dreamy influence seems to hang over the land, and to pervade the very atmosphere. Some say that the place was bewitched by a High German doctor, during the early days of the settlement; others, that an old Indian chief, the prophet or wizard of his tribe, held his powwows there before the country was discovered by Master Hendrick Hudson. Certain it is, the place still continues under the sway of some witching power, that holds a spell over the minds of the good people, causing them to walk in a continual reverie. They are given to all kinds of marvellous beliefs, are subject to trances and visions, and frequently see strange sights, and hear music and voices in the air. The whole neighborhood abounds with local tales, haunted spots, and twilight superstitions; stars shoot and meteors glare oftener across the valley than in any other part of the country, and the nightmare, with her whole ninefold, seems to make it the favorite scene of her gambols.

The dominant spirit, however, that haunts this enchanted region, and seems to be commander-in-chief of all the powers of the air, is the apparition of a figure on horseback, without a head. It is said by some to be the ghost of a Hessian trooper, whose head had been carried away by a cannon-ball, in some nameless battle during the Revolutionary War, and who is ever and anon seen by the country folk hurrying along in the gloom of night, as if on the wings of the wind. His haunts are not confined to the valley, but extend at times to the adjacent roads, and especially to the vicinity of a church at no great distance. Indeed, certain of the most authentic historians of those parts, who have been careful in collecting and collating the floating facts concerning this spectre, allege that the body of the trooper having been buried in the churchyard, the ghost rides forth to the scene of battle in nightly quest of his head, and that the rushing speed with which he sometimes passes along the Hollow, like a midnight blast, is owing to his being belated, and in a hurry to get back to the churchyard before daybreak.

Such is the general purport of this legendary superstition, which has furnished materials for many a wild story in that region of shadows; and the spectre is known at all the country firesides, by the name of the Headless Horseman of Sleepy Hollow.

It is remarkable that the visionary propensity I have mentioned is not confined to the native inhabitants of the valley, but is unconsciously imbibed by every one who resides there for a time. However wide awake they may have been before they entered that sleepy region, they are sure, in a little time, to inhale the witching influence of the air, and begin to grow imaginative, to dream dreams, and see apparitions.

I mention this peaceful spot with all possible laud, for it is in such little retired Dutch valleys, found here and there embosomed in the great State of New York, that population, manners, and customs remain fixed, while the great torrent of migration and improvement, which is making such incessant changes in other parts of this restless country, sweeps by them unobserved. They are like those little nooks of still water, which border a rapid stream, where we may see the straw and bubble riding quietly at anchor, or slowly revolving in their mimic harbor, undisturbed by the rush of the passing current. Though many years have elapsed since I trod the drowsy shades of Sleepy Hollow, yet I question whether I should not still find the same trees and the same families vegetating in its sheltered bosom.

In this by-place of nature there abode, in a remote period of American history, that is to say, some thirty years since, a worthy wight of the name of Ichabod Crane, who sojourned, or, as he expressed it, "tarried," in Sleepy Hollow, for the purpose of instructing the children of the vicinity. He was a native of Connecticut, a State which supplies the Union with pioneers for the mind as well as for the forest, and sends forth yearly its legions of frontier woodmen and country schoolmasters. The cognomen of Crane was not inapplicable to his person. He was tall, but exceedingly lank, with narrow shoulders, long arms and legs, hands that dangled a mile out of his sleeves, feet that might have served for shovels, and his whole frame most loosely hung together. His head was small, and flat at top, with huge ears, large green glassy eyes, and a long snipe nose, so that it looked like a weather-cock perched upon his spindle neck to tell which way the wind blew. To see him striding along the profile of a hill on a windy day, with his clothes bagging and fluttering about him, one might have mistaken him for the genius of famine descending upon the earth, or some scarecrow eloped from a cornfield.

His schoolhouse was a low building of one large room, rudely constructed of logs; the windows partly glazed, and partly patched with leaves of old copybooks. It was most ingeniously secured at vacant hours, by a withe twisted in the handle of the door, and stakes set against the window shutters; so that though a thief might get in with perfect ease, he would find some embarrassment in getting out,—an idea most probably borrowed by the architect, Yost Van Houten, from the mystery of an eelpot. The schoolhouse stood in a rather lonely but pleasant situation, just at the foot of a woody hill, with a brook running close by, and a formidable birch-tree growing at one end of it. From hence the low murmur of his pupils' voices, conning over their lessons, might be heard in a drowsy summer's day, like the hum of a beehive; interrupted now and then by the authoritative voice of the master, in the tone of menace or command, or, peradventure, by the appalling sound of the birch, as he urged some tardy loiterer along the flowery path of knowledge. Truth to say, he was a conscientious man, and ever bore in mind the golden maxim, "Spare the rod and spoil the child." Ichabod Crane's scholars certainly were not spoiled.

I would not have it imagined, however, that he was one of those cruel potentates of the school who joy in the smart of their subjects; on the contrary, he administered justice with discrimination rather than severity; taking the burden off the backs of the weak, and laying it on those of the strong. Your mere puny stripling, that winced at the least flourish of the rod, was passed by with indulgence; but the claims of justice were satisfied by inflicting a double portion on some little tough wrong-headed, broad-skirted Dutch urchin, who sulked and swelled and grew dogged and sullen beneath the birch. All this he called "doing his duty by their parents;" and he never inflicted a chastisement without following it by the assurance, so consolatory to the smarting urchin, that "he would remember it and thank him for it the longest day he had to live."

When school hours were over, he was even the companion and playmate of the larger boys; and on holiday afternoons would convoy some of the smaller ones home, who happened to have pretty sisters, or good housewives for mothers, noted for the comforts of the cupboard. Indeed, it behooved him to keep on good terms with his pupils. The revenue arising from his school was small, and would have been scarcely sufficient to furnish him with daily bread, for he was a huge feeder, and, though lank, had the dilating powers of an anaconda; but to help out his maintenance, he was, according to country custom in those parts, boarded and lodged at the houses of the farmers whose children he instructed. With these he lived successively a week at a time, thus going the rounds of the neighborhood, with all his worldly effects tied up in a cotton handkerchief.

That all this might not be too onerous on the purses of his rustic patrons, who are apt to consider the costs of schooling a grievous burden, and schoolmasters as mere drones, he had various ways of rendering himself both useful and agreeable. He assisted the farmers occasionally in the lighter labors of their farms, helped to make hay, mended the fences, took the horses to water, drove the cows from pasture, and cut wood for the winter fire. He laid aside, too, all the dominant dignity and absolute sway with which he lorded it in his little empire, the school, and became wonderfully gentle and ingratiating. He found favor in the eyes of the mothers by petting the children, particularly the youngest; and like the lion bold, which whilom so magnanimously the lamb did hold, he would sit with a child on one knee, and rock a cradle with his foot for whole hours together.

In addition to his other vocations, he was the singing-master of the neighborhood, and picked up many bright shillings by instructing the young folks in psalmody. It was a matter of no little vanity to him on Sundays, to take his station in front of the church gallery, with a band of chosen singers; where, in his own mind, he completely carried away the palm from the parson. Certain it is, his voice resounded far above all the rest of the congregation; and there are peculiar quavers still to be heard in that church, and which may even be heard half a mile off, quite to the opposite side of the millpond, on a still Sunday morning, which are said to be legitimately descended from the nose of Ichabod Crane. Thus, by divers little makeshifts, in that ingenious way which is commonly denominated "by hook and by crook," the worthy pedagogue got on tolerably enough, and was thought, by all who understood nothing of the labor of headwork, to have a wonderfully easy life of it.

The schoolmaster is generally a man of some importance in the female circle of a rural neighborhood; being considered a kind of idle, gentlemanlike personage, of vastly superior taste and accomplishments to the rough country swains, and, indeed, inferior in learning only to the parson. His appearance, therefore, is apt to occasion some little stir at the tea-table of a farmhouse, and the addition of a supernumerary dish of cakes or sweetmeats, or, peradventure, the parade of a silver teapot. Our man of letters, therefore, was peculiarly happy in the smiles of all the country damsels. How he would figure among them in the churchyard, between services on Sundays; gathering grapes for them from the wild vines that overran the surrounding trees; reciting for their amusement all the epitaphs on the tombstones; or sauntering, with a whole bevy of them, along the banks of the adjacent millpond; while the more bashful country bumpkins hung sheepishly back, envying his superior elegance and address.

From his half-itinerant life, also, he was a kind of travelling gazette, carrying the whole budget of local gossip from house to house, so that his appearance was always greeted with satisfaction. He was, moreover, esteemed by the women as a man of great erudition, for he had read several books quite through, and was a perfect master of Cotton Mather's "History of New England Witchcraft," in which, by the way, he most firmly and potently believed.

He was, in fact, an odd mixture of small shrewdness and simple credulity. His appetite for the marvellous, and his powers of digesting it, were equally extraordinary; and both had been increased by his residence in this spell-bound region. No tale was too gross or monstrous for his capacious swallow. It was often his delight, after his school was dismissed in the afternoon, to stretch himself on the rich bed of clover bordering the little brook that whimpered by his schoolhouse, and there con over old Mather's direful tales, until the gathering dusk of evening made the printed page a mere mist before his eyes. Then, as he wended his way by swamp and stream and awful woodland, to the farmhouse where he happened to be quartered, every sound of nature, at that witching hour, fluttered his excited imagination,—the moan of the whip-poor-will from the hillside, the boding cry of the tree toad, that harbinger of storm, the dreary hooting of the screech owl, or the sudden rustling in the thicket of birds frightened from their roost. The fireflies, too, which sparkled most vividly in the darkest places, now and then startled him, as one of uncommon brightness would stream across his path; and if, by chance, a huge blockhead of a beetle came winging his blundering flight against him, the poor varlet was ready to give up the ghost, with the idea that he was struck with a witch's token. His only resource on such occasions, either to drown thought or drive away evil spirits, was to sing psalm tunes and the good people of Sleepy Hollow, as they sat by their doors of an evening, were often filled with awe at hearing his nasal melody, "in linked sweetness long drawn out," floating from the distant hill, or along the dusky road.

Another of his sources of fearful pleasure was to pass long winter evenings with the old Dutch wives, as they sat spinning by the fire, with a row of apples roasting and spluttering along the hearth, and listen to their marvellous tales of ghosts and goblins, and haunted fields, and haunted brooks, and haunted bridges, and haunted houses, and particularly of the headless horseman, or Galloping Hessian of the Hollow, as they sometimes called him. He would delight them equally by his anecdotes of witchcraft, and of the direful omens and portentous sights and sounds in the air, which prevailed in the earlier times of Connecticut; and would frighten them woefully with speculations upon comets and shooting stars; and with the alarming fact that the world did absolutely turn round, and that they were half the time topsy-turvy!

But if there was a pleasure in all this, while snugly cuddling in the chimney corner of a chamber that was all of a ruddy glow from the crackling wood fire, and where, of course, no spectre dared to show its face, it was dearly purchased by the terrors of his subsequent walk homewards. What fearful shapes and shadows beset his path, amidst the dim and ghastly glare of a snowy night! With what wistful look did he eye every trembling ray of light streaming across the waste fields from some distant window! How often was he appalled by some shrub covered with snow, which, like a sheeted spectre, beset his very path! How often did he shrink with curdling awe at the sound of his own steps on the frosty crust beneath his feet; and dread to look over his shoulder, lest he should behold some uncouth being tramping close behind him! And how often was he thrown into complete dismay by some rushing blast, howling among the trees, in the idea that it was the Galloping Hessian on one of his nightly scourings!

All these, however, were mere terrors of the night, phantoms of the mind that walk in darkness; and though he had seen many spectres in his time, and been more than once beset by Satan in divers shapes, in his lonely perambulations, yet daylight put an end to all these evils; and he would have passed a pleasant life of it, in despite of the Devil and all his works, if his path had not been crossed by a being that causes more perplexity to mortal man than ghosts, goblins, and the whole race of witches put together, and that was—a woman.

Among the musical disciples who assembled, one evening in each week, to receive his instructions in psalmody, was Katrina Van Tassel, the daughter and only child of a substantial Dutch farmer. She was a blooming lass of fresh eighteen; plump as a partridge; ripe and melting and rosy-cheeked as one of her father's peaches, and universally famed, not merely for her beauty, but her vast expectations. She was withal a little of a coquette, as might be perceived even in her dress, which was a mixture of ancient and modern fashions, as most suited to set off her charms. She wore the ornaments of pure yellow gold, which her great-great-grandmother had brought over from Saardam; the tempting stomacher of the olden time, and withal a provokingly short petticoat, to display the prettiest foot and ankle in the country round.

Ichabod Crane had a soft and foolish heart towards the sex; and it is not to be wondered at that so tempting a morsel soon found favor in his eyes, more especially after he had visited her in her paternal mansion. Old Baltus Van Tassel was a perfect picture of a thriving, contented, liberal-hearted farmer. He seldom, it is true, sent either his eyes or his thoughts beyond the boundaries of his own farm; but within those everything was snug, happy and well-conditioned. He was satisfied with his wealth, but not proud of it; and piqued himself upon the hearty abundance, rather than the style in which he lived. His stronghold was situated on the banks of the Hudson, in one of those green, sheltered, fertile nooks in which the Dutch farmers are so fond of nestling. A great elm tree spread its broad branches over it, at the foot of which bubbled up a spring of the softest and sweetest water, in a little well formed of a barrel; and then stole sparkling away through the grass, to a neighboring brook, that babbled along among alders and dwarf willows.

Hard by the farmhouse was a vast barn, that might have served for a church; every window and crevice of which seemed bursting forth with the treasures of the farm; the flail was busily resounding within it from morning to night; swallows and martins skimmed twittering about the eaves; and rows of pigeons, some with one eye turned up, as if watching the weather, some with their heads under their wings or buried in their bosoms, and others swelling, and cooing, and bowing about their dames, were enjoying the sunshine on the roof. Sleek unwieldy porkers were grunting in the repose and abundance of their pens, from whence sallied forth, now and then, troops of sucking pigs, as if to snuff the air. A stately squadron of snowy geese were riding in an adjoining pond, convoying whole fleets of ducks; regiments of turkeys were gobbling through the farmyard, and Guinea fowls fretting about it, like ill-tempered housewives, with their peevish, discontented cry. Before the barn door strutted the gallant cock, that pattern of a husband, a warrior and a fine gentleman, clapping his burnished wings and crowing in the pride and gladness of his heart,—sometimes tearing up the earth with his feet, and then generously calling his ever-hungry family of wives and children to enjoy the rich morsel which he had discovered.

The pedagogue's mouth watered as he looked upon this sumptuous promise of luxurious winter fare. In his devouring mind's eye, he pictured to himself every roasting-pig running about with a pudding in his belly, and an apple in his mouth; the pigeons were snugly put to bed in a comfortable pie, and tucked in with a coverlet of crust; the geese were swimming in their own gravy; and the ducks pairing cosily in dishes, like snug married couples, with a decent competency of onion sauce. In the porkers he saw carved out the future sleek side of bacon, and juicy relishing ham; not a turkey but he beheld daintily trussed up, with its gizzard under its wing, and, peradventure, a necklace of savory sausages; and even bright chanticleer himself lay sprawling on his back, in a side dish, with uplifted claws, as if craving that quarter which his chivalrous spirit disdained to ask while living.

As the enraptured Ichabod fancied all this, and as he rolled his great green eyes over the fat meadow lands, the rich fields of wheat, of rye, of buckwheat, and Indian corn, and the orchards burdened with ruddy fruit, which surrounded the warm tenement of Van Tassel, his heart yearned after the damsel who was to inherit these domains, and his imagination expanded with the idea, how they might be readily turned into cash, and the money invested in immense tracts of wild land, and shingle palaces in the wilderness. Nay, his busy fancy already realized his hopes, and presented to him the blooming Katrina, with a whole family of children, mounted on the top of a wagon loaded with household trumpery, with pots and kettles dangling beneath; and he beheld himself bestriding a pacing mare, with a colt at her heels, setting out for Kentucky, Tennessee,—or the Lord knows where!

When he entered the house, the conquest of his heart was complete. It was one of those spacious farmhouses, with high-ridged but lowly sloping roofs, built in the style handed down from the first Dutch settlers; the low projecting eaves forming a piazza along the front, capable of being closed up in bad weather. Under this were hung flails, harness, various utensils of husbandry, and nets for fishing in the neighboring river. Benches were built along the sides for summer use; and a great spinning-wheel at one end, and a churn at the other, showed the various uses to which this important porch might be devoted. From this piazza the wondering Ichabod entered the hall, which formed the centre of the mansion, and the place of usual residence. Here rows of resplendent pewter, ranged on a long dresser, dazzled his eyes. In one corner stood a huge bag of wool, ready to be spun; in another, a quantity of linsey-woolsey just from the loom; ears of Indian corn, and strings of dried apples and peaches, hung in gay festoons along the walls, mingled with the gaud of red peppers; and a door left ajar gave him a peep into the best parlor, where the claw-footed chairs and dark mahogany tables shone like mirrors; andirons, with their accompanying shovel and tongs, glistened from their covert of asparagus tops; mock-oranges and conch-shells decorated the mantelpiece; strings of various-colored birds eggs were suspended above it; a great ostrich egg was hung from the centre of the room, and a corner cupboard, knowingly left open, displayed immense treasures of old silver and well-mended china.

From the moment Ichabod laid his eyes upon these regions of delight, the peace of his mind was at an end, and his only study was how to gain the affections of the peerless daughter of Van Tassel. In this enterprise, however, he had more real difficulties than generally fell to the lot of a knight-errant of yore, who seldom had anything but giants, enchanters, fiery dragons, and such like easily conquered adversaries, to contend with and had to make his way merely through gates of iron and brass, and walls of adamant to the castle keep, where the lady of his heart was confined; all which he achieved as easily as a man would carve his way to the centre of a

Christmas pie; and then the lady gave him her hand as a matter of course. Ichabod, on the contrary, had to win his way to the heart of a country coquette, beset with a labyrinth of whims and caprices, which were forever presenting new difficulties and impediments; and he had to encounter a host of fearful adversaries of real flesh and blood, the numerous rustic admirers, who beset every portal to her heart, keeping a watchful and angry eye upon each other, but ready to fly out in the common cause against any new competitor.

Among these, the most formidable was a burly, roaring, roystering blade, of the name of Abraham, or, according to the Dutch abbreviation, Brom Van Brunt, the hero of the country round, which rang with his feats of strength and hardihood. He was broad-shouldered and double-jointed, with short curly black hair, and a bluff but not unpleasant countenance, having a mingled air of fun and arrogance. From his Herculean frame and great powers of limb he had received the nickname of BROM BONES, by which he was universally known. He was famed for great knowledge and skill in horsemanship, being as dexterous on horseback as a Tartar. He was foremost at all races and cock fights; and, with the ascendancy which bodily strength always acquires in rustic life, was the umpire in all disputes, setting his hat on one side, and giving his decisions with an air and tone that admitted of no gainsay or appeal. He was always ready for either a fight or a frolic; but had more mischief than ill-will in his composition; and with all his overbearing roughness, there was a strong dash of waggish good humor at bottom. He had three or four boon companions, who regarded him as their model, and at the head of whom he scoured the country, attending every scene of feud or merriment for miles round. In cold weather he was distinguished by a fur cap, surmounted with a flaunting fox's tail; and when the folks at a country gathering descried this well-known crest at a distance, whisking about among a squad of hard riders, they always stood by for a squall. Sometimes his crew would be heard dashing along past the farmhouses at midnight, with whoop and halloo, like a troop of Don Cossacks; and the old dames, startled out of their sleep, would listen for a moment till the hurry-scurry had clattered by, and then exclaim, "Ay, there goes Brom Bones and his gang!" The neighbors looked upon him with a mixture of awe, admiration, and good-will; and, when any madcap prank or rustic brawl occurred in the vicinity, always shook their heads, and warranted Brom Bones was at the bottom of it.

This rantipole hero had for some time singled out the blooming Katrina for the object of his uncouth gallantries, and though his amorous toyings were something like the gentle caresses and endearments of a bear, yet it was whispered that she did not altogether discourage his hopes. Certain it is, his advances were signals for rival candidates to retire, who felt no inclination to cross a lion in his amours; insomuch, that when his horse was seen tied to Van Tassel's paling, on a Sunday night, a sure sign that his master was courting, or, as it is termed, "sparking," within, all other suitors passed by in despair, and carried the war into other quarters.

Such was the formidable rival with whom Ichabod Crane had to contend, and, considering all things, a stouter man than he would have shrunk from the competition, and a wiser man would have despaired. He had, however, a happy mixture of pliability and perseverance in his nature; he was in form and spirit like a supple-jack—yielding, but tough; though he bent, he never broke; and though he bowed beneath the slightest pressure, yet, the moment it was away—jerk!—he was as erect, and carried his head as high as ever.

To have taken the field openly against his rival would have been madness; for he was not a man to be thwarted in his amours, any more than that stormy lover, Achilles. Ichabod, therefore, made his advances in a quiet and gently insinuating manner. Under cover of his character of singing-master, he made frequent visits at the farmhouse; not that he had anything to apprehend from the meddlesome interference of parents, which is so often a stumbling-block in the path of lovers. Balt Van Tassel was an easy indulgent soul; he loved his daughter better even than his pipe, and, like a reasonable man and an excellent father, let her have her way in everything. His notable little wife, too, had enough to do to attend to her housekeeping and manage her poultry; for, as she sagely observed, ducks and geese are foolish things, and must be looked after, but girls can take care of themselves. Thus, while the busy dame bustled about the house, or plied her spinning-wheel at one end of the piazza, honest Balt would sit smoking his evening pipe at the other, watching the achievements of a little wooden warrior, who, armed with a sword in each hand, was most valiantly fighting the wind on the pinnacle of the barn. In the mean time, Ichabod would carry on his suit with the daughter by the side of the spring under the great elm, or sauntering along in the twilight, that hour so favorable to the lover's eloquence.

I profess not to know how women's hearts are wooed and won. To me they have always been matters of riddle and admiration. Some seem to have but one vulnerable point, or door of access; while others have a thousand avenues, and may be captured in a thousand different ways. It is a great triumph of skill to gain the former, but a still greater proof of generalship to maintain possession of the latter, for man must battle for his fortress at every door and window. He who wins a thousand common hearts is therefore entitled to some renown; but he who keeps undisputed sway over the heart of a coquette is indeed a hero. Certain it is, this was not the case with the redoubtable Brom Bones; and from the moment Ichabod Crane made his advances, the interests of the former evidently declined: his horse was no longer seen tied to the palings on Sunday nights, and a deadly feud gradually arose between him and the preceptor of Sleepy Hollow.

Brom, who had a degree of rough chivalry in his nature, would fain have carried matters to open warfare and have settled their pretensions to the lady, according to the mode of those most concise and simple reasoners, the knights-errant of yore,—by single combat; but Ichabod was too conscious of the superior might of his adversary to enter the lists against him; he had overheard a boast of Bones, that he would "double the schoolmaster up, and lay him on a shelf of his own schoolhouse;" and he was too wary to give him an opportunity. There was something extremely provoking in this obstinately pacific system; it left Brom no alternative but to draw upon the funds of rustic waggery in his disposition, and to play off boorish practical jokes upon his rival. Ichabod became the object of whimsical persecution to Bones and his gang of rough riders. They harried his hitherto peaceful domains; smoked out his singing school by stopping up the chimney; broke into the schoolhouse at night, in spite of its formidable fastenings of withe and window stakes, and turned everything topsy-turvy, so that the poor schoolmaster began to think all the witches in the country held their meetings there. But what was still more annoying, Brom took all opportunities of turning him into ridicule in presence of his mistress, and had a scoundrel dog whom he taught to whine in the most ludicrous manner, and introduced as a rival of Ichabod's, to instruct her in psalmody.

In this way matters went on for some time, without producing any material effect on the relative situations of the contending powers. On a fine autumnal afternoon, Ichabod, in pensive mood, sat enthroned on the lofty stool from whence he usually watched all the concerns of his little literary realm. In his hand he swayed a ferule, that sceptre of despotic power; the birch of justice reposed on three nails behind the throne, a constant terror to evil doers, while on the desk before him might be seen sundry contraband articles and prohibited weapons, detected upon the persons of idle urchins, such as half-munched apples, popguns, whirligigs, fly-cages, and whole legions of rampant little paper gamecocks. Apparently there had been some appalling act of justice recently inflicted, for his scholars were all busily intent upon their books, or slyly whispering behind them with one eye kept upon the master; and a kind of buzzing stillness reigned throughout the schoolroom. It was suddenly interrupted by the appearance of a negro in tow-cloth jacket and trowsers, a round-crowned fragment of a hat, like the cap of Mercury, and mounted on the back of a ragged, wild, half-broken colt, which he managed with a rope by way of halter. He came clattering up to the school door with an invitation to Ichabod to attend a merry-making or "quilting frolic," to be held that evening at Mynheer Van Tassel's; and having delivered his message with that air of importance, and effort at fine language, which a negro is apt to display on petty embassies of the kind, he dashed over the brook, and was seen scampering away up the hollow, full of the importance and hurry of his mission.

All was now bustle and hubbub in the late quiet schoolroom. The scholars were hurried through their lessons without stopping at trifles; those who were nimble skipped over half with impunity, and those who were tardy had a smart application now and then in the rear, to quicken their speed or help them over a tall word. Books were flung aside without being put away on the shelves, inkstands were overturned, benches thrown down, and the whole school was turned loose an hour before the usual time, bursting forth like a legion of young imps, yelping and racketing about the green in joy at their early emancipation.

The gallant Ichabod now spent at least an extra half hour at his toilet, brushing and furbishing up his best, and indeed only suit of rusty black, and arranging his locks by a bit of broken looking-glass that hung up in the schoolhouse. That he might make his appearance before his mistress in the true style of a cavalier, he borrowed a horse from the farmer with whom he was domiciliated, a choleric old Dutchman of the name of Hans Van Ripper, and, thus gallantly mounted, issued forth like a knight-errant in quest of adventures. But it is meet I should, in the true spirit of romantic story, give some account of the looks and equipments of my hero and his steed. The animal he bestrode was a broken-down plow-horse, that had outlived almost everything but its viciousness. He was gaunt and shagged, with a ewe neck, and a head like a hammer; his rusty mane and tail were tangled and knotted with burs; one eye had lost its pupil, and was glaring and spectral, but the other had the gleam of a genuine devil in it. Still he must have had fire and mettle in his day, if we may judge from the name he bore of Gunpowder. He had, in fact, been a favorite steed of his master's, the choleric Van Ripper, who was a furious rider, and had infused, very probably, some of his own spirit into the animal; for, old and broken-down as he looked, there was more of the lurking devil in him than in any young filly in the country.

Ichabod was a suitable figure for such a steed. He rode with short stirrups, which brought his knees nearly up to the pommel of the saddle; his sharp elbows stuck out like grasshoppers'; he carried his whip perpendicularly in his hand, like a sceptre, and as his horse jogged on, the motion of his arms was not unlike the flapping of a pair of wings. A small wool hat rested on the top of his nose, for so his scanty strip of forehead might be called, and the skirts of his black coat fluttered out almost to the horses tail. Such was the appearance of Ichabod and his steed as they shambled out of the gate of Hans Van Ripper, and it was altogether such an apparition as is seldom to be met with in broad daylight.

It was, as I have said, a fine autumnal day; the sky was clear and serene, and nature wore that rich and golden livery which we always associate with the idea of abundance. The forests had put on their sober brown and yellow, while some trees of the tenderer kind had been nipped by the frosts into brilliant dyes of orange, purple, and scarlet. Streaming files of wild ducks began to make their appearance high in the air; the bark of the squirrel might be heard from the groves of beech and hickory-nuts, and the pensive whistle of the quail at intervals from the neighboring stubble field.

The small birds were taking their farewell banquets. In the fullness of their revelry, they fluttered, chirping and frolicking from bush to bush, and tree to tree, capricious from the very profusion and variety around them. There was the honest cock robin, the favorite game of stripling sportsmen, with its loud querulous note; and the twittering blackbirds flying in sable clouds; and the golden-winged woodpecker with his crimson crest, his broad black gorget, and splendid plumage; and the cedar bird, with its red-tipt wings and yellow-tipt tail and its little monteiro cap of feathers; and the blue jay, that noisy coxcomb, in his gay light blue coat and white underclothes, screaming and chattering, nodding and bobbing and bowing, and pretending to be on good terms with every songster of the grove.

As Ichabod jogged slowly on his way, his eye, ever open to every symptom of culinary abundance, ranged with delight over the treasures of jolly autumn. On all sides he beheld vast store of apples; some hanging in oppressive opulence on the trees; some gathered into baskets and barrels for the market; others heaped up in rich piles for the cider-press. Farther on he beheld great fields of Indian corn, with its golden ears peeping from their leafy coverts, and holding out the promise of cakes and hasty-pudding; and the yellow pumpkins lying beneath them, turning up their fair round bellies to the sun, and giving ample prospects of the most luxurious of pies; and anon he passed the fragrant buckwheat fields breathing the odor of the beehive, and as he beheld them, soft anticipations stole over his mind of dainty slapjacks, well buttered, and garnished with honey or treacle, by the delicate little dimpled hand of Katrina Van Tassel.

Thus feeding his mind with many sweet thoughts and "sugared suppositions," he journeyed along the sides of a range of hills which look out upon some of the goodliest scenes of the mighty Hudson. The sun gradually wheeled his broad disk down in the west. The wide bosom of the Tappan Zee lay motionless and glassy, excepting that here and there a gentle undulation waved and prolonged the blue shadow of the distant mountain. A few amber clouds floated in the sky, without a breath of air to move them. The horizon was of a fine golden tint, changing gradually into a pure apple green, and from that into the deep blue of the mid-heaven. A slanting ray lingered on the woody crests of the precipices that overhung some parts of the river, giving greater depth to the dark gray and purple of their rocky sides. A sloop was loitering in the distance, dropping slowly down with the tide, her sail hanging uselessly against the mast; and as the reflection of the sky gleamed along the still water, it seemed as if the vessel was suspended in the air.

It was toward evening that Ichabod arrived at the castle of the Heer Van Tassel, which he found thronged with the pride and flower of the adjacent country. Old farmers, a spare leathern-faced race, in homespun coats and breeches, blue stockings, huge shoes, and magnificent pewter buckles. Their brisk, withered little dames, in close-crimped caps, long-waisted short gowns, homespun petticoats, with scissors and pincushions, and gay calico pockets hanging on the outside. Buxom lasses, almost as antiquated as their mothers, excepting where a straw hat, a fine ribbon, or perhaps a white frock, gave symptoms of city innovation. The sons, in short square-skirted coats, with rows of stupendous brass buttons, and their hair generally queued in the fashion of the times, especially if they could procure an eel-skin for the purpose, it being esteemed throughout the country as a potent nourisher and strengthener of the hair.

Brom Bones, however, was the hero of the scene, having come to the gathering on his favorite steed Daredevil, a creature, like himself, full of mettle and mischief, and which no one but himself could manage. He was, in fact, noted for preferring vicious animals, given to all kinds of tricks which kept the rider in constant risk of his neck, for he held a tractable, well-broken horse as unworthy of a lad of spirit.

Fain would I pause to dwell upon the world of charms that burst upon the enraptured gaze of my hero, as he entered the state parlor of Van Tassel's mansion. Not those of the bevy of buxom lasses, with their luxurious display of red and white; but the ample charms of a genuine Dutch country tea-table, in the sumptuous time of autumn. Such heaped up platters of cakes of various and almost indescribable kinds, known only to experienced Dutch housewives! There was the doughty doughnut, the tender oly koek, and the crisp and crumbling cruller; sweet cakes and short cakes, ginger cakes and honey cakes, and the whole family of cakes. And then there were apple pies, and peach pies, and pumpkin pies; besides slices of ham and smoked beef; and moreover delectable dishes of preserved plums, and peaches, and pears, and quinces; not to mention broiled shad and roasted chickens; together with bowls of milk and cream, all mingled higgledy-piggledy, pretty much as I have enumerated them, with the motherly teapot sending up its clouds of vapor from the midst—Heaven bless the mark! I want breath and time to discuss this banquet as it deserves, and am too eager to get on with my story. Happily, Ichabod Crane was not in so great a hurry as his historian, but did ample justice to every dainty.

He was a kind and thankful creature, whose heart dilated in proportion as his skin was filled with good cheer, and whose spirits rose with eating, as some men's do with drink. He could not help, too, rolling his large eyes round him as he ate, and chuckling with the possibility that he might one day be lord of all this scene of almost unimaginable luxury and splendor.

Then, he thought, how soon he'd turn his back upon the old schoolhouse; snap his fingers in the face of Hans Van Ripper, and every other niggardly patron, and kick any itinerant pedagogue out of doors that should dare to call him comrade!

Old Baltus Van Tassel moved about among his guests with a face dilated with content and good humor, round and jolly as the harvest moon. His hospitable attentions were brief, but expressive, being confined to a shake of the hand, a slap on the shoulder, a loud laugh, and a pressing invitation to "fall to, and help themselves."

And now the sound of the music from the common room, or hall, summoned to the dance. The musician was an old gray-headed negro, who had been the itinerant orchestra of the neighborhood for more than half a century. His instrument was as old and battered as himself. The greater part of the time he scraped on two or three strings, accompanying every movement of the bow with a motion of the head; bowing almost to the ground, and stamping with his foot whenever a fresh couple were to start.

Ichabod prided himself upon his dancing as much as upon his vocal powers. Not a limb, not a fibre about him was idle; and to have seen his loosely hung frame in full motion, and clattering about the room, you would have thought St. Vitus himself, that blessed patron of the dance, was figuring before you in person. He was the admiration of all the negroes; who, having gathered, of all ages and sizes, from the farm and the neighborhood, stood forming a pyramid of shining black faces at every door and window, gazing with delight at the scene, rolling their white eyeballs, and showing grinning rows of ivory from ear to ear. How could the flogger of urchins be otherwise than animated and joyous? The lady of his heart was his partner in the dance, and smiling graciously in reply to all his amorous oglings; while Brom Bones, sorely smitten with love and jealousy, sat brooding by himself in one corner.

When the dance was at an end, Ichabod was attracted to a knot of the sager folks, who, with Old Van Tassel, sat smoking at one end of the piazza, gossiping over former times, and drawing out long stories about the war.

This neighborhood, at the time of which I am speaking, was one of those highly favored places which abound with chronicle and great men. The British and American line had run near it during the war; it had, therefore, been the scene of marauding and infested with refugees, cowboys, and all kinds of border chivalry. Just sufficient time had elapsed to enable each storyteller to dress up his tale with a little becoming fiction, and, in the indistinctness of his recollection, to make himself the hero of every exploit.

There was the story of Doffue Martling, a large blue-bearded Dutchman, who had nearly taken a British frigate with an old iron nine-pounder from a mud breastwork, only that his gun burst at the sixth discharge. And there was an old gentleman who shall be nameless, being too rich a mynheer to be lightly mentioned, who, in the battle of White Plains, being an excellent master of defence, parried a musket-ball with a small sword, insomuch that he absolutely felt it whiz round the blade, and glance off at the hilt; in proof of which he was ready at any time to show the sword, with the hilt a little bent. There were several more that had been equally great in the field, not one of whom but was persuaded that he had a considerable hand in bringing the war to a happy termination.

But all these were nothing to the tales of ghosts and apparitions that succeeded. The neighborhood is rich in legendary treasures of the kind. Local tales and superstitions thrive best in these sheltered, long-settled retreats; but are trampled under foot by the shifting throng that forms the population of most of our country places. Besides, there is no encouragement for ghosts in most of our villages, for they have scarcely had time to finish their first nap and turn themselves in their graves, before their surviving friends have travelled away from the neighborhood; so that when they turn out at night to walk their rounds, they have no acquaintance left to call upon. This is perhaps the reason why we so seldom hear of ghosts except in our long-established Dutch communities.

The immediate cause, however, of the prevalence of supernatural stories in these parts, was doubtless owing to the vicinity of Sleepy Hollow. There was a contagion in the very air that blew from that haunted region; it breathed forth an atmosphere of dreams and fancies infecting all the land. Several of the Sleepy Hollow people were present at Van Tassel's, and, as usual, were doling out their wild and wonderful legends. Many dismal tales were told about funeral trains, and mourning cries and wailings heard and seen about the great tree where the unfortunate Major André was taken, and which stood in the neighborhood. Some mention was made also of the woman in white, that haunted the dark glen at Raven Rock, and was often heard to shriek on winter nights before a storm, having perished there in the snow. The chief part of the stories, however, turned upon the favorite spectre of Sleepy Hollow, the Headless Horseman, who had been heard several times of late, patrolling the country; and, it was said, tethered his horse nightly among the graves in the churchyard.

The sequestered situation of this church seems always to have made it a favorite haunt of troubled spirits. It stands on a knoll, surrounded by locust-trees and lofty elms, from among which its decent, whitewashed walls shine modestly forth, like Christian purity beaming through the shades of retirement. A gentle slope descends from it to a silver sheet of water, bordered by high trees, between which, peeps may be caught at the blue hills of the Hudson. To look upon its grass-grown yard, where the sunbeams seem to sleep so quietly, one would think that there at least the dead might rest in peace. On one side of the church extends a wide woody dell, along which raves a large brook among broken rocks and trunks of fallen trees. Over a deep black part of the stream, not far from the church, was formerly thrown a wooden bridge; the road that led to it, and the bridge itself, were thickly shaded by overhanging trees, which cast a gloom about it, even in the daytime; but occasioned a fearful darkness at night. Such was one of the favorite haunts of the Headless Horseman, and the place where he was most frequently encountered. The tale was told of old Brouwer, a most heretical disbeliever in ghosts, how he met the Horseman returning from his foray into Sleepy Hollow, and was obliged to get up behind him; how they galloped over bush and brake, over hill and swamp, until they reached the bridge; when the Horseman suddenly turned into a skeleton, threw old Brouwer into the brook, and sprang away over the tree-tops with a clap of thunder.

This story was immediately matched by a thrice marvellous adventure of Brom Bones, who made light of the Galloping Hessian as an arrant jockey. He affirmed that on returning one night from the neighboring village of Sing Sing, he had been overtaken by this midnight trooper; that he had offered to race with him for a bowl of punch, and should have won it too, for Daredevil beat the goblin horse all hollow, but just as they came to the church bridge, the Hessian bolted, and vanished in a flash of fire.

All these tales, told in that drowsy undertone with which men talk in the dark, the countenances of the listeners only now and then receiving a casual gleam from the glare of a pipe, sank deep in the mind of Ichabod. He repaid them in kind with large extracts from his invaluable author, Cotton Mather, and added many marvellous events that had taken place in his native State of Connecticut, and fearful sights which he had seen in his nightly walks about Sleepy Hollow.

The revel now gradually broke up. The old farmers gathered together their families in their wagons, and were heard for some time rattling along the hollow roads, and over the distant hills. Some of the damsels mounted on pillions behind their favorite swains, and their light-hearted laughter, mingling with the clatter of hoofs, echoed along the silent woodlands, sounding fainter and fainter, until they gradually died away,—and the late scene of noise and frolic was all silent and deserted. Ichabod only lingered behind, according to the custom of country lovers, to have a tête-à-tête with the heiress; fully convinced that he was now on the high road to success. What passed at this interview I will not pretend to say, for in fact I do not know. Something, however, I fear me, must have gone wrong, for he certainly sallied forth, after no very great interval, with an air quite desolate and chapfallen. Oh, these women! these women! Could that girl have been playing off any of her coquettish tricks? Was her encouragement of the poor pedagogue all a mere sham to secure her conquest of his rival? Heaven only knows, not I! Let it suffice to say, Ichabod stole forth with the air of one who had been sacking a henroost, rather than a fair lady's heart. Without looking to the right or left to notice the scene of rural wealth, on which he had so often gloated, he went straight to the stable, and with several hearty cuffs and kicks roused his steed most uncourteously from the comfortable quarters in which he was soundly sleeping, dreaming of mountains of corn and oats, and whole valleys of timothy and clover.

It was the very witching time of night that Ichabod, heavy-hearted and crestfallen, pursued his travels homewards, along the sides of the lofty hills which rise above Tarry Town, and which he had traversed so cheerily in the afternoon. The hour was as dismal as himself. Far below him the Tappan Zee spread its dusky and indistinct waste of waters, with here and there the tall mast of a sloop, riding quietly at anchor under the land. In the dead hush of midnight, he could even hear the barking of the watchdog from the opposite shore of the Hudson; but it was so vague and faint as only to give an idea of his distance from this faithful companion of man. Now and then, too, the long-drawn crowing of a cock, accidentally awakened, would sound far, far off, from some farmhouse away among the hills—but it was like a dreaming sound in his ear. No signs of life occurred near him, but occasionally the melancholy chirp of a cricket, or perhaps the guttural twang of a bullfrog from a neighboring marsh, as if sleeping uncomfortably and turning suddenly in his bed.

All the stories of ghosts and goblins that he had heard in the afternoon now came crowding upon his recollection. The night grew darker and darker; the stars seemed to sink deeper in the sky, and driving clouds occasionally hid them from his sight. He had never felt so lonely and dismal. He was, moreover, approaching the very place where many of the scenes of the ghost stories had been laid. In the centre of the road stood an enormous tulip-tree, which towered like a giant above all the other trees of the neighborhood, and formed a kind of landmark. Its limbs were gnarled and fantastic, large enough to form trunks for ordinary trees, twisting down almost to the earth, and rising again into the air. It was connected with the tragical story of the unfortunate André, who had been taken prisoner hard by; and was universally known by the name of Major André's tree. The common people regarded it with a mixture of respect and superstition, partly out of sympathy for the fate of its ill-starred namesake, and partly from the tales of strange sights, and doleful lamentations, told concerning it.

As Ichabod approached this fearful tree, he began to whistle; he thought his whistle was answered; it was but a blast sweeping sharply through the dry branches. As he approached a little nearer, he thought he saw something white, hanging in the midst of the tree: he paused and ceased whistling but, on looking more narrowly, perceived that it was a place where the tree had been scathed by lightning, and the white wood laid bare. Suddenly he heard a groan—his teeth chattered, and his knees smote against the saddle: it was but the rubbing of one huge bough upon another, as they were swayed about by the breeze. He passed the tree in safety, but new perils lay before him.

About two hundred yards from the tree, a small brook crossed the road, and ran into a marshy and thickly-wooded glen, known by the name of Wiley's Swamp. A few rough logs, laid side by side, served for a bridge over this stream. On that side of the road where the brook entered the wood, a group of oaks and chestnuts, matted thick with wild grape-vines, threw a cavernous gloom over it. To pass this bridge was the severest trial. It was at this identical spot that the unfortunate André was captured, and under the covert of those chestnuts and vines were the sturdy yeomen concealed who surprised him. This has ever since been considered a haunted stream, and fearful are the feelings of the schoolboy who has to pass it alone after dark.

As he approached the stream, his heart began to thump; he summoned up, however, all his resolution, gave his horse half a score of kicks in the ribs, and attempted to dash briskly across the bridge; but instead of starting forward, the perverse old animal made a lateral movement, and ran broadside against the fence. Ichabod, whose fears increased with the delay, jerked the reins on the other side, and kicked lustily with the contrary foot: it was all in vain; his steed started, it is true, but it was only to plunge to the opposite side of the road into a thicket of brambles and alder bushes. The schoolmaster now bestowed both whip and heel upon the starveling ribs of old Gunpowder, who dashed forward, snuffling and snorting, but came to a stand just by the bridge, with a suddenness that had nearly sent his rider sprawling over his head. Just at this moment a plashy tramp by the side of the bridge caught the sensitive ear of Ichabod. In the dark shadow of the grove, on the margin of the brook, he beheld something huge, misshapen and towering. It stirred not, but seemed gathered up in the gloom, like some gigantic monster ready to spring upon the traveller.

The hair of the affrighted pedagogue rose upon his head with terror. What was to be done? To turn and fly was now too late; and besides, what chance was there of escaping ghost or goblin, if such it was, which could ride upon the wings of the wind? Summoning up, therefore, a show of courage, he demanded in stammering accents, "Who are you?" He received no reply. He repeated his demand in a still more agitated voice. Still there was no answer. Once more he cudgelled the sides of the inflexible Gunpowder, and, shutting his eyes, broke forth with involuntary fervor into a psalm tune. Just then the shadowy object of alarm put itself in motion, and with a scramble and a bound stood at once in the middle of the road. Though the night was dark and dismal, yet the form of the unknown might now in some degree be ascertained. He appeared to be a horseman of large dimensions, and mounted on a black horse of powerful frame. He made no offer of molestation or sociability, but kept aloof on one side of the road, jogging along on the blind side of old Gunpowder, who had now got over his fright and waywardness.

Ichabod, who had no relish for this strange midnight companion, and bethought himself of the adventure of Brom Bones with the Galloping Hessian, now quickened his steed in hopes of leaving him behind. The stranger, however, quickened his horse to an equal pace. Ichabod pulled up, and fell into a walk, thinking to lag behind,—the other did the same.

His heart began to sink within him; he endeavored to resume his psalm tune, but his parched tongue clove to the roof of his mouth, and he could not utter a stave. There was something in the moody and dogged silence of this pertinacious companion that was mysterious and appalling. It was soon fearfully accounted for. On mounting a rising ground, which brought the figure of his fellow-traveller in relief against the sky, gigantic in height, and muffled in a cloak, Ichabod was horror-struck on perceiving that he was headless!—but his horror was still more increased on observing that the head, which should have rested on his shoulders, was carried before him on the pommel of his saddle! His terror rose to desperation; he rained a shower of kicks and blows upon Gunpowder, hoping by a sudden movement to give his companion the slip; but the spectre started full jump with him. Away, then, they dashed through thick and thin; stones flying and sparks flashing at every bound. Ichabod's flimsy garments fluttered in the air, as he stretched his long lank body away over his horse's head, in the eagerness of his flight.

They had now reached the road which turns off to Sleepy Hollow; but Gunpowder, who seemed possessed with a demon, instead of keeping up it, made an opposite turn, and plunged headlong downhill to the left. This road leads through a sandy hollow shaded by trees for about a quarter of a mile, where it crosses the bridge famous in goblin story; and just beyond swells the green knoll on which stands the whitewashed church.

As yet the panic of the steed had given his unskilful rider an apparent advantage in the chase, but just as he had got half way through the hollow, the girths of the saddle gave way, and he felt it slipping from under him. He seized it by the pommel, and endeavored to hold it firm, but in vain; and had just time to save himself by clasping old Gunpowder round the neck, when the saddle fell to the earth, and he heard it trampled under foot by his pursuer. For a moment the terror of Hans Van Ripper's wrath passed across his mind,—for it was his Sunday saddle; but this was no time for petty fears; the goblin was hard on his haunches; and (unskilful rider that he was!) he had much ado to maintain his seat; sometimes slipping on one side, sometimes on another, and sometimes jolted on the high ridge of his horse's backbone, with a violence that he verily feared would cleave him asunder.

An opening in the trees now cheered him with the hopes that the church bridge was at hand. The wavering reflection of a silver star in the bosom of the brook told him that he was not mistaken. He saw the walls of the church dimly glaring under the trees beyond. He recollected the place where Brom Bones's ghostly competitor had disappeared. "If I can but reach that bridge," thought Ichabod, "I am safe." Just then he heard the black steed panting and blowing close behind him; he even fancied that he felt his hot breath. Another convulsive kick in the ribs, and old Gunpowder sprang upon the bridge; he thundered over the resounding planks; he gained the opposite side; and now Ichabod cast a look behind to see if his pursuer should vanish, according to rule, in a flash of fire and brimstone. Just then he saw the goblin rising in his stirrups, and in the very act of hurling his head at him. Ichabod endeavored to dodge the horrible missile, but too late. It encountered his cranium with a tremendous crash,—he was tumbled headlong into the dust, and Gunpowder, the black steed, and the goblin rider, passed by like a whirlwind.

The next morning the old horse was found without his saddle, and with the bridle under his feet, soberly cropping the grass at his master's gate. Ichabod did not make his appearance at breakfast; dinner-hour came, but no Ichabod. The boys assembled at the schoolhouse, and strolled idly about the banks of the brook; but no schoolmaster. Hans Van Ripper now began to feel some uneasiness about the fate of poor Ichabod, and his saddle. An inquiry was set on foot, and after diligent investigation they came upon his traces. In one part of the road leading to the church was found the saddle trampled in the dirt; the tracks of horses' hoofs deeply dented in the road, and evidently at furious speed, were traced to the bridge, beyond which, on the bank of a broad part of the brook, where the water ran deep and black, was found the hat of the unfortunate Ichabod, and close beside it a shattered pumpkin.

The brook was searched, but the body of the schoolmaster was not to be discovered. Hans Van Ripper as executor of his estate, examined the bundle which contained all his worldly effects. They consisted of two shirts and a half; two stocks for the neck; a pair or two of worsted stockings; an old pair of corduroy small-clothes; a rusty razor; a book of psalm tunes full of dog's-ears; and a broken pitch-pipe. As to the books and furniture of the schoolhouse, they belonged to the community, excepting Cotton Mather's "History of Witchcraft," a "New England Almanac," and a book of dreams and fortune-telling; in which last was a sheet of foolscap much scribbled and blotted in several fruitless attempts to make a copy of verses in honor of the heiress of Van Tassel. These magic books and the poetic scrawl were forthwith consigned to the flames by Hans Van Ripper; who, from that time forward, determined to send his children no more to school, observing that he never knew any good come of this same reading and writing. Whatever money the schoolmaster possessed, and he had received his quarter's pay but a day or two before, he must have had about his person at the time of his disappearance.

The mysterious event caused much speculation at the church on the following Sunday. Knots of gazers and gossips were collected in the churchyard, at the bridge, and at the spot where the hat and pumpkin had been found. The stories of Brouwer, of Bones, and a whole budget of others were called to mind; and when they had diligently considered them all, and compared them with the symptoms of the present case, they shook their heads, and came to the conclusion that Ichabod had been carried off by the Galloping Hessian. As he was a bachelor, and in nobody's debt, nobody troubled his head any more about him; the school was removed to a different quarter of the hollow, and another pedagogue reigned in his stead.

It is true, an old farmer, who had been down to New York on a visit several years after, and from whom this account of the ghostly adventure was received, brought home the intelligence that Ichabod Crane was still alive; that he had left the neighborhood partly through fear of the goblin and Hans Van Ripper, and partly in mortification at having been suddenly dismissed by the heiress; that he had changed his quarters to a distant part of the country; had kept school and studied law at the same time; had been admitted to the bar; turned politician; electioneered; written for the newspapers; and finally had been made a justice of the Ten Pound Court. Brom Bones, too, who, shortly after his rival's disappearance conducted the blooming Katrina in triumph to the altar, was observed to look exceedingly knowing whenever the story of Ichabod was related, and always burst into a hearty laugh at the mention of the pumpkin; which led some to suspect that he knew more about the matter than he chose to tell.

The old country wives, however, who are the best judges of these matters, maintain to this day that Ichabod was spirited away by supernatural means; and it is a favorite story often told about the neighborhood round the winter evening fire. The bridge became more than ever an object of superstitious awe; and that may be the reason why the road has been altered of late years, so as to approach the church by the border of the millpond.

The schoolhouse being deserted soon fell to decay, and was reported to be haunted by the ghost of the unfortunate pedagogue and the plowboy, loitering homeward of a still summer evening, has often fancied his voice at a distance, chanting a melancholy psalm tune among the tranquil solitudes of Sleepy Hollow.

POSTSCRIPT

Found in the Handwriting of Mr. Knickerbocker.

The preceding tale is given almost in the precise words in which I heard it related at a Corporation meeting at the ancient city of Manhattoes, at which were present many of its sagest and most illustrious burghers. The narrator was a pleasant, shabby, gentlemanly old fellow, in pepper-and-salt clothes, with a sadly humourous face, and one whom I strongly suspected of being poor—he made such efforts to be entertaining. When his story was concluded, there was much laughter and approbation, particularly from two or three deputy aldermen, who had been asleep the greater part of the time. There was, however, one tall, dry-looking old gentleman, with beetling eyebrows, who maintained a grave and rather severe face throughout, now and then folding his arms, inclining his head, and looking down upon the floor, as if turning a doubt over in his mind. He was one of your wary men, who never laugh but upon good grounds—when they have reason and law on their side. When the mirth of the rest of the company had subsided, and silence was restored, he leaned one arm on the elbow of his chair, and sticking the other akimbo, demanded, with a slight, but exceedingly sage motion of the head, and contraction of the brow, what was the moral of the story, and what it went to prove?

The story-teller, who was just putting a glass of wine to his lips, as a refreshment after his toils, paused for a moment, looked at his inquirer with an air of infinite deference, and, lowering the glass slowly to the table, observed that the story was intended most logically to prove—

"That there is no situation in life but has its advantages and pleasures—provided we will but take a joke as we find it:

"That, therefore, he that runs races with goblin troopers is likely to have rough riding of it.

"Ergo, for a country schoolmaster to be refused the hand of a Dutch heiress is a certain step to high preferment in the state."

The cautious old gentleman knit his brows tenfold closer after this explanation, being sorely puzzled by the ratiocination of the syllogism, while, methought, the one in pepper-and-salt eyed him with something of a triumphant leer. At length he observed that all this was very well, but still he thought the story a little on the extravagant—there were one or two points on which he had his doubts.

"Faith, sir," replied the story-teller, "as to that matter, I don't believe one-half of it myself." D. K.

2

Rip Van Winkle

Whoever has made a voyage up the Hudson must remember the Kaatskill mountains. They are a dismembered branch of the great Appalachian family, and are seen away to the west of the river, swelling up to a noble height, and lording it over the surrounding country. Every change of season, every change of weather, indeed, every hour of the day, produces some change in the magical hues and shapes of these mountains, and they are regarded by all the good wives, far and near, as perfect barometers. When the weather is fair and settled, they are clothed in blue and purple, and print their bold outlines on the clear evening sky; but sometimes, when the rest of the landscape is cloudless, they will gather a hood of grey vapours about their summits, which, in the last rays of the setting sun, will glow and light up like a crown of glory.

At the foot of these fairy mountains, the voyager may have descried the light smoke curling up from a village, whose shingle-roofs gleam among the trees, just where the blue tints of the upland melt away into the fresh green of the nearer landscape. It is a little village, of great antiquity, having been founded by some of the Dutch colonists in the early times of the province, just about the beginning of the government of the good Peter Stuyvesant (may he rest in peace!), and there were some of the houses of the original settlers standing within a few years, built of small yellow bricks brought from Holland, having latticed windows and gable fronts, surmounted with weathercocks.

In that same village and in one of these very houses (which, to tell the precise truth, was sadly time-worn and weather-beaten), there lived, many years since, while the country was yet a province of Great Britain, a simple, good-natured fellow, of the name of Rip Van Winkle. He was a descendant of the Van Winkles who figured so gallantly in the chivalrous days of Peter Stuyvesant, and accompanied him to the siege of Fort Christina. He inherited, however, but little of the martial character of his ancestors. I have observed that he was a simple, good-natured man; he was, moreover, a kind neighbour, and an obedient, hen-pecked husband. Indeed, to the latter circumstance might be owing that meekness of spirit which gained him such universal popularity; for those men are apt to be obsequious and conciliating abroad, who are under the discipline of shrews at home. Their tempers, doubtless, are rendered pliant and malleable in the fiery furnace of domestic tribulation; and a curtain-lecture is worth all the sermons in the world for teaching the virtues of patience and long-suffering. A termagant wife may, therefore, in some respects, be considered a tolerable blessing; and if so, Rip Van Winkle was thrice blessed.

Certain it is that he was a great favourite among all the good wives of the village, who, as usual with the amiable sex, took his part in all family squabbles; and never failed, whenever they talked those matters over in their evening gossipings, to lay all the blame on Dame Van Winkle. The children of the village, too, would shout with joy whenever he approached. He assisted at their sports, made their playthings, taught them to fly kites and shoot marbles, and told them long stories of ghosts, witches, and Indians. Whenever he went dodging about the village, he was surrounded by a troop of them, hanging on his skirts, clambering on his back, and playing a thousand tricks on him with impunity; and not a dog would bark at him throughout the neighbourhood.

The great error in Rip's composition was an insuperable aversion to all kinds of profitable labour. It could not be for want of assiduity or perseverance; for he would sit on a wet rock, with a rod as long and heavy as a Tartar's lance, and fish all day without a murmur, even though he should not be encouraged by a single nibble. He would carry a fowling-piece on his shoulder for hours together, trudging through woods and swamps, and up hill and down dale, to shoot a few squirrels or wild pigeons. He would never refuse to assist a neighbour even in the roughest toil, and was a foremost man in all country frolics for husking Indian corn, or building stone fences; the women of the village, too, used to employ him to run their errands, and to do such little odd jobs as their less obliging husbands would not do for them. In a word, Rip was ready to attend to anybody's business but his own; but as to doing family duty, and keeping his farm in order, he found it impossible.

In fact, he declared it was of no use to work on his farm; it was the most pestilent little piece of ground in the whole country; everything about it went wrong, in spite of him. His fences were continually falling to pieces; his cow would either go astray, or get among the cabbages; weeds were sure to grow quicker in his fields than anywhere else; the rain always made a point of setting in just as he had some outdoor work to do; so that though his patrimonial estate had dwindled away under his management, acre by acre, until there was little more left than a mere patch of Indian corn and potatoes, yet it was the worst-conditioned farm in the neighbourhood.

His children, too, were as ragged and wild as if they belonged to nobody. His son Rip, an urchin begotten in his own likeness, promised to inherit the habits, with the old clothes, of his father. He was generally seen trooping like a colt at his mother's heels, equipped in a pair of his father's cast-off galligaskins, which he had much ado to hold up with one hand, as a fine lady does her train in bad weather.

Rip Van Winkle, however, was one of those happy mortals, of foolish, well-oiled dispositions, who take the world easy, eat white bread or brown, whichever can be got with least thought or trouble, and would rather starve on a penny than work for a pound. If left to himself, he would have whistled life away in perfect contentment; but his wife kept continually dinning in his ears about his idleness, his carelessness, and the ruin he was bringing on his family. Morning, noon, and night, her tongue was incessantly going, and everything he said or did was sure to produce a torrent of household eloquence. Rip had but one way of replying to all lectures of the kind, and that, by frequent use, had grown into a habit. He shrugged his shoulders, shook his head, cast up his eyes, but said nothing. This, however, always provoked a fresh volley from his wife; so that he was fain to draw off his forces, and take to the outside of the house—the only side which, in truth, belongs to a hen-pecked husband.

Rip's sole domestic adherent was his dog Wolf, who was as much hen-pecked as his master; for Dame Van Winkle regarded them as companions in idleness, and even looked upon Wolf with an evil eye, as the cause of his master's going so often astray. True it is, in all points of spirit befitting an honourable dog, he was as courageous an animal as ever scoured the woods—but what courage can withstand the evil-doing and all-besetting terrors of a woman's tongue? The moment Wolf entered the house his chest fell, his tail drooped to the ground or curled between his legs, he sneaked about with a gallows air, casting many a sidelong glance at Dame Van Winkle, and at the least flourish of a broomstick or ladle he would fly to the door with yelping precipitation.

Times grew worse and worse with Rip Van Winkle as years of matrimony rolled on; a tart temper never mellows with age, and a sharp tongue is the only edged tool that grows keener with constant use. For a long while he used to console himself, when driven from home, by frequenting a kind of perpetual club of the sages, philosophers and other idle personages of the village, which held its sessions on a bench before a small inn, designated by a rubicund portrait of His Majesty George the Third. Here they used to sit in the shade through a long, lazy summer's day, talking listlessly over village gossip, or telling endless, sleepy stories about nothing. But it would have been worth any statesman's money to have heard the profound discussions that sometimes took place, when by chance an old newspaper fell into their hands from some passing traveller. How solemnly they would listen to the contents, as drawled out by Derrick Van Bummel, the schoolmaster, a dapper, learned little man, who was not to be daunted by the most gigantic word in the dictionary; and how sagely they would deliberate upon public events some months after they had taken place.

The opinions of this junto were completely controlled by Nicholas Vedder, a patriarch of the village, and landlord of the inn, at the door of which he took his seat from morning till night, just moving sufficiently to avoid the sun and keep in the shade of a large tree; so that the neighbours could tell the hour by his movements as accurately as by a sun-dial. It is true he was rarely heard to speak, but smoked his pipe incessantly. His adherents, however (for every great man has his adherents), perfectly understood him, and knew how to gather his opinions. When anything that was read or related displeased him, he was observed to smoke his pipe vehemently, and to send forth short, frequent, and angry puffs; but when pleased, he would inhale the smoke slowly and tranquilly, and emit it in light and placid clouds; and sometimes, taking the pipe from his mouth, and letting the fragrant vapour curl about his nose, would gravely nod his head in token of perfect approbation.

From even this stronghold the unlucky Rip was at length routed by his termagant wife, who would suddenly break in upon the tranquillity of the assemblage and call the members all to naught; nor was that august personage, Nicholas Vedder himself, sacred from the daring tongue of this terrible virago, who charged him outright with encouraging her husband in habits of idleness.

Poor Rip was at last reduced almost to despair; and his only alternative, to escape from the labour of the farm and clamour of his wife, was to take gun in hand and stroll away into the woods. Here he would sometimes seat himself at the foot of a tree, and share the contents of his wallet with Wolf, with whom he sympathised as a fellow-sufferer in persecution. "Poor Wolf," he would say, "thy mistress leads thee a dog's life of it; but never mind, my lad, whilst I live thou shalt never want a friend to stand by thee!" Wolf would wag his tail, look wistfully in his master's face; and, if dogs can feel pity, I verily believe he reciprocated the sentiment with all his heart.

In a long ramble of the kind on a fine autumnal day, Rip had unconsciously scrambled to one of the highest parts of the Kaatskill Mountains. He was after his favourite sport of squirrel shooting, and the still solitudes had echoed and re-echoed with the reports of his gun. Panting and fatigued, he threw himself, late in the afternoon, on a green knoll, covered with mountain herbage, that crowned the brow of a precipice. From an opening between the trees he could overlook all the lower country for many a mile of rich woodland. He saw at a distance the lordly Hudson, far, far below him, moving on its silent but majestic course, with the reflection of a purple cloud, or the sail of a lagging bark, here and there sleeping on its glassy bosom, and at last losing itself in the blue highlands.

On the other side he looked down into a deep mountain glen, wild, lonely, and shagged, the bottom filled with fragments from the impending cliffs, and scarcely lighted by the reflected rays of the setting sun. For some time Rip lay musing on this scene; evening was gradually advancing; the mountains began to throw their long blue shadows over the valleys; he saw that it would be dark long before he could reach the village, and he heaved a heavy sigh when he thought of encountering the terrors of Dame Van Winkle.

As he was about to descend, he heard a voice from a distance, hallooing: "Rip Van Winkle! Rip Van Winkle!" He looked round, but could see nothing but a crow winging its solitary flight across the mountain. He thought his fancy must have deceived him, and turned again to descend, when he heard the same cry ring through the still evening air: "Rip Van Winkle! Rip Van Winkle!" At the same time Wolf bristled up his back, and giving a low growl, skulked to his master's side, looking fearfully down into the glen. Rip now felt a vague apprehension stealing over him; he looked anxiously in the same direction, and perceived a strange figure slowly toiling up the rocks, and bending under the weight of something he carried on his back. He was surprised to see any human being in this lonely and unfrequented place; but supposing it to be some one of the neighbourhood in need of his assistance, he hastened down to yield it.

On nearer approach he was still more surprised at the singularity of the stranger's appearance. He was a short, square-built old fellow, with thick bushy hair, and a grizzled beard. His dress was of the antique Dutch fashion: a cloth jerkin strapped round the waist—several pair of breeches, the outer one of ample volume, decorated with rows of buttons down the sides, and bunches at the knees. He bore on his shoulder a stout keg, that seemed full of liquor, and made signs for Rip to approach and assist him with the load. Though rather shy and distrustful of his new acquaintance, Rip complied with his usual alacrity; and mutually relieving one another, they clambered up a narrow gully, apparently the dry bed of a mountain torrent. As they ascended, Rip every now and then heard long, rolling peals, like distant thunder, that seemed to issue out of a deep ravine, or rather cleft, between lofty rocks, toward which their ragged path conducted. He paused for an instant, but supposing it to be the muttering of one of those transient thunder-showers which often take place in mountain heights, he proceeded. Passing through the ravine, they came to a hollow, like a small amphitheatre, surrounded by perpendicular precipices, over the brinks of which impending trees shot their branches, so that you only caught glimpses of the azure sky and the bright evening cloud. During the whole time Rip and his companion had laboured on in silence; for though the former marvelled greatly what could be the object of carrying a keg of liquor up this wild mountain, yet there was something strange and incomprehensible about the unknown, that inspired awe and checked familiarity.

On entering the amphitheatre, new objects of wonder presented themselves. On a level spot in the centre was a company of odd-looking personages playing at ninepins. They were dressed in a quaint, outlandish fashion; some wore short doublets, others jerkins, with long knives in their belts, and most of them had enormous breeches, of similar style with that of the guide's. Their visages, too, were peculiar; one had a large beard, broad face, and small piggish eyes; the face of another seemed to consist entirely of nose, and was surmounted by a white sugar-loaf hat, set off with a little red cock's tail. They all had beards, of various shapes and colours. There was one who seemed to be the commander. He was a stout old gentleman, with a weather-beaten countenance; he wore a laced doublet, broad belt and hanger, high-crowned hat and feather, red stockings, and high-heeled shoes, with roses in them. The whole group reminded Rip of the figures in an old Flemish painting, in the parlour of Dominie Van Shaick, the village parson, and which had been brought over from Holland at the time of the settlement.

What seemed particularly odd to Rip was, that these folks were evidently amusing themselves, yet they maintained the gravest faces, the most mysterious silence, and were, withal, the most melancholy party of pleasure he had ever witnessed. Nothing interrupted the stillness of the scene but the noise of the balls, which, whenever they were rolled, echoed along the mountains like rumbling peals of thunder.

As Rip and his companion approached them, they suddenly desisted from their play, and stared at him with such fixed, statue-like gaze, and such strange, uncouth, lack-lustre countenances, that his heart turned within him, and his knees smote together. His companion now emptied the contents of the keg into large flagons, and made signs to him to wait upon the company. He obeyed with fear and trembling; they quaffed the liquor in profound silence, and then returned to their game.

By degrees Rip's awe and apprehension subsided. He even ventured, when no eye was fixed upon him, to taste the beverage, which he found had much of the flavour of excellent Hollands. He was naturally a thirsty soul, and was soon tempted to repeat the draught. One taste provoked another; and he reiterated his visits to the flagon so often that at length his senses were overpowered, his eyes swam in his head, his head gradually declined, and he fell into a deep sleep.

On waking, he found himself on the green knoll whence he had first seen the old man of the glen. He rubbed his eyes—it was a bright sunny morning. The birds were hopping and twittering among the bushes, and the eagle was wheeling aloft, and breasting the pure mountain breeze.

"Surely," thought Rip, "I have not slept here all night." He recalled the occurrences before he fell asleep. The strange man with a keg of liquor—the mountain ravine—the wild retreat among the rocks—the woebegone party at ninepins—the flagon—"Oh! that flagon! that wicked flagon!" thought Rip,—"what excuse shall I make to Dame Van Winkle?"

He looked round for his gun, but in place of the clean, well-oiled fowling-piece, he found an old firelock lying by him, the barrel incrusted with rust, the lock falling off, and the stock worm-eaten. He now suspected that the grave roysterers of the mountains had put a trick upon him, and, having dosed him with liquor, had robbed him of his gun. Wolf, too, had disappeared, but he might have strayed away after a squirrel or partridge. He whistled after him, and shouted his name, but all in vain; the echoes repeated his whistle and shout, but no dog was to be seen.

He determined to revisit the scene of the last evening's gambol, and if he met with any of the party, to demand his dog and gun. As he rose to walk, he found himself stiff in the joints, and wanting in his usual activity. "These mountain beds do not agree with me," thought Rip, "and if this frolic should lay me up with a fit of the rheumatism, I shall have a blessed time with Dame Van Winkle." With some difficulty he got down into the glen: he found the gully up which he and his companion had ascended the preceding evening; but to his astonishment a mountain stream was now foaming down it, leaping from rock to rock, and filling the glen with babbling murmurs. He, however, made shift to scramble up its sides, working his toilsome way through thickets of birch, sassafras, and witch-hazel, and sometimes tripped up or entangled by the wild grape-vines that twisted their coils or tendrils from tree to tree, and spread a kind of network in his path.

At length he reached to where the ravine had opened through the cliffs to the amphitheatre; but no traces of such opening remained. The rocks presented a high, impenetrable wall, over which the torrent came tumbling in a sheet of feathery foam, and fell into a broad deep basin, black from the shadows of the surrounding forest. Here, then, poor Rip was brought to a stand. He again called and whistled after his dog; he was only answered by the cawing of a flock of idle crows, sporting high in the air about a dry tree that overhung a sunny precipice; and who, secure in their elevation, seemed to look down and scoff at the poor man's perplexities. What was to be done? the morning was passing away, and Rip felt famished for want of his breakfast. He grieved to give up his dog and gun; he dreaded to meet his wife; but it would not do to starve among the mountains. He shook his head, shouldered the rusty firelock, and, with a heart full of trouble and anxiety, turned his steps homeward.

As he approached the village he met a number of people, but none whom he knew, which somewhat surprised him, for he had thought himself acquainted with every one in the country round. Their dress, too, was of a different fashion from that to which he was accustomed. They all stared at him with equal marks of surprise, and whenever they cast their eyes upon him, invariably stroked their chins. The constant recurrence of this gesture induced Rip, involuntarily, to do the same, when, to his astonishment, he found his beard had grown a foot long!

He had now entered the skirts of the village. A troop of strange children ran at his heels, hooting after him, and pointing at his grey beard. The dogs, too, not one of whom he recognised for an old acquaintance, barked at him as he passed. The very village was altered; it was larger and more populous. There were rows of houses which he had never seen before, and those which had been his familiar haunts had disappeared. Strange names were over the doors—strange faces at the windows—everything was strange. His mind now misgave him; he began to doubt whether both he and the world around him were not bewitched. Surely this was his native village, which he had left but the day before. There stood the Kaatskill Mountains—there ran the silver Hudson at a distance—there was every hill and dale precisely as it had always been. Rip was sorely perplexed. "That flagon last night," thought he, "has addled my poor head sadly!"

It was with some difficulty that he found the way to his own house, which he approached with silent awe, expecting every moment to hear the shrill voice of Dame Van Winkle. He found the house gone to decay—the roof had fallen in, the windows shattered, and the doors off the hinges. A half-starved dog that looked like Wolf was skulking about it. Rip called him by name, but the cur snarled, showed his teeth, and passed on. This was an unkind cut indeed. "My very dog," sighed poor Rip, "has forgotten me!"

He entered the house, which, to tell the truth, Dame Van Winkle had always kept in neat order. It was empty, forlorn, and apparently abandoned. This desolateness overcame all his connubial fears—he called loudly for his wife and children—the lonely chambers rang for a moment with his voice, and then all again was silence.

He now hurried forth, and hastened to his old resort, the village inn—but it too was gone. A large rickety wooden building stood in its place, with great gaping windows, some of them broken and mended with old hats and petticoats, and over the door was painted, "The Union Hotel, by Jonathan Doolittle." Instead of the great tree that used to shelter the quiet little Dutch inn of yore, there now was reared a tall, naked pole, with something on the top that looked like a red nightcap, and from it was fluttering a flag, on which was a singular assemblage of stars and stripes;—all this was strange and incomprehensible. He recognised on the sign, however, the ruby face of King George, under which he had smoked so many a peaceful pipe; but even this was singularly metamorphosed. The red coat was changed for one of blue and buff, a sword was held in the hand instead of a sceptre, the head was decorated with a cocked hat, and underneath was painted in large characters, "General Washington."

There was, as usual, a crowd of folk about the door, but none that Rip recollected. The very character of the people seemed changed. There was a busy, bustling, disputatious tone about it, instead of the accustomed phlegm and drowsy tranquillity. He looked in vain for the sage Nicholas Vedder, with his broad face, double chin, and fair long pipe, uttering clouds of tobacco-smoke instead of idle speeches; or Van Bummel, the schoolmaster, doling forth the contents of an ancient newspaper. In place of these, a lean, bilious-looking fellow, with his pockets full of handbills, was haranguing vehemently about rights of citizens—elections—members of congress—liberty—Bunker's Hill—heroes of seventy-six—and other words, which were a perfect Babylonish jargon to the bewildered Van Winkle.

The appearance of Rip, with his long, grizzled beard, his rusty fowling-piece, his uncouth dress, and an army of women and children at his heels, soon attracted the attention of the tavern politicians. They crowded round him, eyeing him from head to foot with great curiosity. The orator bustled up to him, and, drawing him partly aside, inquired "On which side he voted?" Rip stared in vacant stupidity. Another short but busy little fellow pulled him by the arm, and, rising on tiptoe, inquired in his ear, "Whether he was Federal or Democrat?" Rip was equally at a loss to comprehend the question; when a knowing, self-important old gentleman, in a sharp cocked hat, made his way through the crowd, putting them to the right and left with his elbows as he passed, and planting himself before Van Winkle, with one arm akimbo, the other resting on his cane, his keen eyes and sharp hat penetrating, as it were, into his very soul, demanded in an austere tone, "What brought him to the election with a gun on his shoulder, and a mob at his heels; and whether he meant to breed a riot in the village?" "Alas! gentlemen," cried Rip, somewhat dismayed, "I am a poor quiet man, a native of the place, and a loyal subject of the king, God bless him!"

Here a general shout burst from the bystanders—"A tory! a tory! a spy! a refugee! hustle him! away with him!" It was with great difficulty that the self-important man in the cocked hat restored order; and, having assumed a tenfold austerity of brow, demanded again of the unknown culprit, what he came there for, and whom he was seeking? The poor man humbly assured him that he meant no harm, but merely came there in search of some of his neighbours, who used to keep about the tavern.

"Well—who are they?—name them."

Rip bethought himself a moment, and inquired: "Where's Nicholas Vedder?"

There was a silence for a little while, when an old man replied, in a thin, piping voice, "Nicholas Vedder! why, he is dead and gone these eighteen years! There was a wooden tombstone in the churchyard that used to tell all about him, but that's rotten and gone too."

"Where's Brom Dutcher?"

"Oh, he went off to the army in the beginning of the war; some say he was killed at the storming of Stony Point—others say he was drowned in a squall at the foot of Antony's Nose. I don't know—he never came back again."

"Where's Van Bummel, the schoolmaster?"

"He went off to the wars too, was a great militia general, and is now in congress."

Rip's heart died away at hearing of these sad changes in his home and friends, and finding himself thus alone in the world. Every answer puzzled him too, by treating of such enormous lapses of time, and of matters which he could not understand: war—congress—Stony Point;—he had no courage to ask after any more friends, but cried out in despair: "Does nobody here know Rip Van Winkle?"

"Oh, Rip Van Winkle!" exclaimed two or three, "oh, to be sure! that's Rip Van Winkle yonder, leaning against the tree."

Rip looked, and beheld a precise counterpart of himself, as he went up the mountain; apparently as lazy, and certainly as ragged. The poor fellow was now completely confounded. He doubted his own identity, and whether he was himself or another man. In the midst of his bewilderment, the man in the cocked hat demanded who he was, and what was his name.

"God knows!" exclaimed he, at his wit's end; "I'm not myself—I'm somebody else—that's me yonder—no—that's somebody else got into my shoes—I was myself last night, but I fell asleep on the mountain, and they've changed my gun, and everything's changed, and I can't tell what's my name, or who I am!"

The bystanders began now to look at each other, nod, wink significantly, and tap their fingers against their foreheads. There was a whisper, also, about securing the gun, and keeping the old fellow from doing mischief, at the very suggestion of which the self-important man in the cocked hat retired with some precipitation. At this critical moment a fresh, comely woman pressed through the throng to get a peep at the grey-bearded man. She had a chubby child in her arms, which, frightened at his looks, began to cry. "Hush, Rip," cried she, "hush, you little fool; the old man won't hurt you." The name of the child, the air of the mother, the tone of her voice, all awakened a train of recollections in his mind. "What is your name, my good woman?" asked he.

"Judith Gardenier."

"And your father's name?"

"Ah, poor man, Rip Van Winkle was his name, but it's twenty years since he went away from home with his gun, and never has been heard of since,—his dog came home without him; but whether he shot himself, or was carried away by the Indians, nobody can tell. I was then but a little girl."

Rip had but one question more to ask; but he put it with a faltering voice:

"Where's your mother?"

"Oh, she too had died but a short time since; she broke a blood vessel in a fit of passion at a New-England pedler."

There was a drop of comfort, at least, in this intelligence. The honest man could contain himself no longer. He caught his daughter and her child in his arms. "I am your father!" cried he—"Young Rip Van Winkle once—old Rip Van Winkle now!—Does nobody know poor Rip Van Winkle?"

All stood amazed, until an old woman, tottering out from among the crowd, put her hand to her brow, and peering under it in his face for a moment, exclaimed: "Sure enough! it is Rip Van Winkle—it is himself!

Welcome home again, old neighbour. Why, where have you been these twenty long years?"

Rip's story was soon told, for the whole twenty years had seemed to him as but one night. The neighbours stared when they heard it; some were seen to wink at each other, and put their tongues in their cheeks; and the self-important man in the cocked hat, who, when the alarm was over, had returned to the field, screwed down the corners of his mouth, and shook his head—upon which there was a general shaking of the head throughout the assemblage.

It was determined, however, to take the opinion of old Peter Vanderdonk, who was seen slowly advancing up the road. He was a descendant of the historian of that name, who wrote one of the earliest accounts of the province. Peter was the most ancient inhabitant of the village, and well versed in all the wonderful events and traditions of the neighbourhood. He recollected Rip at once, and corroborated his story in the most satisfactory manner. He assured the company that it was a fact, handed down from his ancestor the historian, that the Kaatskill mountains had always been haunted by strange beings. That it was affirmed that the great Hendrick Hudson, the first discoverer of the river and country, kept a kind of vigil there every twenty years, with his crew of the Half-moon; being permitted in this way to revisit the scenes of his enterprise, and keep a guardian eye upon the river and the great city called by his name. That his father had once seen them in their old Dutch dresses playing at ninepins in a hollow of the mountain; and that he himself had heard, one summer afternoon, the sound of their balls, like distant peals of thunder.

To make a long story short, the company broke up and returned to the more important concerns of the election. Rip's daughter took him home to live with her; she had a snug, well-furnished house, and a stout, cheery farmer for a husband, whom Rip recollected for one of the urchins that used to climb upon his back. As to Rip's son and heir, who was the ditto of himself, seen leaning against the tree, he was employed to work on the farm; but evinced an hereditary disposition to attend to anything else but his business.

Rip now resumed his old walks and habits; he soon found many of his former cronies, though all rather the worse for the wear and tear of time; and preferred making friends among the rising generation, with whom he soon grew into great favour.

Having nothing to do at home, and being arrived at that happy age when a man can be idle with impunity, he took his place once more on the bench at the inn-door, and was reverenced as one of the patriarchs of the village, and a chronicle of the old times "before the war." It was some time before he could get into the regular track of gossip, or could be made to comprehend the strange events that had taken place during his torpor. How that there had been a revolutionary war,—that the country had thrown off the yoke of old England,—and that, instead of being a subject of his Majesty George the Third, he was now a free citizen of the United States. Rip, in fact, was no politician; the changes of states and empires made but little impression on him; but there was one species of despotism under which he had long groaned, and that was—petticoat government. Happily that was at an end; he had got his neck out of the yoke of matrimony, and could go in and out whenever he pleased, without dreading the tyranny of Dame Van Winkle. Whenever her name was mentioned, however, he shook his head, shrugged his shoulders, and cast up his eyes; which might pass either for an expression of resignation to his fate, or joy at his deliverance.

He used to tell his story to every stranger that arrived at Mr. Doolittle's hotel. He was observed, at first, to vary on some points every time he told it, which was, doubtless, owing to his having so recently awaked. It at last settled down precisely to the tale I have related, and not a man, woman, or child in the neighbourhood but knew it by heart. Some always pretended to doubt the reality of it, and insisted that Rip had been out of his head, and that this was one point on which he always remained flighty. The old Dutch inhabitants, however, almost universally gave it full credit. Even to this day they never hear a thunder-storm of a summer afternoon about the Kaatskill, but they say Hendrick Hudson and his crew are at their game of ninepins; and it is a common wish of all hen-pecked husbands in the neighbourhood, when life hangs heavy on their hands, that they might have a quieting draught out of Rip Van Winkle's flagon.

NOTE

The foregoing tale, one would suspect, had been suggested to Mr. Knickerbocker by a little German superstition about the Emperor Frederick *der Rothbart*, and the Kypphäuser mountain; the subjoined note, however, which he had appended to the tale, shows that it is an absolute fact, narrated with his usual fidelity.

"The story of Rip Van Winkle may seem incredible to many, but nevertheless I give it my full belief, for I know the vicinity of our old Dutch settlements to have been very subject to marvellous events and appearances. Indeed, I have heard many stranger stories than this, in the villages along the Hudson, all of which were too well authenticated to admit of a doubt. I have even talked with Rip Van Winkle myself, who, when last I saw him, was a very venerable old man, and so perfectly rational and consistent on every other point, that I think no conscientious person could refuse to take this into the bargain; nay, I have seen a certificate on the subject taken before a country justice and signed with a cross, in the justice's own handwriting. The story, therefore, is beyond the possibility of doubt.

"D. K."

POSTSCRIPT

The following are travelling notes from a memorandum-book of Mr. Knickerbocker.

The Kaatsberg or Catskill mountains have always been a region full of fable. The Indians considered them the abode of spirits, who influenced the weather, spreading sunshine or clouds over the landscape, and sending good or bad hunting seasons. They were ruled by an old squaw spirit, said to be their mother. She dwelt on the highest peak of the Catskills, and had charge of the doors of day and night to open and shut them at the proper hour. She hung up the new moons in the skies, and cut up the old ones into stars. In times of drought, if properly propitiated, she would spin light summer clouds out of cobwebs and morning dew, and send them off from the crest of the mountain, flake after flake, like flakes of carded cotton, to float in the air, until, dissolved by the heat of the sun, they would fall in gentle showers, causing the grass to spring, the fruits to ripen, and the corn to grow an inch an hour. If displeased, however, she would brew up clouds black as ink, sitting in the midst of them like a bottle-bellied spider in the midst of its web; and when these clouds broke, woe betide the valleys!

In old times, say the Indian traditions, there was a kind of Manitou or Spirit, who kept about the wildest recesses of the Catskill mountains, and took a mischievous pleasure in wreaking all kinds of evils and vexations upon the red men. Sometimes he would assume the form of a bear, a panther, or a deer, lead the bewildered hunter a weary chase through tangled forests and among ragged rocks, and then spring off with a loud ho! ho! leaving him aghast on the brink of a beetling precipice or raging torrent.

The favourite abode of this Manitou is still shown. It is a great rock or cliff on the loneliest part of the mountains, and, from the flowering vines which clamber about it, and the wild flowers which abound in its neighbourhood, is known by the name of the Garden Rock. Near the foot of it is a small lake, the haunt of the solitary bittern, with water-snakes basking in the sun on the leaves of the pond-lilies which lie on the surface. This place was held in great awe by the Indians, insomuch that the boldest hunter would not pursue his game within its precincts. Once upon a time, however, a hunter who had lost his way penetrated to the Garden Rock, where he beheld a number of gourds placed in the crotches of trees. One of these he seized and made off with it, but in the hurry of his retreat he let it fall among the rocks, when a great stream gushed forth, which washed him away and swept him down precipices, where he was dashed to pieces, and the stream made its way to the Hudson, and continues to flow to the present day, being the identical stream known by the name of the Kaaters-kill.

AMBROSE BIERCE

1

An Occurrence at the Owl Creek Bridge

I

A man stood upon a railroad bridge in northern Alabama, looking down into the swift water twenty feet below. The man's hands were behind his back, the wrists bound with a cord. A rope closely encircled his neck. It was attached to a stout cross-timber above his head and the slack fell to the level of his knees. Some loose boards laid upon the ties supporting the rails of the railway supplied a footing for him and his executioners—two private soldiers of the Federal army, directed by a sergeant who in civil life may have been a deputy sheriff. At a short remove upon the same temporary platform was an officer in the uniform of his rank, armed. He was a captain. A sentinel at each end of the bridge stood with his rifle in the position known as 'support,' that is to say, vertical in front of the left shoulder, the hammer resting on the forearm thrown straight across the chest—a formal and unnatural position, enforcing an erect carriage of the body. It did not appear to be the duty of these two men to know what was occurring at the center of the bridge; they merely blockaded the two ends of the foot planking that traversed it.

Beyond one of the sentinels nobody was in sight; the railroad ran straight away into a forest for a hundred yards, then, curving, was lost to view. Doubtless there was an outpost farther along. The other bank of the stream was open ground—a gentle slope topped with a stockade of vertical tree trunks, loopholed for rifles, with a single embrasure through which protruded the muzzle of a brass cannon commanding the bridge. Midway up the slope between the bridge and fort were the spectators—a single company of infantry in line, at 'parade rest,' the butts of their rifles on the ground, the barrels inclining slightly backward against the right shoulder, the hands crossed upon the stock. A lieutenant stood at the right of the line, the point of his sword upon the ground, his left hand resting upon his right. Excepting the group of four at the center of the bridge, not a man moved. The company faced the bridge, staring stonily, motionless. The sentinels, facing the banks of the stream, might have been statues to adorn the bridge. The captain stood with folded arms, silent, observing the work of his subordinates, but making no sign. Death is a dignitary who when he comes announced is to be received with formal manifestations of respect, even by those most familiar with him. In the code of military etiquette silence and fixity are forms of deference.

The man who was engaged in being hanged was apparently about thirty-five years of age. He was a civilian, if one might judge from his habit, which was that of a planter. His features were good—a straight nose, firm mouth, broad forehead, from which his long, dark hair was combed straight back, falling behind his ears to the collar of his well fitting frock coat. He wore a moustache and pointed beard, but no whiskers; his eyes were large and dark gray, and had a kindly expression which one would hardly have expected in one whose neck was in the hemp. Evidently this was no vulgar assassin. The liberal military code makes provision for hanging many kinds of persons, and gentlemen are not excluded.

The preparations being complete, the two private soldiers stepped aside and each drew away the plank upon which he had been standing. The sergeant turned to the captain, saluted and placed himself immediately behind that officer, who in turn moved apart one pace. These movements left the condemned man and the sergeant standing on the two ends of the same plank, which spanned three of the cross-ties of the bridge. The end upon which the civilian stood almost, but not quite, reached a fourth. This plank had been held in place by the weight of the captain; it was now held by that of the sergeant. At a signal from the former the latter would step aside, the plank would tilt and the condemned man go down between two ties. The arrangement commended itself to his judgement as simple and effective. His face had not been covered nor his eyes bandaged. He looked a moment at his 'unsteadfast footing,' then let his gaze wander to the swirling water of the stream racing madly beneath his feet. A piece of dancing driftwood caught his attention and his eyes followed it down the current. How slowly it appeared to move! What a sluggish stream!

He closed his eyes in order to fix his last thoughts upon his wife and children. The water, touched to gold by the early sun, the brooding mists under the banks at some distance down the stream, the fort, the soldiers, the piece of drift—all had distracted him. And now he became conscious of a new disturbance. Striking through the thought of his dear ones was sound which he could neither ignore nor understand, a sharp, distinct, metallic percussion like the stroke of a blacksmith's hammer upon the anvil; it had the same ringing quality. He wondered what it was, and whether immeasurably distant or near by—it seemed both. Its recurrence was regular, but as slow as the tolling of a death knell. He awaited each new stroke with impatience and—he knew not why—apprehension. The intervals of silence grew progressively longer; the delays became maddening. With their greater infrequency the sounds increased in strength and sharpness. They hurt his ear like the thrust of a knife; he feared he would shriek. What he heard was the ticking of his watch.

He unclosed his eyes and saw again the water below him. "If I could free my hands," he thought, "I might throw off the noose and spring into the stream. By diving I could evade the bullets and, swimming vigorously, reach the bank, take to the woods and get away home. My home, thank God, is as yet outside their lines; my wife and little ones are still beyond the invader's farthest advance."

As these thoughts, which have here to be set down in words, were flashed into the doomed man's brain rather than evolved from it the captain nodded to the sergeant. The sergeant stepped aside.

II

Peyton Farquhar was a well to do planter, of an old and highly respected Alabama family. Being a slave owner and like other slave owners a politician, he was naturally an original secessionist and ardently devoted to the Southern cause. Circumstances of an imperious nature, which it is unnecessary to relate here, had prevented him from taking service with that gallant army which had fought the disastrous campaigns ending with the fall of Corinth, and he chafed under the inglorious restraint, longing for the release of his energies, the larger life of the soldier, the opportunity for distinction. That opportunity, he felt, would come, as it comes to all in wartime. Meanwhile he did what he could. No service was too humble for him to perform in the aid of the South, no adventure too perilous for him to undertake if consistent with the character of a civilian who was at heart a soldier, and who in good faith and without too much qualification assented to at least a part of the frankly villainous dictum that all is fair in love and war.

One evening while Farquhar and his wife were sitting on a rustic bench near the entrance to his grounds, a gray-clad soldier rode up to the gate and asked for a drink of water. Mrs. Farquhar was only too happy to serve him with her own white hands. While she was fetching the water her husband approached the dusty horseman and inquired eagerly for news from the front.

"The Yanks are repairing the railroads," said the man, "and are getting ready for another advance. They have reached the Owl Creek bridge, put it in order and built a stockade on the north bank. The commandant has issued an order, which is posted everywhere, declaring that any civilian caught interfering with the railroad, its bridges, tunnels, or trains will be summarily hanged. I saw the order."

"How far is it to the Owl Creek bridge?" Farquhar asked.

"About thirty miles."

"Is there no force on this side of the creek?"

"Only a picket post half a mile out, on the railroad, and a single sentinel at this end of the bridge."

"Suppose a man—a civilian and student of hanging—should elude the picket post and perhaps get the better of the sentinel," said Farquhar, smiling, "what could he accomplish?"

The soldier reflected. "I was there a month ago," he replied. "I observed that the flood of last winter had lodged a great quantity of driftwood against the wooden pier at this end of the bridge. It is now dry and would burn like tinder."

The lady had now brought the water, which the soldier drank. He thanked her ceremoniously, bowed to her husband and rode away. An hour later, after nightfall, he repassed the plantation, going northward in the direction from which he had come. He was a Federal scout.

III

As Peyton Farquhar fell straight downward through the bridge he lost consciousness and was as one already dead. From this state he was awakened—ages later, it seemed to him—by the pain of a sharp pressure upon his throat, followed by a sense of suffocation. Keen, poignant agonies seemed to shoot from his neck downward through every fiber of his body and limbs. These pains appeared to flash along well defined lines of ramification and to beat with an inconceivably rapid periodicity. They seemed like streams of pulsating fire heating him to an intolerable temperature. As to his head, he was conscious of nothing but a feeling of fullness—of congestion. These sensations were unaccompanied by thought. The intellectual part of his nature was already effaced; he had power only to feel, and feeling was torment. He was conscious of motion. Encompassed in a luminous cloud, of which he was now merely the fiery heart, without material substance, he swung through unthinkable arcs of oscillation, like a vast pendulum. Then all at once, with terrible suddenness, the light about him shot upward with the noise of a loud splash; a frightful roaring was in his ears, and all was cold and dark. The power of thought was restored; he knew that the rope had broken and he had fallen into the stream. There was no additional strangulation; the noose about his neck was already suffocating him and kept the water from his lungs. To die of hanging at the bottom of a river!—the idea seemed to him ludicrous. He opened his eyes in the darkness and saw above him a gleam of light, but how distant, how inaccessible! He was still sinking, for the light became fainter and fainter until it was a mere glimmer. Then it began to grow and brighten, and he knew that he was rising toward the surface—knew it with reluctance, for he was now very comfortable. "To be hanged and drowned," he thought, "that is not so bad; but I do not wish to be shot. No; I will not be shot; that is not fair."

He was not conscious of an effort, but a sharp pain in his wrist apprised him that he was trying to free his hands. He gave the struggle his attention, as an idler might observe the feat of a juggler, without interest in the outcome. What splendid effort!—what magnificent, what superhuman strength! Ah, that was a fine endeavour! Bravo! The cord fell away; his arms parted and floated upward, the hands dimly seen on each side in the growing light. He watched them with a new interest as first one and then the other pounced upon the noose at his neck. They tore it away and thrust it fiercely aside, its undulations resembling those of a water snake. "Put it back, put it back!" He thought he shouted these words to his hands, for the undoing of the noose had been succeeded by the direst pang that he had yet experienced. His neck ached horribly; his brain was on fire, his heart, which had been fluttering faintly, gave a great leap, trying to force itself out at his mouth. His whole body was racked and wrenched with an insupportable anguish! But his disobedient hands gave no heed to the command. They beat the water vigorously with quick, downward strokes, forcing him to the surface. He felt his head emerge; his eyes were blinded by the sunlight; his chest expanded convulsively, and with a supreme and crowning agony his lungs engulfed a great draught of air, which instantly he expelled in a shriek!

He was now in full possession of his physical senses. They were, indeed, preternaturally keen and alert. Something in the awful disturbance of his organic system had so exalted and refined them that they made record of things never before perceived. He felt the ripples upon his face and heard their separate sounds as they struck. He looked at the forest on the bank of the stream, saw the individual trees, the leaves and the veining of each leaf—he saw the very insects upon them: the locusts, the brilliant bodied flies, the gray spiders stretching their webs from twig to twig. He noted the prismatic colours in all the dewdrops upon a million blades of grass. The humming of the gnats that danced above the eddies of the stream, the beating of the dragon flies' wings, the strokes of the water spiders' legs, like oars which had lifted their boat—all these made audible music. A fish slid along beneath his eyes and he heard the rush of its body parting the water.

He had come to the surface facing down the stream; in a moment the visible world seemed to wheel slowly round, himself the pivotal point, and he saw the bridge, the fort, the soldiers upon the bridge, the captain, the sergeant, the two privates, his executioners. They were in silhouette against the blue sky. They shouted and gesticulated, pointing at him. The captain had drawn his pistol, but did not fire; the others were unarmed. Their movements were grotesque and horrible, their forms gigantic.

Suddenly he heard a sharp report and something struck the water smartly within a few inches of his head, spattering his face with spray. He heard a second report, and saw one of the sentinels with his rifle at his shoulder, a light cloud of blue smoke rising from the muzzle. The man in the water saw the eye of the man on the bridge gazing into his own through the sights of the rifle. He observed that it was a gray eye and remembered having read that gray eyes were keenest, and that all famous marksmen had them. Nevertheless, this one had missed.

A counter-swirl had caught Farquhar and turned him half round; he was again looking at the forest on the bank opposite the fort. The sound of a clear, high voice in a monotonous singsong now rang out behind him and came across the water with a distinctness that pierced and subdued all other sounds, even the beating of the ripples in his ears. Although no soldier, he had frequented camps enough to know the dread significance of that deliberate, drawling, aspirated chant; the lieutenant on shore was taking a part in the morning's work. How coldly and pitilessly—with what an even, calm intonation, presaging, and enforcing tranquility in the men—with what accurately measured interval fell those cruel words:

"Company! . . . Attention! . . . Shoulder arms! . . . Ready! . . . Aim! . . . Fire!"

Farquhar dived—dived as deeply as he could. The water roared in his ears like the voice of Niagara, yet he heard the dull thunder of the volley and, rising again toward the surface, met shining bits of metal, singularly flattened, oscillating slowly downward. Some of them touched him on the face and hands, then fell away, continuing their descent. One lodged between his collar and neck; it was uncomfortably warm and he snatched it out.

As he rose to the surface, gasping for breath, he saw that he had been a long time under water; he was perceptibly farther downstream—nearer to safety. The soldiers had almost finished reloading; the metal ramrods flashed all at once in the sunshine as they were drawn from the barrels, turned in the air, and thrust into their sockets. The two sentinels fired again, independently and ineffectually.

The hunted man saw all this over his shoulder; he was now swimming vigorously with the current. His brain was as energetic as his arms and legs; he thought with the rapidity of lightning:

"The officer," he reasoned, "will not make that martinet's error a second time. It is as easy to dodge a volley as a single shot. He has probably already given the command to fire at will. God help me, I cannot dodge them all!"

An appalling splash within two yards of him was followed by a loud, rushing sound, DIMINUENDO, which seemed to travel back through the air to the fort and died in an explosion which stirred the very river to its deeps! A rising sheet of water curved over him, fell down upon him, blinded him, strangled him! The cannon had taken a hand in the game. As he shook his head free from the commotion of the smitten water he heard the deflected shot humming through the air ahead, and in an instant it was cracking and smashing the branches in the forest beyond.

"They will not do that again," he thought; "the next time they will use a charge of grape. I must keep my eye upon the gun; the smoke will apprise me—the report arrives too late; it lags behind the missile. That is a good gun."

Suddenly he felt himself whirled round and round—spinning like a top. The water, the banks, the forests, the now distant bridge, fort and men, all were commingled and blurred. Objects were represented by their colours only; circular horizontal streaks of colour—that was all he saw. He had been caught in a vortex and was being whirled on with a velocity of advance and gyration that made him giddy and sick. In few moments he was flung upon the gravel at the foot of the left bank of the stream—the southern bank—and behind a projecting point which concealed him from his enemies. The sudden arrest of his motion, the abrasion of one of his hands on the gravel, restored him, and he wept with delight. He dug his fingers into the sand, threw it over himself in handfuls and audibly blessed it. It looked like diamonds, rubies, emeralds; he could think of nothing beautiful which it did not resemble. The trees upon the bank were giant garden plants; he noted a definite order in their arrangement, inhaled the fragrance of their blooms. A strange roseate light shone through the spaces among their trunks and the wind made in their branches the music of Aeolian harps. He had not wish to perfect his escape—he was content to remain in that enchanting spot until retaken.

A whiz and a rattle of grapeshot among the branches high above his head roused him from his dream. The baffled cannoneer had fired him a random farewell. He sprang to his feet, rushed up the sloping bank, and plunged into the forest.

All that day he traveled, laying his course by the rounding sun. The forest seemed interminable; nowhere did he discover a break in it, not even a woodman's road. He had not known that he lived in so wild a region. There was something uncanny in the revelation.

By nightfall he was fatigued, footsore, famished. The thought of his wife and children urged him on. At last he found a road which led him in what he knew to be the right direction. It was as wide and straight as a city street, yet it seemed untraveled. No fields bordered it, no dwelling anywhere. Not so much as the barking of a dog suggested human habitation. The black bodies of the trees formed a straight wall on both sides, terminating on the horizon in a point, like a diagram in a lesson in perspective. Overhead, as he looked up through this rift in the wood, shone great golden stars looking unfamiliar and grouped in strange constellations. He was sure they were arranged in some order which had a secret and malign significance. The wood on either side was full of singular noises, among which—once, twice, and again—he distinctly heard whispers in an unknown tongue.

His neck was in pain and lifting his hand to it found it horribly swollen. He knew that it had a circle of black where the rope had bruised it. His eyes felt congested; he could no longer close them. His tongue was swollen with thirst; he relieved its fever by thrusting it forward from between his teeth into the cold air. How softly the turf had carpeted the untraveled avenue—he could no longer feel the roadway beneath his feet!

Doubtless, despite his suffering, he had fallen asleep while walking, for now he sees another scene—perhaps he has merely recovered from a delirium. He stands at the gate of his own home. All is as he left it, and all bright and beautiful in the morning sunshine. He must have traveled the entire night. As he pushes open the gate and passes up the wide white walk, he sees a flutter of female garments; his wife, looking fresh and cool and sweet, steps down from the veranda to meet him. At the bottom of the steps she stands waiting, with a smile of ineffable joy, an attitude of matchless grace and dignity. Ah, how beautiful she is! He springs forwards with extended arms. As he is about to clasp her he feels a stunning blow upon the back of the neck; a blinding white light blazes all about him with a sound like the shock of a cannon—then all is darkness and silence!

Peyton Farquhar was dead; his body, with a broken neck, swung gently from side to side beneath the timbers of the Owl Creek bridge.

2

The Stranger

A man stepped out of the darkness into the little illuminated circle about our failing campfire and seated himself upon a rock.

"You are not the first to explore this region," he said, gravely.

Nobody controverted his statement; he was himself proof of its truth, for he was not of our party and must have been somewhere near when we camped. Moreover, he must have companions not far away; it was not a place where one would be living or traveling alone. For more than a week we had seen, besides ourselves and our animals, only such living things as rattlesnakes and horned toads. In an Arizona desert one does not long coexist with only such creatures as these: one must have pack animals, supplies, arms—'an outfit.' And all these imply comrades. It was perhaps a doubt as to what manner of men this unceremonious stranger's comrades might be, together with something in his words interpretable as a challenge, that caused every man of our half-dozen 'gentlemen adventurers' to rise to a sitting posture and lay his hand upon a weapon—an act signifying, in that time and place, a policy of expectation. The stranger gave the matter no attention and began again to speak in the same deliberate, uninflected monotone in which he had delivered his first sentence:

"Thirty years ago Ramon Gallegos, William Shaw, George W. Kent and Berry Davis, all of Tucson, crossed the Santa Catalina mountains and traveled due west, as nearly as the configuration of the country permitted. We were prospecting and it was our intention, if we found nothing, to push through to the Gila river at some point near Big Bend, where we understood there was a settlement. We had a good outfit but no guide—just Ramon Gallegos, William Shaw, George W. Kent and Berry Davis."

The man repeated the names slowly and distinctly, as if to fix them in the memories of his audience, every member of which was now attentively observing him, but with a slackened apprehension regarding his possible companions somewhere in the darkness that seemed to enclose us like a black wall; in the manner of this volunteer historian was no suggestion of an unfriendly purpose. His act was rather that of a harmless lunatic than an enemy. We were not so new to the country as not to know that the solitary life of many a plainsman had a tendency to develop eccentricities of conduct and character not always easily distinguishable from mental aberration. A man is like a tree: in a forest of his fellows he will grow as straight as his generic and individual nature permits; alone in the open, he yields to the deforming stresses and tortions that environ him. Some such thoughts were in my mind as I watched the man from the shadow of my hat, pulled low to shut out the firelight. A witless fellow, no doubt, but what could he be doing there in the heart of a desert?

Having undertaken to tell this story, I wish that I could describe the man's appearance; that would be a natural thing to do. Unfortunately, and somewhat strangely, I find myself unable to do so with any degree of confidence, for afterward no two of us agreed as to what he wore and how he looked; and when I try to set down my own impressions they elude me. Anyone can tell some kind of story; narration is one of the elemental powers of the race. But the talent for description is a gift.

Nobody having broken silence the visitor went on to say:

"This country was not then what it is now. There was not a ranch between the Gila and the Gulf. There was a little game here and there in the mountains, and near the infrequent water-holes grass enough to keep our animals from starvation. If we should be so fortunate as to encounter no Indians we might get through. But within a week the purpose of the expedition had altered from discovery of wealth to preservation of life. We had gone too far to go back, for what was ahead could be no worse than what was behind; so we pushed on, riding by night to avoid Indians and the intolerable heat, and concealing ourselves by day as best we could.

Sometimes, having exhausted our supply of wild meat and emptied our casks, we were days without food or drink; then a water-hole or a shallow pool in the bottom of an arroyo so restored our strength and sanity that we were able to shoot some of the wild animals that sought it also. Sometimes it was a bear, sometimes an antelope, a coyote, a cougar—that was as God pleased; all were food.

"One morning as we skirted a mountain range, seeking a practicable pass, we were attacked by a band of Apaches who had followed our trail up a gulch—it is not far from here. Knowing that they outnumbered us ten to one, they took none of their usual cowardly precautions, but dashed upon us at a gallop, firing and yelling. Fighting was out of the question: we urged our feeble animals up the gulch as far as there was footing for a hoof, then threw ourselves out of our saddles and took to the chaparral on one of the slopes, abandoning our entire outfit to the enemy. But we retained our rifles, every man—Ramon Gallegos, William Shaw, George W. Kent and Berry Davis."

"Same old crowd," said the humorist of our party. He was an Eastern man, unfamiliar with the decent observances of social intercourse. A gesture of disapproval from our leader silenced him and the stranger proceeded with his tale:

"The savages dismounted also, and some of them ran up the gulch beyond the point at which we had left it, cutting off further retreat in that direction and forcing us on up the side. Unfortunately the chaparral extended only a short distance up the slope, and as we came into the open ground above we took the fire of a dozen rifles; but Apaches shoot badly when in a hurry, and God so willed it that none of us fell. Twenty yards up the slope, beyond the edge of the brush, were vertical cliffs, in which, directly in front of us, was a narrow opening. Into that we ran, finding ourselves in a cavern about as large as an ordinary room in a house. Here for a time we were safe: a single man with a repeating rifle could defend the entrance against all the Apaches in the land. But against hunger and thirst we had no defense. Courage we still had, but hope was a memory.

"Not one of those Indians did we afterward see, but by the smoke and glare of their fires in the gulch we knew that by day and by night they watched with ready rifles in the edge of the bush—knew that if we made a sortie not a man of us would live to take three steps into the open. For three days, watching in turn, we held out before our suffering became insupportable. Then—it was the morning of the fourth day—Ramon Gallegos said:

"'Senores, I know not well of the good God and what please him. I have live without religion, and I am not acquaint with that of you. Pardon, senores, if I shock you, but for me the time is come to beat the game of the Apache.'

"He knelt upon the rock floor of the cave and pressed his pistol against his temple. 'Madre de Dios,' he said, 'comes now the soul of Ramon Gallegos.'

"And so he left us—William Shaw, George W. Kent and Berry Davis.

"I was the leader: it was for me to speak.

"'He was a brave man,' I said—'he knew when to die, and how. It is foolish to go mad from thirst and fall by Apache bullets, or be skinned alive—it is in bad taste. Let us join Ramon Gallegos.'

"'That is right,' said William Shaw.

"'That is right,' said George W. Kent.

"I straightened the limbs of Ramon Gallegos and put a handkerchief over his face. Then William Shaw said: 'I should like to look like that—a little while.'

"And George W. Kent said that he felt that way, too.

"'It shall be so,' I said: 'the red devils will wait a week. William Shaw and George W. Kent, draw and kneel.'

"They did so and I stood before them.

"'Almighty God, our Father,' said I.

"'Almighty God, our Father,' said William Shaw.

"'Almighty God, our Father,' said George W. Kent.

"'Forgive us our sins,' said I.

"'Forgive us our sins,' said they.

"'And receive our souls.'

"'And receive our souls.'

"'Amen!'

"'Amen!'

"I laid them beside Ramon Gallegos and covered their faces."

There was a quick commotion on the opposite side of the campfire: one of our party had sprung to his feet, pistol in hand.

"And you!" he shouted—"YOU dared to escape?—You dare to be alive? You cowardly hound, I'll send you to join them if I hang for it!"

But with the leap of a panther the captain was upon him, grasping his wrist. "Hold it in, Sam Yountsey, hold it in!"

We were now all upon our feet—except the stranger, who sat motionless and apparently inattentive. Some one seized Yountsey's other arm.

"Captain," I said, "there is something wrong here. This fellow is either a lunatic or merely a liar—just a plain, every-day liar whom Yountsey has no call to kill. If this man was of that party it had five members, one of whom—probably himself—he has not named."

"Yes," said the captain, releasing the insurgent, who sat down, "there is something—unusual. Years ago four dead bodies of white men, scalped and shamefully mutilated, were found about the mouth of that cave. They are buried there; I have seen the graves—we shall all see them tomorrow."

The stranger rose, standing tall in the light of the expiring fire, which in our breathless attention to his story we had neglected to keep going.

"There were four," he said—"Ramon Gallegos, William Shaw, George W. Kent and Berry Davis."

With this reiterated roll-call of the dead he walked into the darkness and we saw him no more.

At that moment one of our party, who had been on guard, strode in among us, rifle in hand and somewhat excited.

"Captain," he said, "for the last half-hour three men have been standing out there on the mesa." He pointed in the direction taken by the stranger. "I could see them distinctly, for the moon is up, but as they had no guns and I had them covered with mine I thought it was their move. They have made none, but, damn it! they have got on to my nerves."

"Go back to your post, and stay till you see them again," said the captain. "The rest of you lie down again, or I'll kick you all into the fire."

The sentinel obediently withdrew, swearing, and did not return. As we were arranging our blankets the fiery Yountsey said: "I beg your pardon, Captain, but who the devil do you take them to be?"

"Ramon Gallegos, William Shaw and George W. Kent."

"But how about Berry Davis? I ought to have shot him."

"Quite needless; you couldn't have made him any deader. Go to sleep."

NATHANIEL HAWTHRONE

1

Young Goodman Brown

Young Goodman Brown came forth at sunset into the street at Salem village; but put his head back, after crossing the threshold, to exchange a parting kiss with his young wife. And Faith, as the wife was aptly named, thrust her own pretty head into the street, letting the wind play with the pink ribbons of her cap while she called to Goodman Brown.

"Dearest heart," whispered she, softly and rather sadly, when her lips were close to his ear, "prithee put off your journey until sunrise and sleep in your own bed to-night. A lone woman is troubled with such dreams and such thoughts that she's afeard of herself sometimes. Pray tarry with me this night, dear husband, of all nights in the year."

"My love and my Faith," replied young Goodman Brown, "of all nights in the year, this one night must I tarry away from thee. My journey, as thou callest it, forth and back again, must needs be done 'twixt now and sunrise. What, my sweet, pretty wife, dost thou doubt me already, and we but three months married?"

"Then God bless you!" said Faith, with the pink ribbons; "and may you find all well when you come back."

"Amen!" cried Goodman Brown. "Say thy prayers, dear Faith, and go to bed at dusk, and no harm will come to thee."

So they parted; and the young man pursued his way until, being about to turn the corner by the meeting-house, he looked back and saw the head of Faith still peeping after him with a melancholy air, in spite of her pink ribbons.

"Poor little Faith!" thought he, for his heart smote him. "What a wretch am I to leave her on such an errand! She talks of dreams, too. Methought as she spoke there was trouble in her face, as if a dream had warned her what work is to be done tonight. But no, no; 'twould kill her to think it. Well, she's a blessed angel on earth; and after this one night I'll cling to her skirts and follow her to heaven."

With this excellent resolve for the future, Goodman Brown felt himself justified in making more haste on his present evil purpose. He had taken a dreary road, darkened by all the gloomiest trees of the forest, which barely stood aside to let the narrow path creep through, and closed immediately behind. It was all as lonely as could be; and there is this peculiarity in such a solitude, that the traveller knows not who may be concealed by the innumerable trunks and the thick boughs overhead; so that with lonely footsteps he may yet be passing through an unseen multitude.

"There may be a devilish Indian behind every tree," said Goodman Brown to himself; and he glanced fearfully behind him as he added, "What if the devil himself should be at my very elbow!"

His head being turned back, he passed a crook of the road, and, looking forward again, beheld the figure of a man, in grave and decent attire, seated at the foot of an old tree. He arose at Goodman Brown's approach and walked onward side by side with him.

"You are late, Goodman Brown," said he. "The clock of the Old South was striking as I came through Boston, and that is full fifteen minutes agone."

"Faith kept me back a while," replied the young man, with a tremor in his voice, caused by the sudden appearance of his companion, though not wholly unexpected.

It was now deep dusk in the forest, and deepest in that part of it where these two were journeying. As nearly as could be discerned, the second traveller was about fifty years old, apparently in the same rank of life as Goodman Brown, and bearing a considerable resemblance to him, though perhaps more in expression than features. Still they might have been taken for father and son. And yet, though the elder person was as simply clad as the younger, and as simple in manner too, he had an indescribable air of one who knew the world, and who would not have felt abashed at the governor's dinner table or in King William's court, were it possible that his affairs should call him thither. But the only thing about him that could be fixed upon as remarkable was his staff, which bore the likeness of a great black snake, so curiously wrought that it might almost be seen to twist and wriggle itself like a living serpent. This, of course, must have been an ocular deception, assisted by the uncertain light.

"Come, Goodman Brown," cried his fellow-traveller, "this is a dull pace for the beginning of a journey. Take my staff, if you are so soon weary."

"Friend," said the other, exchanging his slow pace for a full stop, "having kept covenant by meeting thee here, it is my purpose now to return whence I came. I have scruples touching the matter thou wot'st of."

"Sayest thou so?" replied he of the serpent, smiling apart. "Let us walk on, nevertheless, reasoning as we go; and if I convince thee not thou shalt turn back. We are but a little way in the forest yet."

"Too far! too far!" exclaimed the goodman, unconsciously resuming his walk. "My father never went into the woods on such an errand, nor his father before him. We have been a race of honest men and good Christians since the days of the martyrs; and shall I be the first of the name of Brown that ever took this path and kept—"

"Such company, thou wouldst say," observed the elder person, interpreting his pause. "Well said, Goodman Brown! I have been as well acquainted with your family as with ever a one among the Puritans; and that's no trifle to say. I helped your grandfather, the constable, when he lashed the Quaker woman so smartly through the streets of Salem; and it was I that brought your father a pitch-pine knot, kindled at my own hearth, to set fire to an Indian village, in King Philip's war. They were my good friends, both; and many a pleasant walk have we had along this path, and returned merrily after midnight. I would fain be friends with you for their sake."

"If it be as thou sayest," replied Goodman Brown, "I marvel they never spoke of these matters; or, verily, I marvel not, seeing that the least rumor of the sort would have driven them from New England. We are a people of prayer, and good works to boot, and abide no such wickedness."

"Wickedness or not," said the traveller with the twisted staff, "I have a very general acquaintance here in New England. The deacons of many a church have drunk the communion wine with me; the selectmen of divers towns make me their chairman; and a majority of the Great and General

Court are firm supporters of my interest. The governor and I, too—But these are state secrets."

"Can this be so?" cried Goodman Brown, with a stare of amazement at his undisturbed companion. "Howbeit, I have nothing to do with the governor and council; they have their own ways, and are no rule for a simple husbandman like me. But, were I to go on with thee, how should I meet the eye of that good old man, our minister, at Salem village? Oh, his voice would make me tremble both Sabbath day and lecture day."

Thus far the elder traveller had listened with due gravity; but now burst into a fit of irrepressible mirth, shaking himself so violently that his snake-like staff actually seemed to wriggle in sympathy.

"Ha! ha! ha!" shouted he again and again; then composing himself, "Well, go on, Goodman Brown, go on; but, prithee, don't kill me with laughing."

"Well, then, to end the matter at once," said Goodman Brown, considerably nettled, "there is my wife, Faith. It would break her dear little heart; and I'd rather break my own."

"Nay, if that be the case," answered the other, "e'en go thy ways, Goodman Brown. I would not for twenty old women like the one hobbling before us that Faith should come to any harm."

As he spoke he pointed his staff at a female figure on the path, in whom Goodman Brown recognized a very pious and exemplary dame, who had taught him his catechism in youth, and was still his moral and spiritual adviser, jointly with the minister and Deacon Gookin.

"A marvel, truly, that Goody Cloyse should be so far in the wilderness at nightfall," said he. "But with your leave, friend, I shall take a cut through the woods until we have left this Christian woman behind. Being a stranger to you, she might ask whom I was consorting with and whither I was going."

"Be it so," said his fellow-traveller. "Betake you to the woods, and let me keep the path."

Accordingly the young man turned aside, but took care to watch his companion, who advanced softly along the road until he had come within a staff's length of the old dame. She, meanwhile, was making the best of her way, with singular speed for so aged a woman, and mumbling some indistinct words—a prayer, doubtless—as she went. The traveller put forth his staff and touched her withered neck with what seemed the serpent's tail.

"The devil!" screamed the pious old lady.

"Then Goody Cloyse knows her old friend?" observed the traveller, confronting her and leaning on his writhing stick.

"Ah, forsooth, and is it your worship indeed?" cried the good dame. "Yea, truly is it, and in the very image of my old gossip, Goodman Brown, the grandfather of the silly fellow that now is. But—would your worship believe it?—my broomstick hath strangely disappeared, stolen, as I suspect, by that unhanged witch, Goody Cory, and that, too, when I was all anointed with the juice of smallage, and cinquefoil, and wolf's bane."

"Mingled with fine wheat and the fat of a new-born babe," said the shape of old Goodman Brown.

"Ah, your worship knows the recipe," cried the old lady, cackling aloud. "So, as I was saying, being all ready for the meeting, and no horse to ride on, I made up my mind to foot it; for they tell me there is a nice young man to be taken into communion to-night. But now your good worship will lend me your arm, and we shall be there in a twinkling."

"That can hardly be," answered her friend. "I may not spare you my arm, Goody Cloyse; but here is my staff, if you will."

So saying, he threw it down at her feet, where, perhaps, it assumed life, being one of the rods which its owner had formerly lent to the Egyptian magi. Of this fact, however, Goodman Brown could not take cognizance. He had cast up his eyes in astonishment, and, looking down again, beheld neither Goody Cloyse nor the serpentine staff, but his fellow-traveller alone, who waited for him as calmly as if nothing had happened.

"That old woman taught me my catechism," said the young man; and there was a world of meaning in this simple comment.

They continued to walk onward, while the elder traveller exhorted his companion to make good speed and persevere in the path, discoursing so aptly that his arguments seemed rather to spring up in the bosom of his auditor than to be suggested by himself. As they went, he plucked a branch of maple to serve for a walking stick, and began to strip it of the twigs and little boughs, which were wet with evening dew. The moment his fingers touched them they became strangely withered and dried up as with a week's sunshine. Thus the pair proceeded, at a good free pace, until suddenly, in a gloomy hollow of the road, Goodman Brown sat himself down on the stump of a tree and refused to go any farther.

"Friend," said he, stubbornly, "my mind is made up. Not another step will I budge on this errand. What if a wretched old woman do choose to go to the devil when I thought she was going to heaven: is that any reason why I should quit my dear Faith and go after her?"

"You will think better of this by and by," said his acquaintance, composedly. "Sit here and rest yourself a while; and when you feel like moving again, there is my staff to help you along."

Without more words, he threw his companion the maple stick, and was as speedily out of sight as if he had vanished into the deepening gloom. The young man sat a few moments by the roadside, applauding himself greatly, and thinking with how clear a conscience he should meet the minister in his morning walk, nor shrink from the eye of good old Deacon Gookin. And what calm sleep would be his that very night, which was to have been spent so wickedly, but so purely and sweetly now, in the arms of Faith! Amidst these pleasant and praiseworthy meditations, Goodman Brown heard the tramp of horses along the road, and deemed it advisable to conceal himself within the verge of the forest, conscious of the guilty purpose that had brought him thither, though now so happily turned from it.

On came the hoof tramps and the voices of the riders, two grave old voices, conversing soberly as they drew near. These mingled sounds appeared to pass along the road, within a few yards of the young man's hiding-place; but, owing doubtless to the depth of the gloom at that particular spot, neither the travellers nor their steeds were visible. Though their figures brushed the small boughs by the wayside, it could not be seen that they intercepted, even for a moment, the faint gleam from the strip of bright sky athwart which they must have passed. Goodman Brown alternately crouched and stood on tiptoe, pulling aside the branches and thrusting forth his head as far as he durst without discerning so much as a shadow. It vexed him the more, because he could have sworn, were such a thing possible, that he recognized the voices of the minister and Deacon Gookin, jogging along quietly, as they were wont to do, when bound to some ordination or ecclesiastical council. While yet within hearing, one of the riders stopped to pluck a switch.

"Of the two, reverend sir," said the voice like the deacon's, "I had rather miss an ordination dinner than to-night's meeting. They tell me that some of our community are to be here from Falmouth and beyond, and others from Connecticut and Rhode Island, besides several of the Indian powwows, who, after their fashion, know almost as much deviltry as the best of us. Moreover, there is a goodly young woman to be taken into communion."

"Mighty well, Deacon Gookin!" replied the solemn old tones of the minister. "Spur up, or we shall be late. Nothing can be done, you know, until I get on the ground."

The hoofs clattered again; and the voices, talking so strangely in the empty air, passed on through the forest, where no church had ever been gathered or solitary Christian prayed. Whither, then, could these holy men be journeying so deep into the heathen wilderness? Young Goodman Brown caught hold of a tree for support, being ready to sink down on the ground, faint and overburdened with the heavy sickness of his heart. He looked up to the sky, doubting whether there really was a heaven above him. Yet there was the blue arch, and the stars brightening in it.

"With heaven above and Faith below, I will yet stand firm against the devil!" cried Goodman Brown.

While he still gazed upward into the deep arch of the firmament and had lifted his hands to pray, a cloud, though no wind was stirring, hurried across the zenith and hid the brightening stars. The blue sky was still visible, except directly overhead, where this black mass of cloud was sweeping swiftly northward. Aloft in the air, as if from the depths of the cloud, came a confused and doubtful sound of voices. Once the listener fancied that he could distinguish the accents of towns-people of his own, men and women, both pious and ungodly, many of whom he had met at the communion table, and had seen others rioting at the tavern. The next moment, so indistinct were the sounds, he doubted whether he had heard aught but the murmur of the old forest, whispering without a wind. Then came a stronger swell of those familiar tones, heard daily in the sunshine at Salem village, but never until now from a cloud of night There was one voice of a young woman, uttering lamentations, yet with an uncertain sorrow, and entreating for some favor, which, perhaps, it would grieve her to obtain; and all the unseen multitude, both saints and sinners, seemed to encourage her onward.

"Faith!" shouted Goodman Brown, in a voice of agony and desperation; and the echoes of the forest mocked him, crying, "Faith! Faith!" as if bewildered wretches were seeking her all through the wilderness.

The cry of grief, rage, and terror was yet piercing the night, when the unhappy husband held his breath for a response. There was a scream, drowned immediately in a louder murmur of voices, fading into far-off laughter, as the dark cloud swept away, leaving the clear and silent sky above Goodman Brown. But something fluttered lightly down through the air and caught on the branch of a tree. The young man seized it, and beheld a pink ribbon.

"My Faith is gone!" cried he, after one stupefied moment. "There is no good on earth; and sin is but a name. Come, devil; for to thee is this world given."

And, maddened with despair, so that he laughed loud and long, did Goodman Brown grasp his staff and set forth again, at such a rate that he seemed to fly along the forest path rather than to walk or run. The road grew wilder and drearier and more faintly traced, and vanished at length, leaving him in the heart of the dark wilderness, still rushing onward with the instinct that guides mortal man to evil. The whole forest was peopled with frightful sounds—the creaking of the trees, the howling of wild beasts, and the yell of Indians; while sometimes the wind tolled like a distant church bell, and sometimes gave a broad roar around the traveller, as if all Nature were laughing him to scorn. But he was himself the chief horror of the scene, and shrank not from its other horrors.

"Ha! ha! ha!" roared Goodman Brown when the wind laughed at him.

"Let us hear which will laugh loudest. Think not to frighten me with your deviltry. Come witch, come wizard, come Indian powwow, come devil himself, and here comes Goodman Brown. You may as well fear him as he fear you."

In truth, all through the haunted forest there could be nothing more frightful than the figure of Goodman Brown. On he flew among the black pines, brandishing his staff with frenzied gestures, now giving vent to an inspiration of horrid blasphemy, and now shouting forth such laughter as set all the echoes of the forest laughing like demons around him. The fiend in his own shape is less hideous than when he rages in the breast of man. Thus sped the demoniac on his course, until, quivering among the trees, he saw a red light before him, as when the felled trunks and branches of a clearing have been set on fire, and throw up their lurid blaze against the sky, at the hour of midnight. He paused, in a lull of the tempest that had driven him onward, and heard the swell of what seemed a hymn, rolling solemnly from a distance with the weight of many voices. He knew the tune; it was a familiar one in the choir of the village meeting-house. The verse died heavily away, and was lengthened by a chorus, not of human voices, but of all the sounds of the benighted wilderness pealing in awful harmony together. Goodman Brown cried out, and his cry was lost to his own ear by its unison with the cry of the desert.

In the interval of silence he stole forward until the light glared full upon his eyes. At one extremity of an open space, hemmed in by the dark wall of the forest, arose a rock, bearing some rude, natural resemblance either to an altar or a pulpit, and surrounded by four blazing pines, their tops aflame, their stems untouched, like candles at an evening meeting. The mass of foliage that had overgrown the summit of the rock was all on fire, blazing high into the night and fitfully illuminating the whole field. Each pendent twig and leafy festoon was in a blaze. As the red light arose and fell, a numerous congregation alternately shone forth, then disappeared in shadow, and again grew, as it were, out of the darkness, peopling the heart of the solitary woods at once.

"A grave and dark-clad company," quoth Goodman Brown.

In truth they were such. Among them, quivering to and fro between gloom and splendor, appeared faces that would be seen next day at the council board of the province, and others which, Sabbath after Sabbath, looked devoutly heavenward, and benignantly over the crowded pews, from the holiest pulpits in the land. Some affirm that the lady of the governor was there. At least there were high dames well known to her, and wives of honored husbands, and widows, a great multitude, and ancient maidens, all of excellent repute, and fair young girls, who trembled lest their mothers should espy them. Either the sudden gleams of light flashing over the obscure field bedazzled Goodman Brown, or he recognized a score of the church members of Salem village famous for their especial sanctity. Good old Deacon Gookin had arrived, and waited at the skirts of that venerable saint, his revered pastor. But, irreverently consorting with these grave, reputable, and pious people, these elders of the church, these chaste dames and dewy virgins, there were men of dissolute lives and women of spotted fame, wretches given over to all mean and filthy vice, and suspected even of horrid crimes. It was strange to see that the good shrank not from the wicked, nor were the sinners abashed by the saints. Scattered also among their pale-faced enemies were the Indian priests, or powwows, who had often scared their native forest with more hideous incantations than any known to English witchcraft.

"But where is Faith?" thought Goodman Brown; and, as hope came into his heart, he trembled.

Another verse of the hymn arose, a slow and mournful strain, such as the pious love, but joined to words which expressed all that our nature can conceive of sin, and darkly hinted at far more. Unfathomable to mere mortals is the lore of fiends. Verse after verse was sung; and still the chorus of the desert swelled between like the deepest tone of a mighty organ; and with the final peal of that dreadful anthem there came a sound, as if the roaring wind, the rushing streams, the howling beasts, and every other voice of the unconcerted wilderness were mingling and according with the voice of guilty man in homage to the prince of all. The four blazing pines threw up a loftier flame, and obscurely discovered shapes and visages of horror on the smoke wreaths above the impious assembly. At the same moment the fire on the rock shot redly forth and formed a glowing arch above its base, where now appeared a figure. With reverence be it spoken, the figure bore no slight similitude, both in garb and manner, to some grave divine of the New England churches.

"Bring forth the converts!" cried a voice that echoed through the field and rolled into the forest.

At the word, Goodman Brown stepped forth from the shadow of the trees and approached the congregation, with whom he felt a loathful brotherhood by the sympathy of all that was wicked in his heart. He could have well-nigh sworn that the shape of his own dead father beckoned him to advance, looking downward from a smoke wreath, while a woman, with dim features of despair, threw out her hand to warn him back. Was it his mother? But he had no power to retreat one step, nor to resist, even in thought, when the minister and good old Deacon Gookin seized his arms and led him to the blazing rock. Thither came also the slender form of a veiled female, led between Goody Cloyse, that pious teacher of the catechism, and Martha Carrier, who had received the devil's promise to be queen of hell. A rampant hag was she. And there stood the proselytes beneath the canopy of fire.

"Welcome, my children," said the dark figure, "to the communion of your race. Ye have found thus young your nature and your destiny. My children, look behind you!"

They turned; and flashing forth, as it were, in a sheet of flame, the fiend worshippers were seen; the smile of welcome gleamed darkly on every visage.

"There," resumed the sable form, "are all whom ye have reverenced from youth. Ye deemed them holier than yourselves, and shrank from your own sin, contrasting it with their lives of righteousness and prayerful aspirations heavenward. Yet here are they all in my worshipping assembly. This night it shall be granted you to know their secret deeds: how hoary-bearded elders of the church have whispered wanton words to the young maids of their households; how many a woman, eager for widows' weeds, has given her husband a drink at bedtime and let him sleep his last sleep in her bosom; how beardless youths have made haste to inherit their fathers' wealth; and how fair damsels—blush not, sweet ones—have dug little graves in the garden, and bidden me, the sole guest to an infant's funeral. By the sympathy of your human hearts for sin ye shall scent out all the places—whether in church, bedchamber, street, field, or forest—where crime has been committed, and shall exult to behold the whole earth one stain of guilt, one mighty blood spot. Far more than this. It shall be yours to penetrate, in every bosom, the deep mystery of sin, the fountain of all wicked arts, and which inexhaustibly supplies more evil impulses than human power—than my power at its utmost—can make manifest in deeds. And now, my children, look upon each other."

They did so; and, by the blaze of the hell-kindled torches, the wretched man beheld his Faith, and the wife her husband, trembling before that unhallowed altar.

"Lo, there ye stand, my children," said the figure, in a deep and solemn tone, almost sad with its despairing awfulness, as if his once angelic nature could yet mourn for our miserable race. "Depending upon one another's hearts, ye had still hoped that virtue were not all a dream. Now are ye undeceived. Evil is the nature of mankind. Evil must be your only happiness. Welcome again, my children, to the communion of your race."

"Welcome," repeated the fiend worshippers, in one cry of despair and triumph.

And there they stood, the only pair, as it seemed, who were yet hesitating on the verge of wickedness in this dark world. A basin was hollowed, naturally, in the rock. Did it contain water, reddened by the lurid light? or was it blood? or, perchance, a liquid flame? Herein did the shape of evil dip his hand and prepare to lay the mark of baptism upon their foreheads, that they might be partakers of the mystery of sin, more conscious of the secret guilt of others, both in deed and thought, than they could now be of their own. The husband cast one look at his pale wife, and Faith at him. What polluted wretches would the next glance show them to each other, shuddering alike at what they disclosed and what they saw!

"Faith! Faith!" cried the husband, "look up to heaven, and resist the wicked one."

Whether Faith obeyed he knew not. Hardly had he spoken when he found himself amid calm night and solitude, listening to a roar of the wind which died heavily away through the forest. He staggered against the rock, and felt it chill and damp; while a hanging twig, that had been all on fire, besprinkled his cheek with the coldest dew.

The next morning young Goodman Brown came slowly into the street of Salem village, staring around him like a bewildered man. The good old minister was taking a walk along the graveyard to get an appetite for breakfast and meditate his sermon, and bestowed a blessing, as he passed, on Goodman Brown. He shrank from the venerable saint as if to avoid an anathema. Old Deacon Gookin was at domestic worship, and the holy words of his prayer were heard through the open window. "What God doth the wizard pray to?" quoth Goodman Brown. Goody Cloyse, that excellent old Christian, stood in the early sunshine at her own lattice, catechizing a little girl who had brought her a pint of morning's milk. Goodman Brown snatched away the child as from the grasp of the fiend himself. Turning the corner by the meeting-house, he spied the head of Faith, with the pink ribbons, gazing anxiously forth, and bursting into such joy at sight of him that she skipped along the street and almost kissed her husband before the whole village. But Goodman Brown looked sternly and sadly into her face, and passed on without a greeting.

Had Goodman Brown fallen asleep in the forest and only dreamed a wild dream of a witch-meeting?

Be it so if you will; but, alas! it was a dream of evil omen for young Goodman Brown. A stern, a sad, a darkly meditative, a distrustful, if not a desperate man did he become from the night of that fearful dream. On the Sabbath day, when the congregation were singing a holy psalm, he could not listen because an anthem of sin rushed loudly upon his ear and drowned all the blessed strain. When the minister spoke from the pulpit with power and fervid eloquence, and, with his hand on the open Bible, of the sacred truths of our religion, and of saint-like lives and triumphant deaths, and of future bliss or misery unutterable, then did Goodman Brown turn pale, dreading lest the roof should thunder down upon the gray blasphemer and his hearers. Often, waking suddenly at midnight, he shrank from the bosom of Faith; and at morning or eventide, when the family knelt down at prayer, he scowled and muttered to himself, and gazed sternly at his wife, and turned away. And when he had lived long, and was borne to his grave a hoary corpse, followed by Faith, an aged woman, and children and grandchildren, a goodly procession, besides neighbors not a few, they carved no hopeful verse upon his tombstone, for his dying hour was gloom.

2

The Birth-Mark

In the latter part of the last century there lived a man of science, an eminent proficient in every branch of natural philosophy, who not long before our story opens had made experience of a spiritual affinity more attractive than any chemical one. He had left his laboratory to the care of an assistant, cleared his fine countenance from the furnace smoke, washed the stain of acids from his fingers, and persuaded a beautiful woman to become his wife. In those days when the comparatively recent discovery of electricity and other kindred mysteries of Nature seemed to open paths into the region of miracle, it was not unusual for the love of science to rival the love of woman in its depth and absorbing energy. The higher intellect, the imagination, the spirit, and even the heart might all find their congenial aliment in pursuits which, as some of their ardent votaries believed, would ascend from one step of powerful intelligence to another, until the philosopher should lay his hand on the secret of creative force and perhaps make new worlds for himself. We know not whether Aylmer possessed this degree of faith in man's ultimate control over Nature. He had devoted himself, however, too unreservedly to scientific studies ever to be weaned from them by any second passion. His love for his young wife might prove the stronger of the two; but it could only be by intertwining itself with his love of science, and uniting the strength of the latter to his own.

Such a union accordingly took place, and was attended with truly remarkable consequences and a deeply impressive moral. One day, very soon after their marriage, Aylmer sat gazing at his wife with a trouble in his countenance that grew stronger until he spoke.

"Georgiana," said he, "has it never occurred to you that the mark upon your cheek might be removed?"

"No, indeed," said she, smiling; but perceiving the seriousness of his manner, she blushed deeply. "To tell you the truth it has been so often called a charm that I was simple enough to imagine it might be so."

"Ah, upon another face perhaps it might," replied her husband; "but never on yours. No, dearest Georgiana, you came so nearly perfect from the hand of Nature that this slightest possible defect, which we hesitate whether to term a defect or a beauty, shocks me, as being the visible mark of earthly imperfection."

"Shocks you, my husband!" cried Georgiana, deeply hurt; at first reddening with momentary anger, but then bursting into tears. "Then why did you take me from my mother's side? You cannot love what shocks you!"

To explain this conversation it must be mentioned that in the centre of Georgiana's left cheek there was a singular mark, deeply interwoven, as it were, with the texture and substance of her face. In the usual state of her complexion—a healthy though delicate bloom—the mark wore a tint of deeper crimson, which imperfectly defined its shape amid the surrounding rosiness. When she blushed it gradually became more indistinct, and finally vanished amid the triumphant rush of blood that bathed the whole cheek with its brilliant glow. But if any shifting motion caused her to turn pale there was the mark again, a crimson stain upon the snow, in what Aylmer sometimes deemed an almost fearful distinctness. Its shape bore not a little similarity to the human hand, though of the smallest pygmy size. Georgiana's lovers were wont to say that some fairy at her birth hour had laid her tiny hand upon the infant's cheek, and left this impress there in token of the magic endowments that were to give her such sway over all hearts. Many a desperate swain would have risked life for the privilege of pressing his lips to the mysterious hand. It must not be concealed, however, that the impression wrought by this fairy sign manual varied exceedingly, according to the difference of temperament in the beholders. Some fastidious persons—but they were exclusively of her own sex—affirmed that the bloody hand, as they chose to call it, quite destroyed the effect of Georgiana's beauty, and rendered her countenance even hideous. But it would be as reasonable to say that one of those small blue stains which sometimes occur in the purest statuary marble would convert the Eve of Powers to a monster. Masculine observers, if the birthmark did not heighten their admiration, contented themselves with wishing it away, that the world might possess one living specimen of ideal loveliness without the semblance of a flaw. After his marriage,—for he thought little or nothing of the matter before,—Aylmer discovered that this was the case with himself.

Had she been less beautiful,—if Envy's self could have found aught else to sneer at,—he might have felt his affection heightened by the prettiness of this mimic hand, now vaguely portrayed, now lost, now stealing forth again and glimmering to and fro with every pulse of emotion that throbbed within her heart; but seeing her otherwise so perfect, he found this one defect grow more and more intolerable with every moment of their united lives. It was the fatal flaw of humanity which Nature, in one shape or another, stamps ineffaceably on all her productions, either to imply that they are temporary and finite, or that their perfection must be wrought by toil and pain. The crimson hand expressed the ineludible gripe in which mortality clutches the highest and purest of earthly mould, degrading them into kindred with the lowest, and even with the very brutes, like whom their visible frames return to dust. In this manner, selecting it as the symbol of his wife's liability to sin, sorrow, decay, and death, Aylmer's sombre imagination was not long in rendering the birthmark a frightful object, causing him more trouble and horror than ever Georgiana's beauty, whether of soul or sense, had given him delight.

At all the seasons which should have been their happiest, he invariably and without intending it, nay, in spite of a purpose to the contrary, reverted to this one disastrous topic. Trifling as it at first appeared, it so connected itself with innumerable trains of thought and modes of feeling that it became the central point of all. With the morning twilight Aylmer opened his eyes upon his wife's face and recognized the symbol of imperfection; and when they sat together at the evening hearth his eyes wandered stealthily to her cheek, and beheld, flickering with the blaze of the wood fire, the spectral hand that wrote mortality where he would fain have worshipped. Georgiana soon learned to shudder at his gaze. It needed but a glance with the peculiar expression that his face often wore to change the roses of her cheek into a deathlike paleness, amid which the crimson hand was brought strongly out, like a bass-relief of ruby on the whitest marble.

Late one night when the lights were growing dim, so as hardly to betray the stain on the poor wife's cheek, she herself, for the first time, voluntarily took up the subject.

"Do you remember, my dear Aylmer," said she, with a feeble attempt at a smile, "have you any recollection of a dream last night about this odious hand?"

"None! none whatever!" replied Aylmer, starting; but then he added, in a dry, cold tone, affected for the sake of concealing the real depth of his emotion, "I might well dream of it; for before I fell asleep it had taken a pretty firm hold of my fancy."

"And you did dream of it?" continued Georgiana, hastily; for she dreaded lest a gush of tears should interrupt what she had to say. "A terrible dream! I wonder that you can forget it. Is it possible to forget this one expression?—'It is in her heart now; we must have it out!' Reflect, my husband; for by all means I would have you recall that dream."

The mind is in a sad state when Sleep, the all-involving, cannot confine her spectres within the dim region of her sway, but suffers them to break forth, affrighting this actual life with secrets that perchance belong to a deeper one. Aylmer now remembered his dream. He had fancied himself with his servant Aminadab, attempting an operation for the removal of the birthmark; but the deeper went the knife, the deeper sank the hand, until at length its tiny grasp appeared to have caught hold of Georgiana's heart; whence, however, her husband was inexorably resolved to cut or wrench it away.

When the dream had shaped itself perfectly in his memory, Aylmer sat in his wife's presence with a guilty feeling. Truth often finds its way to the mind close muffled in robes of sleep, and then speaks with uncompromising directness of matters in regard to which we practise an unconscious self-deception during our waking moments. Until now he had not been aware of the tyrannizing influence acquired by one idea over his mind, and of the lengths which he might find in his heart to go for the sake of giving himself peace.

"Aylmer," resumed Georgiana, solemnly, "I know not what may be the cost to both of us to rid me of this fatal birthmark. Perhaps its removal may cause cureless deformity; or it may be the stain goes as deep as life itself. Again: do we know that there is a possibility, on any terms, of unclasping the firm gripe of this little hand which was laid upon me before I came into the world?"

"Dearest Georgiana, I have spent much thought upon the subject," hastily interrupted Aylmer. "I am convinced of the perfect practicability of its removal."

"If there be the remotest possibility of it," continued Georgiana, "let the attempt be made at whatever risk. Danger is nothing to me; for life, while this hateful mark makes me the object of your horror and disgust,—life is a burden which I would fling down with joy. Either remove this dreadful hand, or take my wretched life! You have deep science. All the world bears witness of it. You have achieved great wonders. Cannot you remove this little, little mark, which I cover with the tips of two small fingers? Is this beyond your power, for the sake of your own peace, and to save your poor wife from madness?"

"Noblest, dearest, tenderest wife," cried Aylmer, rapturously, "doubt not my power. I have already given this matter the deepest thought—thought which might almost have enlightened me to create a being less perfect than yourself. Georgiana, you have led me deeper than ever into the heart of science. I feel myself fully competent to render this dear cheek as faultless as its fellow; and then, most beloved, what will be my triumph when I shall have corrected what Nature left imperfect in her fairest work! Even Pygmalion, when his sculptured woman assumed life, felt not greater ecstasy than mine will be."

"It is resolved, then," said Georgiana, faintly smiling. "And, Aylmer, spare me not, though you should find the birthmark take refuge in my heart at last."

Her husband tenderly kissed her cheek—her right cheek—not that which bore the impress of the crimson hand.

The next day Aylmer apprised his wife of a plan that he had formed whereby he might have opportunity for the intense thought and constant watchfulness which the proposed operation would require; while Georgiana, likewise, would enjoy the perfect repose essential to its success. They were to seclude themselves in the extensive apartments occupied by Aylmer as a laboratory, and where, during his toilsome youth, he had made discoveries in the elemental powers of Nature that had roused the admiration of all the learned societies in Europe. Seated calmly in this laboratory, the pale philosopher had investigated the secrets of the highest cloud region and of the profoundest mines; he had satisfied himself of the causes that kindled and kept alive the fires of the volcano; and had explained the mystery of fountains, and how it is that they gush forth, some so bright and pure, and others with such rich medicinal virtues, from the dark bosom of the earth. Here, too, at an earlier period, he had studied the wonders of the human frame, and attempted to fathom the very process by which Nature assimilates all her precious influences from earth and air, and from the spiritual world, to create and foster man, her masterpiece. The latter pursuit, however, Aylmer had long laid aside in unwilling recognition of the truth—against which all seekers sooner or later stumble—that our great creative Mother, while she amuses us with apparently working in the broadest sunshine, is yet severely careful to keep her own secrets, and, in spite of her pretended openness, shows us nothing but results. She permits us, indeed, to mar, but seldom to mend, and, like a jealous patentee, on no account to make. Now, however, Aylmer resumed these half-forgotten investigations; not, of course, with such hopes or wishes as first suggested them; but because they involved much physiological truth and lay in the path of his proposed scheme for the treatment of Georgiana.

As he led her over the threshold of the laboratory, Georgiana was cold and tremulous. Aylmer looked cheerfully into her face, with intent to reassure her, but was so startled with the intense glow of the birthmark upon the whiteness of her cheek that he could not restrain a strong convulsive shudder. His wife fainted.

"Aminadab! Aminadab!" shouted Aylmer, stamping violently on the floor.

Forthwith there issued from an inner apartment a man of low stature, but bulky frame, with shaggy hair hanging about his visage, which was grimed with the vapors of the furnace. This personage had been Aylmer's underworker during his whole scientific career, and was admirably fitted for that office by his great mechanical readiness, and the skill with which, while incapable of comprehending a single principle, he executed all the details of his master's experiments. With his vast strength, his shaggy hair, his smoky aspect, and the indescribable earthiness that incrusted him, he seemed to represent man's physical nature; while Aylmer's slender figure, and pale, intellectual face, were no less apt a type of the spiritual element.

"Throw open the door of the boudoir, Aminadab," said Aylmer, "and burn a pastil."

"Yes, master," answered Aminadab, looking intently at the lifeless form of Georgiana; and then he muttered to himself, "If she were my wife, I'd never part with that birthmark."

When Georgiana recovered consciousness she found herself breathing an atmosphere of penetrating fragrance, the gentle potency of which had recalled her from her deathlike faintness. The scene around her looked like enchantment. Aylmer had converted those smoky, dingy, sombre rooms, where he had spent his brightest years in recondite pursuits, into a series of beautiful apartments not unfit to be the secluded abode of a lovely woman. The walls were hung with gorgeous curtains, which imparted the combination of grandeur and grace that no other species of adornment can achieve; and as they fell from the ceiling to the floor, their rich and ponderous folds, concealing all angles and straight lines, appeared to shut in the scene from infinite space. For aught Georgiana knew, it might be a pavilion among the clouds. And Aylmer, excluding the sunshine, which would have interfered with his chemical processes, had supplied its place with perfumed lamps, emitting flames of various hue, but all uniting in a soft, impurpled radiance. He now knelt by his wife's side, watching her earnestly, but without alarm; for he was confident in his science, and felt that he could draw a magic circle round her within which no evil might intrude.

"Where am I? Ah, I remember," said Georgiana, faintly; and she placed her hand over her cheek to hide the terrible mark from her husband's eyes.

"Fear not, dearest!" exclaimed he. "Do not shrink from me! Believe me, Georgiana, I even rejoice in this single imperfection, since it will be such a rapture to remove it."

"Oh, spare me!" sadly replied his wife. "Pray do not look at it again. I never can forget that convulsive shudder."

In order to soothe Georgiana, and, as it were, to release her mind from the burden of actual things, Aylmer now put in practice some of the light and playful secrets which science had taught him among its profounder lore. Airy figures, absolutely bodiless ideas, and forms of unsubstantial beauty came and danced before her, imprinting their momentary footsteps on beams of light. Though she had some indistinct idea of the method of these optical phenomena, still the illusion was almost perfect enough to warrant the belief that her husband possessed sway over the spiritual world. Then again, when she felt a wish to look forth from her seclusion, immediately, as if her thoughts were answered, the procession of external existence flitted across a screen. The scenery and the figures of actual life were perfectly represented, but with that bewitching, yet indescribable difference which always makes a picture, an image, or a shadow so much more attractive than the original. When wearied of this, Aylmer bade her cast her eyes upon a vessel containing a quantity of earth. She did so, with little interest at first; but was soon startled to perceive the germ of a plant shooting upward from the soil. Then came the slender stalk; the leaves gradually unfolded themselves; and amid them was a perfect and lovely flower.

"It is magical!" cried Georgiana. "I dare not touch it."

"Nay, pluck it," answered Aylmer,—"pluck it, and inhale its brief perfume while you may. The flower will wither in a few moments and leave nothing save its brown seed vessels; but thence may be perpetuated a race as ephemeral as itself."

But Georgiana had no sooner touched the flower than the whole plant suffered a blight, its leaves turning coal-black as if by the agency of fire.

"There was too powerful a stimulus," said Aylmer, thoughtfully.

To make up for this abortive experiment, he proposed to take her portrait by a scientific process of his own invention. It was to be effected by rays of light striking upon a polished plate of metal. Georgiana assented; but, on looking at the result, was affrighted to find the features of the portrait blurred and indefinable; while the minute figure of a hand appeared where the cheek should have been. Aylmer snatched the metallic plate and threw it into a jar of corrosive acid.

Soon, however, he forgot these mortifying failures. In the intervals of study and chemical experiment he came to her flushed and exhausted, but seemed invigorated by her presence, and spoke in glowing language of the resources of his art. He gave a history of the long dynasty of the alchemists, who spent so many ages in quest of the universal solvent by which the golden principle might be elicited from all things vile and base. Aylmer appeared to believe that, by the plainest scientific logic, it was altogether within the limits of possibility to discover this long-sought medium; "but," he added, "a philosopher who should go deep enough to acquire the power would attain too lofty a wisdom to stoop to the exercise of it." Not less singular were his opinions in regard to the elixir vitae. He more than intimated that it was at his option to concoct a liquid that should prolong life for years, perhaps interminably; but that it would produce a discord in Nature which all the world, and chiefly the quaffer of the immortal nostrum, would find cause to curse.

"Aylmer, are you in earnest?" asked Georgiana, looking at him with amazement and fear. "It is terrible to possess such power, or even to dream of possessing it."

"Oh, do not tremble, my love," said her husband. "I would not wrong either you or myself by working such inharmonious effects upon our lives; but I would have you consider how trifling, in comparison, is the skill requisite to remove this little hand."

At the mention of the birthmark, Georgiana, as usual, shrank as if a redhot iron had touched her cheek.

Again Aylmer applied himself to his labors. She could hear his voice in the distant furnace room giving directions to Aminadab, whose harsh, uncouth, misshapen tones were audible in response, more like the grunt or growl of a brute than human speech. After hours of absence, Aylmer reappeared and proposed that she should now examine his cabinet of chemical products and natural treasures of the earth. Among the former he showed her a small vial, in which, he remarked, was contained a gentle yet most powerful fragrance, capable of impregnating all the breezes that blow across a kingdom. They were of inestimable value, the contents of that little vial; and, as he said so, he threw some of the perfume into the air and filled the room with piercing and invigorating delight.

"And what is this?" asked Georgiana, pointing to a small crystal globe containing a gold-colored liquid. "It is so beautiful to the eye that I could imagine it the elixir of life."

"In one sense it is," replied Aylmer; "or, rather, the elixir of immortality. It is the most precious poison that ever was concocted in this world. By its aid I could apportion the lifetime of any mortal at whom you might point your finger. The strength of the dose would determine whether he were to linger out years, or drop dead in the midst of a breath. No king on his guarded throne could keep his life if I, in my private station, should deem that the welfare of millions justified me in depriving him of it."

"Why do you keep such a terrific drug?" inquired Georgiana in horror.

"Do not mistrust me, dearest," said her husband, smiling; "its virtuous potency is yet greater than its harmful one. But see! here is a powerful cosmetic. With a few drops of this in a vase of water, freckles may be washed away as easily as the hands are cleansed. A stronger infusion would take the blood out of the cheek, and leave the rosiest beauty a pale ghost."

"Is it with this lotion that you intend to bathe my cheek?" asked Georgiana, anxiously.

"Oh, no," hastily replied her husband; "this is merely superficial. Your case demands a remedy that shall go deeper."

In his interviews with Georgiana, Aylmer generally made minute inquiries as to her sensations and whether the confinement of the rooms and the temperature of the atmosphere agreed with her. These questions had such a particular drift that Georgiana began to conjecture that she was already subjected to certain physical influences, either breathed in with the fragrant air or taken with her food. She fancied likewise, but it might be altogether fancy, that there was a stirring up of her system—a strange, indefinite sensation creeping through her veins, and tingling, half painfully, half pleasurably, at her heart. Still, whenever she dared to look into the mirror, there she beheld herself pale as a white rose and with the crimson birthmark stamped upon her cheek. Not even Aylmer now hated it so much as she.

To dispel the tedium of the hours which her husband found it necessary to devote to the processes of combination and analysis, Georgiana turned over the volumes of his scientific library. In many dark old tomes she met with chapters full of romance and poetry. They were the works of philosophers of the middle ages, such as Albertus Magnus, Cornelius Agrippa, Paracelsus, and the famous friar who created the prophetic Brazen Head. All these antique naturalists stood in advance of their centuries, yet were imbued with some of their credulity, and therefore were believed, and perhaps imagined themselves to have acquired from the investigation of Nature a power above Nature, and from physics a sway over the spiritual world. Hardly less curious and imaginative were the early volumes of the Transactions of the Royal Society, in which the members, knowing little of the limits of natural possibility, were continually recording wonders or proposing methods whereby wonders might be wrought.

But to Georgiana the most engrossing volume was a large folio from her husband's own hand, in which he had recorded every experiment of his scientific career, its original aim, the methods adopted for its development, and its final success or failure, with the circumstances to which either event was attributable. The book, in truth, was both the history and emblem of his ardent, ambitious, imaginative, yet practical and laborious life. He handled physical details as if there were nothing beyond them; yet spiritualized them all, and redeemed himself from materialism by his strong and eager aspiration towards the infinite. In his grasp the veriest clod of earth assumed a soul. Georgiana, as she read, reverenced Aylmer and loved him more profoundly than ever, but with a less entire dependence on his judgment than heretofore. Much as he had accomplished, she could not but observe that his most splendid successes were almost invariably failures, if compared with the ideal at which he aimed. His brightest diamonds were the merest pebbles, and felt to be so by himself, in comparison with the inestimable gems which lay hidden beyond his reach. The volume, rich with achievements that had won renown for its author, was yet as melancholy a record as ever mortal hand had penned. It was the sad confession and continual exemplification of the shortcomings of the composite man, the spirit burdened with clay and working in matter, and of the despair that assails the higher nature at finding itself so miserably thwarted by the earthly part. Perhaps every man of genius in whatever sphere might recognize the image of his own experience in Aylmer's journal.

So deeply did these reflections affect Georgiana that she laid her face upon the open volume and burst into tears. In this situation she was found by her husband.

"It is dangerous to read in a sorcerer's books," said he with a smile, though his countenance was uneasy and displeased. "Georgiana, there are pages in that volume which I can scarcely glance over and keep my senses. Take heed lest it prove as detrimental to you."

"It has made me worship you more than ever," said she.

"Ah, wait for this one success," rejoined he, "then worship me if you will. I shall deem myself hardly unworthy of it. But come, I have sought you for the luxury of your voice. Sing to me, dearest."

So she poured out the liquid music of her voice to quench the thirst of his spirit. He then took his leave with a boyish exuberance of gayety, assuring her that her seclusion would endure but a little longer, and that the result was already certain. Scarcely had he departed when Georgiana felt irresistibly impelled to follow him. She had forgotten to inform Aylmer of a symptom which for two or three hours past had begun to excite her attention. It was a sensation in the fatal birthmark, not painful, but which induced a restlessness throughout her system. Hastening after her husband, she intruded for the first time into the laboratory.

The first thing that struck her eye was the furnace, that hot and feverish worker, with the intense glow of its fire, which by the quantities of soot clustered above it seemed to have been burning for ages. There was a distilling apparatus in full operation. Around the room were retorts, tubes, cylinders, crucibles, and other apparatus of chemical research. An electrical machine stood ready for immediate use. The atmosphere felt oppressively close, and was tainted with gaseous odors which had been tormented forth by the processes of science. The severe and homely simplicity of the apartment, with its naked walls and brick pavement, looked strange, accustomed as Georgiana had become to the fantastic elegance of her boudoir. But what chiefly, indeed almost solely, drew her attention, was the aspect of Aylmer himself.

He was pale as death, anxious and absorbed, and hung over the furnace as if it depended upon his utmost watchfulness whether the liquid which it was distilling should be the draught of immortal happiness or misery. How different from the sanguine and joyous mien that he had assumed for Georgiana's encouragement!

"Carefully now, Aminadab; carefully, thou human machine; carefully, thou man of clay!" muttered Aylmer, more to himself than his assistant. "Now, if there be a thought too much or too little, it is all over."

"Ho! ho!" mumbled Aminadab. "Look, master! look!"

Aylmer raised his eyes hastily, and at first reddened, then grew paler than ever, on beholding Georgiana. He rushed towards her and seized her arm with a gripe that left the print of his fingers upon it.

"Why do you come hither? Have you no trust in your husband?" cried he, impetuously. "Would you throw the blight of that fatal birthmark over my labors? It is not well done. Go, prying woman, go!"

"Nay, Aylmer," said Georgiana with the firmness of which she possessed no stinted endowment, "it is not you that have a right to complain. You mistrust your wife; you have concealed the anxiety with which you watch the development of this experiment. Think not so unworthily of me, my husband. Tell me all the risk we run, and fear not that I shall shrink; for my share in it is far less than your own."

"No, no, Georgiana!" said Aylmer, impatiently; "it must not be."

"I submit," replied she calmly. "And, Aylmer, I shall quaff whatever draught you bring me; but it will be on the same principle that would induce me to take a dose of poison if offered by your hand."

"My noble wife," said Aylmer, deeply moved, "I knew not the height and depth of your nature until now. Nothing shall be concealed. Know, then, that this crimson hand, superficial as it seems, has clutched its grasp into your being with a strength of which I had no previous conception. I have already administered agents powerful enough to do aught except to change your entire physical system. Only one thing remains to be tried. If that fail us we are ruined."

"Why did you hesitate to tell me this?" asked she.

"Because, Georgiana," said Aylmer, in a low voice, "there is danger."

"Danger? There is but one danger—that this horrible stigma shall be left upon my cheek!" cried Georgiana. "Remove it, remove it, whatever be the cost, or we shall both go mad!"

"Heaven knows your words are too true," said Aylmer, sadly. "And now, dearest, return to your boudoir. In a little while all will be tested."

He conducted her back and took leave of her with a solemn tenderness which spoke far more than his words how much was now at stake. After his departure Georgiana became rapt in musings. She considered the character of Aylmer, and did it completer justice than at any previous moment. Her heart exulted, while it trembled, at his honorable love—so pure and lofty that it would accept nothing less than perfection nor miserably make itself contented with an earthlier nature than he had dreamed of. She felt how much more precious was such a sentiment than that meaner kind which would have borne with the imperfection for her sake, and have been guilty of treason to holy love by degrading its perfect idea to the level of the actual; and with her whole spirit she prayed that, for a single moment, she might satisfy his highest and deepest conception. Longer than one moment she well knew it could not be; for his spirit was ever on the march, ever ascending, and each instant required something that was beyond the scope of the instant before.

The sound of her husband's footsteps aroused her. He bore a crystal goblet containing a liquor colorless as water, but bright enough to be the draught of immortality. Aylmer was pale; but it seemed rather the consequence of a highly-wrought state of mind and tension of spirit than of fear or doubt.

"The concoction of the draught has been perfect," said he, in answer to Georgiana's look. "Unless all my science have deceived me, it cannot fail."

"Save on your account, my dearest Aylmer," observed his wife, "I might wish to put off this birthmark of mortality by relinquishing mortality itself in preference to any other mode. Life is but a sad possession to those who have attained precisely the degree of moral advancement at which I stand. Were I weaker and blinder it might be happiness. Were I stronger, it might be endured hopefully. But, being what I find myself, methinks I am of all mortals the most fit to die."

"You are fit for heaven without tasting death!" replied her husband "But why do we speak of dying? The draught cannot fail. Behold its effect upon this plant."

On the window seat there stood a geranium diseased with yellow blotches, which had overspread all its leaves. Aylmer poured a small quantity of the liquid upon the soil in which it grew. In a little time, when the roots of the plant had taken up the moisture, the unsightly blotches began to be extinguished in a living verdure.

"There needed no proof," said Georgiana, quietly. "Give me the goblet I joyfully stake all upon your word."

"Drink, then, thou lofty creature!" exclaimed Aylmer, with fervid admiration. "There is no taint of imperfection on thy spirit. Thy sensible frame, too, shall soon be all perfect."

She quaffed the liquid and returned the goblet to his hand.

"It is grateful," said she with a placid smile. "Methinks it is like water from a heavenly fountain; for it contains I know not what of unobtrusive fragrance and deliciousness. It allays a feverish thirst that had parched me for many days. Now, dearest, let me sleep. My earthly senses are closing over my spirit like the leaves around the heart of a rose at sunset."

She spoke the last words with a gentle reluctance, as if it required almost more energy than she could command to pronounce the faint and lingering syllables. Scarcely had they loitered through her lips ere she was lost in slumber. Aylmer sat by her side, watching her aspect with the emotions proper to a man the whole value of whose existence was involved in the process now to be tested. Mingled with this mood, however, was the philosophic investigation characteristic of the man of science. Not the minutest symptom escaped him. A heightened flush of the cheek, a slight irregularity of breath, a quiver of the eyelid, a hardly perceptible tremor through the frame,—such were the details which, as the moments passed, he wrote down in his folio volume. Intense thought had set its stamp upon every previous page of that volume, but the thoughts of years were all concentrated upon the last.

While thus employed, he failed not to gaze often at the fatal hand, and not without a shudder. Yet once, by a strange and unaccountable impulse he pressed it with his lips. His spirit recoiled, however, in the very act, and Georgiana, out of the midst of her deep sleep, moved uneasily and murmured as if in remonstrance. Again Aylmer resumed his watch. Nor was it without avail. The crimson hand, which at first had been strongly visible upon the marble paleness of Georgiana's cheek, now grew more faintly outlined. She remained not less pale than ever; but the birthmark with every breath that came and went, lost somewhat of its former distinctness. Its presence had been awful; its departure was more awful still. Watch the stain of the rainbow fading out the sky, and you will know how that mysterious symbol passed away.

"By Heaven! it is well-nigh gone!" said Aylmer to himself, in almost irrepressible ecstasy. "I can scarcely trace it now. Success! success! And now it is like the faintest rose color. The lightest flush of blood across her cheek would overcome it. But she is so pale!"

He drew aside the window curtain and suffered the light of natural day to fall into the room and rest upon her cheek. At the same time he heard a gross, hoarse chuckle, which he had long known as his servant Aminadab's expression of delight.

"Ah, clod! ah, earthly mass!" cried Aylmer, laughing in a sort of frenzy, "you have served me well! Matter and spirit—earth and heaven—have both done their part in this! Laugh, thing of the senses! You have earned the right to laugh."

These exclamations broke Georgiana's sleep. She slowly unclosed her eyes and gazed into the mirror which her husband had arranged for that purpose. A faint smile flitted over her lips when she recognized how barely perceptible was now that crimson hand which had once blazed forth with such disastrous brilliancy as to scare away all their happiness. But then her eyes sought Aylmer's face with a trouble and anxiety that he could by no means account for.

"My poor Aylmer!" murmured she.

"Poor? Nay, richest, happiest, most favored!" exclaimed he. "My peerless bride, it is successful! You are perfect!"

"My poor Aylmer," she repeated, with a more than human tenderness, "you have aimed loftily; you have done nobly. Do not repent that with so high and pure a feeling, you have rejected the best the earth could offer. Aylmer, dearest Aylmer, I am dying!"

Alas! it was too true! The fatal hand had grappled with the mystery of life, and was the bond by which an angelic spirit kept itself in union with a mortal frame. As the last crimson tint of the birthmark—that sole token of human imperfection—faded from her cheek, the parting breath of the now perfect woman passed into the atmosphere, and her soul, lingering a moment near her husband, took its heavenward flight. Then a hoarse, chuckling laugh was heard again! Thus ever does the gross fatality of earth exult in its invariable triumph over the immortal essence which, in this dim sphere of half development, demands the completeness of a higher state. Yet, had Alymer reached a profounder wisdom, he need not thus have flung away the happiness which would have woven his mortal life of the selfsame texture with the celestial. The momentary circumstance was too strong for him; he failed to look beyond the shadowy scope of time, and, living once for all in eternity, to find the perfect future in the present.

EDITH WHARTON

1

Afterward

January 1910

I

"Oh, there is one, of course, but you'll never know it."

The assertion, laughingly flung out six months earlier in a bright June garden, came back to Mary Boyne with a sharp perception of its latent significance as she stood, in the December dusk, waiting for the lamps to be brought into the library.

The words had been spoken by their friend Alida Stair, as they sat at tea on her lawn at Pangbourne, in reference to the very house of which the library in question was the central, the pivotal "feature." Mary Boyne and her husband, in quest of a country place in one of the southern or southwestern counties, had, on their arrival in England, carried their problem straight to Alida Stair, who had successfully solved it in her own case; but it was not until they had rejected, almost capriciously, several practical and judicious suggestions that she threw it out: "Well, there's Lyng, in Dorsetshire. It belongs to Hugo's cousins, and you can get it for a song."

The reasons she gave for its being obtainable on these terms—its remoteness from a station, its lack of electric light, hot-water pipes, and other vulgar necessities—were exactly those pleading in its favor with two romantic Americans perversely in search of the economic drawbacks which were associated, in their tradition, with unusual architectural felicities.

"I should never believe I was living in an old house unless I was thoroughly uncomfortable," Ned Boyne, the more extravagant of the two, had jocosely insisted; "the least hint of 'convenience' would make me think it had been bought out of an exhibition, with the pieces numbered, and set up again." And they had proceeded to enumerate, with humorous precision, their various suspicions and exactions, refusing to believe that the house their cousin recommended was really Tudor till they learned it had no heating system, or that the village church was literally in the grounds till she assured them of the deplorable uncertainty of the water-supply.

"It's too uncomfortable to be true!" Edward Boyne had continued to exult as the avowal of each disadvantage was successively wrung from her; but he had cut short his rhapsody to ask, with a sudden relapse to distrust: "And the ghost? You've been concealing from us the fact that there is no ghost!"

Mary, at the moment, had laughed with him, yet almost with her laugh, being possessed of several sets of independent perceptions, had noted a sudden flatness of tone in Alida's answering hilarity.

"Oh, Dorsetshire's full of ghosts, you know."

"Yes, yes; but that won't do. I don't want to have to drive ten miles to see somebody else's ghost. I want one of my own on the premises. Is there a ghost at Lyng?"

His rejoinder had made Alida laugh again, and it was then that she had flung back tantalizingly: "Oh, there is one, of course, but you'll never know it."

"Never know it?" Boyne pulled her up. "But what in the world constitutes a ghost except the fact of its being known for one?"

"I can't say. But that's the story."

"That there's a ghost, but that nobody knows it's a ghost?"

"Well—not till afterward, at any rate."

"Till afterward?"

"Not till long, long afterward."

"But if it's once been identified as an unearthly visitant, why hasn't its signalement been handed down in the family? How has it managed to preserve its incognito?"

Alida could only shake her head. "Don't ask me. But it has."

"And then suddenly—" Mary spoke up as if from some cavernous depth of divination—"suddenly, long afterward, one says to one's self, 'that was it?'"

She was oddly startled at the sepulchral sound with which her question fell on the banter of the other two, and she saw the shadow of the same surprise flit across Alida's clear pupils. "I suppose so. One just has to wait."

"Oh, hang waiting!" Ned broke in. "Life's too short for a ghost who can only be enjoyed in retrospect. Can't we do better than that, Mary?"

But it turned out that in the event they were not destined to, for within three months of their conversation with Mrs. Stair they were established at Lyng, and the life they had yearned for to the point of planning it out in all its daily details had actually begun for them.

It was to sit, in the thick December dusk, by just such a wide-hooded fireplace, under just such black oak rafters, with the sense that beyond the mullioned panes the downs were darkening to a deeper solitude: it was for the ultimate indulgence in such sensations that Mary Boyne had endured for nearly fourteen years the soul-deadening ugliness of the Middle West, and that Boyne had ground on doggedly at his engineering till, with a suddenness that still made her blink, the prodigious windfall of the Blue Star Mine had put them at a stroke in possession of life and the leisure to taste it. They had never for a moment meant their new state to be one of idleness; but they meant to give themselves only to harmonious activities. She had her vision of painting and gardening (against a background of gray walls), he dreamed of the production of his long-planned book on the "Economic Basis of Culture"; and with such absorbing work ahead no existence could be too sequestered; they could not get far enough from the world, or plunge deep enough into the past.

Dorsetshire had attracted them from the first by a semblance of remoteness out of all proportion to its geographical position. But to the Boynes it was one of the ever-recurring wonders of the whole incredibly compressed island—a nest of counties, as they put it—that for the production of its effects so little of a given quality went so far: that so few miles made a distance, and so short a distance a difference.

"It's that," Ned had once enthusiastically explained, "that gives such depth to their effects, such relief to their least contrasts. They've been able to lay the butter so thick on every exquisite mouthful."

The butter had certainly been laid on thick at Lyng: the old gray house, hidden under a shoulder of the downs, had almost all the finer marks of commerce with a protracted past. The mere fact that it was neither large nor exceptional made it, to the Boynes, abound the more richly in its special sense—the sense of having been for centuries a deep, dim reservoir of life. The life had probably not been of the most vivid order: for long periods, no doubt, it had fallen as noiselessly into the past as the quiet drizzle of autumn fell, hour after hour, into the green fish-pond between the yews; but these back-waters of existence sometimes breed, in their sluggish depths, strange acuities of emotion, and Mary Boyne had felt from the first the occasional brush of an intenser memory.

The feeling had never been stronger than on the December afternoon when, waiting in the library for the belated lamps, she rose from her seat and stood among the shadows of the hearth. Her husband had gone off, after luncheon, for one of his long tramps on the downs. She had noticed of late that he preferred to be unaccompanied on these occasions; and, in the tried security of their personal relations, had been driven to conclude that his book was bothering him, and that he needed the afternoons to turn over in solitude the problems left from the morning's work. Certainly the book was not going as smoothly as she had imagined it would, and the lines of perplexity between his eyes had never been there in his engineering days. Then he had often looked fagged to the verge of illness, but the native demon of "worry" had never branded his brow. Yet the few pages he had so far read to her—the introduction, and a synopsis of the opening chapter—gave evidences of a firm possession of his subject, and a deepening confidence in his powers.

The fact threw her into deeper perplexity, since, now that he had done with "business" and its disturbing contingencies, the one other possible element of anxiety was eliminated. Unless it were his health, then? But physically he had gained since they had come to Dorsetshire, grown robuster, ruddier, and fresher-eyed. It was only within a week that she had felt in him the undefinable change that made her restless in his absence, and as tongue-tied in his presence as though it were she who had a secret to keep from him!

The thought that there was a secret somewhere between them struck her with a sudden smart rap of wonder, and she looked about her down the dim, long room.

"Can it be the house?" she mused.

The room itself might have been full of secrets. They seemed to be piling themselves up, as evening fell, like the layers and layers of velvet shadow dropping from the low ceiling, the dusky walls of books, the smoke-blurred sculpture of the hooded hearth.

"Why, of course—the house is haunted!" she reflected.

The ghost—Alida's imperceptible ghost—after figuring largely in the banter of their first month or two at Lyng, had been gradually discarded as too ineffectual for imaginative use. Mary had, indeed, as became the tenant of a haunted house, made the customary inquiries among her few rural neighbors, but, beyond a vague, "They du say so, Ma'am," the villagers had nothing to impart. The elusive specter had apparently never had sufficient identity for a legend to crystallize about it, and after a time the Boynes had laughingly set the matter down to their profit-and-loss account, agreeing that Lyng was one of the few houses good enough in itself to dispense with supernatural enhancements.

"And I suppose, poor, ineffectual demon, that's why it beats its beautiful wings in vain in the void," Mary had laughingly concluded.

"Or, rather," Ned answered, in the same strain, "why, amid so much that's ghostly, it can never affirm its separate existence as the ghost." And thereupon their invisible housemate had finally dropped out of their references, which were numerous enough to make them promptly unaware of the loss.

Now, as she stood on the hearth, the subject of their earlier curiosity revived in her with a new sense of its meaning—a sense gradually acquired through close daily contact with the scene of the lurking mystery. It was the house itself, of course, that possessed the ghost-seeing faculty, that communed visually but secretly with its own past; and if one could only get into close enough communion with the house, one might surprise its secret, and acquire the ghost-sight on one's own account. Perhaps, in his long solitary hours in this very room, where she never trespassed till the afternoon, her husband had acquired it already, and was silently carrying the dread weight of whatever it had revealed to him. Mary was too well-versed in the code of the spectral world not to know that one could not talk about the ghosts one saw: to do so was almost as great a breach of good-breeding as to name a lady in a club. But this explanation did not really satisfy her. "What, after all, except for the fun of the frisson," she reflected, "would he really care for any of their old ghosts?" And thence she was thrown back once more on the fundamental dilemma: the fact that one's greater or less susceptibility to spectral influences had no particular bearing on the case, since, when one did see a ghost at Lyng, one did not know it.

"Not till long afterward," Alida Stair had said. Well, supposing Ned had seen one when they first came, and had known only within the last week what had happened to him? More and more under the spell of the hour, she threw back her searching thoughts to the early days of their tenancy, but at first only to recall a gay confusion of unpacking, settling, arranging of books, and calling to each other from remote corners of the house as treasure after treasure of their habitation revealed itself to them. It was in this particular connection that she presently recalled a certain soft afternoon of the previous October, when, passing from the first rapturous flurry of exploration to a detailed inspection of the old house, she had pressed (like a novel heroine) a panel that opened at her touch, on a narrow flight of stairs leading to an unsuspected flat ledge of the roof—the roof which, from below, seemed to slope away on all sides too abruptly for any but practised feet to scale.

The view from this hidden coign was enchanting, and she had flown down to snatch Ned from his papers and give him the freedom of her discovery. She remembered still how, standing on the narrow ledge, he had passed his arm about her while their gaze flew to the long, tossed horizon-line of the downs, and then dropped contentedly back to trace the arabesque of yew hedges about the fish-pond, and the shadow of the cedar on the lawn.

"And now the other way," he had said, gently turning her about within his arm; and closely pressed to him, she had absorbed, like some long, satisfying draft, the picture of the gray-walled court, the squat lions on the gates, and the lime-avenue reaching up to the highroad under the downs.

It was just then, while they gazed and held each other, that she had felt his arm relax, and heard a sharp "Hullo!" that made her turn to glance at him.

Distinctly, yes, she now recalled she had seen, as she glanced, a shadow of anxiety, of perplexity, rather, fall across his face; and, following his eyes, had beheld the figure of a man—a man in loose, grayish clothes, as it appeared to her—who was sauntering down the lime-avenue to the court with the tentative gait of a stranger seeking his way. Her short-sighted eyes had given her but a blurred impression of slightness and grayness, with something foreign, or at least unlocal, in the cut of the figure or its garb; but her husband had apparently seen more—seen enough to make him push past her with a sharp "Wait!" and dash down the twisting stairs without pausing to give her a hand for the descent.

A slight tendency to dizziness obliged her, after a provisional clutch at the chimney against which they had been leaning, to follow him down more cautiously; and when she had reached the attic landing she paused again for a less definite reason, leaning over the oak banister to strain her eyes through the silence of the brown, sun-flecked depths below. She lingered there till, somewhere in those depths, she heard the closing of a door; then, mechanically impelled, she went down the shallow flights of steps till she reached the lower hall.

The front door stood open on the mild sunlight of the court, and hall and court were empty. The library door was open, too, and after listening in vain for any sound of voices within, she quickly crossed the threshold, and found her husband alone, vaguely fingering the papers on his desk.

He looked up, as if surprised at her precipitate entrance, but the shadow of anxiety had passed from his face, leaving it even, as she fancied, a little brighter and clearer than usual.

"What was it? Who was it?" she asked.

"Who?" he repeated, with the surprise still all on his side.

"The man we saw coming toward the house."

He seemed honestly to reflect. "The man? Why, I thought I saw Peters; I dashed after him to say a word about the stable-drains, but he had disappeared before I could get down."

"Disappeared? Why, he seemed to be walking so slowly when we saw him."

Boyne shrugged his shoulders. "So I thought; but he must have got up steam in the interval. What do you say to our trying a scramble up Meldon Steep before sunset?"

That was all. At the time the occurrence had been less than nothing, had, indeed, been immediately obliterated by the magic of their first vision from Meldon Steep, a height which they had dreamed of climbing ever since they had first seen its bare spine heaving itself above the low roof of Lyng. Doubtless it was the mere fact of the other incident's having occurred on the very day of their ascent to Meldon that had kept it stored away in the unconscious fold of association from which it now emerged; for in itself it had no mark of the portentous. At the moment there could have been nothing more natural than that Ned should dash himself from the roof in the pursuit of dilatory tradesmen. It was the period when they were always on the watch for one or the other of the specialists employed about the place; always lying in wait for them, and dashing out at them with questions, reproaches, or reminders. And certainly in the distance the gray figure had looked like Peters.

Yet now, as she reviewed the rapid scene, she felt her husband's explanation of it to have been invalidated by the look of anxiety on his face. Why had the familiar appearance of Peters made him anxious? Why, above all, if it was of such prime necessity to confer with that authority on the subject of the stable-drains, had the failure to find him produced such a look of relief? Mary could not say that any one of these considerations had occurred to her at the time, yet, from the promptness with which they now marshaled themselves at her summons, she had a sudden sense that they must all along have been there, waiting their hour.

II

Weary with her thoughts, she moved toward the window. The library was now completely dark, and she was surprised to see how much faint light the outer world still held.

As she peered out into it across the court, a figure shaped itself in the tapering perspective of bare lines: it looked a mere blot of deeper gray in the grayness, and for an instant, as it moved toward her, her heart thumped to the thought, "It's the ghost!"

She had time, in that long instant, to feel suddenly that the man of whom, two months earlier, she had a brief distant vision from the roof was now, at his predestined hour, about to reveal himself as not having been Peters; and her spirit sank under the impending fear of the disclosure. But almost with the next tick of the clock the ambiguous figure, gaining substance and character, showed itself even to her weak sight as her husband's; and she turned away to meet him, as he entered, with the confession of her folly.

"It's really too absurd," she laughed out from the threshold, "but I never can remember!"

"Remember what?" Boyne questioned as they drew together.

"That when one sees the Lyng ghost one never knows it."

Her hand was on his sleeve, and he kept it there, but with no response in his gesture or in the lines of his fagged, preoccupied face.

"Did you think you'd seen it?" he asked, after an appreciable interval.

"Why, I actually took you for it, my dear, in my mad determination to spot it!"

"Me—just now?" His arm dropped away, and he turned from her with a faint echo of her laugh. "Really, dearest, you'd better give it up, if that's the best you can do."

"Yes, I give it up—I give it up. Have you?" she asked, turning round on him abruptly.

The parlor-maid had entered with letters and a lamp, and the light struck up into Boyne's face as he bent above the tray she presented.

"Have you?" Mary perversely insisted, when the servant had disappeared on her errand of illumination.

"Have I what?" he rejoined absently, the light bringing out the sharp stamp of worry between his brows as he turned over the letters.

"Given up trying to see the ghost." Her heart beat a little at the experiment she was making.

Her husband, laying his letters aside, moved away into the shadow of the hearth.

"I never tried," he said, tearing open the wrapper of a newspaper.

"Well, of course," Mary persisted, "the exasperating thing is that there's no use trying, since one can't be sure till so long afterward."

He was unfolding the paper as if he had hardly heard her; but after a pause, during which the sheets rustled spasmodically between his hands, he lifted his head to say abruptly, "Have you any idea how long?"

Mary had sunk into a low chair beside the fireplace. From her seat she looked up, startled, at her husband's profile, which was darkly projected against the circle of lamplight.

"No; none. Have you?" she retorted, repeating her former phrase with an added keenness of intention.

Boyne crumpled the paper into a bunch, and then inconsequently turned back with it toward the lamp.

"Lord, no! I only meant," he explained, with a faint tinge of impatience, "is there any legend, any tradition, as to that?"

"Not that I know of," she answered; but the impulse to add, "What makes you ask?" was checked by the reappearance of the parlor-maid with tea and a second lamp.

With the dispersal of shadows, and the repetition of the daily domestic office, Mary Boyne felt herself less oppressed by that sense of something mutely imminent which had darkened her solitary afternoon. For a few moments she gave herself silently to the details of her task, and when she looked up from it she was struck to the point of bewilderment by the change in her husband's face. He had seated himself near the farther lamp, and was absorbed in the perusal of his letters; but was it something he had found in them, or merely the shifting of her own point of view, that had restored his features to their normal aspect? The longer she looked, the more definitely the change affirmed itself. The lines of painful tension had vanished, and such traces of fatigue as lingered were of the kind easily attributable to steady mental effort. He glanced up, as if drawn by her gaze, and met her eyes with a smile.

"I'm dying for my tea, you know; and here's a letter for you," he said.

She took the letter he held out in exchange for the cup she proffered him, and, returning to her seat, broke the seal with the languid gesture of the reader whose interests are all inclosed in the circle of one cherished presence.

Her next conscious motion was that of starting to her feet, the letter falling to them as she rose, while she held out to her husband a long newspaper clipping.

"Ned! What's this? What does it mean?"

He had risen at the same instant, almost as if hearing her cry before she uttered it; and for a perceptible space of time he and she studied each other, like adversaries watching for an advantage, across the space between her chair and his desk.

"What's what? You fairly made me jump!" Boyne said at length, moving toward her with a sudden, half-exasperated laugh. The shadow of apprehension was on his face again, not now a look of fixed foreboding, but a shifting vigilance of lips and eyes that gave her the sense of his feeling himself invisibly surrounded.

Her hand shook so that she could hardly give him the clipping.

"This article—from the 'Waukesha Sentinel'—that a man named Elwell has brought suit against you—that there was something wrong about the Blue Star Mine. I can't understand more than half."

They continued to face each other as she spoke, and to her astonishment, she saw that her words had the almost immediate effect of dissipating the strained watchfulness of his look.

"Oh, that!" He glanced down the printed slip, and then folded it with the gesture of one who handles something harmless and familiar. "What's the matter with you this afternoon, Mary? I thought you'd got bad news."

She stood before him with her undefinable terror subsiding slowly under the reassuring touch of his composure.

"You knew about this, then—it's all right?"

"Certainly I knew about it; and it's all right."

"But what is it? I don't understand. What does this man accuse you of?"

"Oh, pretty nearly every crime in the calendar." Boyne had tossed the clipping down, and thrown himself comfortably into an arm-chair near the fire. "Do you want to hear the story? It's not particularly interesting—just a squabble over interests in the Blue Star."

"But who is this Elwell? I don't know the name."

"Oh, he's a fellow I put into it—gave him a hand up. I told you all about him at the time."

"I daresay. I must have forgotten." Vainly she strained back among her memories. "But if you helped him, why does he make this return?"

"Oh, probably some shyster lawyer got hold of him and talked him over. It's all rather technical and complicated. I thought that kind of thing bored you."

His wife felt a sting of compunction. Theoretically, she deprecated the American wife's detachment from her husband's professional interests, but in practice she had always found it difficult to fix her attention on Boyne's report of the transactions in which his varied interests involved him. Besides, she had felt from the first that, in a community where the amenities of living could be obtained only at the cost of efforts as arduous as her husband's professional labors, such brief leisure as they could command should be used as an escape from immediate preoccupations, a flight to the life they always dreamed of living. Once or twice, now that this new life had actually drawn its magic circle about them, she had asked herself if she had done right; but hitherto such conjectures had been no more than the retrospective excursions of an active fancy. Now, for the first time, it startled her a little to find how little she knew of the material foundation on which her happiness was built.

She glanced again at her husband, and was reassured by the composure of his face; yet she felt the need of more definite grounds for her reassurance.

"But doesn't this suit worry you? Why have you never spoken to me about it?"

He answered both questions at once: "I didn't speak of it at first because it did worry me—annoyed me, rather. But it's all ancient history now. Your correspondent must have got hold of a back number of the 'Sentinel.'"

She felt a quick thrill of relief. "You mean it's over? He's lost his case?"

There was a just perceptible delay in Boyne's reply. "The suit's been withdrawn—that's all."

But she persisted, as if to exonerate herself from the inward charge of being too easily put off. "Withdrawn because he saw he had no chance?"

"Oh, he had no chance," Boyne answered.

She was still struggling with a dimly felt perplexity at the back of her thoughts.

"How long ago was it withdrawn?"

He paused, as if with a slight return of his former uncertainty. "I've just had the news now; but I've been expecting it."

"Just now—in one of your letters?"

"Yes; in one of my letters."

She made no answer, and was aware only, after a short interval of waiting, that he had risen, and strolling across the room, had placed himself on the sofa at her side. She felt him, as he did so, pass an arm about her, she felt his hand seek hers and clasp it, and turning slowly, drawn by the warmth of his cheek, she met the smiling clearness of his eyes.

"It's all right—it's all right?" she questioned, through the flood of her dissolving doubts; and "I give you my word it never was righter!" he laughed back at her, holding her close.

III

One of the strangest things she was afterward to recall out of all the next day's incredible strangeness was the sudden and complete recovery of her sense of security.

It was in the air when she woke in her low-ceilinged, dusky room; it accompanied her down-stairs to the breakfast-table, flashed out at her from the fire, and re-duplicated itself brightly from the flanks of the urn and the sturdy flutings of the Georgian teapot. It was as if, in some roundabout way, all her diffused apprehensions of the previous day, with their moment of sharp concentration about the newspaper article,—as if this dim questioning of the future, and startled return upon the past,—had between them liquidated the arrears of some haunting moral obligation. If she had indeed been careless of her husband's affairs, it was, her new state seemed to prove, because her faith in him instinctively justified such carelessness; and his right to her faith had overwhelmingly affirmed itself in the very face of menace and suspicion. She had never seen him more untroubled, more naturally and unconsciously in possession of himself, than after the cross-examination to which she had subjected him: it was almost as if he had been aware of her lurking doubts, and had wanted the air cleared as much as she did.

It was as clear, thank Heaven! as the bright outer light that surprised her almost with a touch of summer when she issued from the house for her daily round of the gardens. She had left Boyne at his desk, indulging herself, as she passed the library door, by a last peep at his quiet face, where he bent, pipe in his mouth, above his papers, and now she had her own morning's task to perform. The task involved on such charmed winter days almost as much delighted loitering about the different quarters of her demesne as if spring were already at work on shrubs and borders. There were such inexhaustible possibilities still before her, such opportunities to bring out the latent graces of the old place, without a single irreverent touch of alteration, that the winter months were all too short to plan what spring and autumn executed. And her recovered sense of safety gave, on this particular morning, a peculiar zest to her progress through the sweet, still place. She went first to the kitchen-garden, where the espaliered pear-trees drew complicated patterns on the walls, and pigeons were fluttering and preening about the silvery-slated roof of their cot. There was something wrong about the piping of the hothouse, and she was expecting an authority from Dorchester, who was to drive out between trains and make a diagnosis of the boiler. But when she dipped into the damp heat of the greenhouses, among the spiced scents and waxy pinks and reds of old-fashioned exotics,—even the flora of Lyng was in the note!—she learned that the great man had not arrived, and the day being too rare to waste in an artificial atmosphere, she came out again and paced slowly along the springy turf of the bowling-green to the gardens behind the house.

At their farther end rose a grass terrace, commanding, over the fish-pond and the yew hedges, a view of the long house-front, with its twisted chimney-stacks and the blue shadows of its roof angles, all drenched in the pale gold moisture of the air.

Seen thus, across the level tracery of the yews, under the suffused, mild light, it sent her, from its open windows and hospitably smoking chimneys, the look of some warm human presence, of a mind slowly ripened on a sunny wall of experience. She had never before had so deep a sense of her intimacy with it, such a conviction that its secrets were all beneficent, kept, as they said to children, "for one's good," so complete a trust in its power to gather up her life and Ned's into the harmonious pattern of the long, long story it sat there weaving in the sun.

She heard steps behind her, and turned, expecting to see the gardener, accompanied by the engineer from Dorchester. But only one figure was in sight, that of a youngish, slightly built man, who, for reasons she could not on the spot have specified, did not remotely resemble her preconceived notion of an authority on hot-house boilers. The new-comer, on seeing her, lifted his hat, and paused with the air of a gentleman—perhaps a traveler—desirous of having it immediately known that his intrusion is involuntary. The local fame of Lyng occasionally attracted the more intelligent sight-seer, and Mary half-expected to see the stranger dissemble a camera, or justify his presence by producing it. But he made no gesture of any sort, and after a moment she asked, in a tone responding to the courteous deprecation of his attitude: "Is there any one you wish to see?"

"I came to see Mr. Boyne," he replied. His intonation, rather than his accent, was faintly American, and Mary, at the familiar note, looked at him more closely. The brim of his soft felt hat cast a shade on his face, which, thus obscured, wore to her short-sighted gaze a look of seriousness, as of a person arriving "on business," and civilly but firmly aware of his rights.

Past experience had made Mary equally sensible to such claims; but she was jealous of her husband's morning hours, and doubtful of his having given any one the right to intrude on them.

"Have you an appointment with Mr. Boyne?" she asked.

He hesitated, as if unprepared for the question.

"Not exactly an appointment," he replied.

"Then I'm afraid, this being his working-time, that he can't receive you now. Will you give me a message, or come back later?"

The visitor, again lifting his hat, briefly replied that he would come back later, and walked away, as if to regain the front of the house. As his figure receded down the walk between the yew hedges, Mary saw him pause and look up an instant at the peaceful house-front bathed in faint winter sunshine; and it struck her, with a tardy touch of compunction, that it would have been more humane to ask if he had come from a distance, and to offer, in that case, to inquire if her husband could receive him. But as the thought occurred to her he passed out of sight behind a pyramidal yew, and at the same moment her attention was distracted by the approach of the gardener, attended by the bearded pepper-and-salt figure of the boiler-maker from Dorchester.

The encounter with this authority led to such far-reaching issues that they resulted in his finding it expedient to ignore his train, and beguiled Mary into spending the remainder of the morning in absorbed confabulation among the greenhouses. She was startled to find, when the colloquy ended, that it was nearly luncheon-time, and she half expected, as she hurried back to the house, to see her husband coming out to meet her. But she found no one in the court but an under-gardener raking the gravel, and the hall, when she entered it, was so silent that she guessed Boyne to be still at work behind the closed door of the library.

Not wishing to disturb him, she turned into the drawing-room, and there, at her writing-table, lost herself in renewed calculations of the outlay to which the morning's conference had committed her. The knowledge that she could permit herself such follies had not yet lost its novelty; and somehow, in contrast to the vague apprehensions of the previous days, it now seemed an element of her recovered security, of the sense that, as Ned had said, things in general had never been "righter."

She was still luxuriating in a lavish play of figures when the parlor-maid, from the threshold, roused her with a dubiously worded inquiry as to the expediency of serving luncheon. It was one of their jokes that Trimmle announced luncheon as if she were divulging a state secret, and Mary, intent upon her papers, merely murmured an absent-minded assent.

She felt Trimmle wavering expressively on the threshold as if in rebuke of such offhand acquiescence; then her retreating steps sounded down the passage, and Mary, pushing away her papers, crossed the hall, and went to the library door. It was still closed, and she wavered in her turn, disliking to disturb her husband, yet anxious that he should not exceed his normal measure of work. As she stood there, balancing her impulses, the esoteric Trimmle returned with the announcement of luncheon, and Mary, thus impelled, opened the door and went into the library.

Boyne was not at his desk, and she peered about her, expecting to discover him at the book-shelves, somewhere down the length of the room; but her call brought no response, and gradually it became clear to her that he was not in the library.

She turned back to the parlor-maid.

"Mr. Boyne must be up-stairs. Please tell him that luncheon is ready."

The parlor-maid appeared to hesitate between the obvious duty of obeying orders and an equally obvious conviction of the foolishness of the injunction laid upon her. The struggle resulted in her saying doubtfully, "If you please, Madam, Mr. Boyne's not up-stairs."

"Not in his room? Are you sure?"

"I'm sure, Madam."

Mary consulted the clock. "Where is he, then?"

"He's gone out," Trimmle announced, with the superior air of one who has respectfully waited for the question that a well-ordered mind would have first propounded.

Mary's previous conjecture had been right, then. Boyne must have gone to the gardens to meet her, and since she had missed him, it was clear that he had taken the shorter way by the south door, instead of going round to the court. She crossed the hall to the glass portal opening directly on the yew garden, but the parlor-maid, after another moment of inner conflict, decided to bring out recklessly, "Please, Madam, Mr. Boyne didn't go that way."

Mary turned back. "Where did he go? And when?"

"He went out of the front door, up the drive, Madam." It was a matter of principle with Trimmle never to answer more than one question at a time.

"Up the drive? At this hour?" Mary went to the door herself, and glanced across the court through the long tunnel of bare limes. But its perspective was as empty as when she had scanned it on entering the house.

"Did Mr. Boyne leave no message?" she asked.

Trimmle seemed to surrender herself to a last struggle with the forces of chaos.

"No, Madam. He just went out with the gentleman."

"The gentleman? What gentleman?" Mary wheeled about, as if to front this new factor.

"The gentleman who called, Madam," said Trimmle, resignedly.

"When did a gentleman call? Do explain yourself, Trimmle!"

Only the fact that Mary was very hungry, and that she wanted to consult her husband about the greenhouses, would have caused her to lay so unusual an injunction on her attendant; and even now she was detached enough to note in Trimmle's eye the dawning defiance of the respectful subordinate who has been pressed too hard.

"I couldn't exactly say the hour, Madam, because I didn't let the gentleman in," she replied, with the air of magnanimously ignoring the irregularity of her mistress's course.

"You didn't let him in?"

"No, Madam. When the bell rang I was dressing, and Agnes—"

"Go and ask Agnes, then," Mary interjected. Trimmle still wore her look of patient magnanimity. "Agnes would not know, Madam, for she had unfortunately burnt her hand in trying the wick of the new lamp from town—" Trimmle, as Mary was aware, had always been opposed to the new lamp—"and so Mrs. Dockett sent the kitchen-maid instead."

Mary looked again at the clock. "It's after two! Go and ask the kitchen-maid if Mr. Boyne left any word."

She went into luncheon without waiting, and Trimmle presently brought her there the kitchen-maid's statement that the gentleman had called about one o'clock, that Mr. Boyne had gone out with him without leaving any message. The kitchen-maid did not even know the caller's name, for he had written it on a slip of paper, which he had folded and handed to her, with the injunction to deliver it at once to Mr. Boyne.

Mary finished her luncheon, still wondering, and when it was over, and Trimmle had brought the coffee to the drawing-room, her wonder had deepened to a first faint tinge of disquietude. It was unlike Boyne to absent himself without explanation at so unwonted an hour, and the difficulty of identifying the visitor whose summons he had apparently obeyed made his disappearance the more unaccountable. Mary Boyne's experience as the wife of a busy engineer, subject to sudden calls and compelled to keep irregular hours, had trained her to the philosophic acceptance of surprises; but since Boyne's withdrawal from business he had adopted a Benedictine regularity of life. As if to make up for the dispersed and agitated years, with their "stand-up" lunches and dinners rattled down to the joltings of the dining-car, he cultivated the last refinements of punctuality and monotony, discouraging his wife's fancy for the unexpected; and declaring that to a delicate taste there were infinite gradations of pleasure in the fixed recurrences of habit.

Still, since no life can completely defend itself from the unforeseen, it was evident that all Boyne's precautions would sooner or later prove unavailable, and Mary concluded that he had cut short a tiresome visit by walking with his caller to the station, or at least accompanying him for part of the way.

This conclusion relieved her from farther preoccupation, and she went out herself to take up her conference with the gardener. Thence she walked to the village post-office, a mile or so away; and when she turned toward home, the early twilight was setting in.

She had taken a foot-path across the downs, and as Boyne, meanwhile, had probably returned from the station by the highroad, there was little likelihood of their meeting on the way. She felt sure, however, of his having reached the house before her; so sure that, when she entered it herself, without even pausing to inquire of Trimmle, she made directly for the library. But the library was still empty, and with an unwonted precision of visual memory she immediately observed that the papers on her husband's desk lay precisely as they had lain when she had gone in to call him to luncheon.

Then of a sudden she was seized by a vague dread of the unknown. She had closed the door behind her on entering, and as she stood alone in the long, silent, shadowy room, her dread seemed to take shape and sound, to be there audibly breathing and lurking among the shadows. Her short-sighted eyes strained through them, half-discerning an actual presence, something aloof, that watched and knew; and in the recoil from that intangible propinquity she threw herself suddenly on the bell-rope and gave it a desperate pull.

The long, quavering summons brought Trimmle in precipitately with a lamp, and Mary breathed again at this sobering reappearance of the usual.

"You may bring tea if Mr. Boyne is in," she said, to justify her ring.

"Very well, Madam. But Mr. Boyne is not in," said Trimmle, putting down the lamp.

"Not in? You mean he's come back and gone out again?"

"No, Madam. He's never been back."

The dread stirred again, and Mary knew that now it had her fast.

"Not since he went out with—the gentleman?"

"Not since he went out with the gentleman."

"But who was the gentleman?" Mary gasped out, with the sharp note of some one trying to be heard through a confusion of meaningless noises.

"That I couldn't say, Madam." Trimmle, standing there by the lamp, seemed suddenly to grow less round and rosy, as though eclipsed by the same creeping shade of apprehension.

"But the kitchen-maid knows—wasn't it the kitchen-maid who let him in?"

"She doesn't know either, Madam, for he wrote his name on a folded paper."

Mary, through her agitation, was aware that they were both designating the unknown visitor by a vague pronoun, instead of the conventional formula which, till then, had kept their allusions within the bounds of custom. And at the same moment her mind caught at the suggestion of the folded paper.

"But he must have a name! Where is the paper?"

She moved to the desk, and began to turn over the scattered documents that littered it. The first that caught her eye was an unfinished letter in her husband's hand, with his pen lying across it, as though dropped there at a sudden summons.

"My dear Parvis,"—who was Parvis?—"I have just received your letter announcing Elwell's death, and while I suppose there is now no farther risk of trouble, it might be safer—"

She tossed the sheet aside, and continued her search; but no folded paper was discoverable among the letters and pages of manuscript which had been swept together in a promiscuous heap, as if by a hurried or a startled gesture.

"But the kitchen-maid saw him. Send her here," she commanded, wondering at her dullness in not thinking sooner of so simple a solution.

Trimmle, at the behest, vanished in a flash, as if thankful to be out of the room, and when she reappeared, conducting the agitated underling, Mary had regained her self-possession, and had her questions pat.

The gentleman was a stranger, yes—that she understood. But what had he said? And, above all, what had he looked like? The first question was easily enough answered, for the disconcerting reason that he had said so little—had merely asked for Mr. Boyne, and, scribbling something on a bit of paper, had requested that it should at once be carried in to him.

"Then you don't know what he wrote? You're not sure it was his name?"

The kitchen-maid was not sure, but supposed it was, since he had written it in answer to her inquiry as to whom she should announce.

"And when you carried the paper in to Mr. Boyne, what did he say?"

The kitchen-maid did not think that Mr. Boyne had said anything, but she could not be sure, for just as she had handed him the paper and he was opening it, she had become aware that the visitor had followed her into the library, and she had slipped out, leaving the two gentlemen together.

"But then, if you left them in the library, how do you know that they went out of the house?"

This question plunged the witness into momentary inarticulateness, from which she was rescued by Trimmle, who, by means of ingenious circumlocutions, elicited the statement that before she could cross the hall to the back passage she had heard the gentlemen behind her, and had seen them go out of the front door together.

"Then, if you saw the gentleman twice, you must be able to tell me what he looked like."

But with this final challenge to her powers of expression it became clear that the limit of the kitchen-maid's endurance had been reached. The obligation of going to the front door to "show in" a visitor was in itself so subversive of the fundamental order of things that it had thrown her faculties into hopeless disarray, and she could only stammer out, after various panting efforts at evocation, "His hat, mum, was different-like, as you might say—"

"Different? How different?" Mary flashed out at her, her own mind, in the same instant, leaping back to an image left on it that morning, but temporarily lost under layers of subsequent impressions.

"His hat had a wide brim, you mean? and his face was pale—a youngish face?" Mary pressed her, with a white-lipped intensity of interrogation. But if the kitchen-maid found any adequate answer to this challenge, it was swept away for her listener down the rushing current of her own convictions. The stranger—the stranger in the garden! Why had Mary not thought of him before? She needed no one now to tell her that it was he who had called for her husband and gone away with him. But who was he, and why had Boyne obeyed his call?

IV

It leaped out at her suddenly, like a grin out of the dark, that they had often called England so little—"such a confoundedly hard place to get lost in."

A confoundedly hard place to get lost in! That had been her husband's phrase. And now, with the whole machinery of official investigation sweeping its flash-lights from shore to shore, and across the dividing straits; now, with Boyne's name blazing from the walls of every town and village, his portrait (how that wrung her!) hawked up and down the country like the image of a hunted criminal; now the little compact, populous island, so policed, surveyed, and administered, revealed itself as a Sphinx-like guardian of abysmal mysteries, staring back into his wife's anguished eyes as if with the malicious joy of knowing something they would never know!

In the fortnight since Boyne's disappearance there had been no word of him, no trace of his movements. Even the usual misleading reports that raise expectancy in tortured bosoms had been few and fleeting. No one but the bewildered kitchen-maid had seen him leave the house, and no one else had seen "the gentleman" who accompanied him. All inquiries in the neighborhood failed to elicit the memory of a stranger's presence that day in the neighborhood of Lyng. And no one had met Edward Boyne, either alone or in company, in any of the neighboring villages, or on the road across the downs, or at either of the local railway-stations. The sunny English noon had swallowed him as completely as if he had gone out into Cimmerian night.

Mary, while every external means of investigation was working at its highest pressure, had ransacked her husband's papers for any trace of antecedent complications, of entanglements or obligations unknown to her, that might throw a faint ray into the darkness. But if any such had existed in the background of Boyne's life, they had disappeared as completely as the slip of paper on which the visitor had written his name. There remained no possible thread of guidance except—if it were indeed an exception—the letter which Boyne had apparently been in the act of writing when he received his mysterious summons. That letter, read and reread by his wife, and submitted by her to the police, yielded little enough for conjecture to feed on.

"I have just heard of Elwell's death, and while I suppose there is now no farther risk of trouble, it might be safer—" That was all. The "risk of trouble" was easily explained by the newspaper clipping which had apprised Mary of the suit brought against her husband by one of his associates in the Blue Star enterprise. The only new information conveyed in the letter was the fact of its showing Boyne, when he wrote it, to be still apprehensive of the results of the suit, though he had assured his wife that it had been withdrawn, and though the letter itself declared that the plaintiff was dead. It took several weeks of exhaustive cabling to fix the identity of the "Parvis" to whom the fragmentary communication was addressed, but even after these inquiries had shown him to be a Waukesha lawyer, no new facts concerning the Elwell suit were elicited. He appeared to have had no direct concern in it, but to have been conversant with the facts merely as an acquaintance, and possible intermediary; and he declared himself unable to divine with what object Boyne intended to seek his assistance.

This negative information, sole fruit of the first fortnight's feverish search, was not increased by a jot during the slow weeks that followed. Mary knew that the investigations were still being carried on, but she had a vague sense of their gradually slackening, as the actual march of time seemed to slacken. It was as though the days, flying horror-struck from the shrouded image of the one inscrutable day, gained assurance as the distance lengthened, till at last they fell back into their normal gait. And so with the human imaginations at work on the dark event. No doubt it occupied them still, but week by week and hour by hour it grew less absorbing, took up less space, was slowly but inevitably crowded out of the foreground of consciousness by the new problems perpetually bubbling up from the vaporous caldron of human experience.

Even Mary Boyne's consciousness gradually felt the same lowering of velocity. It still swayed with the incessant oscillations of conjecture; but they were slower, more rhythmical in their beat. There were moments of overwhelming lassitude when, like the victim of some poison which leaves the brain clear, but holds the body motionless, she saw herself domesticated with the Horror, accepting its perpetual presence as one of the fixed conditions of life.

These moments lengthened into hours and days, till she passed into a phase of stolid acquiescence. She watched the familiar routine of life with the incurious eye of a savage on whom the meaningless processes of civilization make but the faintest impression. She had come to regard herself as part of the routine, a spoke of the wheel, revolving with its motion; she felt almost like the furniture of the room in which she sat, an insensate object to be dusted and pushed about with the chairs and tables. And this deepening apathy held her fast at Lyng, in spite of the urgent entreaties of friends and the usual medical recommendation of "change." Her friends supposed that her refusal to move was inspired by the belief that her husband would one day return to the spot from which he had vanished, and a beautiful legend grew up about this imaginary state of waiting. But in reality she had no such belief: the depths of anguish inclosing her were no longer lighted by flashes of hope. She was sure that Boyne would never come back, that he had gone out of her sight as completely as if Death itself had waited that day on the threshold. She had even renounced, one by one, the various theories as to his disappearance which had been advanced by the press, the police, and her own agonized imagination. In sheer lassitude her mind turned from these alternatives of horror, and sank back into the blank fact that he was gone.

No, she would never know what had become of him—no one would ever know. But the house knew; the library in which she spent her long, lonely evenings knew. For it was here that the last scene had been enacted, here that the stranger had come, and spoken the word which had caused Boyne to rise and follow him. The floor she trod had felt his tread; the books on the shelves had seen his face; and there were moments when the intense consciousness of the old, dusky walls seemed about to break out into some audible revelation of their secret. But the revelation never came, and she knew it would never come. Lyng was not one of the garrulous old houses that betray the secrets intrusted to them. Its very legend proved that it had always been the mute accomplice, the incorruptible custodian of the mysteries it had surprised. And Mary Boyne, sitting face to face with its portentous silence, felt the futility of seeking to break it by any human means.

V

"I don't say it wasn't straight, yet don't say it was straight. It was business."

Mary, at the words, lifted her head with a start, and looked intently at the speaker.

When, half an hour before, a card with "Mr. Parvis" on it had been brought up to her, she had been immediately aware that the name had been a part of her consciousness ever since she had read it at the head of Boyne's unfinished letter. In the library she had found awaiting her a small neutral-tinted man with a bald head and gold eye-glasses, and it sent a strange tremor through her to know that this was the person to whom her husband's last known thought had been directed.

Parvis, civilly, but without vain preamble,—in the manner of a man who has his watch in his hand,—had set forth the object of his visit. He had "run over" to England on business, and finding himself in the neighborhood of Dorchester, had not wished to leave it without paying his respects to Mrs. Boyne; without asking her, if the occasion offered, what she meant to do about Bob Elwell's family.

The words touched the spring of some obscure dread in Mary's bosom. Did her visitor, after all, know what Boyne had meant by his unfinished phrase? She asked for an elucidation of his question, and noticed at once that he seemed surprised at her continued ignorance of the subject. Was it possible that she really knew as little as she said?

"I know nothing—you must tell me," she faltered out; and her visitor thereupon proceeded to unfold his story. It threw, even to her confused perceptions, and imperfectly initiated vision, a lurid glare on the whole hazy episode of the Blue Star Mine. Her husband had made his money in that brilliant speculation at the cost of "getting ahead" of some one less alert to seize the chance; the victim of his ingenuity was young Robert Elwell, who had "put him on" to the Blue Star scheme.

Parvis, at Mary's first startled cry, had thrown her a sobering glance through his impartial glasses.

"Bob Elwell wasn't smart enough, that's all; if he had been, he might have turned round and served Boyne the same way. It's the kind of thing that happens every day in business. I guess it's what the scientists call the survival of the fittest," said Mr. Parvis, evidently pleased with the aptness of his analogy.

Mary felt a physical shrinking from the next question she tried to frame; it was as though the words on her lips had a taste that nauseated her.

"But then—you accuse my husband of doing something dishonorable?"

Mr. Parvis surveyed the question dispassionately. "Oh, no, I don't. I don't even say it wasn't straight." He glanced up and down the long lines of books, as if one of them might have supplied him with the definition he sought. "I don't say it wasn't straight, and yet I don't say it was straight.

It was business." After all, no definition in his category could be more comprehensive than that.

Mary sat staring at him with a look of terror. He seemed to her like the indifferent, implacable emissary of some dark, formless power.

"But Mr. Elwell's lawyers apparently did not take your view, since I suppose the suit was withdrawn by their advice."

"Oh, yes, they knew he hadn't a leg to stand on, technically. It was when they advised him to withdraw the suit that he got desperate. You see, he'd borrowed most of the money he lost in the Blue Star, and he was up a tree. That's why he shot himself when they told him he had no show."

The horror was sweeping over Mary in great, deafening waves.

"He shot himself? He killed himself because of that?"

"Well, he didn't kill himself, exactly. He dragged on two months before he died." Parvis emitted the statement as unemotionally as a gramophone grinding out its "record."

"You mean that he tried to kill himself, and failed? And tried again?"

"Oh, he didn't have to try again," said Parvis, grimly.

They sat opposite each other in silence, he swinging his eye-glass thoughtfully about his finger, she, motionless, her arms stretched along her knees in an attitude of rigid tension.

"But if you knew all this," she began at length, hardly able to force her voice above a whisper, "how is it that when I wrote you at the time of my husband's disappearance you said you didn't understand his letter?"

Parvis received this without perceptible discomfiture. "Why, I didn't understand it—strictly speaking. And it wasn't the time to talk about it, if I had. The Elwell business was settled when the suit was withdrawn. Nothing I could have told you would have helped you to find your husband."

Mary continued to scrutinize him. "Then why are you telling me now?"

Still Parvis did not hesitate. "Well, to begin with, I supposed you knew more than you appear to—I mean about the circumstances of Elwell's death. And then people are talking of it now; the whole matter's been raked up again. And I thought, if you didn't know, you ought to."

She remained silent, and he continued: "You see, it's only come out lately what a bad state Elwell's affairs were in. His wife's a proud woman, and she fought on as long as she could, going out to work, and taking sewing at home, when she got too sick—something with the heart, I believe.

But she had his bedridden mother to look after, and the children, and she broke down under it, and finally had to ask for help. That attracted attention to the case, and the papers took it up, and a subscription was started. Everybody out there liked Bob Elwell, and most of the prominent names in the place are down on the list, and people began to wonder why—"

Parvis broke off to fumble in an inner pocket. "Here," he continued, "here's an account of the whole thing from the 'Sentinel'—a little sensational, of course. But I guess you'd better look it over."

He held out a newspaper to Mary, who unfolded it slowly, remembering, as she did so, the evening when, in that same room, the perusal of a clipping from the "Sentinel" had first shaken the depths of her security.

As she opened the paper, her eyes, shrinking from the glaring headlines, "Widow of Boyne's Victim Forced to Appeal for Aid," ran down the column of text to two portraits inserted in it. The first was her husband's, taken from a photograph made the year they had come to England. It was the picture of him that she liked best, the one that stood on the writing-table up-stairs in her bedroom. As the eyes in the photograph met hers, she felt it would be impossible to read what was said of him, and closed her lids with the sharpness of the pain.

"I thought if you felt disposed to put your name down—" she heard Parvis continue.

She opened her eyes with an effort, and they fell on the other portrait. It was that of a youngish man, slightly built, in rough clothes, with features somewhat blurred by the shadow of a projecting hat-brim. Where had she seen that outline before? She stared at it confusedly, her heart hammering in her throat and ears. Then she gave a cry.

"This is the man—the man who came for my husband!"

She heard Parvis start to his feet, and was dimly aware that she had slipped backward into the corner of the sofa, and that he was bending above her in alarm. With an intense effort she straightened herself, and reached out for the paper, which she had dropped.

"It's the man! I should know him anywhere!" she cried in a voice that sounded in her own ears like a scream.

Parvis's voice seemed to come to her from far off, down endless, fog-muffled windings.

"Mrs. Boyne, you're not very well. Shall I call somebody? Shall I get a glass of water?"

"No, no, no!" She threw herself toward him, her hand frantically clenching the newspaper. "I tell you, it's the man! I know him! He spoke to me in the garden!"

Parvis took the journal from her, directing his glasses to the portrait. "It can't be, Mrs. Boyne. It's Robert Elwell."

"Robert Elwell?" Her white stare seemed to travel into space. "Then it was Robert Elwell who came for him."

"Came for Boyne? The day he went away?" Parvis's voice dropped as hers rose. He bent over, laying a fraternal hand on her, as if to coax her gently back into her seat. "Why, Elwell was dead! Don't you remember?"

Mary sat with her eyes fixed on the picture, unconscious of what he was saying.

"Don't you remember Boyne's unfinished letter to me—the one you found on his desk that day? It was written just after he'd heard of Elwell's death." She noticed an odd shake in Parvis's unemotional voice. "Surely you remember that!" he urged her.

Yes, she remembered: that was the profoundest horror of it. Elwell had died the day before her husband's disappearance; and this was Elwell's portrait; and it was the portrait of the man who had spoken to her in the garden. She lifted her head and looked slowly about the library. The library could have borne witness that it was also the portrait of the man who had come in that day to call Boyne from his unfinished letter. Through the misty surgings of her brain she heard the faint boom of half-forgotten words—words spoken by Alida Stair on the lawn at Pangbourne before Boyne and his wife had ever seen the house at Lyng, or had imagined that they might one day live there.

"This was the man who spoke to me," she repeated.

She looked again at Parvis. He was trying to conceal his disturbance under what he imagined to be an expression of indulgent commiseration; but the edges of his lips were blue. "He thinks me mad; but I'm not mad," she reflected; and suddenly there flashed upon her a way of justifying her strange affirmation.

She sat quiet, controlling the quiver of her lips, and waiting till she could trust her voice to keep its habitual level; then she said, looking straight at Parvis: "Will you answer me one question, please? When was it that Robert Elwell tried to kill himself?"

"When—when?" Parvis stammered.

"Yes; the date. Please try to remember."

She saw that he was growing still more afraid of her. "I have a reason," she insisted gently.

"Yes, yes. Only I can't remember. About two months before, I should say."

"I want the date," she repeated.

Parvis picked up the newspaper. "We might see here," he said, still humoring her. He ran his eyes down the page. "Here it is. Last October—the—"

She caught the words from him. "The 20th, wasn't it?" With a sharp look at her, he verified. "Yes, the 20th. Then you did know?"

"I know now." Her white stare continued to travel past him. "Sunday, the 20th—that was the day he came first."

Parvis's voice was almost inaudible. "Came here first?"

"Yes."

"You saw him twice, then?"

"Yes, twice." She breathed it at him with dilated eyes. "He came first on the 20th of October. I remember the date because it was the day we went up Meldon Steep for the first time." She felt a faint gasp of inward laughter at the thought that but for that she might have forgotten.

Parvis continued to scrutinize her, as if trying to intercept her gaze.

"We saw him from the roof," she went on. "He came down the lime-avenue toward the house. He was dressed just as he is in that picture. My husband saw him first. He was frightened, and ran down ahead of me; but there was no one there. He had vanished."

"Elwell had vanished?" Parvis faltered.

"Yes." Their two whispers seemed to grope for each other. "I couldn't think what had happened. I see now. He tried to come then; but he wasn't dead enough—he couldn't reach us. He had to wait for two months; and then he came back again—and Ned went with him."

She nodded at Parvis with the look of triumph of a child who has successfully worked out a difficult puzzle. But suddenly she lifted her hands with a desperate gesture, pressing them to her bursting temples.

"Oh, my God! I sent him to Ned—I told him where to go! I sent him to this room!" she screamed out.

She felt the walls of the room rush toward her, like inward falling ruins; and she heard Parvis, a long way off, as if through the ruins, crying to her, and struggling to get at her. But she was numb to his touch, she did not know what he was saying. Through the tumult she heard but one clear note, the voice of Alida Stair, speaking on the lawn at Pangbourne.

"You won't know till afterward," it said. "You won't know till long, long afterward."

2

The Eyes

I

We had been put in the mood for ghosts, that evening, after an excellent dinner at our old friend Culwin's, by a tale of Fred Murchard's—the narrative of a strange personal visitation.

Seen through the haze of our cigars, and by the drowsy gleam of a coal fire, Culwin's library, with its oak walls and dark old bindings, made a good setting for such evocations; and ghostly experiences at first hand being, after Murchard's brilliant opening, the only kind acceptable to us, we proceeded to take stock of our group and tax each member for a contribution. There were eight of us, and seven contrived, in a manner more or less adequate, to fulfil the condition imposed. It surprised us all to find that we could muster such a show of supernatural impressions, for none of us, excepting Murchard himself and young Phil Frenham—whose story was the slightest of the lot—had the habit of sending our souls into the invisible. So that, on the whole, we had every reason to be proud of our seven "exhibits," and none of us would have dreamed of expecting an eighth from our host.

Our old friend, Mr. Andrew Culwin, who had sat back in his arm-chair, listening and blinking through the smoke circles with the cheerful tolerance of a wise old idol, was not the kind of man likely to be favoured with such contacts, though he had imagination enough to enjoy, without envying, the superior privileges of his guests. By age and by education he belonged to the stout Positivist tradition, and his habit of thought had been formed in the days of the epic struggle between physics and metaphysics. But he had been, then and always, essentially a spectator, a humorous detached observer of the immense muddled variety show of life, slipping out of his seat now and then for a brief dip into the convivialities at the back of the house, but never, as far as one knew, showing the least desire to jump on the stage and do a "turn."

Among his contemporaries there lingered a vague tradition of his having, at a remote period, and in a romantic clime, been wounded in a duel; but this legend no more tallied with what we younger men knew of his character than my mother's assertion that he had once been "a charming little man with nice eyes" corresponded to any possible reconstitution of his dry thwarted physiognomy.

"He never can have looked like anything but a bundle of sticks," Murchard had once said of him. "Or a phosphorescent log, rather," some one else amended; and we recognized the happiness of this description of his small squat trunk, with the red blink of the eyes in a face like mottled bark. He had always been possessed of a leisure which he had nursed and protected, instead of squandering it in vain activities. His carefully guarded hours had been devoted to the cultivation of a fine intelligence and a few judiciously chosen habits; and none of the disturbances common to human experience seemed to have crossed his sky. Nevertheless, his dispassionate survey of the universe had not raised his opinion of that costly experiment, and his study of the human race seemed to have resulted in the conclusion that all men were superfluous, and women necessary only because some one had to do the cooking. On the importance of this point his convictions were absolute, and gastronomy was the only science which he revered as dogma. It must be owned that his little dinners were a strong argument in favour of this view, besides being a reason—though not the main one—for the fidelity of his friends.

Mentally he exercised a hospitality less seductive but no less stimulating. His mind was like a forum, or some open meeting-place for the exchange of ideas: somewhat cold and draughty, but light, spacious and orderly—a kind of academic grove from which all the leaves had fallen. In this privileged area a dozen of us were wont to stretch our muscles and expand our lungs; and, as if to prolong as much as possible the tradition of what we felt to be a vanishing institution, one or two neophytes were now and then added to our band.

Young Phil Frenham was the last, and the most interesting, of these recruits, and a good example of Murchard's somewhat morbid assertion that our old friend "liked 'em juicy." It was indeed a fact that Culwin, for all his mental dryness, specially tasted the lyric qualities in youth. As he was far too good an Epicurean to nip the flowers of soul which he gathered for his garden, his friendship was not a disintegrating influence: on the contrary, it forced the young idea to robuster bloom. And in Phil Frenham he had a fine subject for experimentation. The boy was really intelligent, and the soundness of his nature was like the pure paste under a delicate glaze. Culwin had fished him out of a thick fog of family dulness, and pulled him up to a peak in Darien; and the adventure hadn't hurt him a bit. Indeed, the skill with which Culwin had contrived to stimulate his curiosities without robbing them of their young bloom of awe seemed to me a sufficient answer to Murchard's ogreish metaphor. There was nothing hectic in Frenham's efflorescence, and his old friend had not laid even a finger-tip on the sacred stupidities. One wanted no better proof of that than the fact that Frenham still reverenced them in Culwin.

"There's a side of him you fellows don't see. I believe that story about the duel!" he declared; and it was of the very essence of this belief that it should impel him—just as our little party was dispersing—to turn back to our host with the absurd demand: "And now you've got to tell us about your ghost!"

The outer door had closed on Murchard and the others; only Frenham and I remained; and the vigilant servant who presided over Culwin's destinies, having brought a fresh supply of soda-water, had been laconically ordered to bed.

Culwin's sociability was a night-blooming flower, and we knew that he expected the nucleus of his group to tighten around him after midnight. But Frenham's appeal seemed to disconcert him comically, and he rose from the chair in which he had just reseated himself after his farewells in the hall.

"My ghost? Do you suppose I'm fool enough to go to the expense of keeping one of my own, when there are so many charming ones in my friends' closets?—Take another cigar," he said, revolving toward me with a laugh.

Frenham laughed too, pulling up his slender height before the chimney-piece as he turned to face his short bristling friend.

"Oh," he said, "you'd never be content to share if you met one you really liked."

Culwin had dropped back into his armchair, his shock head embedded in its habitual hollow, his little eyes glimmering over a fresh cigar.

"Liked—liked? Good Lord!" he growled.

"Ah, you have, then!" Frenham pounced on him in the same instant, with a sidewise glance of victory at me; but Culwin cowered gnomelike among his cushions, dissembling himself in a protective cloud of smoke.

"What's the use of denying it? You've seen everything, so of course you've seen a ghost!" his young friend persisted, talking intrepidly into the cloud. "Or, if you haven't seen one, it's only because you've seen two!"

The form of the challenge seemed to strike our host. He shot his head out of the mist with a queer tortoise-like motion he sometimes had, and blinked approvingly at Frenham.

"Yes," he suddenly flung at us on a shrill jerk of laughter; "it's only because I've seen two!"

The words were so unexpected that they dropped down and down into a fathomless silence, while we continued to stare at each other over Culwin's head, and Culwin stared at his ghosts. At length Frenham, without speaking, threw himself into the chair on the other side of the hearth, and leaned forward with his listening smile . . .

II

"OH, of course they're not show ghosts—a collector wouldn't think anything of them . . . Don't let me raise your hopes . . . their one merit is their numerical strength: the exceptional fact of their being two. But, as against this, I'm bound to admit that at any moment I could probably have exorcised them both by asking my doctor for a prescription, or my oculist for a pair of spectacles. Only, as I never could make up my mind whether to go to the doctor or the oculist—whether I was afflicted by an optical or a digestive delusion—I left them to pursue their interesting double life, though at times they made mine exceedingly comfortable . . .

"Yes—uncomfortable; and you know how I hate to be uncomfortable!

But it was part of my stupid pride, when the thing began, not to admit that I could be disturbed by the trifling matter of seeing two—

"And then I'd no reason, really, to suppose I was ill. As far as I knew I was simply bored—horribly bored. But it was part of my boredom—I remember—that I was feeling so uncommonly well, and didn't know how on earth to work off my surplus energy. I had come back from a long journey—down in South America and Mexico—and had settled down for the winter near New York, with an old aunt who had known Washington Irving and corresponded with N. P. Willis. She lived, not far from Irvington, in a damp Gothic villa, overhung by Norway spruces, and looking exactly like a memorial emblem done in hair. Her personal appearance was in keeping with this image, and her own hair—of which there was little left—might have been sacrificed to the manufacture of the emblem.

"I had just reached the end of an agitated year, with considerable arrears to make up in money and emotion; and theoretically it seemed as though my aunt's mild hospitality would be as beneficial to my nerves as to my purse. But the deuce of it was that as soon as I felt myself safe and sheltered my energy began to revive; and how was I to work it off inside of a memorial emblem? I had, at that time, the agreeable illusion that sustained intellectual effort could engage a man's whole activity; and I decided to write a great book—I forget about what. My aunt, impressed by my plan, gave up to me her Gothic library, filled with classics in black cloth and daguerrotypes of faded celebrities; and I sat down at my desk to make myself a place among their number. And to facilitate my task she lent me a cousin to copy my manuscript.

"The cousin was a nice girl, and I had an idea that a nice girl was just what I needed to restore my faith in human nature, and principally in myself. She was neither beautiful nor intelligent—poor Alice Nowell!—but it interested me to see any woman content to be so uninteresting, and I wanted to find out the secret of her content. In doing this I handled it rather rashly, and put it out of joint—oh, just for a moment! There's no fatuity in telling you this, for the poor girl had never seen any one but cousins . . .

"Well, I was sorry for what I'd done, of course, and confoundedly bothered as to how I should put it straight. She was staying in the house, and one evening, after my aunt had gone to bed, she came down to the library to fetch a book she'd mislaid, like any artless heroine on the shelves behind us. She was pink-nosed and flustered, and it suddenly occurred to me that her hair, though it was fairly thick and pretty, would look exactly like my aunt's when she grew older. I was glad I had noticed this, for it made it easier for me to do what was right; and when I had found the book she hadn't lost I told her I was leaving for Europe that week.

"Europe was terribly far off in those days, and Alice knew at once what I meant. She didn't take it in the least as I'd expected—it would have been easier if she had. She held her book very tight, and turned away a moment to wind up the lamp on my desk—it had a ground glass shade with vine leaves, and glass drops around the edge, I remember. Then she came back, held out her hand, and said: 'Good-bye.' And as she said it she looked straight at me and kissed me. I had never felt anything as fresh and shy and brave as her kiss. It was worse than any reproach, and it made me ashamed to deserve a reproach from her. I said to myself: 'I'll marry her, and when my aunt dies she'll leave us this house, and I'll sit here at the desk and go on with my book; and Alice will sit over there with her embroidery and look at me as she's looking now. And life will go on like that for any number of years.' The prospect frightened me a little, but at the time it didn't frighten me as much as doing anything to hurt her; and ten minutes later she had my seal ring on my finger, and my promise that when I went abroad she should go with me.

"You'll wonder why I'm enlarging on this familiar incident. It's because the evening on which it took place was the very evening on which I first saw the queer sight I've spoken of. Being at that time an ardent believer in a necessary sequence between cause and effect I naturally tried to trace some kind of link between what had just happened to me in my aunt's library, and what was to happen a few hours later on the same night; and so the coincidence between the two events always remained in my mind.

"I went up to bed with rather a heavy heart, for I was bowed under the weight of the first good action I had ever consciously committed; and young as I was, I saw the gravity of my situation. Don't imagine from this that I had hitherto been an instrument of destruction. I had been merely a harmless young man, who had followed his bent and declined all collaboration with Providence. Now I had suddenly undertaken to promote the moral order of the world, and I felt a good deal like the trustful spectator who has given his gold watch to the conjurer, and doesn't know in what shape he'll get it back when the trick is over . . . Still, a glow of self-righteousness tempered my fears, and I said to myself as I undressed that when I'd got used to being good it probably wouldn't make me as nervous as it did at the start. And by the time I was in bed, and had blown out my candle, I felt that I really was getting used to it, and that, as far as I'd got, it was not unlike sinking down into one of my aunt's very softest wool mattresses.

"I closed my eyes on this image, and when I opened them it must have been a good deal later, for my room had grown cold, and the night was intensely still. I was waked suddenly by the feeling we all know—the feeling that there was something near me that hadn't been there when I fell asleep. I sat up and strained my eyes into the darkness. The room was pitch black, and at first I saw nothing; but gradually a vague glimmer at the foot of the bed turned into two eyes staring back at me. I couldn't see the face attached to them—on account of the darkness, I imagined—but as I looked the eyes grew more and more distinct: they gave out a light of their own.

"The sensation of being thus gazed at was far from pleasant, and you might suppose that my first impulse would have been to jump out of bed and hurl myself on the invisible figure attached to the eyes. But it wasn't—my impulse was simply to lie still . . . I can't say whether this was due to an immediate sense of the uncanny nature of the apparition—to the certainty that if I did jump out of bed I should hurl myself on nothing—or merely to the benumbing effect of the eyes themselves. They were the very worst eyes I've ever seen: a man's eyes—but what a man! My first thought was that he must be frightfully old. The orbits were sunk, and the thick red-lined lids hung over the eyeballs like blinds of which the cords are broken. One lid drooped a little lower than the other, with the effect of a crooked leer; and between these pulpy folds of flesh, with their scant bristle of lashes, the eyes themselves, small glassy disks with an agate-like rim about the pupils, looked like sea-pebbles in the grip of a starfish.

"But the age of the eyes was not the most unpleasant thing about them. What turned me sick was their expression of vicious security. I don't know how else to describe the fact that they seemed to belong to a man who had done a lot of harm in his life, but had always kept just inside the danger lines. They were not the eyes of a coward, but of some one much too clever to take risks; and my gorge rose at their look of base astuteness. Yet even that wasn't the worst; for as we continued to scan each other I saw in them a tinge of faint derision, and felt myself to be its object.

"At that I was seized by an impulse of rage that jerked me out of bed and pitched me straight on the unseen figure at its foot. But of course there wasn't any figure there, and my fists struck at emptiness. Ashamed and cold, I groped about for a match and lit the candles. The room looked just as usual—as I had known it would; and I crawled back to bed, and blew out the lights.

"As soon as the room was dark again the eyes reappeared; and I now applied myself to explaining them on scientific principles. At first I thought the illusion might have been caused by the glow of the last embers in the chimney; but the fire-place was on the other side of my bed, and so placed that the fire could not possibly be reflected in my toilet glass, which was the only mirror in the room. Then it occurred to me that I might have been tricked by the reflection of the embers in some polished bit of wood or metal; and though I couldn't discover any object of the sort in my line of vision, I got up again, groped my way to the hearth, and covered what was left of the fire. But as soon as I was back in bed the eyes were back at its foot.

"They were an hallucination, then: that was plain. But the fact that they were not due to any external dupery didn't make them a bit pleasanter to see. For if they were a projection of my inner consciousness, what the deuce was the matter with that organ? I had gone deeply enough into the mystery of morbid pathological states to picture the conditions under which an exploring mind might lay itself open to such a midnight admonition; but I couldn't fit it to my present case. I had never felt more normal, mentally and physically; and the only unusual fact in my situation—that of having assured the happiness of an amiable girl—did not seem of a kind to summon unclean spirits about my pillow. But there were the eyes still looking at me . . .

"I shut mine, and tried to evoke a vision of Alice Nowell's. They were not remarkable eyes, but they were as wholesome as fresh water, and if she had had more imagination—or longer lashes—their expression might have been interesting. As it was, they did not prove very efficacious, and in a few moments I perceived that they had mysteriously changed into the eyes at the foot of the bed. It exasperated me more to feel these glaring at me through my shut lids than to see them, and I opened my eyes again and looked straight into their hateful stare . . .

"And so it went on all night. I can't tell you what that night was, nor how long it lasted. Have you ever lain in bed, hopelessly wide awake, and tried to keep your eyes shut, knowing that if you opened 'em you'd see something you dreaded and loathed? It sounds easy, but it's devilish hard. Those eyes hung there and drew me. I had the vertige de l'abime, and their red lids were the edge of my abyss. . . . I had known nervous hours before: hours when I'd felt the wind of danger in my neck; but never this kind of strain. It wasn't that the eyes were so awful; they hadn't the majesty of the powers of darkness. But they had—how shall I say?—a physical effect that was the equivalent of a bad smell: their look left a smear like a snail's. And I didn't see what business they had with me, anyhow—and I stared and stared, trying to find out . . .

"I don't know what effect they were trying to produce; but the effect they did produce was that of making me pack my portmanteau and bolt to town early the next morning. I left a note for my aunt, explaining that I was ill and had gone to see my doctor; and as a matter of fact I did feel uncommonly ill—the night seemed to have pumped all the blood out of me. But when I reached town I didn't go to the doctor's. I went to a friend's rooms, and threw myself on a bed, and slept for ten heavenly hours. When I woke it was the middle of the night, and I turned cold at the thought of what might be waiting for me. I sat up, shaking, and stared into the darkness; but there wasn't a break in its blessed surface, and when I saw that the eyes were not there I dropped back into another long sleep.

"I had left no word for Alice when I fled, because I meant to go back the next morning. But the next morning I was too exhausted to stir. As the day went on the exhaustion increased, instead of wearing off like the lassitude left by an ordinary night of insomnia: the effect of the eyes seemed to be cumulative, and the thought of seeing them again grew intolerable. For two days I struggled with my dread; but on the third evening I pulled myself together and decided to go back the next morning. I felt a good deal happier as soon as I'd decided, for I knew that my abrupt disappearance, and the strangeness of my not writing, must have been very painful for poor Alice. That night I went to bed with an easy mind, and fell asleep at once; but in the middle of the night I woke, and there were the eyes . . .

"Well, I simply couldn't face them; and instead of going back to my aunt's I bundled a few things into a trunk and jumped onto the first steamer for England. I was so dead tired when I got on board that I crawled straight into my berth, and slept most of the way over; and I can't tell you the bliss it was to wake from those long stretches of dreamless sleep and look fearlessly into the darkness, knowing that I shouldn't see the eyes . . .

"I stayed abroad for a year, and then I stayed for another; and during that time I never had a glimpse of them. That was enough reason for prolonging my stay if I'd been on a desert island. Another was, of course, that I had perfectly come to see, on the voyage over, the folly, complete impossibility, of my marrying Alice Nowell. The fact that I had been so slow in making this discovery annoyed me, and made me want to avoid explanations. The bliss of escaping at one stroke from the eyes, and from this other embarrassment, gave my freedom an extraordinary zest; and the longer I savoured it the better I liked its taste.

"The eyes had burned such a hole in my consciousness that for a long time I went on puzzling over the nature of the apparition, and wondering nervously if it would ever come back. But as time passed I lost this dread, and retained only the precision of the image. Then that faded in its turn.

"The second year found me settled in Rome, where I was planning, I believe, to write another great book—a definitive work on Etruscan influences in Italian art. At any rate, I'd found some pretext of the kind for taking a sunny apartment in the Piazza di Spagna and dabbling about indefinitely in the Forum; and there, one morning, a charming youth came to me. As he stood there in the warm light, slender and smooth and hyacinthine, he might have stepped from a ruined altar—one to Antinous, say—but he'd come instead from New York, with a letter (of all people) from Alice Nowell. The letter—the first I'd had from her since our break—was simply a line introducing her young cousin, Gilbert Noyes, and appealing to me to befriend him. It appeared, poor lad, that he 'had talent,' and 'wanted to write'; and, an obdurate family having insisted that his calligraphy should take the form of double entry, Alice had intervened to win him six months' respite, during which he was to travel on a meagre pittance, and somehow prove his ultimate ability to increase it by his pen. The quaint conditions of the test struck me first: it seemed about as conclusive as a mediaeval 'ordeal.' Then I was touched by her having sent him to me. I had always wanted to do her some service, to justify myself in my own eyes rather than hers; and here was a beautiful embodiment of my chance.

"Well, I imagine it's safe to lay down the general principle that predestined geniuses don't, as a rule, appear before one in the spring sunshine of the Forum looking like one of its banished gods. At any rate, poor Noyes wasn't a predestined genius. But he was beautiful to see, and charming as a comrade too. It was only when he began to talk literature that my heart failed me. I knew all the symptoms so well—the things he had 'in him,' and the things outside him that impinged! There's the real test, after all. It was always—punctually, inevitably, with the inexorableness of a mechanical law—it was always the wrong thing that struck him. I grew to find a certain grim fascination in deciding in advance exactly which wrong thing he'd select; and I acquired an astonishing skill at the game . . .

"The worst of it was that his betise wasn't of the too obvious sort. Ladies who met him at picnics thought him intellectual; and even at dinners he passed for clever. I, who had him under the microscope, fancied now and then that he might develop some kind of a slim talent, something that he could make 'do' and be happy on; and wasn't that, after all, what I was concerned with? He was so charming—he continued to be so charming—that he called forth all my charity in support of this argument; and for the first few months I really believed there was a chance for him . . .

"Those months were delightful. Noyes was constantly with me, and the more I saw of him the better I liked him. His stupidity was a natural grace—it was as beautiful, really, as his eye-lashes. And he was so gay, so affectionate, and so happy with me, that telling him the truth would have been about as pleasant as slitting the throat of some artless animal. At first I used to wonder what had put into that radiant head the detestable delusion that it held a brain. Then I began to see that it was simply protective mimicry—an instinctive ruse to get away from family life and an office desk. Not that Gilbert didn't—dear lad!—believe in himself. There wasn't a trace of hypocrisy in his composition. He was sure that his 'call' was irresistible, while to me it was the saving grace of his situation that it wasn't, and that a little money, a little leisure, a little pleasure would have turned him into an inoffensive idler. Unluckily, however, there was no hope of money, and with the grim alternative of the office desk before him he couldn't postpone his attempt at literature. The stuff he turned out was deplorable, and I see now that I knew it from the first. Still, the absurdity of deciding a man's whole future on a first trial seemed to justify me in withholding my verdict, and perhaps even in encouraging him a little, on the ground that the human plant generally needs warmth to flower.

"At any rate, I proceeded on that principle, and carried it to the point of getting his term of probation extended. When I left Rome he went with me, and we idled away a delicious summer between Capri and Venice. I said to myself: 'If he has anything in him, it will come out now; and it did. He was never more enchanting and enchanted. There were moments of our pilgrimage when beauty born of murmuring sound seemed actually to pass into his face—but only to issue forth in a shallow flood of the palest ink . . .

"Well the time came to turn off the tap; and I knew there was no hand but mine to do it. We were back in Rome, and I had taken him to stay with me, not wanting him to be alone in his dismal pension when he had to face the necessity of renouncing his ambition. I hadn't, of course, relied solely on my own judgment in deciding to advise him to drop literature. I had sent his stuff to various people—editors and critics—and they had always sent it back with the same chilling lack of comment. Really there was nothing on earth to say about it—

"I confess I never felt more shabbily than I did on the day when I decided to have it out with Gilbert. It was well enough to tell myself that it was my duty to knock the poor boy's hopes into splinters—but I'd like to know what act of gratuitous cruelty hasn't been justified on that plea? I've always shrunk from usurping the functions of Providence, and when I have to exercise them I decidedly prefer that it shouldn't be on an errand of destruction. Besides, in the last issue, who was I to decide, even after a year's trial, if poor Gilbert had it in him or not?

"The more I looked at the part I'd resolved to play, the less I liked it; and I liked it still less when Gilbert sat opposite me, with his head thrown back in the lamplight, just as Phil's is now . . . I'd been going over his last manuscript, and he knew it, and he knew that his future hung on my verdict—we'd tacitly agreed to that. The manuscript lay between us, on my table—a novel, his first novel, if you please!—and he reached over and laid his hand on it, and looked up at me with all his life in the look.

"I stood up and cleared my throat, trying to keep my eyes away from his face and on the manuscript.

"'The fact is, my dear Gilbert,' I began—

"I saw him turn pale, but he was up and facing me in an instant.

"'Oh, look here, don't take on so, my dear fellow! I'm not so awfully cut up as all that!' His hands were on my shoulders, and he was laughing down on me from his full height, with a kind of mortally-stricken gaiety that drove the knife into my side.

"He was too beautifully brave for me to keep up any humbug about my duty. And it came over me suddenly how I should hurt others in hurting him: myself first, since sending him home meant losing him; but more particularly poor Alice Nowell, to whom I had so uneasily longed to prove my good faith and my immense desire to serve her. It really seemed like failing her twice to fail Gilbert—

"But my intuition was like one of those lightning flashes that encircle the whole horizon, and in the same instant I saw what I might be letting myself in for if I didn't tell the truth. I said to myself: 'I shall have him for life'—and I'd never yet seen any one, man or woman, whom I was quite sure of wanting on those terms. Well, this impulse of egotism decided me. I was ashamed of it, and to get away from it I took a leap that landed me straight in Gilbert's arms.

"'The thing's all right, and you're all wrong!' I shouted up at him; and as he hugged me, and I laughed and shook in his incredulous clutch, I had for a minute the sense of self-complacency that is supposed to attend the footsteps of the just. Hang it all, making people happy has its charms—

"Gilbert, of course, was for celebrating his emancipation in some spectacular manner; but I sent him away alone to explode his emotions, and went to bed to sleep off mine. As I undressed I began to wonder what their after-taste would be—so many of the finest don't keep! Still, I wasn't sorry, and I meant to empty the bottle, even if it did turn a trifle flat.

"After I got into bed I lay for a long time smiling at the memory of his eyes—his blissful eyes . . . Then I fell asleep, and when I woke the room was deathly cold, and I sat up with a jerk—and there were the other eyes . . .

"It was three years since I'd seen them, but I'd thought of them so often that I fancied they could never take me unawares again. Now, with their red sneer on me, I knew that I had never really believed they would come back, and that I was as defenceless as ever against them . . . As before, it was the insane irrelevance of their coming that made it so horrible. What the deuce were they after, to leap out at me at such a time? I had lived more or less carelessly in the years since I'd seen them, though my worst indiscretions were not dark enough to invite the searchings of their infernal glare; but at this particular moment I was really in what might have been called a state of grace; and I can't tell you how the fact added to their horror . . .

"But it's not enough to say they were as bad as before: they were worse. Worse by just so much as I'd learned of life in the interval; by all the damnable implications my wider experience read into them. I saw now what I hadn't seen before: that they were eyes which had grown hideous gradually, which had built up their baseness coral-wise, bit by bit, out of a series of small turpitudes slowly accumulated through the industrious years. Yes—it came to me that what made them so bad was that they'd grown bad so slowly . . .

"There they hung in the darkness, their swollen lids dropped across the little watery bulbs rolling loose in the orbits, and the puff of fat flesh making a muddy shadow underneath—and as their filmy stare moved with my movements, there came over me a sense of their tacit complicity, of a deep hidden understanding between us that was worse than the first shock of their strangeness. Not that I understood them; but that they made it so clear that some day I should . . . Yes, that was the worst part of it, decidedly; and it was the feeling that became stronger each time they came back to me . . .

"For they got into the damnable habit of coming back. They reminded me of vampires with a taste for young flesh, they seemed so to gloat over the taste of a good conscience. Every night for a month they came to claim their morsel of mine: since I'd made Gilbert happy they simply wouldn't loosen their fangs. The coincidence almost made me hate him, poor lad, fortuitous as I felt it to be. I puzzled over it a good deal, but couldn't find any hint of an explanation except in the chance of his association with Alice Nowell. But then the eyes had let up on me the moment I had abandoned her, so they could hardly be the emissaries of a woman scorned, even if one could have pictured poor Alice charging such spirits to avenge her. That set me thinking, and I began to wonder if they would let up on me if I abandoned Gilbert. The temptation was insidious, and I had to stiffen myself against it; but really, dear boy! he was too charming to be sacrificed to such demons. And so, after all, I never found out what they wanted . . ."

III

THE fire crumbled, sending up a flash which threw into relief the narrator's gnarled red face under its grey-black stubble. Pressed into the hollow of the dark leather armchair, it stood out an instant like an intaglio of yellowish red-veined stone, with spots of enamel for the eyes; then the fire sank and in the shaded lamp-light it became once more a dim Rembrandtish blur.

Phil Frenham, sitting in a low chair on the opposite side of the hearth, one long arm propped on the table behind him, one hand supporting his thrown-back head, and his eyes steadily fixed on his old friend's face, had not moved since the tale began. He continued to maintain his silent immobility after Culwin had ceased to speak, and it was I who, with a vague sense of disappointment at the sudden drop of the story, finally asked: "But how long did you keep on seeing them?"

Culwin, so sunk into his chair that he seemed like a heap of his own empty clothes, stirred a little, as if in surprise at my question. He appeared to have half-forgotten what he had been telling us.

"How long? Oh, off and on all that winter. It was infernal. I never got used to them. I grew really ill."

Frenham shifted his attitude silently, and as he did so his elbow struck against a small mirror in a bronze frame standing on the table behind him. He turned and changed its angle slightly; then he resumed his former attitude, his dark head thrown back on his lifted palm, his eyes intent on Culwin's face. Something in his stare embarrassed me, and as if to divert attention from it I pressed on with another question:

"And you never tried sacrificing Noyes?"

"Oh, no. The fact is I didn't have to. He did it for me, poor infatuated boy!"

"Did it for you? How do you mean?"

"He wore me out—wore everybody out. He kept on pouring out his lamentable twaddle, and hawking it up and down the place till he became a thing of terror. I tried to wean him from writing—oh, ever so gently, you understand, by throwing him with agreeable people, giving him a chance to make himself felt, to come to a sense of what he really had to give. I'd foreseen this solution from the beginning—felt sure that, once the first ardour of authorship was quenched, he'd drop into his place as a charming parasitic thing, the kind of chronic Cherubino for whom, in old societies, there's always a seat at table, and a shelter behind the ladies' skirts. I saw him take his place as 'the poet': the poet who doesn't write. One knows the type in every drawing-room. Living in that way doesn't cost much—I'd worked it all out in my mind, and felt sure that, with a little help, he could manage it for the next few years; and meanwhile he'd be sure to marry. I saw him married to a widow, rather older, with a good cook and a well-run house. And I actually had my eye on the widow . . . Meanwhile I did everything to facilitate the transition—lent him money to ease his conscience, introduced him to pretty women to make him forget his vows. But nothing would do him: he had but one idea in his beautiful obstinate head. He wanted the laurel and not the rose, and he kept on repeating Gautier's axiom, and battering and filing at his limp prose till he'd spread it out over Lord knows how many thousand sloppy pages. Now and then he would send a pailful to a publisher, and of course it would always come back.

"At first it didn't matter—he thought he was 'misunderstood.' He took the attitudes of genius, and whenever an opus came home he wrote another to keep it company. Then he had a reaction of despair, and accused me of deceiving him, and Lord knows what. I got angry at that, and told him it was he who had deceived himself. He'd come to me determined to write, and I'd done my best to help him. That was the extent of my offence, and I'd done it for his cousin's sake, not his.

"That seemed to strike home, and he didn't answer for a minute. Then he said: 'My time's up and my money's up. What do you think I'd better do?'

"'I think you'd better not be an ass,' I said.

"He turned red, and asked: 'What do you mean by being an ass?'

"I took a letter from my desk and held it out to him.

"'I mean refusing this offer of Mrs. Ellinger's: to be her secretary at a salary of five thousand dollars. There may be a lot more in it than that.'

"He flung out his hand with a violence that struck the letter from mine. 'Oh, I know well enough what's in it!' he said, scarlet to the roots of his hair.

"'And what's your answer, if you know?' I asked.

"He made none at the minute, but turned away slowly to the door. There, with his hand on the threshold, he stopped to ask, almost under his breath: 'Then you really think my stuff's no good?'

"I was tired and exasperated, and I laughed. I don't defend my laugh—it was in wretched taste. But I must plead in extenuation that the boy was a fool, and that I'd done my best for him—I really had.

"He went out of the room, shutting the door quietly after him. That afternoon I left for Frascati, where I'd promised to spend the Sunday with some friends. I was glad to escape from Gilbert, and by the same token, as I learned that night, I had also escaped from the eyes. I dropped into the same lethargic sleep that had come to me before when their visitations ceased; and when I woke the next morning, in my peaceful painted room above the ilexes, I felt the utter weariness and deep relief that always followed on that repairing slumber. I put in two blessed nights at Frascati, and when I got back to my rooms in Rome I found that Gilbert had gone . . . Oh, nothing tragic had happened—the episode never rose to that. He'd simply packed his manuscripts and left for America—for his family and the Wall Street desk. He left a decent little note to tell me of his decision, and behaved altogether, in the circumstances, as little like a fool as it's possible for a fool to behave . . ."

IV

CULWIN paused again, and again Frenham sat motionless, the dusky contour of his young head reflected in the mirror at his back.

"And what became of Noyes afterward?" I finally asked, still disquieted by a sense of incompleteness, by the need of some connecting thread between the parallel lines of the tale.

Culwin twitched his shoulders. "Oh, nothing became of him—because he became nothing. There could be no question of 'becoming' about it. He vegetated in an office, I believe, and finally got a clerkship in a consulate, and married drearily in China. I saw him once in Hong Kong, years afterward. He was fat and hadn't shaved. I was told he drank. He didn't recognize me."

"And the eyes?" I asked, after another pause which Frenham's continued silence made oppressive.

Culwin, stroking his chin, blinked at me meditatively through the shadows. "I never saw them after my last talk with Gilbert. Put two and two together if you can. For my part, I haven't found the link."

He rose stiffly, his hands in his pockets, and walked over to the table on which reviving drinks had been set out.

"You must be parched after this dry tale. Here, help yourself, my dear fellow. Here, Phil—" He turned back to the hearth.

Frenham still sat in his low chair, making no response to his host's hospitable summons. But as Culwin advanced toward him, their eyes met in a long look; after which, to my intense surprise, the young man, turning suddenly in his seat, flung his arms across the table, and dropped his face upon them.

Culwin, at the unexpected gesture, stopped short, a flush on his face.

"Phil—what the deuce? Why, have the eyes scared you? My dear boy—my dear fellow—I never had such a tribute to my literary ability, never!"

He broke into a chuckle at the thought, and halted on the hearth-rug, his hands still in his pockets, gazing down in honest perplexity at the youth's bowed head. Then, as Frenham still made no answer, he moved a step or two nearer.

"Cheer up, my dear Phil! It's years since I've seen them—apparently I've done nothing lately bad enough to call them out of chaos. Unless my present evocation of them has made you see them; which would be their worst stroke yet!"

His bantering appeal quivered off into an uneasy laugh, and he moved still nearer, bending over Frenham, and laying his gouty hands on the lad's shoulders.

"Phil, my dear boy, really—what's the matter? Why don't you answer? Have you seen the eyes?"

Frenham's face was still pressed against his arms, and from where I stood behind Culwin I saw the latter, as if under the rebuff of this unaccountable attitude, draw back slowly from his friend. As he did so, the light of the lamp on the table fell full on his perplexed congested face, and I caught its sudden reflection in the mirror behind Frenham's head.

Culwin saw the reflection also. He paused, his face level with the mirror, as if scarcely recognizing the countenance in it as his own. But as he looked his expression gradually changed, and for an appreciable space of time he and the image in the glass confronted each other with a glare of slowly gathering hate. Then Culwin let go of Frenham's shoulders, and drew back a step, covering his eyes with his hands . . .

Frenham, his face still hidden, did not stir.

3

The Bolted Door

I

HUBERT GRANICE, pacing the length of his pleasant lamp-lit library, paused to compare his watch with the clock on the chimney-piece.

Three minutes to eight.

In exactly three minutes Mr. Peter Ascham, of the eminent legal firm of Ascham and Pettilow, would have his punctual hand on the door-bell of the flat. It was a comfort to reflect that Ascham was so punctual—the suspense was beginning to make his host nervous. And the sound of the door-bell would be the beginning of the end—after that there'd be no going back, by God—no going back!

Granice resumed his pacing. Each time he reached the end of the room opposite the door he caught his reflection in the Florentine mirror above the fine old walnut credence he had picked up at Dijon—saw himself spare, quick-moving, carefully brushed and dressed, but furrowed, gray about the temples, with a stoop which he corrected by a spasmodic straightening of the shoulders whenever a glass confronted him: a tired middle-aged man, baffled, beaten, worn out.

As he summed himself up thus for the third or fourth time the door opened and he turned with a thrill of relief to greet his guest.

But it was only the man-servant who entered, advancing silently over the mossy surface of the old Turkey rug.

"Mr. Ascham telephones, sir, to say he's unexpectedly detained and can't be here till eight-thirty."

Granice made a curt gesture of annoyance. It was becoming harder and harder for him to control these reflexes. He turned on his heel, tossing to the servant over his shoulder: "Very good. Put off dinner."

Down his spine he felt the man's injured stare. Mr. Granice had always been so mild-spoken to his people—no doubt the odd change in his manner had already been noticed and discussed below stairs. And very likely they suspected the cause. He stood drumming on the writing-table till he heard the servant go out; then he threw himself into a chair, propping his elbows on the table and resting his chin on his locked hands.

Another half hour alone with it!

He wondered irritably what could have detained his guest. Some professional matter, no doubt—the punctilious lawyer would have allowed nothing less to interfere with a dinner engagement, more especially since Granice, in his note, had said: "I shall want a little business chat afterward."

But what professional matter could have come up at that unprofessional hour? Perhaps some other soul in misery had called on the lawyer; and, after all, Granice's note had given no hint of his own need! No doubt Ascham thought he merely wanted to make another change in his will. Since he had come into his little property, ten years earlier, Granice had been perpetually tinkering with his will.

Suddenly another thought pulled him up, sending a flush to his sallow temples. He remembered a word he had tossed to the lawyer some six weeks earlier, at the Century Club. "Yes—my play's as good as taken. I shall be calling on you soon to go over the contract. Those theatrical chaps are so slippery—I won't trust anybody but you to tie the knot for me!" That, of course, was what Ascham would think he was wanted for. Granice, at the idea, broke into an audible laugh—a queer stage-laugh, like the cackle of a baffled villain in a melodrama. The absurdity, the unnaturalness of the sound abashed him, and he compressed his lips angrily. Would he take to soliloquy next?

He lowered his arms and pulled open the upper drawer of the writing-table. In the right-hand corner lay a thick manuscript, bound in paper folders, and tied with a string beneath which a letter had been slipped. Next to the manuscript was a small revolver. Granice stared a moment at these oddly associated objects; then he took the letter from under the string and slowly began to open it. He had known he should do so from the moment his hand touched the drawer. Whenever his eye fell on that letter some relentless force compelled him to re-read it.

It was dated about four weeks back, under the letter-head of "The Diversity Theatre."

"MY DEAR MR. GRANICE:

"I have given the matter my best consideration for the last month, and it's no use—the play won't do. I have talked it over with Miss Melrose—and you know there isn't a gamer artist on our stage—and I regret to tell you she feels just as I do about it. It isn't the poetry that scares her—or me either. We both want to do all we can to help along the poetic drama—we believe the public's ready for it, and we're willing to take a big financial risk in order to be the first to give them what they want. But we don't believe they could be made to want this. The fact is, there isn't enough drama in your play to the allowance of poetry—the thing drags all through. You've got a big idea, but it's not out of swaddling clothes.

"If this was your first play I'd say: Try again. But it has been just the same with all the others you've shown me. And you remember the result of 'The Lee Shore,' where you carried all the expenses of production yourself, and we couldn't fill the theatre for a week. Yet 'The Lee Shore' was a modern problem play—much easier to swing than blank verse. It isn't as if you hadn't tried all kinds—"

Granice folded the letter and put it carefully back into the envelope. Why on earth was he re-reading it, when he knew every phrase in it by heart, when for a month past he had seen it, night after night, stand out in letters of flame against the darkness of his sleepless lids?

"It has been just the same with all the others you've shown me."

That was the way they dismissed ten years of passionate unremitting work!

"You remember the result of 'The Lee Shore.'"

Good God—as if he were likely to forget it! He re-lived it all now in a drowning flash: the persistent rejection of the play, his sudden resolve to put it on at his own cost, to spend ten thousand dollars of his inheritance on testing his chance of success—the fever of preparation, the dry-mouthed agony of the "first night," the flat fall, the stupid press, his secret rush to Europe to escape the condolence of his friends!

"It isn't as if you hadn't tried all kinds."

No—he had tried all kinds: comedy, tragedy, prose and verse, the light curtain-raiser, the short sharp drama, the bourgeois-realistic and the lyrical-romantic—finally deciding that he would no longer "prostitute his talent" to win popularity, but would impose on the public his own theory of art in the form of five acts of blank verse. Yes, he had offered them everything—and always with the same result.

Ten years of it—ten years of dogged work and unrelieved failure. The ten years from forty to fifty—the best ten years of his life! And if one counted the years before, the silent years of dreams, assimilation, preparation—then call it half a man's life-time: half a man's life-time thrown away!

And what was he to do with the remaining half? Well, he had settled that, thank God! He turned and glanced anxiously at the clock. Ten minutes past eight—only ten minutes had been consumed in that stormy rush through his whole past! And he must wait another twenty minutes for Ascham. It was one of the worst symptoms of his case that, in proportion as he had grown to shrink from human company, he dreaded more and more to be alone. . . . But why the devil was he waiting for Ascham? Why didn't he cut the knot himself? Since he was so unutterably sick of the whole business, why did he have to call in an outsider to rid him of this nightmare of living?

He opened the drawer again and laid his hand on the revolver. It was a small slim ivory toy—just the instrument for a tired sufferer to give himself a "hypodermic" with. Granice raised it slowly in one hand, while with the other he felt under the thin hair at the back of his head, between the ear and the nape. He knew just where to place the muzzle: he had once got a young surgeon to show him. And as he found the spot, and lifted the revolver to it, the inevitable phenomenon occurred. The hand that held the weapon began to shake, the tremor communicated itself to his arm, his heart gave a wild leap which sent up a wave of deadly nausea to his throat, he smelt the powder, he sickened at the crash of the bullet through his skull, and a sweat of fear broke out over his forehead and ran down his quivering face . . .

He laid away the revolver with an oath and, pulling out a cologne-scented handkerchief, passed it tremulously over his brow and temples. It was no use—he knew he could never do it in that way. His attempts at self-destruction were as futile as his snatches at fame! He couldn't make himself a real life, and he couldn't get rid of the life he had. And that was why he had sent for Ascham to help him . . .

The lawyer, over the Camembert and Burgundy, began to excuse himself for his delay.

"I didn't like to say anything while your man was about—but the fact is, I was sent for on a rather unusual matter—"

"Oh, it's all right," said Granice cheerfully. He was beginning to feel the usual reaction that food and company produced. It was not any recovered pleasure in life that he felt, but only a deeper withdrawal into himself. It was easier to go on automatically with the social gestures than to uncover to any human eye the abyss within him.

"My dear fellow, it's sacrilege to keep a dinner waiting—especially the production of an artist like yours." Mr. Ascham sipped his Burgundy luxuriously. "But the fact is, Mrs. Ashgrove sent for me."

Granice raised his head with a quick movement of surprise. For a moment he was shaken out of his self-absorption.

"Mrs. Ashgrove?"

Ascham smiled. "I thought you'd be interested; I know your passion for causes celebres. And this promises to be one. Of course it's out of our line entirely—we never touch criminal cases. But she wanted to consult me as a friend. Ashgrove was a distant connection of my wife's. And, by Jove, it is a queer case!" The servant re-entered, and Ascham snapped his lips shut.

Would the gentlemen have their coffee in the dining-room?

"No—serve it in the library," said Granice, rising. He led the way back to the curtained confidential room. He was really curious to hear what Ascham had to tell him.

While the coffee and cigars were being served he fidgeted about the library, glancing at his letters—the usual meaningless notes and bills—and picking up the evening paper. As he unfolded it a headline caught his eye.

"ROSE MELROSE WANTS TO PLAY POETRY.

"THINKS SHE HAS FOUND HER POET."

He read on with a thumping heart—found the name of a young author he had barely heard of, saw the title of a play, a "poetic drama," dance before his eyes, and dropped the paper, sick, disgusted. It was true, then—she was "game"—it was not the manner but the matter she mistrusted!

Granice turned to the servant, who seemed to be purposely lingering. "I shan't need you this evening, Flint. I'll lock up myself."

He fancied the man's acquiescence implied surprise. What was going on, Flint seemed to wonder, that Mr. Granice should want him out of the way? Probably he would find a pretext for coming back to see. Granice suddenly felt himself enveloped in a network of espionage.

As the door closed he threw himself into an armchair and leaned forward to take a light from Ascham's cigar.

"Tell me about Mrs. Ashgrove," he said, seeming to himself to speak stiffly, as if his lips were cracked.

"Mrs. Ashgrove? Well, there's not much to tell."

"And you couldn't if there were?" Granice smiled.

"Probably not. As a matter of fact, she wanted my advice about her choice of counsel. There was nothing especially confidential in our talk."

"And what's your impression, now you've seen her?"

"My impression is, very distinctly, that nothing will ever be known."

"Ah—?" Granice murmured, puffing at his cigar.

"I'm more and more convinced that whoever poisoned Ashgrove knew his business, and will consequently never be found out. That's a capital cigar you've given me."

"You like it? I get them over from Cuba." Granice examined his own reflectively. "Then you believe in the theory that the clever criminals never are caught?"

"Of course I do. Look about you—look back for the last dozen years—none of the big murder problems are ever solved." The lawyer ruminated behind his blue cloud. "Why, take the instance in your own family: I'd forgotten I had an illustration at hand! Take old Joseph Lenman's murder—do you suppose that will ever be explained?"

As the words dropped from Ascham's lips his host looked slowly about the library, and every object in it stared back at him with a stale unescapable familiarity. How sick he was of looking at that room! It was as dull as the face of a wife one has wearied of. He cleared his throat slowly; then he turned his head to the lawyer and said: "I could explain the Lenman murder myself."

Ascham's eye kindled: he shared Granice's interest in criminal cases.

"By Jove! You've had a theory all this time? It's odd you never mentioned it. Go ahead and tell me. There are certain features in the Lenman case not unlike this Ashgrove affair, and your idea may be a help."

Granice paused and his eye reverted instinctively to the table drawer in which the revolver and the manuscript lay side by side. What if he were to try another appeal to Rose Melrose? Then he looked at the notes and bills on the table, and the horror of taking up again the lifeless routine of life—of performing the same automatic gestures another day—displaced his fleeting vision.

"I haven't a theory. I know who murdered Joseph Lenman."

Ascham settled himself comfortably in his chair, prepared for enjoyment.

"You know? Well, who did?" he laughed.

"I did," said Granice, rising.

He stood before Ascham, and the lawyer lay back staring up at him. Then he broke into another laugh.

"Why, this is glorious! You murdered him, did you? To inherit his money, I suppose? Better and better! Go on, my boy! Unbosom yourself! Tell me all about it! Confession is good for the soul."

Granice waited till the lawyer had shaken the last peal of laughter from his throat; then he repeated doggedly: "I murdered him."

The two men looked at each other for a long moment, and this time Ascham did not laugh.

"Granice!"

"I murdered him—to get his money, as you say."

There was another pause, and Granice, with a vague underlying sense of amusement, saw his guest's look change from pleasantry to apprehension.

"What's the joke, my dear fellow? I fail to see."

"It's not a joke. It's the truth. I murdered him." He had spoken painfully at first, as if there were a knot in his throat; but each time he repeated the words he found they were easier to say.

Ascham laid down his extinct cigar.

"What's the matter? Aren't you well? What on earth are you driving at?"

"I'm perfectly well. But I murdered my cousin, Joseph Lenman, and I want it known that I murdered him."

"You want it known?"

"Yes. That's why I sent for you. I'm sick of living, and when I try to kill myself I funk it." He spoke quite naturally now, as if the knot in his throat had been untied.

"Good Lord—good Lord," the lawyer gasped.

"But I suppose," Granice continued, "there's no doubt this would be murder in the first degree? I'm sure of the chair if I own up?"

Ascham drew a long breath; then he said slowly: "Sit down, Granice. Let's talk."

II

GRANICE told his story simply, connectedly.

He began by a quick survey of his early years—the years of drudgery and privation. His father, a charming man who could never say "no," had so signally failed to say it on certain essential occasions that when he died he left an illegitimate family and a mortgaged estate. His lawful kin found themselves hanging over a gulf of debt, and young Granice, to support his mother and sister, had to leave Harvard and bury himself at eighteen in a broker's office. He loathed his work, and he was always poor, always worried and in ill-health. A few years later his mother died, but his sister, an ineffectual neurasthenic, remained on his hands. His own health gave out, and he had to go away for six months, and work harder than ever when he came back. He had no knack for business, no head for figures, no dimmest insight into the mysteries of commerce. He wanted to travel and write—those were his inmost longings. And as the years dragged on, and he neared middle-age without making any more money, or acquiring any firmer health, a sick despair possessed him. He tried writing, but he always came home from the office so tired that his brain could not work. For half the year he did not reach his dim up-town flat till after dark, and could only "brush up" for dinner, and afterward lie on the lounge with his pipe, while his sister droned through the evening paper. Sometimes he spent an evening at the theatre; or he dined out, or, more rarely, strayed off with an acquaintance or two in quest of what is known as "pleasure." And in summer, when he and Kate went to the sea-side for a month, he dozed through the days in utter weariness. Once he fell in love with a charming girl—but what had he to offer her, in God's name? She seemed to like him, and in common decency he had to drop out of the running. Apparently no one replaced him, for she never married, but grew stoutish, grayish, philanthropic—yet how sweet she had been when he had first kissed her! One more wasted life, he reflected . . .

But the stage had always been his master-passion. He would have sold his soul for the time and freedom to write plays! It was in him—he could not remember when it had not been his deepest-seated instinct. As the years passed it became a morbid, a relentless obsession—yet with every year the material conditions were more and more against it. He felt himself growing middle-aged, and he watched the reflection of the process in his sister's wasted face. At eighteen she had been pretty, and as full of enthusiasm as he. Now she was sour, trivial, insignificant—she had missed her chance of life. And she had no resources, poor creature, was fashioned simply for the primitive functions she had been denied the chance to fulfil! It exasperated him to think of it—and to reflect that even now a little travel, a little health, a little money, might transform her, make her young and desirable . . . The chief fruit of his experience was that there is no such fixed state as age or youth—there is only health as against sickness, wealth as against poverty; and age or youth as the outcome of the lot one draws.

At this point in his narrative Granice stood up, and went to lean against the mantel-piece, looking down at Ascham, who had not moved from his seat, or changed his attitude of rigid fascinated attention.

"Then came the summer when we went to Wrenfield to be near old Lenman—my mother's cousin, as you know. Some of the family always mounted guard over him—generally a niece or so. But that year they were all scattered, and one of the nieces offered to lend us her cottage if we'd relieve her of duty for two months. It was a nuisance for me, of course, for Wrenfield is two hours from town; but my mother, who was a slave to family observances, had always been good to the old man, so it was natural we should be called on—and there was the saving of rent and the good air for Kate. So we went.

"You never knew Joseph Lenman? Well, picture to yourself an amoeba or some primitive organism of that sort, under a Titan's microscope. He was large, undifferentiated, inert—since I could remember him he had done nothing but take his temperature and read the Churchman. Oh, and cultivate melons—that was his hobby. Not vulgar, out-of-door melons—his were grown under glass. He had miles of it at Wrenfield—his big kitchen-garden was surrounded by blinking battalions of green-houses. And in nearly all of them melons were grown—early melons and late, French, English, domestic—dwarf melons and monsters: every shape, colour and variety. They were petted and nursed like children—a staff of trained attendants waited on them. I'm not sure they didn't have a doctor to take their temperature—at any rate the place was full of thermometers. And they didn't sprawl on the ground like ordinary melons; they were trained against the glass like nectarines, and each melon hung in a net which sustained its weight and left it free on all sides to the sun and air . . .

"It used to strike me sometimes that old Lenman was just like one of his own melons—the pale-fleshed English kind. His life, apathetic and motionless, hung in a net of gold, in an equable warm ventilated atmosphere, high above sordid earthly worries. The cardinal rule of his existence was not to let himself be 'worried.' . . I remember his advising me to try it myself, one day when I spoke to him about Kate's bad health, and her need of a change. 'I never let myself worry,' he said complacently. 'It's the worst thing for the liver—and you look to me as if you had a liver. Take my advice and be cheerful. You'll make yourself happier and others too.' And all he had to do was to write a cheque, and send the poor girl off for a holiday!

"The hardest part of it was that the money half-belonged to us already. The old skin-flint only had it for life, in trust for us and the others. But his life was a good deal sounder than mine or Kate's—and one could picture him taking extra care of it for the joke of keeping us waiting. I always felt that the sight of our hungry eyes was a tonic to him.

"Well, I tried to see if I couldn't reach him through his vanity. I flattered him, feigned a passionate interest in his melons. And he was taken in, and used to discourse on them by the hour. On fine days he was driven to the green-houses in his pony-chair, and waddled through them, prodding and leering at the fruit, like a fat Turk in his seraglio. When he bragged to me of the expense of growing them I was reminded of a hideous old Lothario bragging of what his pleasures cost. And the resemblance was completed by the fact that he couldn't eat as much as a mouthful of his melons—had lived for years on buttermilk and toast. 'But, after all, it's my only hobby—why shouldn't I indulge it?' he said sentimentally. As if I'd ever been able to indulge any of mine! On the keep of those melons Kate and I could have lived like gods . . .

"One day toward the end of the summer, when Kate was too unwell to drag herself up to the big house, she asked me to go and spend the afternoon with cousin Joseph. It was a lovely soft September afternoon—a day to lie under a Roman stone-pine, with one's eyes on the sky, and let the cosmic harmonies rush through one. Perhaps the vision was suggested by the fact that, as I entered cousin Joseph's hideous black walnut library, I passed one of the under-gardeners, a handsome full-throated Italian, who dashed out in such a hurry that he nearly knocked me down. I remember thinking it queer that the fellow, whom I had often seen about the melon-houses, did not bow to me, or even seem to see me.

"Cousin Joseph sat in his usual seat, behind the darkened windows, his fat hands folded on his protuberant waistcoat, the last number of the Churchman at his elbow, and near it, on a huge dish, a fat melon—the fattest melon I'd ever seen. As I looked at it I pictured the ecstasy of contemplation from which I must have roused him, and congratulated myself on finding him in such a mood, since I had made up my mind to ask him a favour. Then I noticed that his face, instead of looking as calm as an egg-shell, was distorted and whimpering—and without stopping to greet me he pointed passionately to the melon.

"'Look at it, look at it—did you ever see such a beauty? Such firmness—roundness—such delicious smoothness to the touch?' It was as if he had said 'she' instead of 'it,' and when he put out his senile hand and touched the melon I positively had to look the other way.

"Then he told me what had happened. The Italian under-gardener, who had been specially recommended for the melon-houses—though it was against my cousin's principles to employ a Papist—had been assigned to the care of the monster: for it had revealed itself, early in its existence, as destined to become a monster, to surpass its plumpest, pulpiest sisters, carry off prizes at agricultural shows, and be photographed and celebrated in every gardening paper in the land. The Italian had done well—seemed to have a sense of responsibility. And that very morning he had been ordered to pick the melon, which was to be shown next day at the county fair, and to bring it in for Mr. Lenman to gaze on its blonde virginity. But in picking it, what had the damned scoundrelly Jesuit done but drop it—drop it crash on the sharp spout of a watering-pot, so that it received a deep gash in its firm pale rotundity, and was henceforth but a bruised, ruined, fallen melon?

"The old man's rage was fearful in its impotence—he shook, spluttered and strangled with it. He had just had the Italian up and had sacked him on the spot, without wages or character—had threatened to have him arrested if he was ever caught prowling about Wrenfield. 'By God, and I'll do it—I'll write to Washington—I'll have the pauper scoundrel deported! I'll show him what money can do!' As likely as not there was some murderous Black-hand business under it—it would be found that the fellow was a member of a 'gang.' Those Italians would murder you for a quarter. He meant to have the police look into it . . . And then he grew frightened at his own excitement. 'But I must calm myself,' he said. He took his temperature, rang for his drops, and turned to the Churchman. He had been reading an article on Nestorianism when the melon was brought in. He asked me to go on with it, and I read to him for an hour, in the dim close room, with a fat fly buzzing stealthily about the fallen melon.

"All the while one phrase of the old man's buzzed in my brain like the fly about the melon. 'I'll show him what money can do!' Good heaven! If I could but show the old man! If I could make him see his power of giving happiness as a new outlet for his monstrous egotism! I tried to tell him something about my situation and Kate's—spoke of my ill-health, my unsuccessful drudgery, my longing to write, to make myself a name—I stammered out an entreaty for a loan. 'I can guarantee to repay you, sir—I've a half-written play as security . . .'

"I shall never forget his glassy stare. His face had grown as smooth as an egg-shell again—his eyes peered over his fat cheeks like sentinels over a slippery rampart.

"'A half-written play—a play of yours as security?' He looked at me almost fearfully, as if detecting the first symptoms of insanity. 'Do you understand anything of business?' he enquired mildly. I laughed and answered: 'No, not much.'

"He leaned back with closed lids. 'All this excitement has been too much for me,' he said. 'If you'll excuse me, I'll prepare for my nap.' And I stumbled out of the room, blindly, like the Italian."

Granice moved away from the mantel-piece, and walked across to the tray set out with decanters and soda-water. He poured himself a tall glass of soda-water, emptied it, and glanced at Ascham's dead cigar.

"Better light another," he suggested.

The lawyer shook his head, and Granice went on with his tale. He told of his mounting obsession—how the murderous impulse had waked in him on the instant of his cousin's refusal, and he had muttered to himself: "By God, if you won't, I'll make you." He spoke more tranquilly as the narrative proceeded, as though his rage had died down once the resolve to act on it was taken. He applied his whole mind to the question of how the old man was to be "disposed of." Suddenly he remembered the outcry: "Those Italians will murder you for a quarter!" But no definite project presented itself: he simply waited for an inspiration.

Granice and his sister moved to town a day or two after the incident of the melon. But the cousins, who had returned, kept them informed of the old man's condition. One day, about three weeks later, Granice, on getting home, found Kate excited over a report from Wrenfield. The Italian had been there again—had somehow slipped into the house, made his way up to the library, and "used threatening language." The house-keeper found cousin Joseph gasping, the whites of his eyes showing "something awful." The doctor was sent for, and the attack warded off; and the police had ordered the Italian from the neighbourhood.

But cousin Joseph, thereafter, languished, had "nerves," and lost his taste for toast and butter-milk. The doctor called in a colleague, and the consultation amused and excited the old man—he became once more an important figure. The medical men reassured the family—too completely!—and to the patient they recommended a more varied diet: advised him to take whatever "tempted him." And so one day, tremulously, prayerfully, he decided on a tiny bit of melon. It was brought up with ceremony, and consumed in the presence of the house-keeper and a hovering cousin; and twenty minutes later he was dead . . .

"But you remember the circumstances," Granice went on; "how suspicion turned at once on the Italian? In spite of the hint the police had given him he had been seen hanging about the house since 'the scene.' It was said that he had tender relations with the kitchen-maid, and the rest seemed easy to explain. But when they looked round to ask him for the explanation he was gone—gone clean out of sight. He had been 'warned' to leave Wrenfield, and he had taken the warning so to heart that no one ever laid eyes on him again."

Granice paused. He had dropped into a chair opposite the lawyer's, and he sat for a moment, his head thrown back, looking about the familiar room. Everything in it had grown grimacing and alien, and each strange insistent object seemed craning forward from its place to hear him.

"It was I who put the stuff in the melon," he said. "And I don't want you to think I'm sorry for it. This isn't 'remorse,' understand. I'm glad the old skin-flint is dead—I'm glad the others have their money. But mine's no use to me any more. My sister married miserably, and died. And I've never had what I wanted."

Ascham continued to stare; then he said: "What on earth was your object, then?"

"Why, to get what I wanted—what I fancied was in reach! I wanted change, rest, life, for both of us—wanted, above all, for myself, the chance to write! I travelled, got back my health, and came home to tie myself up to my work. And I've slaved at it steadily for ten years without reward—without the most distant hope of success! Nobody will look at my stuff. And now I'm fifty, and I'm beaten, and I know it." His chin dropped forward on his breast. "I want to chuck the whole business," he ended.

III

IT was after midnight when Ascham left.

His hand on Granice's shoulder, as he turned to go—"District Attorney be hanged; see a doctor, see a doctor!" he had cried; and so, with an exaggerated laugh, had pulled on his coat and departed.

Granice turned back into the library. It had never occurred to him that Ascham would not believe his story. For three hours he had explained, elucidated, patiently and painfully gone over every detail—but without once breaking down the iron incredulity of the lawyer's eye.

At first Ascham had feigned to be convinced—but that, as Granice now perceived, was simply to get him to expose himself, to entrap him into contradictions. And when the attempt failed, when Granice triumphantly met and refuted each disconcerting question, the lawyer dropped the mask suddenly, and said with a good-humoured laugh: "By Jove, Granice you'll write a successful play yet. The way you've worked this all out is a marvel."

Granice swung about furiously—that last sneer about the play inflamed him. Was all the world in a conspiracy to deride his failure?

"I did it, I did it," he muttered sullenly, his rage spending itself against the impenetrable surface of the other's mockery; and Ascham answered with a smile: "Ever read any of those books on hallucination? I've got a fairly good medico-legal library. I could send you one or two if you like . . ."

Left alone, Granice cowered down in the chair before his writing-table. He understood that Ascham thought him off his head.

"Good God—what if they all think me crazy?"

The horror of it broke out over him in a cold sweat—he sat there and shook, his eyes hidden in his icy hands. But gradually, as he began to rehearse his story for the thousandth time, he saw again how incontrovertible it was, and felt sure that any criminal lawyer would believe him.

"That's the trouble—Ascham's not a criminal lawyer. And then he's a friend. What a fool I was to talk to a friend! Even if he did believe me, he'd never let me see it—his instinct would be to cover the whole thing up . . . But in that case—if he did believe me—he might think it a kindness to get me shut up in an asylum . . ." Granice began to tremble again. "Good heaven! If he should bring in an expert—one of those damned alienists! Ascham and Pettilow can do anything—their word always goes. If Ascham drops a hint that I'd better be shut up, I'll be in a strait-jacket by to-morrow! And he'd do it from the kindest motives—be quite right to do it if he thinks I'm a murderer!"

The vision froze him to his chair. He pressed his fists to his bursting temples and tried to think. For the first time he hoped that Ascham had not believed his story.

"But he did—he did! I can see it now—I noticed what a queer eye he cocked at me. Good God, what shall I do—what shall I do?"

He started up and looked at the clock. Half-past one. What if Ascham should think the case urgent, rout out an alienist, and come back with him? Granice jumped to his feet, and his sudden gesture brushed the morning paper from the table. Mechanically he stooped to pick it up, and the movement started a new train of association.

He sat down again, and reached for the telephone book in the rack by his chair.

"Give me three-o-ten . . . yes."

The new idea in his mind had revived his flagging energy. He would act—act at once. It was only by thus planning ahead, committing himself to some unavoidable line of conduct, that he could pull himself through the meaningless days. Each time he reached a fresh decision it was like coming out of a foggy weltering sea into a calm harbour with lights. One of the queerest phases of his long agony was the intense relief produced by these momentary lulls.

"That the office of the Investigator? Yes? Give me Mr. Denver, please . . . Hallo, Denver . . . Yes, Hubert Granice. . . . Just caught you? Going straight home? Can I come and see you . . . yes, now . . . have a talk? It's rather urgent . . . yes, might give you some first-rate 'copy.' . . . All right!" He hung up the receiver with a laugh. It had been a happy thought to call up the editor of the Investigator—Robert Denver was the very man he needed . . .

Granice put out the lights in the library—it was odd how the automatic gestures persisted!—went into the hall, put on his hat and overcoat, and let himself out of the flat. In the hall, a sleepy elevator boy blinked at him and then dropped his head on his folded arms. Granice passed out into the street. At the corner of Fifth Avenue he hailed a crawling cab, and called out an up-town address. The long thoroughfare stretched before him, dim and deserted, like an ancient avenue of tombs. But from Denver's house a friendly beam fell on the pavement; and as Granice sprang from his cab the editor's electric turned the corner.

The two men grasped hands, and Denver, feeling for his latch-key, ushered Granice into the brightly-lit hall.

"Disturb me? Not a bit. You might have, at ten to-morrow morning . . . but this is my liveliest hour . . . you know my habits of old."

Granice had known Robert Denver for fifteen years—watched his rise through all the stages of journalism to the Olympian pinnacle of the Investigator's editorial office. In the thick-set man with grizzling hair there were few traces left of the hungry-eyed young reporter who, on his way home in the small hours, used to "bob in" on Granice, while the latter sat grinding at his plays. Denver had to pass Granice's flat on the way to his own, and it became a habit, if he saw a light in the window, and Granice's shadow against the blind, to go in, smoke a pipe, and discuss the universe.

"Well—this is like old times—a good old habit reversed." The editor smote his visitor genially on the shoulder. "Reminds me of the nights when I used to rout you out . . . How's the play, by the way? There is a play, I suppose? It's as safe to ask you that as to say to some men: 'How's the baby?'"

Denver laughed good-naturedly, and Granice thought how thick and heavy he had grown. It was evident, even to Granice's tortured nerves, that the words had not been uttered in malice—and the fact gave him a new measure of his insignificance. Denver did not even know that he had been a failure! The fact hurt more than Ascham's irony.

"Come in—come in." The editor led the way into a small cheerful room, where there were cigars and decanters. He pushed an arm-chair toward his visitor, and dropped into another with a comfortable groan.

"Now, then—help yourself. And let's hear all about it."

He beamed at Granice over his pipe-bowl, and the latter, lighting his cigar, said to himself: "Success makes men comfortable, but it makes them stupid."

Then he turned, and began: "Denver, I want to tell you—"

The clock ticked rhythmically on the mantel-piece. The room was gradually filled with drifting blue layers of smoke, and through them the editor's face came and went like the moon through a moving sky. Once the hour struck—then the rhythmical ticking began again. The atmosphere grew denser and heavier, and beads of perspiration began to roll from Granice's forehead.

"Do you mind if I open the window?"

"No. It is stuffy in here. Wait—I'll do it myself." Denver pushed down the upper sash, and returned to his chair. "Well—go on," he said, filling another pipe. His composure exasperated Granice.

"There's no use in my going on if you don't believe me."

The editor remained unmoved. "Who says I don't believe you? And how can I tell till you've finished?"

Granice went on, ashamed of his outburst. "It was simple enough, as you'll see. From the day the old man said to me, 'Those Italians would murder you for a quarter,' I dropped everything and just worked at my scheme. It struck me at once that I must find a way of getting to Wrenfield and back in a night—and that led to the idea of a motor. A motor—that never occurred to you? You wonder where I got the money, I suppose. Well, I had a thousand or so put by, and I nosed around till I found what I wanted—a second-hand racer. I knew how to drive a car, and I tried the thing and found it was all right. Times were bad, and I bought it for my price, and stored it away. Where? Why, in one of those no-questions-asked garages where they keep motors that are not for family use. I had a lively cousin who had put me up to that dodge, and I looked about till I found a queer hole where they took in my car like a baby in a foundling asylum . . . Then I practiced running to Wrenfield and back in a night. I knew the way pretty well, for I'd done it often with the same lively cousin—and in the small hours, too. The distance is over ninety miles, and on the third trial I did it under two hours. But my arms were so lame that I could hardly get dressed the next morning . . .

"Well, then came the report about the Italian's threats, and I saw I must act at once . . . I meant to break into the old man's room, shoot him, and get away again. It was a big risk, but I thought I could manage it. Then we heard that he was ill—that there'd been a consultation. Perhaps the fates were going to do it for me! Good Lord, if that could only be! . . ."

Granice stopped and wiped his forehead: the open window did not seem to have cooled the room.

"Then came word that he was better; and the day after, when I came up from my office, I found Kate laughing over the news that he was to try a bit of melon. The house-keeper had just telephoned her—all Wrenfield was in a flutter. The doctor himself had picked out the melon, one of the little French ones that are hardly bigger than a large tomato—and the patient was to eat it at his breakfast the next morning.

"In a flash I saw my chance. It was a bare chance, no more. But I knew the ways of the house—I was sure the melon would be brought in over night and put in the pantry ice-box. If there were only one melon in the ice-box I could be fairly sure it was the one I wanted. Melons didn't lie around loose in that house—every one was known, numbered, catalogued. The old man was beset by the dread that the servants would eat them, and he took a hundred mean precautions to prevent it. Yes, I felt pretty sure of my melon . . . and poisoning was much safer than shooting. It would have been the devil and all to get into the old man's bedroom without his rousing the house; but I ought to be able to break into the pantry without much trouble.

"It was a cloudy night, too—everything served me. I dined quietly, and sat down at my desk. Kate had one of her usual headaches, and went to bed early. As soon as she was gone I slipped out. I had got together a sort of disguise—red beard and queer-looking ulster. I shoved them into a bag, and went round to the garage. There was no one there but a half-drunken machinist whom I'd never seen before. That served me, too. They were always changing machinists, and this new fellow didn't even bother to ask if the car belonged to me. It was a very easy-going place . . .

"Well, I jumped in, ran up Broadway, and let the car go as soon as I was out of Harlem. Dark as it was, I could trust myself to strike a sharp pace. In the shadow of a wood I stopped a second and got into the beard and ulster. Then away again—it was just eleven-thirty when I got to Wrenfield.

"I left the car in a dark lane behind the Lenman place, and slipped through the kitchen-garden. The melon-houses winked at me through the dark—I remember thinking that they knew what I wanted to know. . . . By the stable a dog came out growling—but he nosed me out, jumped on me, and went back . . . The house was as dark as the grave. I knew everybody went to bed by ten. But there might be a prowling servant—the kitchen-maid might have come down to let in her Italian. I had to risk that, of course. I crept around by the back door and hid in the shrubbery. Then I listened. It was all as silent as death. I crossed over to the house, pried open the pantry window and climbed in. I had a little electric lamp in my pocket, and shielding it with my cap I groped my way to the ice-box, opened it—and there was the little French melon . . . only one.

"I stopped to listen—I was quite cool. Then I pulled out my bottle of stuff and my syringe, and gave each section of the melon a hypodermic. It was all done inside of three minutes—at ten minutes to twelve I was back in the car. I got out of the lane as quietly as I could, struck a back road that skirted the village, and let the car out as soon as I was beyond the last houses. I only stopped once on the way in, to drop the beard and ulster into a pond. I had a big stone ready to weight them with and they went down plump, like a dead body—and at two o'clock I was back at my desk."

Granice stopped speaking and looked across the smoke-fumes at his listener; but Denver's face remained inscrutable.

At length he said: "Why did you want to tell me this?"

The question startled Granice. He was about to explain, as he had explained to Ascham; but suddenly it occurred to him that if his motive had not seemed convincing to the lawyer it would carry much less weight with Denver. Both were successful men, and success does not understand the subtle agony of failure. Granice cast about for another reason.

"Why, I—the thing haunts me . . . remorse, I suppose you'd call it . . ."

Denver struck the ashes from his empty pipe.

"Remorse? Bosh!" he said energetically.

Granice's heart sank. "You don't believe in—remorse?"

"Not an atom: in the man of action. The mere fact of your talking of remorse proves to me that you're not the man to have planned and put through such a job."

Granice groaned. "Well—I lied to you about remorse. I've never felt any."

Denver's lips tightened sceptically about his freshly-filled pipe. "What was your motive, then? You must have had one."

"I'll tell you—" And Granice began again to rehearse the story of his failure, of his loathing for life. "Don't say you don't believe me this time . . . that this isn't a real reason!" he stammered out piteously as he ended.

Denver meditated. "No, I won't say that. I've seen too many queer things. There's always a reason for wanting to get out of life—the wonder is that we find so many for staying in!"

Granice's heart grew light. "Then you do believe me?" he faltered.

"Believe that you're sick of the job? Yes. And that you haven't the nerve to pull the trigger? Oh, yes—that's easy enough, too. But all that doesn't make you a murderer—though I don't say it proves you could never have been one."

"I have been one, Denver—I swear to you."

"Perhaps." He meditated. "Just tell me one or two things."

"Oh, go ahead. You won't stump me!" Granice heard himself say with a laugh.

"Well—how did you make all those trial trips without exciting your sister's curiosity? I knew your night habits pretty well at that time, remember. You were very seldom out late. Didn't the change in your ways surprise her?"

"No; because she was away at the time. She went to pay several visits in the country soon after we came back from Wrenfield, and was only in town for a night or two before—before I did the job."

"And that night she went to bed early with a headache?"

"Yes—blinding. She didn't know anything when she had that kind. And her room was at the back of the flat."

Denver again meditated. "And when you got back—she didn't hear you? You got in without her knowing it?"

"Yes. I went straight to my work—took it up at the word where I'd left off—why, Denver, don't you remember?" Granice suddenly, passionately interjected.

"Remember—?"

"Yes; how you found me—when you looked in that morning, between two and three . . . your usual hour . . .?"

"Yes," the editor nodded.

Granice gave a short laugh. "In my old coat—with my pipe: looked as if I'd been working all night, didn't I? Well, I hadn't been in my chair ten minutes!"

Denver uncrossed his legs and then crossed them again. "I didn't know whether you remembered that."

"What?"

"My coming in that particular night—or morning."

Granice swung round in his chair. "Why, man alive! That's why I'm here now. Because it was you who spoke for me at the inquest, when they looked round to see what all the old man's heirs had been doing that night—you who testified to having dropped in and found me at my desk as usual. . . . I thought that would appeal to your journalistic sense if nothing else would!"

Denver smiled. "Oh, my journalistic sense is still susceptible enough—and the idea's picturesque, I grant you: asking the man who proved your alibi to establish your guilt."

"That's it—that's it!" Granice's laugh had a ring of triumph.

"Well, but how about the other chap's testimony—I mean that young doctor: what was his name? Ned Ranney. Don't you remember my testifying that I'd met him at the elevated station, and told him I was on my way to smoke a pipe with you, and his saying: 'All right; you'll find him in. I passed the house two hours ago, and saw his shadow against the blind, as usual.' And the lady with the toothache in the flat across the way: she corroborated his statement, you remember."

"Yes; I remember."

"Well, then?"

"Simple enough. Before starting I rigged up a kind of mannikin with old coats and a cushion—something to cast a shadow on the blind. All you fellows were used to seeing my shadow there in the small hours—I counted on that, and knew you'd take any vague outline as mine."

"Simple enough, as you say. But the woman with the toothache saw the shadow move—you remember she said she saw you sink forward, as if you'd fallen asleep."

"Yes; and she was right. It did move. I suppose some extra-heavy dray must have jolted by the flimsy building—at any rate, something gave my mannikin a jar, and when I came back he had sunk forward, half over the table."

There was a long silence between the two men. Granice, with a throbbing heart, watched Denver refill his pipe. The editor, at any rate, did not sneer and flout him. After all, journalism gave a deeper insight than the law into the fantastic possibilities of life, prepared one better to allow for the incalculableness of human impulses.

"Well?" Granice faltered out.

Denver stood up with a shrug. "Look here, man—what's wrong with you? Make a clean breast of it! Nerves gone to smash? I'd like to take you to see a chap I know—an ex-prize-fighter—who's a wonder at pulling fellows in your state out of their hole—"

"Oh, oh—" Granice broke in. He stood up also, and the two men eyed each other. "You don't believe me, then?"

"This yarn—how can I? There wasn't a flaw in your alibi."

"But haven't I filled it full of them now?"

Denver shook his head. "I might think so if I hadn't happened to know that you wanted to. There's the hitch, don't you see?"

Granice groaned. "No, I didn't. You mean my wanting to be found guilty—?"

"Of course! If somebody else had accused you, the story might have been worth looking into. As it is, a child could have invented it. It doesn't do much credit to your ingenuity."

Granice turned sullenly toward the door. What was the use of arguing? But on the threshold a sudden impulse drew him back. "Look here, Denver—I daresay you're right. But will you do just one thing to prove it? Put my statement in the Investigator, just as I've made it. Ridicule it as much as you like. Only give the other fellows a chance at it—men who don't know anything about me. Set them talking and looking about. I don't care a damn whether you believe me—what I want is to convince the Grand Jury! I oughtn't to have come to a man who knows me—your cursed incredulity is infectious. I don't put my case well, because I know in advance it's discredited, and I almost end by not believing it myself. That's why I can't convince you. It's a vicious circle." He laid a hand on Denver's arm. "Send a stenographer, and put my statement in the paper."

But Denver did not warm to the idea. "My dear fellow, you seem to forget that all the evidence was pretty thoroughly sifted at the time, every possible clue followed up. The public would have been ready enough then to believe that you murdered old Lenman—you or anybody else. All they wanted was a murderer—the most improbable would have served. But your alibi was too confoundedly complete. And nothing you've told me has shaken it." Denver laid his cool hand over the other's burning fingers. "Look here, old fellow, go home and work up a better case—then come in and submit it to the Investigator."

IV

THE perspiration was rolling off Granice's forehead. Every few minutes he had to draw out his handkerchief and wipe the moisture from his haggard face.

For an hour and a half he had been talking steadily, putting his case to the District Attorney. Luckily he had a speaking acquaintance with Allonby, and had obtained, without much difficulty, a private audience on the very day after his talk with Robert Denver. In the interval between he had hurried home, got out of his evening clothes, and gone forth again at once into the dreary dawn. His fear of Ascham and the alienist made it impossible for him to remain in his rooms. And it seemed to him that the only way of averting that hideous peril was by establishing, in some sane impartial mind, the proof of his guilt. Even if he had not been so incurably sick of life, the electric chair seemed now the only alternative to the strait-jacket.

As he paused to wipe his forehead he saw the District Attorney glance at his watch. The gesture was significant, and Granice lifted an appealing hand. "I don't expect you to believe me now—but can't you put me under arrest, and have the thing looked into?"

Allonby smiled faintly under his heavy grayish moustache. He had a ruddy face, full and jovial, in which his keen professional eyes seemed to keep watch over impulses not strictly professional.

"Well, I don't know that we need lock you up just yet. But of course I'm bound to look into your statement—"

Granice rose with an exquisite sense of relief. Surely Allonby wouldn't have said that if he hadn't believed him!

"That's all right. Then I needn't detain you. I can be found at any time at my apartment." He gave the address.

The District Attorney smiled again, more openly. "What do you say to leaving it for an hour or two this evening? I'm giving a little supper at Rector's—quiet, little affair, you understand: just Miss Melrose—I think you know her—and a friend or two; and if you'll join us . . ."

Granice stumbled out of the office without knowing what reply he had made.

He waited for four days—four days of concentrated horror. During the first twenty-four hours the fear of Ascham's alienist dogged him; and as that subsided, it was replaced by the exasperating sense that his avowal had made no impression on the District Attorney. Evidently, if he had been going to look into the case, Allonby would have been heard from before now. . . . And that mocking invitation to supper showed clearly enough how little the story had impressed him!

Granice was overcome by the futility of any farther attempt to inculpate himself. He was chained to life—a "prisoner of consciousness." Where was it he had read the phrase? Well, he was learning what it meant. In the glaring night-hours, when his brain seemed ablaze, he was visited by a sense of his fixed identity, of his irreducible, inexpugnable selfness, keener, more insidious, more unescapable, than any sensation he had ever known. He had not guessed that the mind was capable of such intricacies of self-realization, of penetrating so deep into its own dark windings. Often he woke from his brief snatches of sleep with the feeling that something material was clinging to him, was on his hands and face, and in his throat—and as his brain cleared he understood that it was the sense of his own loathed personality that stuck to him like some thick viscous substance.

Then, in the first morning hours, he would rise and look out of his window at the awakening activities of the street—at the street-cleaners, the ash-cart drivers, and the other dingy workers flitting hurriedly by through the sallow winter light. Oh, to be one of them—any of them—to take his chance in any of their skins! They were the toilers—the men whose lot was pitied—the victims wept over and ranted about by altruists and economists; and how gladly he would have taken up the load of any one of them, if only he might have shaken off his own! But, no—the iron circle of consciousness held them too: each one was hand-cuffed to his own hideous ego. Why wish to be any one man rather than another? The only absolute good was not to be . . . And Flint, coming in to draw his bath, would ask if he preferred his eggs scrambled or poached that morning?

On the fifth day he wrote a long urgent letter to Allonby; and for the succeeding two days he had the occupation of waiting for an answer. He hardly stirred from his rooms, in his fear of missing the letter by a moment; but would the District Attorney write, or send a representative: a policeman, a "secret agent," or some other mysterious emissary of the law?

On the third morning Flint, stepping softly—as if, confound it! his master were ill—entered the library where Granice sat behind an unread newspaper, and proferred a card on a tray.

Granice read the name—J. B. Hewson—and underneath, in pencil,

"From the District Attorney's office." He started up with a thumping heart, and signed an assent to the servant.

Mr. Hewson was a slight sallow nondescript man of about fifty—the kind of man of whom one is sure to see a specimen in any crowd. "Just the type of the successful detective," Granice reflected as he shook hands with his visitor.

And it was in that character that Mr. Hewson briefly introduced himself. He had been sent by the District Attorney to have "a quiet talk" with Mr. Granice—to ask him to repeat the statement he had made about the Lenman murder.

His manner was so quiet, so reasonable and receptive, that Granice's self-confidence returned. Here was a sensible man—a man who knew his business—it would be easy enough to make him see through that ridiculous alibi! Granice offered Mr. Hewson a cigar, and lighting one himself—to prove his coolness—began again to tell his story.

He was conscious, as he proceeded, of telling it better than ever before. Practice helped, no doubt; and his listener's detached, impartial attitude helped still more. He could see that Hewson, at least, had not decided in advance to disbelieve him, and the sense of being trusted made him more lucid and more consecutive. Yes, this time his words would certainly carry conviction . . .

V

DESPAIRINGLY, Granice gazed up and down the shabby street. Beside him stood a young man with bright prominent eyes, a smooth but not too smoothly-shaven face, and an Irish smile. The young man's nimble glance followed Granice's.

"Sure of the number, are you?" he asked briskly.

"Oh, yes—it was 104."

"Well, then, the new building has swallowed it up—that's certain."

He tilted his head back and surveyed the half-finished front of a brick and limestone flat-house that reared its flimsy elegance above a row of tottering tenements and stables.

"Dead sure?" he repeated.

"Yes," said Granice, discouraged. "And even if I hadn't been, I know the garage was just opposite Leffler's over there." He pointed across the street to a tumble-down stable with a blotched sign on which the words "Livery and Boarding" were still faintly discernible.

The young man dashed across to the opposite pavement. "Well, that's something—may get a clue there. Leffler's—same name there, anyhow. You remember that name?"

"Yes—distinctly."

Granice had felt a return of confidence since he had enlisted the interest of the Explorer's "smartest" reporter. If there were moments when he hardly believed his own story, there were others when it seemed impossible that every one should not believe it; and young Peter McCarren, peering, listening, questioning, jotting down notes, inspired him with an exquisite sense of security. McCarren had fastened on the case at once, "like a leech," as he phrased it—jumped at it, thrilled to it, and settled down to "draw the last drop of fact from it, and had not let go till he had." No one else had treated Granice in that way—even Allonby's detective had not taken a single note. And though a week had elapsed since the visit of that authorized official, nothing had been heard from the District Attorney's office: Allonby had apparently dropped the matter again. But McCarren wasn't going to drop it—not he! He positively hung on Granice's footsteps. They had spent the greater part of the previous day together, and now they were off again, running down clues.

But at Leffler's they got none, after all. Leffler's was no longer a stable. It was condemned to demolition, and in the respite between sentence and execution it had become a vague place of storage, a hospital for broken-down carriages and carts, presided over by a blear-eyed old woman who knew nothing of Flood's garage across the way—did not even remember what had stood there before the new flat-house began to rise.

"Well—we may run Leffler down somewhere; I've seen harder jobs done," said McCarren, cheerfully noting down the name.

As they walked back toward Sixth Avenue he added, in a less sanguine tone: "I'd undertake now to put the thing through if you could only put me on the track of that cyanide."

Granice's heart sank. Yes—there was the weak spot; he had felt it from the first! But he still hoped to convince McCarren that his case was strong enough without it; and he urged the reporter to come back to his rooms and sum up the facts with him again.

"Sorry, Mr. Granice, but I'm due at the office now. Besides, it'd be no use till I get some fresh stuff to work on. Suppose I call you up tomorrow or next day?"

He plunged into a trolley and left Granice gazing desolately after him.

Two days later he reappeared at the apartment, a shade less jaunty in demeanor.

"Well, Mr. Granice, the stars in their courses are against you, as the bard says. Can't get a trace of Flood, or of Leffler either. And you say you bought the motor through Flood, and sold it through him, too?"

"Yes," said Granice wearily.

"Who bought it, do you know?"

Granice wrinkled his brows. "Why, Flood—yes, Flood himself. I sold it back to him three months later."

"Flood? The devil! And I've ransacked the town for Flood. That kind of business disappears as if the earth had swallowed it."

Granice, discouraged, kept silence.

"That brings us back to the poison," McCarren continued, his note-book out. "Just go over that again, will you?"

And Granice went over it again. It had all been so simple at the time—and he had been so clever in covering up his traces! As soon as he decided on poison he looked about for an acquaintance who manufactured chemicals; and there was Jim Dawes, a Harvard classmate, in the dyeing business—just the man. But at the last moment it occurred to him that suspicion might turn toward so obvious an opportunity, and he decided on a more tortuous course. Another friend, Carrick Venn, a student of medicine whom irremediable ill-health had kept from the practice of his profession, amused his leisure with experiments in physics, for the exercise of which he had set up a simple laboratory. Granice had the habit of dropping in to smoke a cigar with him on Sunday afternoons, and the friends generally sat in Venn's work-shop, at the back of the old family house in Stuyvesant Square. Off this work-shop was the cupboard of supplies, with its row of deadly bottles. Carrick Venn was an original, a man of restless curious tastes, and his place, on a Sunday, was often full of visitors: a cheerful crowd of journalists, scribblers, painters, experimenters in divers forms of expression. Coming and going among so many, it was easy enough to pass unperceived; and one afternoon Granice, arriving before Venn had returned home, found himself alone in the work-shop, and quickly slipping into the cupboard, transferred the drug to his pocket.

But that had happened ten years ago; and Venn, poor fellow, was long since dead of his dragging ailment. His old father was dead, too, the house in Stuyvesant Square had been turned into a boarding-house, and the shifting life of New York had passed its rapid sponge over every trace of their obscure little history. Even the optimistic McCarren seemed to acknowledge the hopelessness of seeking for proof in that direction.

"And there's the third door slammed in our faces." He shut his note-book, and throwing back his head, rested his bright inquisitive eyes on Granice's furrowed face.

"Look here, Mr. Granice—you see the weak spot, don't you?"

The other made a despairing motion. "I see so many!"

"Yes: but the one that weakens all the others. Why the deuce do you want this thing known? Why do you want to put your head into the noose?"

Granice looked at him hopelessly, trying to take the measure of his quick light irreverent mind. No one so full of a cheerful animal life would believe in the craving for death as a sufficient motive; and Granice racked his brain for one more convincing. But suddenly he saw the reporter's face soften, and melt to a naive sentimentalism.

"Mr. Granice—has the memory of it always haunted you?"

Granice stared a moment, and then leapt at the opening. "That's it—the memory of it . . . always . . ."

McCarren nodded vehemently. "Dogged your steps, eh? Wouldn't let you sleep? The time came when you had to make a clean breast of it?"

"I had to. Can't you understand?"

The reporter struck his fist on the table. "God, sir! I don't suppose there's a human being with a drop of warm blood in him that can't picture the deadly horrors of remorse—"

The Celtic imagination was aflame, and Granice mutely thanked him for the word. What neither Ascham nor Denver would accept as a conceivable motive the Irish reporter seized on as the most adequate; and, as he said, once one could find a convincing motive, the difficulties of the case became so many incentives to effort.

"Remorse—remorse," he repeated, rolling the word under his tongue with an accent that was a clue to the psychology of the popular drama; and Granice, perversely, said to himself: "If I could only have struck that note I should have been running in six theatres at once."

He saw that from that moment McCarren's professional zeal would be fanned by emotional curiosity; and he profited by the fact to propose that they should dine together, and go on afterward to some music-hall or theatre. It was becoming necessary to Granice to feel himself an object of pre-occupation, to find himself in another mind. He took a kind of gray penumbral pleasure in riveting McCarren's attention on his case; and to feign the grimaces of moral anguish became a passionately engrossing game. He had not entered a theatre for months; but he sat out the meaningless performance in rigid tolerance, sustained by the sense of the reporter's observation.

Between the acts, McCarren amused him with anecdotes about the audience: he knew every one by sight, and could lift the curtain from every physiognomy. Granice listened indulgently. He had lost all interest in his kind, but he knew that he was himself the real centre of McCarren's attention, and that every word the latter spoke had an indirect bearing on his own problem.

"See that fellow over there—the little dried-up man in the third row, pulling his moustache? His memoirs would be worth publishing," McCarren said suddenly in the last entr'acte.

Granice, following his glance, recognized the detective from Allonby's office. For a moment he had the thrilling sense that he was being shadowed.

"Caesar, if he could talk—!" McCarren continued. "Know who he is, of course? Dr. John B. Stell, the biggest alienist in the country—"

Granice, with a start, bent again between the heads in front of him. "That man—the fourth from the aisle? You're mistaken. That's not Dr. Stell."

McCarren laughed. "Well, I guess I've been in court enough to know Stell when I see him. He testifies in nearly all the big cases where they plead insanity."

A cold shiver ran down Granice's spine, but he repeated obstinately: "That's not Dr. Stell."

"Not Stell? Why, man, I know him. Look—here he comes. If it isn't Stell, he won't speak to me."

The little dried-up man was moving slowly up the aisle. As he neared McCarren he made a slight gesture of recognition.

"How'do, Doctor Stell? Pretty slim show, ain't it?" the reporter cheerfully flung out at him. And Mr. J. B. Hewson, with a nod of amicable assent, passed on.

Granice sat benumbed. He knew he had not been mistaken—the man who had just passed was the same man whom Allonby had sent to see him: a physician disguised as a detective. Allonby, then, had thought him insane, like the others—had regarded his confession as the maundering of a maniac. The discovery froze Granice with horror—he seemed to see the mad-house gaping for him.

"Isn't there a man a good deal like him—a detective named J. B. Hewson?"

But he knew in advance what McCarren's answer would be. "Hewson? J. B. Hewson? Never heard of him. But that was J. B. Stell fast enough—I guess he can be trusted to know himself, and you saw he answered to his name."

VI

SOME days passed before Granice could obtain a word with the District Attorney: he began to think that Allonby avoided him.

But when they were face to face Allonby's jovial countenance showed no sign of embarrassment. He waved his visitor to a chair, and leaned across his desk with the encouraging smile of a consulting physician.

Granice broke out at once: "That detective you sent me the other day—"

Allonby raised a deprecating hand.

"—I know: it was Stell the alienist. Why did you do that, Allonby?"

The other's face did not lose its composure. "Because I looked up your story first—and there's nothing in it."

"Nothing in it?" Granice furiously interposed.

"Absolutely nothing. If there is, why the deuce don't you bring me proofs? I know you've been talking to Peter Ascham, and to Denver, and to that little ferret McCarren of the Explorer. Have any of them been able to make out a case for you? No. Well, what am I to do?"

Granice's lips began to tremble. "Why did you play me that trick?"

"About Stell? I had to, my dear fellow: it's part of my business. Stell is a detective, if you come to that—every doctor is."

The trembling of Granice's lips increased, communicating itself in a long quiver to his facial muscles. He forced a laugh through his dry throat. "Well—and what did he detect?"

"In you? Oh, he thinks it's overwork—overwork and too much smoking. If you look in on him some day at his office he'll show you the record of hundreds of cases like yours, and advise you what treatment to follow. It's one of the commonest forms of hallucination. Have a cigar, all the same."

"But, Allonby, I killed that man!"

The District Attorney's large hand, outstretched on his desk, had an almost imperceptible gesture, and a moment later, as if an answer to the call of an electric bell, a clerk looked in from the outer office.

"Sorry, my dear fellow—lot of people waiting. Drop in on Stell some morning," Allonby said, shaking hands.

McCarren had to own himself beaten: there was absolutely no flaw in the alibi. And since his duty to his journal obviously forbade his wasting time on insoluble mysteries, he ceased to frequent Granice, who dropped back into a deeper isolation. For a day or two after his visit to Allonby he continued to live in dread of Dr. Stell. Why might not Allonby have deceived him as to the alienist's diagnosis? What if he were really being shadowed, not by a police agent but by a mad-doctor? To have the truth out, he suddenly determined to call on Dr. Stell.

The physician received him kindly, and reverted without embarrassment to the conditions of their previous meeting. "We have to do that occasionally, Mr. Granice; it's one of our methods. And you had given Allonby a fright."

Granice was silent. He would have liked to reaffirm his guilt, to produce the fresh arguments which had occurred to him since his last talk with the physician; but he feared his eagerness might be taken for a symptom of derangement, and he affected to smile away Dr. Stell's allusion.

"You think, then, it's a case of brain-fag—nothing more?"

"Nothing more. And I should advise you to knock off tobacco. You smoke a good deal, don't you?"

He developed his treatment, recommending massage, gymnastics, travel, or any form of diversion that did not—that in short—

Granice interrupted him impatiently. "Oh, I loathe all that—and I'm sick of travelling."

"H'm. Then some larger interest—politics, reform, philanthropy? Something to take you out of yourself."

"Yes. I understand," said Granice wearily.

"Above all, don't lose heart. I see hundreds of cases like yours," the doctor added cheerfully from the threshold.

On the doorstep Granice stood still and laughed. Hundreds of cases like his—the case of a man who had committed a murder, who confessed his guilt, and whom no one would believe! Why, there had never been a case like it in the world. What a good figure Stell would have made in a play: the great alienist who couldn't read a man's mind any better than that!

Granice saw huge comic opportunities in the type.

But as he walked away, his fears dispelled, the sense of listlessness returned on him. For the first time since his avowal to Peter Ascham he found himself without an occupation, and understood that he had been carried through the past weeks only by the necessity of constant action. Now his life had once more become a stagnant backwater, and as he stood on the street corner watching the tides of traffic sweep by, he asked himself despairingly how much longer he could endure to float about in the sluggish circle of his consciousness.

The thought of self-destruction recurred to him; but again his flesh recoiled. He yearned for death from other hands, but he could never take it from his own. And, aside from his insuperable physical reluctance, another motive restrained him. He was possessed by the dogged desire to establish the truth of his story. He refused to be swept aside as an irresponsible dreamer—even if he had to kill himself in the end, he would not do so before proving to society that he had deserved death from it.

He began to write long letters to the papers; but after the first had been published and commented on, public curiosity was quelled by a brief statement from the District Attorney's office, and the rest of his communications remained unprinted. Ascham came to see him, and begged him to travel. Robert Denver dropped in, and tried to joke him out of his delusion; till Granice, mistrustful of their motives, began to dread the reappearance of Dr. Stell, and set a guard on his lips. But the words he kept back engendered others and still others in his brain. His inner self became a humming factory of arguments, and he spent long hours reciting and writing down elaborate statements of his crime, which he constantly retouched and developed. Then gradually his activity languished under the lack of an audience, the sense of being buried beneath deepening drifts of indifference. In a passion of resentment he swore that he would prove himself a murderer, even if he had to commit another crime to do it; and for a sleepless night or two the thought flamed red on his darkness. But daylight dispelled it. The determining impulse was lacking and he hated too promiscuously to choose his victim . . . So he was thrown back on the unavailing struggle to impose the truth of his story. As fast as one channel closed on him he tried to pierce another through the sliding sands of incredulity. But every issue seemed blocked, and the whole human race leagued together to cheat one man of the right to die.

Thus viewed, the situation became so monstrous that he lost his last shred of self-restraint in contemplating it. What if he were really the victim of some mocking experiment, the centre of a ring of holiday-makers jeering at a poor creature in its blind dashes against the solid walls of consciousness? But, no—men were not so uniformly cruel: there were flaws in the close surface of their indifference, cracks of weakness and pity here and there . . .

Granice began to think that his mistake lay in having appealed to persons more or less familiar with his past, and to whom the visible conformities of his life seemed a final disproof of its one fierce secret deviation. The general tendency was to take for the whole of life the slit seen between the blinders of habit: and in his walk down that narrow vista Granice cut a correct enough figure. To a vision free to follow his whole orbit his story would be more intelligible: it would be easier to convince a chance idler in the street than the trained intelligence hampered by a sense of his antecedents. This idea shot up in him with the tropic luxuriance of each new seed of thought, and he began to walk the streets, and to frequent out-of-the-way chop-houses and bars in his search for the impartial stranger to whom he should disclose himself.

At first every face looked encouragement; but at the crucial moment he always held back. So much was at stake, and it was so essential that his first choice should be decisive. He dreaded stupidity, timidity, intolerance. The imaginative eye, the furrowed brow, were what he sought. He must reveal himself only to a heart versed in the tortuous motions of the human will; and he began to hate the dull benevolence of the average face. Once or twice, obscurely, allusively, he made a beginning—once sitting down at a man's side in a basement chop-house, another day approaching a lounger on an east-side wharf. But in both cases the premonition of failure checked him on the brink of avowal. His dread of being taken for a man in the clutch of a fixed idea gave him an unnatural keenness in reading the expression of his interlocutors, and he had provided himself in advance with a series of verbal alternatives, trap-doors of evasion from the first dart of ridicule or suspicion.

He passed the greater part of the day in the streets, coming home at irregular hours, dreading the silence and orderliness of his apartment, and the critical scrutiny of Flint. His real life was spent in a world so remote from this familiar setting that he sometimes had the mysterious sense of a living metempsychosis, a furtive passage from one identity to another—yet the other as unescapably himself!

One humiliation he was spared: the desire to live never revived in him. Not for a moment was he tempted to a shabby pact with existing conditions. He wanted to die, wanted it with the fixed unwavering desire which alone attains its end. And still the end eluded him! It would not always, of course—he had full faith in the dark star of his destiny. And he could prove it best by repeating his story, persistently and indefatigably, pouring it into indifferent ears, hammering it into dull brains, till at last it kindled a spark, and some one of the careless millions paused, listened, believed . . .

It was a mild March day, and he had been loitering on the west-side docks, looking at faces. He was becoming an expert in physiognomies: his eagerness no longer made rash darts and awkward recoils. He knew now the face he needed, as clearly as if it had come to him in a vision; and not till he found it would he speak. As he walked eastward through the shabby reeking streets he had a premonition that he should find it that morning. Perhaps it was the promise of spring in the air—certainly he felt calmer than for many days . . .

He turned into Washington Square, struck across it obliquely, and walked up University Place. Its heterogeneous passers always allured him—they were less hurried than in Broadway, less enclosed and classified than in Fifth Avenue. He walked slowly, watching for his face.

At Union Square he felt a sudden relapse into discouragement, like a votary who has watched too long for a sign from the altar. Perhaps, after all, he should never find his face . . . The air was languid, and he felt tired. He walked between the bald grass-plots and the twisted trees, making for an empty seat. Presently he passed a bench on which a girl sat alone, and something as definite as the twitch of a cord made him stop before her. He had never dreamed of telling his story to a girl, had hardly looked at the women's faces as they passed. His case was man's work: how could a woman help him? But this girl's face was extraordinary—quiet and wide as a clear evening sky. It suggested a hundred images of space, distance, mystery, like ships he had seen, as a boy, quietly berthed by a familiar wharf, but with the breath of far seas and strange harbours in their shrouds . . . Certainly this girl would understand. He went up to her quietly, lifting his hat, observing the forms—wishing her to see at once that he was "a gentleman."

"I am a stranger to you," he began, sitting down beside her, "but your face is so extremely intelligent that I feel . . . I feel it is the face I've waited for . . . looked for everywhere; and I want to tell you—"

The girl's eyes widened: she rose to her feet. She was escaping him!

In his dismay he ran a few steps after her, and caught her roughly by the arm.

"Here—wait—listen! Oh, don't scream, you fool!" he shouted out.

He felt a hand on his own arm; turned and confronted a policeman. Instantly he understood that he was being arrested, and something hard within him was loosened and ran to tears.

"Ah, you know—you know I'm guilty!"

He was conscious that a crowd was forming, and that the girl's frightened face had disappeared. But what did he care about her face? It was the policeman who had really understood him. He turned and followed, the crowd at his heels . . .

VII

IN the charming place in which he found himself there were so many sympathetic faces that he felt more than ever convinced of the certainty of making himself heard.

It was a bad blow, at first, to find that he had not been arrested for murder; but Ascham, who had come to him at once, explained that he needed rest, and the time to "review" his statements; it appeared that reiteration had made them a little confused and contradictory. To this end he had willingly acquiesced in his removal to a large quiet establishment, with an open space and trees about it, where he had found a number of intelligent companions, some, like himself, engaged in preparing or reviewing statements of their cases, and others ready to lend an interested ear to his own recital.

For a time he was content to let himself go on the tranquil current of this existence; but although his auditors gave him for the most part an encouraging attention, which, in some, went the length of really brilliant and helpful suggestion, he gradually felt a recurrence of his old doubts. Either his hearers were not sincere, or else they had less power to aid him than they boasted. His interminable conferences resulted in nothing, and as the benefit of the long rest made itself felt, it produced an increased mental lucidity which rendered inaction more and more unbearable. At length he discovered that on certain days visitors from the outer world were admitted to his retreat; and he wrote out long and logically constructed relations of his crime, and furtively slipped them into the hands of these messengers of hope.

This occupation gave him a fresh lease of patience, and he now lived only to watch for the visitors' days, and scan the faces that swept by him like stars seen and lost in the rifts of a hurrying sky.

Mostly, these faces were strange and less intelligent than those of his companions. But they represented his last means of access to the world, a kind of subterranean channel on which he could set his "statements" afloat, like paper boats which the mysterious current might sweep out into the open seas of life.

One day, however, his attention was arrested by a familiar contour, a pair of bright prominent eyes, and a chin insufficiently shaved. He sprang up and stood in the path of Peter McCarren.

The journalist looked at him doubtfully, then held out his hand with a startled deprecating, "Why—?"

"You didn't know me? I'm so changed?" Granice faltered, feeling the rebound of the other's wonder.

"Why, no; but you're looking quieter—smoothed out," McCarren smiled.

"Yes: that's what I'm here for—to rest. And I've taken the opportunity to write out a clearer statement—"

Granice's hand shook so that he could hardly draw the folded paper from his pocket. As he did so he noticed that the reporter was accompanied by a tall man with grave compassionate eyes. It came to Granice in a wild thrill of conviction that this was the face he had waited for . . .

"Perhaps your friend—he is your friend?—would glance over it—or I could put the case in a few words if you have time?" Granice's voice shook like his hand. If this chance escaped him he felt that his last hope was gone. McCarren and the stranger looked at each other, and the former glanced at his watch.

"I'm sorry we can't stay and talk it over now, Mr. Granice; but my friend has an engagement, and we're rather pressed—"

Granice continued to proffer the paper. "I'm sorry—I think I could have explained. But you'll take this, at any rate?"

The stranger looked at him gently. "Certainly—I'll take it." He had his hand out. "Good-bye."

"Good-bye," Granice echoed.

He stood watching the two men move away from him through the long light hall; and as he watched them a tear ran down his face. But as soon as they were out of sight he turned and walked hastily toward his room, beginning to hope again, already planning a new statement.

Outside the building the two men stood still, and the journalist's companion looked up curiously at the long monotonous rows of barred windows.

"So that was Granice?"

"Yes—that was Granice, poor devil," said McCarren.

"Strange case! I suppose there's never been one just like it? He's still absolutely convinced that he committed that murder?"

"Absolutely. Yes."

The stranger reflected. "And there was no conceivable ground for the idea? No one could make out how it started? A quiet conventional sort of fellow like that—where do you suppose he got such a delusion? Did you ever get the least clue to it?"

McCarren stood still, his hands in his pockets, his head cocked up in contemplation of the barred windows. Then he turned his bright hard gaze on his companion.

"That was the queer part of it. I've never spoken of it—but I did get a clue."

"By Jove! That's interesting. What was it?"

McCarren formed his red lips into a whistle. "Why—that it wasn't a delusion."

He produced his effect—the other turned on him with a pallid stare.

"He murdered the man all right. I tumbled on the truth by the merest accident, when I'd pretty nearly chucked the whole job."

"He murdered him—murdered his cousin?"

"Sure as you live. Only don't split on me. It's about the queerest business I ever ran into . . . Do about it? Why, what was I to do? I couldn't hang the poor devil, could I? Lord, but I was glad when they collared him, and had him stowed away safe in there!"

The tall man listened with a grave face, grasping Granice's statement in his hand.

"Here—take this; it makes me sick," he said abruptly, thrusting the paper at the reporter; and the two men turned and walked in silence to the gates.